D0252069

Acclaim for Ian Slater

WORLD WAR III
"Superior to the Tom Clancy genre . . . and the military aspect far more realistic."
—*The Spectator*

MACARTHUR MUST DIE
"A most satisfying what-if thriller . . . The plot [is] a full-speed-ahead page-turner. . . . Flashy, fast fun."
—New York *Daily News*

"Searing suspense . . . [A] rousing, splendidly told adventure."
—*Los Angeles Times*

"Tautly written, this novel is loaded with scenes that will have you grasping the book so tightly your knuckles will turn white. . . . The final scene is a climactic hair-raising thriller."
—*West Coast Review of Books*

*Please turn the page
for more reviews. . . .*

By Ian Slater

FIRESPILL
SEA GOLD
AIR GLOW RED
ORWELL: THE ROAD TO AIRSTRIP ONE
STORM
DEEP CHILL
FORBIDDEN ZONE*
MACARTHUR MUST DIE
WW III*
WW III: RAGE OF BATTLE*
WW III: WORLD IN FLAMES*
WW III: ARCTIC FRONT*
WW III: WARSHOT*
WW III: ASIAN FRONT*
WW III: FORCE OF ARMS*
WW III: SOUTH CHINA SEA*
SHOWDOWN*
BATTLE FRONT*
MANHUNT*
FORCE TEN*
KNOCKOUT*
ORWELL: THE ROAD TO AIRSTRIP ONE
(second revised edition)
WW III: CHOKE POINT*
WW III: PAYBACK*

published by Ballantine Books

WWIII
Darpa Alpha
A Novel

IAN SLATER

PRESIDIO PRESS
BALLANTINE BOOKS • NEW YORK

2007 Presidio Press Mass Market Edition

Published in the United States by Presidio Press, an imprint of The Random House Publishing Group, a division of Random House, Inc., New York.

PRESIDIO PRESS and colophon are registered trademarks of Random House, Inc.

Originally published in hardcover in Great Britain by Greenhill Books in 1997. First published in paperback in Great Britain by Greenhill Books, and in the United States by Stackpole Books, in 2002.

ISBN 978-0-345-49112-1

Cover illustration: Studio Liddell

Printed in the United States of America

www.presidiopress.com

OPM   9 8 7 6 5 4 3 2 1

As always, for Marian, Serena, and Blair

ACKNOWLEDGMENTS

Among the unsung heroines in the world of writers are those women who unselfishly give of their time and talent in support of writer husbands. Such is my wife, Marian. Without her, these books would simply not appear. I would also like to thank Charles Slonecker for his help and support.

CHAPTER ONE

Early Fall—Dusk

"SURE BEATS BINOCULARS," the sergeant opined softly, one hand deftly slipping another stick of odorless gum into his mouth, the other holding a four-inch-square monitor. "Clear as crystal."

Lieutenant Sammy Ramon nodded as he too watched the monitor his sergeant was holding. The live video feed of the lake's research facility a quarter of a mile below was coming in from the twelve-man team's tiny eight-inch MAV recon plane. The micro air vehicle, developed by DARPA, the U.S. Defense Department's Advanced Research and Projects Agency, was made up of collapsible transparent wings and tail and equipped with a Viccol video camera and laser range finder. To get a closer look at the monitor, the lieutenant, using his left hand to remove his "Fritz" Kevlar helmet, his right to slide his M-16 forward to his side, momentarily wiped the beaded perspiration from his drab olive-green face paint, the latter indistinguishable from the camouflage paint of his collapsible Paratrooper mountain bike nearby. For security reasons, the other eleven men in the lieutenant's commando squad hadn't been given the precise in-country coordinates of the enemy naval base below, yet each man, looking down from his hide toward the lake, knew the exact layout of the base, everything from the small data hut on the lake's sandy shoreline to the bigger and more vital research barge offshore.

Though the MAV couldn't be detected by enemy radar because of its stealth-fiber, sharp-edged construction, affording it an extraordinarily small radar signature, it nevertheless gave the lieutenant a start when, for a second, it passed as a black dot across the lemon wafer of the moon that was already visible in the dusk. But any fright the momentary silhouette might have given him was ameliorated by the fact that apart from the lone civilian security guard, which the MAV's infrared vision had detected, there seemed to be no other visible defenses. Once again, the lieutenant had occasion to remind himself of what a fellow soldier, retired U.S. Army General Douglas Freeman, had once said on a CNN interview after 9/11, that base security, indeed security anywhere, is more often a state of mind than a reality, more an assumption than a fact.

As the tiny plane circled the enemy base again, Ramon switched to watching the target through his own videomounted M-16, which gave him a head-on view of it, a lone barge in the fading light. The ninety-foot-long, thirty-foot-wide research barge hadn't changed location, remaining anchored more than a hundred yards offshore from the bungalow-sized hut onshore. Intel had told the lieutenant that while this bungalow would have to be neutralized, it was the barge that contained the data they were after and which would, therefore, be the commando team's primary target. Neither the lieutenant, nor any of the eleven men under his command, had been told what the data were specifically, only that they would be on a disk and how the disk would be labeled. But they had been told that this data was so vital it could irrevocably tip the balance of power in favor of the United States, not only in its ongoing war against terror but also in the face of China's massive buildup of high-tech weaponry following the Chinese leaders' jaw-dropping surprise at witnessing America's delivery of shock and awe in the two Gulf wars.

Lieutenant Ramon's first job was to get his team into the enemy base before he could neutralize the main hut onshore and loot the barge computer's hard drive, as well as the disk which scientists back home could use to reverse-engineer the weapon. Intel had told Ramon the data had originally been spawned by a Russian prototype of the revolutionary technology.

Ramon had told his assault team that they were to approach the naval base with as casual an air as possible—just another case of a friendly visit from U.S. troops coming back from maneuvers during the day—and not to give a damn about the security cameras around the research station's perimeter. Ramon would give a friendly howdy-do to the security guard who was looking bored out of his mind from walking up and down along the quarter-mile chain-link storm fence that enclosed the shore hut and the fifty-foot-long jetty where a small rigid inflatable boat, obviously used for transport to and from the barge, was bobbing up and down in a small chop.

Each of the twelve commandos extracted his collapsible khaki DARPA-designed Paratrooper mountain bike from its canvas shoulder bag, mounted up, and pedaled off.

Some were soon freewheeling and braking, but quietly, as they headed down the blacktop road toward the fence's gate. Sammy Ramon spoke to each man personally as he had before the mission, warning them that if he heard so much as a squeak or squeal coming from these special post-Afghanistan-designed bikes, he'd see to it that the man responsible would be put on a charge. "Absolutely nothing," he'd intoned, "is to go wrong."

Pushing for perfection, the lieutenant had had them endlessly practicing extraction, snap assembly, and disas-
sembly. To qualify, each of the eleven commandos had
to be equally proficient in handling his MOLLE, as the
DARPA-designed state-of-the-art Modular Lightweight
Load-Carrying Equipment pack was known, and which
was equipped with an ergonomically designed plastic
frame capable of hauling a central rucksack plus eighteen
additional pouches of DARPA-designed "goodies," including everything from extra ammunition for the videomounted, red-dot-aiming M-16s to their GPS-updated
inertial navigation system and DARPA-designed MAV.
Every man had to extract his bike from his shoulder pack
and assemble its two folding halves in less than thirty seconds, his MOLLE in under five minutes.

   Using bikes instead of noisy Humvees, Ramon had explained to his team, would enhance their "just passing by"
explanation to the security guard. After all, what could be
more natural than a group of the U.S. Tenth Mountain
Division's bicycle unit out practicing with their bikes and
just waving "hi" to the locals in the spirit of mutual coop-
eration? Ramon and his team knew that what they were
about to do, if all went well, was strictly against all international law, but in the war between America and terrorists, rules were frequently thrown out the window. The
enemy, Intel had assured him, wouldn't be expecting an
attack. But Sammy Ramon's hard experience told him
that HUMINT, human intelligence, and SIGINT, signal
intelligence, could be dead wrong. Look at Tony Blair
and George Bush's search for WMDs. Intel had also told
Ramon that there'd been reports of long copper-mesh
curtains having been erected inside the onshore data-
receiving hut and on board the offshore barge, this being
done, Intel reports had said, in order to block any extra-
neous radio signals that might scramble any of the critical

electronic communication traffic between the hut and off-shore barge while they were calibrating their equipment. All he needed, the lieutenant told his sergeant, was for the guard, a dark, swarthy man with a submachine gun slung about his shoulder, to stand still for a couple of seconds.

"You got the envelope?" asked the sergeant.

The lieutenant patted his battle dress shirt pocket. "I'm set."

As dusk faded, day easing into night, and the breeze that carried the faint smell of algae from the lake became cooler, Ramon watched the moon's pale light sharply silhouetting the onshore hut and the offshore barge. Now they were ten yards from the chain-link gate and the big sign that warned in six languages "KEEP OUT."

"This is it," Ramon said softly to his sergeant as he stopped his column of eleven men, who, as they'd rehearsed it, were doing their damnedest to look tired and disinterested, their expressions suggesting they wanted to get back to their camp rather than waste time while the lieutenant started yakking with the locals.

"How you doin'?" Ramon asked the guard through the chain-link fence. The man, with bushy black eyebrows and deep-set brown eyes, was wearing a cheap, civilian-made security-firm uniform festooned with shoulder patches and crimson epaulettes, no doubt meant to intimidate the locals. He looked grumpy and immediately suspicious, but Ramon took no notice, as if he hadn't seen the man's unwelcoming frown. "Hi, I'm Lieutenant Ramon. We're here to see your director." Ramon took a letter from his pocket and held it up close to his eyes, inclining the paper in the moonlight. "A Doctor—" Ramon's forehead creased in concentration, as if he were trying to read a name on the envelope.

All he needed was a moment or two of confusion, the security guard to cease pacing up and down inside the chain-link fence. But the guard, much shorter than Ramon had first guessed, kept moving right to left behind the wire, taking no notice of the proffered letter of authorization, looking instead beyond Ramon and the sergeant at the eleven other men. He put up his hand, signaling "stop," and began walking away from the fence toward the shoreline hut, at which point Ramon, heart in his mouth, called out, "Hey, standard procedure, man. Check my ID first."

The man paused, looked back, and saw that Ramon was holding a striped ID card against the fence, a fence which Ramon knew was normally linked to motion sensors but the latter, Intel had told him, had been disengaged because of so many false alerts, set off by roaming dogs. Sometimes the alarms were tripped by falcons, which occasionally mistook the ground sensors for rodents.

The guard walked back to the fence and, taking out his flashlight, peered at the striped ID card.

Ramon's sergeant held up his ID card as well. The guard glanced from one to the other, and it was obvious to the lieutenant that the guard didn't recognize either but that his pride was demanding he examine the ID cards as if he knew what he was doing. Ramon hoped Intel was right about the copper shielding thwarting any communication with the barge or hut.

The guard came closer to the fence and stood still, examining the cards. The sergeant shot him point-blank through a diamond-shaped space in the chain-link fence, the spit of the Heckler & Koch 9 mm sidearm barely making a sound. The guard fell backward, thudding to the ground.

In seconds, the tired-looking soldiers standing around with their mountain bikes were galvanized into action.

Within another five seconds, Ramon, kneeling by the chain-link fence, combat gloves on, extracted what looked like the leg of a small camera's tripod from his MOLLE.

It was a one-inch-diameter telescoping extension claw rod with three retractable fishhook talons on it that could be used in this case to hook the dead guard's clothing and drag him closer to the fence. There Ramon pulled out his keys, the stench of the dead guard's involuntarily defecation heavy in the air.

The twelve were through the gate, each of the six two-man teams knowing precisely where to go and what to do and that they had less than ten minutes before local police could be expected to be alerted and arrive. With noise suppressors on their M-16s, Heckler & Koch submachine guns, and sidearms, there should be little noise. And Intel had told them that there should be relatively few people: four science graduate students in the onshore hut, six scientists on the offshore barge. The four students in the shore hut, all male, took no notice of the door opening, probably expecting visitors from the barge. All four were shot quickly, silently, at point-blank range by two of Ramon's sidearm specialists. Ramon's job, with his sergeant and four others, was to make straight for the rigid inflatable, its presence confirmed by the MAV, tied up on the far side of the fifty-foot-long jetty.

Ramon, his sergeant, and the four-man backup team ran toward the wharf, Ramon praying that every one of the six scientists would be inside the barge, a hope stoked by the fact that even though it had been a relatively hot day, the temperature had plummeted as soon as the sun had died, and working conditions now were much more pleasant. But what if one of the scientists were to stroll out for a minute for a cigarette or to relieve himself? Intel had told him there were no facilities on the barge other than an unhandy portable chemical toilet. This meant there was a risk of somebody suddenly wanting to run ashore in the rigid inflatable, which would screw up everybody's timing.

Ramon's squad had reached the jetty and were in the inflatable in seconds, their training, the seemingly endless repetition, paying off. In a few seconds the RIB, emitting a whiff of diesel, was away from the wharf, its outboard initially sounding to the lieutenant like the rip of a light machine gun but only because, apart from the deep throb of a compressor, there was no other noise on the shoreline. In fact, the outboard engine was remarkably quiet, purring along after the initial burp. It was too good, too smooth, to last, thought Ramon. Something must be about to happen. Murphy's Law. The RIB had just nudged into one of the rubber tires that served as a bump rail girding the barge when a door opened. A skewed rectangle of light flooded out onto the black deck, silhouetting Ramon, his sergeant, and the four other men in the RIB sharply against the moonlit lake. The scientist let out a cry. Ramon and the sergeant fired and the man pitched forward, crashing against a spool of cable on the black grit-grip deck. Moving quickly through the acrid smell of cordite into the barge's housing, they burst in to find five startled scientists. Two men in stained white lab coats were bending over a map of the lake, while a woman in a spotless lab coat sat at the mainframe. A second woman, extraordinarily thin, was busy reloading the printer, while a man in his fifties in stain-blotched white coveralls, his balding head and eyeglasses catching the light from the swivel-mounted monitor screen above his computer terminal, looked at them in astonishment.

"Who za hell are you?" demanded the bald man imperiously.

Ramon slammed his gloved fist into the man's face, sending the scientist reeling back past the screaming woman, the scientist crashing into a door three feet behind him and falling down amid a pile of stacked printer paper.

"The Flow-In-Flight file!" demanded Ramon, as the

older man, now lying in shock and bleeding from his teeth, gasped, looking down at his bloodstained hand and at his four companions for help. The four were frozen in fear.

"The Flow-In-Flight file!" Ramon repeated, only more forcefully this time. "I want it. On screen—*now!*" He brought his Heckler & Koch MP5 submachine gun level with the woman, dark-haired and probably in her midtwenties. "Bring it up!" Ramon told her.

She shook her head, a definite no. Ramon shot her, the man bleeding on the floor yelling, *"Nein! Nein!"* The other three scientists, in their late twenties or early thirties, were aghast, faces turning waxen in fright.

"Bring it *UP!*" Ramon said once again. "You started this war. We'll finish it!"

The two male scientists to the left of the computer, and the woman behind them, looked at one another in shock, as if they didn't understand. There was a moment of indecision.

The sergeant glanced anxiously at his watch. Five minutes left before local police could be expected to arrive if any of the staff on the barge or in the onshore data hut had had time to punch an alarm Intel hadn't known about. Ramon fired again, this time at one of the men leaning against the mainframe. It was a head shot, Ramon not wanting to damage the computer. The scientist slid down, his face a stare of utter astonishment. He was bleeding profusely from the back of the head, his two companions huddling together now against the mainframe as if it might give them protection.

"Bring it up or you're a dead man!" Ramon told the next man in line.

The man tried to speak but couldn't, mouth and tongue dry as parchment. He keyed in what Ramon hoped would bring up the file. A millisecond later and there it was, the Flow-In-Flight data, the latest test results. "You have a backup disk," Ramon said. It was a statement more than a question.

The terrified scientist nodded vigorously.

"Put it in the computer and show me!" ordered Ramon.

The scientist did as he was told, Ramon watching closely over his shoulder, and there on the screen appeared the same "Flow-In-Flight Data."

"Put it on the table," Ramon ordered.

The scientist complied.

"Copies?" shouted Ramon.

The man shook his head and found his voice. "No, I swear. No copies."

Ramon shot him dead and turned to the remaining two. "Copies?"

The man whom the lieutenant had knocked down and the remaining woman shook their heads. "No, no!" the woman cried. "I swear to God!"

"Grab the disk!" Ramon ordered his sergeant, and then in two bursts from his Heckler & Koch shot the man and the woman.

Ramon's sergeant picked up the disk, waving it triumphantly to the lieutenant. "We have it, Ramon. Allah is great!"

"Destroy the hard drive!" Ramon told him. "And get out of the U.S. uniforms. Civilian dress. Remember, no Arabic. English only till we're home."

"Yes, sir."

CHAPTER TWO

Monterey

IN MONTEREY IT was still dark, and in a modest bungalow's bedroom, the phone rang—eight times before retired General Douglas Freeman finally relented. Half sitting up, careful not to disturb his wife, Margaret, he glanced at his watch. It was 5:00 A.M. What the hell—? He knew it had to be something wrong with his son Dan, who was posted in the Middle East, for anyone to be calling at this ungodly hour. The "crump" of high surf pounding the beach sounded to him like distant artillery, a creeping barrage. He fumbled sleepily for the phone. "Hello?" he growled, his voice gravelly and nasal in his sudden awakening. *"Hello?"*

"General Freeman?"

"Yes. Who is this?"

"Aussie Lewis," came the jovial voice. In the background was the sound of either a Special Forces team checking weapons or metal crates banging together.

"Aussie? What's wrong?"

"We clear fore and aft, mate?" came Aussie's voice, his Australian twang still distinctive, though he'd been a U.S. Special Forces commando and a naturalized American for fifteen years.

"Yes," said the general. "Clear fore and aft."

"What is it?" pressed the general. Freeman was one of America's legendary commanders but right now all he was was a rather grumpy, impatient retiree who needed his sleep.

"Well," said Aussie Lewis, "there's this old sailor who decides to have a last fling. So, he goes down to the water-front and picks up this lady of the evening. Well, they're goin' at it and he says, 'How'm I doin'?' and she says, 'You're doin' about three knots.'

" 'What d'you mean, three knots?' he asks her and she says, 'Well, you're *not* hard, you're *not* in, and you're *not* gettin' your money back!' "

This was followed by raucous laughter from what sounded like a football team. The metallic sound the general had heard earlier, he decided, must have been the rattle of beer cans.

"Son of a bitch!" said General Douglas Freeman. "You rang to tell me a joke—an *old* joke at that—at 0500?"

"Oh, shite!" came Aussie's response. "I thought it was 0800 hours."

"You must be on the East Coast," said Freeman, "and pissed as usual."

"Yes and no, General," answered Aussie. "A few of the old team got together for an ad hoc reunion. We're seeing the sights in Washington, D.C. Saw the World War II monument yesterday. See where all our friggin' taxes go. The monument's A-okay, though. We all like it. 'Bout time all those people had something to honor them. Anyway, I thought I'd give you a bell, see how you were, you being retired and all. Thought you could do with a bit of a laugh."

Freeman smiled, relaxed, and sat back against the bed's headboard, Margaret stirring sleepily beside him. "Well, thanks, Aussie. And you're right. Ever since the yuppies in the Pentagon *requested* I take retirement because of my—well, what they said was—"

"Your penchant," answered Aussie, "for 'politically incorrect statements.' You called those congressmen on the Appropriations Committee—let's see, what was it? Oh yeah, 'A bunch of broad-banging bureaucrats.' Don't think you can say 'broad' anymore," continued Aussie. "Sexist."

"Hmmm, I suppose," the general conceded ruefully. "Never mind that it was the truth. That bunch on the Appropriations Committee should've voted more money for DARPA."

"That's what the team's been talking about here."

"Where's 'here'—a dive?"

"Of course not, General. We're on top of the roof at the Willard Hotel. Breakfast. We can see the White House from here."

"Hope they can't see you guys. Who's there?"

"In the White House? The president, I guess."

"No, you dork. Who's with you at the Willard?"

"Ah, lessee. Salvini, alias the Brooklyn Dodger, Choir Williams, the bloody Welsh tenor—he's singing, God help us—and yours truly. Couldn't get Eddie Mervyn or Gomez out here. After that Korean stint we did they went home to Mommy. They live on the West Coast."

"I know," said Freeman. He knew exactly where every member of his old team was located and how he could reach them—quickly, if needed—including Medal of Honor winner David Brentwood, who was laid up at the moment with a flare-up of an old shoulder wound.

"Oh," added Aussie, "I'm getting crap for not mentioning Johnny Lee, our multilingual expert. He's here too, pissed out of his mind. That DARPA outfit you were talking about?"

"What about it?" said the general.

"You know," said Aussie. "This B and E at the naval facility."

"Break and enter?" said the general, sitting up higher against the headboard, his face clouding over. He prided himself on being current, particularly in this long, hard war against terror which, as Bush had told the Air Force Academy in Colorado Springs, would be the "work of decades"—how history was once more witnessing a great clash like that of the Cold War. Only this war on terror was a damn sight hotter, and it was for that reason that the general had vociferously argued for more money to be allocated for DARPA's black box stuff. DARPA needed all the funding it could get, even if it meant hiding it so deep within the GAO's—the General Accounting Office's— records that to locate it would be like trying to find the proverbial needle in a bureaucratic haystack. The general was very up-to-date vis-à-vis DARPA, but he hadn't heard anything about a B and E against any DARPA installation.

"What happened?" he asked Aussie.

"No details really," said Aussie. "On the idiot box— breaking news. Oh, guess it must have been about an hour ago. Oh four hundred your time."

"I didn't see anything," said the general. "I was watching a late movie. What channel?"

"CNN."

"Huh," said Freeman. "Those people know more than the CIA half the time."

"Tell me about it," answered Aussie, having to raise his voice against the sound of the beer cans.

"Which facility?" Freeman pressed; he could hear the usually quiet Welshman Choir Williams singing "Goodbye" from *White Horse Inn*.

The Willard wouldn't put up with that for long.

"That's what we've been tossing around over a few beers here," said Aussie. "The location of the facility. Your old CNN flame, Marte Price, broke into the newscast, said there'd been a B and E at a highly sensitive naval base out your way."

"*My* way?" said the general, adding wryly, "You mean somewhere between San Diego and Alaska?"

"Yeah, pretty broad isn't it?" responded Aussie. "I dunno, but we all got the impression it was on the West Coast—somewhere out there. All she said was something about a naval facility '*out west*' but—just hold on a mo, General." Then Freeman heard Aussie asking the others, "She did say it was a naval facility out west, right?"

There was a chorus of boozy agreement.

"Yeah, General," continued Aussie. "She said it was a 'highly classified' naval facility that had been broken into. Security guard killed."

"And—?" pressed Freeman.

"That's it. No film, just the verbal report."

"But they must have aired the story again later? More details?"

"Nada," said Aussie. "We were up playing a few hands of poker. We would've heard any more news about it. My guess is DHS must have come down on CNN like a ton o' bricks to kill the report. 'Course, at the time of the newscast, most people were in bed anyway. That always helps to squelch a story."

"You weren't in bed," said the general.

"Well, you know how it is, General. Team likes to stay up—stay current."

"And I *don't*?" the general joshed.

"Oh no," said Aussie. "We know you're up-to-date. But you've probably been busy staying *up* with your wife."

"Cheeky bastard!"

"Oh no," replied Aussie again, with mock embarrassment. "Oh, I didn't mean anything untoward, General, or anything under *covers*, if you know what I mean?"

"I *do*. You're pissed and you're insolent. Call me back if you hear anything on that DARPA facility—where the hell it is."

"Roger that," said Aussie. "You sleep tight now."

The general put the phone down and shook his head.

"*Who* was *that*?" asked Margaret, opening her eyes. Their brilliant turquoise color always surprised her famous or, perhaps more truthfully nowadays, once-famous husband.

"Ah, the boys," replied the general. "They're tying one on."

Margaret had to think about that phrase. It wasn't one she normally heard amongst her friends at the church socials, even those put on for the benefit of retired service folk who, with so many other Americans, had suffered catastrophic losses, personal and financial, when the family breadwinner had been killed in the long, ongoing war against terror.

"Aren't you coming back to bed?" Margaret murmured, taking a sip of water from the glass on the bedside table as Freeman opened the closet, reaching in for his long gray robe. He didn't answer her, already deep in thought about the DARPA burglary, if that's what it had been, and surfing channels on their bedroom TV as he slipped his feet into his moccasins. Nothing about a break-in at any military base. Perhaps Aussie had glimpsed part of an old documentary tape. Freeman recalled how just the other day he had pulled a newspaper out of the magazine rack and was halfway through reading an article on yet another terrorist raid in Britain before he realized the paper was a month old.

Margaret drew the duvet over her eyes to shut out the flashes of light from the television. "Douglas? What are you doing?"

"Oh, sorry." He stabbed the power button, shutting off

the TV. Something wasn't right. Aussie had said all of them saw it. "Think I'll stay up awhile," he told Margaret. "Get some juice, maybe have a cup of coffee." He glanced at his watch which, from old "in-country" habit he wore so that the face was under his wrist and reflections from its quartz face couldn't be easily seen by the enemy.

"*I'd* like some company," Margaret persisted, "and something in your robe tells me that you would too."

"*Margaret!*" he said, feigning shock but pleased by her sudden sauciness. "Time for me to get up," he added. "Nearly reveille."

"You *are* up," she said. "*C'est magnifique!* I'd like you to come down."

"Mrs. Freeman!" he said, turning and looking down at her. "You astound me. You wouldn't have said that six months ago—in French *or* English!"

"No," she conceded, pulling down the covers invitingly. "I wouldn't, but you know how these sudden conversions can be." She was right. Once Douglas had told her how Catherine, his late wife and Margaret's sister, had hoped that he and Margaret would "get together" should Catherine's melanoma spread and make Douglas a widower, Margaret had experienced a surge of excitement. "I suddenly felt free," she told him now. "That's the truth of it, Douglas. Catherine set me free. Since then I've been—I don't know. I feel like a new woman."

"You are," he said understandingly. She had, he knew, been straining to be free. He was at once enormously flattered that she had so secretly loved him all those years and sorry that the tension created in her by her suppression of her love had more often than not resulted in hostility. "I know. I only hope you're not sorry that you've ended up with this retired old fart who still can't leave the wars behind him."

"You most certainly are *not* an old fart. Why, you jog

more miles in a day than most marathoners. You, Douglas Freeman, are as fit as a young buck." But she could see that, as virile as he was, his mind was elsewhere right now and, sliding back under the pink eiderdown, she said, "Oh all right, I'll wait. I know you won't settle until you check out this DARPA thing."

"You were listening in," he said, pretending shock. "I thought you were asleep."

"I was, my darling, until I felt you sit straight up as if there was a spider in the bed. Go on," she said teasingly. "Go down to your Rolodex."

"Don't you make fun of my Rolodex file, lady. When the power fails on my laptop, I have my cards. Hard copy, Margaret."

"Oh," she said, holding back a laugh.

He smiled as he drew the charcoal-gray *Truman Show* robe, an old gift from his actor nephew, tighter about his waist against the hard slab of his abdominal muscles. "You're very nice," he continued, "as I'm about to redis-cover in that nest of yours once I find out what the—" He hesitated, refusing to use even the most commonplace blasphemy in her presence. It was a leftover from his mar-riage to Catherine. "Once I find out whether a DARPA facility's been penetrated."

"Penetrated?"

"Stop it, woman! Is that all you can think of?"

"Right now, yes."

"Get up and make me some coffee."

"Oh, tush!" she said. "Make it yourself."

Freeman grinned and walked through to the kitchen via the living room, past a portrait of his ancestor, William Douglas Freeman, whose American rifleman's forest green and chocolate brown uniform in the painting con-trasted with the bloodred and white uniforms of the 1812 British regulars. A photo of his twenty-year-old son Dan and his girlfriend was on the lamp table along with a vase of sweet-smelling pink Mojave roses, a birthday gift to Margaret from Dan, who, in the general's view, was finding it difficult to accept that his father had not only remarried but had married his aunt.

He watched CNN. There was nothing about a break-in at any defense base, let alone any DARPA facility. Had Aussie and the other SpecForces seen it on another network? There were so many now. He channel-surfed while Margaret's ancient coffeemaker gurgled and spat. She saved everything. He had a rule: For every new thing that came into the house, an 1,100-square-foot bungalow, some old thing had to go out. In their first real quarrel after getting married she'd suggested *he* be put out. He smiled at how they'd laughed afterward and enjoyed passion-fueled sex that had left the argument in its wake.

On NBC there was yet another story about a series of terrorist alerts throughout the world. In London, a taxi bombing at Heathrow Airport had killed eight—twenty-three injured, six critically—and there was a threat in Washington state, but no reference to a West Coast naval base. Mention of Washington, however, reminded him that the U.S. Navy did have several highly sensitive installations up in Washington state.

Taking his coffee into the hallway, the general, who had been retired by a White House that hadn't appreciated his blunt public description of jihad, studied his wall map of Cascadia, the Pacific Northwest made up of British Columbia, Idaho, Oregon, and Washington state. First there was the extensive sub base on the stunningly beautiful Hood Canal, surely at the top of any terrorist's list. And then there was the huge naval air station on Whidbey Island east of the Canadian-U.S. Strait of Juan de Fuca. The latter, usually mispronounced by Aussie in crude allusions, was the egress channel for the big American Trident boomers and the hunter-killer attack subs out of Bangor, Washington. Then there was the huge Cold War SAC— Strategic Air Command—bomber base at Fairchild near Spokane way out in eastern Washington in the sagebrush country where the gargantuan B-52s flew over the sun-twinkling sprinklers that appeared like white lace across the irrigated farms and dry, coulee-rutted earth. Closer to the coast there was the army's Fort Lewis near Tacoma. It was here on this enormous base that Freeman had last attended a DARPA demonstration, having been accidentally invited by a Pentagon clerk who hadn't realized that the general was now on the "has-been" list.

But, according to Aussie, it hadn't been an army barracks that had been hit but a naval base. He knew there were naval, civilian-staffed bases, secret research stations, tucked away along the coast from San Diego to San Francisco. And there were, since 9/11, several other locations on the West Coast with its thousands of inlets and bays. These mostly consisted of cutting-edge university labs with minimum, if any, real security, the academic community not naturally disposed to the presence of armed guards, arguing, with a good deal of merit, that low profiles in fact afforded more real security than any official display of armed security and high-profile signage, the latter best exemplified by the "Use of Deadly Force Authorized" sign at the entrance to the secret Bangor sub base that everyone knew about.

Freeman thought, as he sipped the strong, black coffee, that right then he couldn't have given Aussie, Margaret, or anyone else a good, rational argument for his suspicion that it was probably the DARPA installation outside Bangor on Puget Sound's Hood Canal or the naval testing lab near Keyport, thirty-five miles west of Hood Canal in Puget Sound, but he felt it in his gut. He called one of his many contacts in the Puget Sound area and discovered that his hunch was, as Aussie would have said, as useful as "tits on a bull." Completely off track.

He did a computer news search of all the major naval establishments on the West Coast. Nothing. Next, he did a specific search on the Net for any current media mention of naval establishments on the East Coast. None had been referred to by either the networks' anchors or their affiliates in the last twenty-four hours, and there was nothing on the main blogs. Of course, he reminded himself, these days the government, citing the Patriot Act in this long war against terror, had annoyingly, if understandably, shut down thousands of Internet sites with hitherto available defense-related information and links. The American Civil Liberties Union was particularly vexed by FBI and Homeland Security "visits" to any blogger who persisted in Internet searches vis-à-vis classified defense establishments.

In frustration, Douglas Freeman decided to call Marte Price. Surely his occasional trysts with her after Catherine died, when Marte was embedded with various units of his overseas, ought to be worth something. Besides, he had never been cavalier with Marte, never treated her as a "ready lay" but as a good-looking, savvy newswoman who, on tough, life-endangering assignments, needed the same kind of sexual release he did. It had been discreet— or as discreet as any liaison can be in the field. It had, of course, been strictly against army rules and regulations, but the war had slammed peacetime propriety hard up against the certainty of their own mortality. He had seen her a few times since and spoken with her on the phone. But now that he was remarried, he knew that a call to an old flame from his own house would not be a good tactical move. And the call would have to be made on a land line. Anyone who used a cellphone these days for anything confidential had no idea of just how pervasive the

National Security Agency phone taps were, especially since 9/11. Not even Voice Over Internet Protocol-encrypted phone data was being respected by the NSA.

"I'm going down to the 7-Eleven for the *Times*," he told Margaret as she walked into the living room.

He'd always preferred the *feel* of a good newspaper, such as the old *International Herald Tribune* that he used to scan every day in Heidelberg during his Cold War posting in Germany. A good newspaper with a second cup of coffee was one of the great pleasures in life, and something he usually enjoyed after each morning's ten-mile run, fantasies of coming in first in the Olympic marathon in his head, the crowd on its feet for his sensational last-minute dash to victory. Well, hell, Georgie Patton had made it to the 1912 Olympics.

"You haven't been for your run," she said at the very moment he'd thought it.

He smiled at the synchronicity. Here was a marriage, he hoped, that would last.

"Ah, I'll run later."

"Oh? This DARPA thing must be important then."

"Well, I don't like stories that are aired once then die, especially given that this is an election year. Something's fishy. Might be something in the papers, though."

"Douglas?"

"Yes?"

"While you're on the phone with her, why don't you invite the old tart around for dinner? I'd love to see the competition."

He stood there stunned, as if a grenade had exploded nearby. Speechless.

"Oh," said Margaret, her arms akimbo, smile gone, her tone acidic. "Why so shocked, Douglas? You two were very chatty last time there was a terrorist attack. I assume you want to chat again."

"Margaret," Freeman began, "I didn't want you to think—"

"I'm already thinking it."

"I'm sorry," said the general. "Honey, honest to God, Margaret, there is no subterfuge in this. I just thought it more—"

"Discreet?" she proffered angrily. "To contact your tart from the 7-Eleven?"

"Don't call her that. She's just an old—"

"Tart," said Margaret. "I know. I have the misfortune to see her regularly on the boob tube because my legendary general of a husband just happens to be obsessed with watching CNN. And guess who is one of the anchors?"

"Margaret, stop it! That's enough, dammit. I merely want to know what happened to a story that was alive and well one moment and dead the next. Smells fishy, and I want to get to the bottom of it. You know as well as I do that I'm still on a Special Forces advisory retainer for the White House. The president himself wanted retirees kept on a potential call-up basis. We're spread—our forces are spread too thinly all over the world. And seeing they've put me on retainer, small though it is, at least they've given me something after pushing me out, and the way I keep that unofficial job, with entrée to the national security adviser, I might add, is to stay current. It's like anything else. If you're not current, you're dead."

Margaret was rigid—glacial ice.

"Ah, dammit, I'll call from here."

"No, go. Go get the papers. Keep *current*. There might be a picture of her in the obituaries."

Son of a bitch, this is getting out of control. All I said was I'm going to the 7-Eleven and, BOOM, I'm in a mine-field!

Margaret turned abruptly, stormed out of the living room, and slammed the bedroom door.

"Shit!" said Freeman. *I'm cut off for a week.*

He put on his jogging suit, grabbed his old SF forage cap and his keys, along with his phone card and ID, and left, thinking again of Rudyard Kipling's poem, the old imperialist's advice to "fill the unforgiving minute with sixty seconds' worth of distance run—" But he knew Margaret was going to need more than sixty seconds. Sixty hours, maybe? Dammit, he should have just called Marte Price from home, just do it in plain sight, with Admiral Horatio Nelson's stratagem in mind: "Never mind maneuvers. Go straight at 'em!"

Well, he thought, this is what you get when you try to do things by stealth, but then again, as a virile, fit man in his sixties, feeling closer to a fit forty, he was hugely flattered by Margaret's jealousy. When she got that cold look, the softer features of her face taking on a distinctively intimidating expression reminiscent of Julia Roberts's in *Erin Brockovich*, she was dauntingly beautiful. He strode down to the 7-Eleven.

"No, Douglas," Marte Price assured him. "I don't know anything about an attack on a navy base. Who told you there was?"

"Aussie Lewis. You remember him. He's one of my old team. You interviewed him after the team cleaned up those gangs of no-hopers on the Olympic Peninsula up in Washington state."

"Oh—wait a minute." Freeman could hear the rustle of papers at her end. "Yes," Marte said, "there was a news feed from some affiliate, something about a breaking and entering caper, but it all proved bogus." Marte laughed. "Embarrassing as hell, really. We had to run a retraction. I don't *think*," she said, laughing, "that the stringer who phoned it in will be paid for anything he or she pitches at our newspeople now. Apparently it was just some rumor. Probably some blogger screwing with us."

"Uh-huh," said the general, wiping his forehead with the heel of his right hand as he held the phone in the other. "And my name, for the record, Marte, is Shirley, and I've got the biggest hooters in Monterey County."

"Good for you, Shirley," she quipped.

"Oh, come on, Marte. Give me a break. Don't give me that stringer rumor crap. CNN has faster intel half the time than No Such Agency." He meant the National Security Agency. "You don't run anything unless it's reliable, has to be fact-checked."

"I'm sorry, Douglas, but I'm telling you the truth. I hate to say it, but sometimes we actually do make mistakes— like that kid in San Diego, remember? Back in forty-one, alone in the newsroom on the Sunday, December seventh? Couldn't get any confirmation, but he was going to run the header 'Japs Bomb San Francisco' until they got it sorted out at the last moment."

"Bad analogy, sweetheart," said Freeman. "The *Japanese*—'Japs' is politically incorrect, Marte—*did* bomb us. The kid just thought it was 'Frisco instead of Pearl Harbor. But there *was* a bombing attack."

"Douglas, I don't want to be rude, but I'm busy. The story is there's no story. *Nothing happened. Nothing.* Bad news source. Nada." She paused. "I hear traffic. Why aren't you calling from home? Afraid your new wife'll find out?"

"Thanks, Marte," he told her. "Take care."

She hung up.

Bitch. Well, not really a bitch, but—a "*bad news source*"? Douglas Freeman gleaned every headline in the 7-Eleven, including those in *USA Today, The New York Times, The Los Angeles Times*, and *La Opinión*. Nada.

He went down to the beach and began his morning run.

He hated jogging in sand but knew it increased his work-out by a factor of two to three and tempered his calf muscles until they were as hard as the new hagfish and Kevlar bulletproof vests he'd championed. As he pounded up and down the dunes, he was confident he'd give any drill instructor anywhere a run for his money—*with* full modern combat pack of fifty to seventy pounds, which just happened to be the same amount of weight as the Roman legionnaires had carried on their twenty-mile-a-day marches. As usual when jogging, he imagined that he was in a history-making race, like Philippides who ran the twenty-six miles from Marathon to Athens to tell the Athenians to hold fast, that their army under General Miltiades, who had just whipped the Persians, was now on its way back to save Athens itself, which it did. Of course Philippides had collapsed and died the second after he'd delivered the fateful message.

By the time he'd reached home, Freeman was in full sweat.

"Sweetie, I'm home."

"I can smell."

Ouch. Maybe she would cut him off for a *month*?

"Sorry, I know I must pong."

"Must *what*?" she asked sharply.

"Pong."

"Is that—" There was a pause, and he thought he heard a stifled laugh, and seized the opportunity.

"Yes, pong—means to really smell bad. An Aussie or Brit word. Not sure which. Aussie Lewis used to use it a lot. Guess I picked it up from him." There was another long pause, and she appeared at the door in a smart fall suit of variegated autumnal tones: nothing too gauche but one that showed her ample bustline to best advantage.

"Where are you off to?" asked the general, a little cap-in-hand, a man who had once commanded thousands of men in the field, and the commander who had electrified America with his momentous "U-turn battle" against the Siberian Sixth Armored Corps during the U.S.-led U.N. "peacekeeping action" in the Transbaikal.

"I'm going out," she said, checking her reflection in the hall mirror. "I told you last week. Linda Rushmein is giving a bridal shower for her niece, Julia."

"Rushmein," mused Freeman. "As in 'rush mein dinner, mein Herr?'"

Margaret didn't smile. "The shower will be later in the day but Linda's asked me to help with the preparations. I won't be back till late. She's coming to pick me up."

"That's a long drive," Freeman noted.

"Don't wait up for me," she said.

"Of course I will."

"I can't imagine why. I'll be tired."

"Then I'll run you a hot bath," Freeman said congenially.

She had put on gold, dolphin-shaped earrings. Freeman idly recalled that dolphins were the symbols of submariners. It got him thinking that perhaps this nonstory about a DARPA facility being attacked had to do with the new submarine base in Alaska. It might be a bit of a stretch, he thought, but a news source could say "West Coast" and still mean Alaska.

"You can stay up for me if you want," said Margaret, "but I'm going straight to bed."

"That's what I mean," he said cheekily, slipping off his jogging shoes. "I'll be *up*!"

"Don't be vulgar, Douglas." She straightened her suit jacket, crimped her hair, then looked straight at him. "You're famous, I'm told, for your commando raids and command of detail, meticulous planning, and concern for your troops. Well, through no fault of your own, you've been pushed into retirement by what Linda tells me is the iPod generation in the Pentagon. And I'm sorry for that, and I'll try my best to be a good, loyal wife, but I'm serious, Douglas, I don't want you flirting with other women. It's something I abhor in men who are married and—"

"Flirting?" he interjected. "Margaret, I was thinking of *you*. I just thought it would be imprudent to be calling Marte Price from home. I'd probably feel the same if you had reason, however sound, to call an old beau, someone *you* had known—"

"Slept with, you mean, like you did with that tart."

"That was *before* I met you—well, I mean, really got to know you after Catherine's death. For Heaven's sake, Margaret, get a grip. You're blowing this way out of proportion. Talk about making a mountain out of a molehill."

"It's the *lie*, Douglas. It's not that you're phoning your old tart."

"I've asked you before. Please don't refer to her like that."

"It's not that you're phoning your old tart. It's this pathetic 7-Eleven cover story. Linda Rushmein tells me that even amongst your enemies in the State Department, whom you've raked over the coals for being professional liars, you're thought to be an honest man. But I caught you in one of your own lies."

His blood pressure was shooting up, and his grim-jawed George C. Scott in *Patton* face was set in Defcon 2—the penultimate defense condition before outright war. "Linda Rushmouth should keep her mouth shut. I did *not* call people in the State Department professional liars. I said that they lied because most diplomats were paid to lie."

"Oh, don't be so tendentious. It's the same thing." She snatched her raincoat from the hall rack.

"All right, all right," he began, "it was foolish of me not to tell you I'd be calling her. It's just that I could see no good reason to tell you and get you all upset. It was wrong of me to do it. I'm sorry. It won't happen again."

There was a horn bipping outside.

"That'll be Linda," said Margaret. "I have to go."

"Can you leave a number where I can reach you? I always like to have a—"

She scribbled the number on the yellow Post-it pad on the hall table.

"I love you, you silly woman," he called after her. "And tell Linda Rushmein to get a muzzle. And don't let her drive you home if she's had too many. Those Krauts like their suds!"

Shouldn't have said that, oaf. He would have bawled out a subordinate for such boorishness. As he looked into the hall mirror, he rebuked himself. *Now you've done it, Freeman. You might be the hero from way back in the Far East against the Siberian Sixth et al. but here in Monterey you're facing a domestic court-martial for a damn fool tactical move.*

He descended to the basement, opened the Rolodex file in the cabinet near his weights, and looked up Alaska—naval bases. Nothing rang a bell. Perhaps this nonstory CNN had broadcast before they'd been obviously sat upon by the heavies from the Department of Homeland Security, the FBI, et al. didn't have anything to do with a naval base at all but was about an air force, army, or marine base, with an unmarked "black box" DARPA facility nearby? The Rolodex listed one DARPA facility attached to El-mendorf, the big air force base adjacent to Anchorage, Alaska, as well as other bases down Canada's adjoining West Coast. Turning on his computer, he did a Net search for all armed forces bases. But there were no reports, not even a suggestion of a B and E, only assurances that the government was doing a good job with your tax dollars.

He called the White House, asking to speak to National

Security Adviser Eleanor Prenty, the only connection he had with the administration as per his contract. He had promised he'd call only on matters of national emergency. He was put on hold. Usually the presidential staff, like those at State, didn't take kindly to Freeman; he was likely to say what he thought, his words unadorned by the usual equivocation of career flip-floppers and yes-men.

He wouldn't have made the call if he'd been able to get even a scrap of information about the "nonstory," but there were no scraps. Still the very idea that terrorists might have penetrated DARPA security had set off his alarm bells. His personal interest in DARPA dated from when he'd sent a memo to the Pentagon, personally championing what otherwise would have been a small item in the press: the development of a hagfish slime-fiber weave vest. The slime's molecular structure, he knew, was so strong that he suggested it be mixed with the latest Kevlar to make what he believed would be the toughest bulletproof vest possible, given the weight-to-load-bearing ratio of America's fighting men and women. DARPA had run with the idea, and he was proved right. Since then, countless American and allied lives had been saved by the vests, and unfortunately the lives of American-hating terrorists who, just as Freeman had warned the Pentagon, had gotten their hands on either the chemical formula or the vests themselves so as to reverse-engineer their own. Of course it was only a matter of time before the DARPA vest went commercial anyway, but he'd hoped to give the Pentagon the heads-up to at least try to restrict the distribution of the vests. Had terrorists penetrated DARPA again? And if so, what was at risk? Or was he way off course, and Marte Price right—that it was nothing more than a badly sourced nonstory, a figment of some eager blogger's imagination?

The White House operator told the general he'd have to

leave a message or call back. Eleanor Prenty was in a meeting right now.

To calm down, he showered, opening his eyes every now and then to check that no one else was in the bathroom. As a youngster, he'd seen Hitchcock's *Psycho* and after that murder in the shower scene he'd harbored a subliminal fear about showering with his eyes shut, training himself to keep his eyes open even while shampooing. It had saved his life in Iraq when a terrorist, breaching the U.S. security ring around Karbala, had come in firing his AK-47. Freeman, having glimpsed him through an eye-stinging film of soapsuds, had dived, quickly knocking the terrorist over, grabbing him in a headlock and plunging the would-be assassin headfirst into a toilet and drowning him.

Hours later, sitting in the living room La-Z-Boy waiting for Margaret to come home and tired of surfing the Net for any possible DARPA connection, Douglas Freeman was starting to have grave doubts about Aussie's story. He had killed the TV and turned to read his favorite passages from Thucydides' *History of the Peloponnesian War*, when the phone's jangle startled him. It was Aussie Lewis.

"Hi, Aussie, what's up?"

"We clear?"

"Clear fore and aft," the general replied, his tone edgy after the fight with Margaret. "What's up?"

"Uh, nothing much, General, but I've got a good bet." There was a pause. "Does Mommy let you bet?"

"I'll bet when I want," said Freeman. It was an old Special Forces team joke that whenever you wanted to rib a guy, you just said, "Will Mommy let you do it?"

"Okay," said Aussie. "This is straight from the trainer's mouth, not the horse's. Very interesting info on the eight horse in the sixth race at Churchill Downs. It's been raining."

The general was more alert now; this was how his SpecWar team's military intelligence often came to him: not from neat official reports but from bits and pieces buried here and there in casual conversation which, because there was no record of it, could be "plausibly denied" by all team members should some snoopy congressman launch a fishing expedition into the financial heart of the General Accounting Office, trolling for black ops budgets.

"It's been raining," Aussie repeated.

"Uh-huh." Horse racing was the team's venue of choice for issuing an alert to the other team members, the track chosen somewhere in the world where there'd been bad weather in the last twenty-four hours.

The general was already Googling Churchill Downs: an inch of precipitation in the last twelve hours.

"The eight horse," Aussie told him, "is a good mudder. So put a packet on him if you want to make a bundle."

"I don't know," said the general, feigning disinterest should his phone be tapped by any of the myriad agencies that were now watching their own citizens more closely than ever before in the ongoing war against terror. "There must be other nags in that race who can run in the mud, Aussie."

"Yeah, but not like this one. Jockey told me this horse loves the mud, digs deep, no slipping and sliding. The mother of all mudders, General."

"I don't know," the general repeated. "Unlike you Aussies, I'm not the betting type. A ticket in the Powerball now and then, maybe, but you know what they say about the lotteries."

"Yeah, yeah, tax on the stupid. Our mate Choir's been singing that song to me for years. 'Course he doesn't gamble," continued Aussie sarcastically. "He *invests*. But he's not on my case today. He's got one hell of a hangover from last night, and has to hightail it to catch a flight back to—where's that burg he lives in in Washington?" It wasn't a burg, it was a small township nestled in the hills on the eastern edge of the Cascade Mountains.

"Winthrop," the general answered, and answered jokingly, "He's not sick already?"

Choir Williams, one of the toughest of the tough in Special Forces, having been trained first by the British SAS, Special Air Service, at Brecon Beacons in Wales. He was notorious for getting motion sickness. Choir, they used to joke, would get sick on an early-morning dew, but, like his grandfather and so many others who'd been violently ill on that gray, ugly morning of June 6, 1944, in Normandy, once he was in action, it was the enemy's turn to suffer.

"He'll be fine," said Aussie, rubbing it in. "I'll give 'im a coupla greasy fried eggs 'fore he leaves."

Choir's terse response could be heard in the background.

"You be sure to make the bet, General," Aussie pressed. "The eight horse. I guarantee it."

"Oh," came the general's retort. "So you'll give me a refund if it doesn't win or place?"

"Stone the crows!" said Aussie. "I'm not *that* stupid."

"I'll think about it, Aussie. Thanks for calling."

When Freeman hung up, he scribbled "8, Churchill Downs" on his bedside Post-it pad and got up to spin the Rolodex file for the team's letter-for-number code that had been disguised on one of the three-by-five-inch index cards. The cards contained everything from specs about the new weapons coming out of DARPA to the dimensions of the new Wasp-class carriers of the kind that the team had used on earlier missions and which housed helos and vertical takeoff and Joint Strike Fighter aircraft. The

Rolodex also held the specifications for the object that looked like a marking pen that the general nearly always carried in his shirt pocket when out of the house.

Consulting the Rolodex's file for this day's one-time pad—that is, this day's number-for-letter code—he wrote down a seven-digit number prefixed by a three-number area code. But to make sure his end was as secure as Aussie's had been, the general would now have to use a landline outside the house. He knew the NSA had hired hundreds of Arab-speaking translators post-9/11, but he suspected some Arab agents must have slipped through the net, using the NSA's intercepts for their own intelligence networks. Such was the paranoia of the world after 9/11.

He grabbed his Windbreaker and zipped it up, feeling a stiff breeze coming off the ocean, and headed down to the 7-Eleven again. He stood impatiently while a lanky, dirty-haired, earring-in-tongue youth of about twenty, who could see that the general was anxious to get on the phone, turned his back on Freeman and proceeded to loll against the wall of the phone booth, indulging himself in a long, banal conversation with his girlfriend, the communication consisting of repetition of "y'know" and "totally" and "like." Like the general would, you know, like to pull the insolent son of a bitch right out of the phone booth and totally put him in the Marine Corps; give him a Parris Island haircut, feed him to the drill instructors, and teach the kid a few manners.

The youth was picking his teeth with a broken fingernail as the general left, cooling down, telling himself he'd been through his own rebellious time as a young man, but assuring himself that he'd not put anything in his body that didn't belong there. As his self-righteous mood abated, he walked off to another phone booth four blocks away to dial the number Aussie had given him.

"Hello?" It sounded like Aussie, but there was a lot of static on the line.

"Clear?" intoned the general.

"Clear," came the reply.

The general hesitated. As his old Special Forces outfit knew, he was a stickler for details. It wasn't only his normal disposition that made him so but the experience of having a mission in Iraq compromised because of an English-speaking insurgent having successfully imitated a U.S. Ranger, calling down mortar rounds on U.S. positions. The interloper had used only "clear" instead of the full "clear fore and aft," but had sounded so much like an American that the SpecFor team had taken out four Rangers before realizing they'd been set up for a blue on blue. And so the general, although he was 90 percent sure it was Aussie on the other end, said, "Clear is insufficient reply. I say again, clear is insufficient reply." The static increased. The general heard, "Clear fore and aft."

"What's up?" asked the general, still on guard. Since 9/11, nothing was safe—voice mail, e-mail, snail mail, and especially text of any kind. What was it J. P. Morgan had advised? "Never write anything down."

"Got a phone message this afternoon. From an old girl-friend of ours."

"Yes?" said Freeman. The static eased up, but then surged.

"Well, she said she couldn't talk earlier because of the pressure of work."

The general still felt uneasy, the static doing nothing to abate his lingering suspicion.

So, thought Freeman, Homeland Security or the FBI *had* gotten to Marte.

"What did she say?" asked Freeman, maintaining a casual, almost bored, tone.

"She said she wished she could have explained more but that her brother had been in the room."

"Uh-huh," said Freeman. *Big Brother. A CNN boss? Or a DHS official?*

"Did she like the card I sent her?" It was the team's phrase for more information.

"Oh yeah. She said it was a little sentimental but every word was true. She loved hearing your story about Eleanor Roosevelt, the French fries, and that kid who told her she had such big ears."

Freeman was so keen to jot down the message, he had at first mistakenly taken out the fake DARPA marking pen from his shirt pocket instead of the regular ballpoint before reminding himself of the "no text" rule. He'd have to commit it to memory.

"Oh yeah," said the general, laughing casually. "I remember that incident—cheeky damn kid. Where was that? On the campaign trail for FDR down in Louisiana?"

"No, you're way off." It was said good-naturedly. "No, remember, the story was that she was flying out west for FDR and it was some VIP's kid on the plane who insulted her."

"Yeah," said Freeman in the tone of one who was just now recalling the full details of an old joke. "And she says to the cheeky kid, 'Never mind my ears. Your nose is longer than a French fry,' right?"

"That was it. But I never believed that bit about her saying that to the kid. From what I remember of my history lessons, Eleanor Roosevelt wasn't like that. So, okay, she mightn't have looked like a Hollywood film starlet, but she was a kind woman and she did a hell of a lot for this country. She was FDR's right-hand woman, right?"

"Right," said Freeman, committing these three things to memory: *Eleanor Roosevelt, the kid's supposed comment about her "big ears,"* and *"French fries."* None of

these words used by Aussie were likely to trigger automatic NSA, FBI, or DHS phone taps. Besides, the
computer-heavy NSA, quite apart from the DHS and the
FBI, simply didn't have enough manpower. The computers were programmed so that certain giveaway phrases
such as "terrorist," "assassination," "attack," and "the
Great Satan" would automatically trigger an NSA computer to record the conversation for later analysis. On the
off chance that any terrorist infiltrator from any of the security agencies had been plugged in, neither Freeman nor
Aussie had made any reference to a DARPA breaking and
entering. And Eleanor Roosevelt, French fries, and big
ears weren't the kind of words that would alert NSA's
terrorist surveillance.

"Gotta go," said Aussie. "Someone else wants to use
this phone."

Back at the house, the general brewed another cup of
"velvet Java," as he liked to call the smooth, black liquid
that dripped from Margaret's old but thorough filtration
system. As he waited for his favorite Pyrex glass mug to
fill, the one with the faded insignia of his old Third Army
on it, he mused over three things. First, Aussie's mention
of "an old girlfriend of ours" clearly referred to Marte
Price. Second, she had felt her message urgent and sensitive enough to call Aussie Lewis, whose number she
would have from one of her interviews with the general's
team following one of their celebrated raids. And third,
she wanted to get the message to Freeman quickly without phoning him directly, having eschewed e-mail, snail
mail, or courier service—all of which could be, and were
being, opened under the Patriot Act. If DHS and the other
agencies had come down on her so hard about this "nonstory," then they were certainly going to check any e-mail
or phone calls from and to her office and home. She had

done the smart thing, obviously having left the office, and chosen a landline to call Aussie. But what in hell did her message mean? He shook his head in ironic acknowledgement of the odd, ofttimes mundane, names that had been used to hide military secrets and the turning points of history: "Climb Mount Nikita," the three words that launched the Japanese sneak attack on Pearl Harbor, and the names Juno, Sword, Omaha, Utah, and Gold, the designations of the four beaches used in the Allied invasion of Normandy, and, for Freeman, the moving line of Paul Verlaine's poetry, " . . . *blessent mon couer d'une langueur monotone*"—". . . wound my heart with a monotonous languor"—being the long-awaited signal that galvanized the Maquis, the French Resistance, to rise en masse against the Nazis. At least Freeman now realized that the original B and E story was true, and that Aussie's phone message from Marte Price was trying to help him identify the base.

All right, then, how about Eleanor Roosevelt? What did her name signify in history? Freeman remembered how Marte had once lamented to him that one of the most depressing things in her career as an investigative reporter and news anchor was discovering just how ignorant Americans are of history. Not only the history of far-off places such as Iraq but the history of our own country as well. And, she'd noted, the ignorance wasn't confined to the United States. She'd told him how she'd had to cover the visit of one of Canada's former prime ministers, Paul Martin, who was giving a televised speech at a military base to celebrate the D-Day landings in Normandy but who called it the "invasion of Norway." And there was the Canadian cabinet minister who didn't know the difference between France's pro-Nazi Vichy government and the famous Battle of *Vimy* Ridge in World War I, where the Canadians had charged and broken the German line.

But Marte hadn't told him anything special, or at least anything that he could remember, about Eleanor Roosevelt. And what on earth had she to do with Aussie's mention of French fries and big ears? Freeman, an avid history buff, had never heard such a story about FDR's wife, and believed that a child's supposed insult to the first lady was a red herring that Aussie had dropped into the conversation merely to get the phrase "big ears" into the message. The general had considered the possibility that a callow youth could have actually said something so rude and hurtful to the first lady; there had certainly been a lot of cruel, if unpublished, allusions to her looks during the war by many who had opposed FDR. It had been bad enough that FDR had polio, the scourge of his generation, and was in iron leg braces and a wheelchair, the press having had a gentleman's agreement that they would never photograph the leg braces or focus in too closely on the two Secret Service men who had to stand by the president at every function, holding him by cupping his elbows. Marte and Freeman had talked about that little-known historical fact and how JFK's severe back pain and his Addison's disease had also been kept from the public.

Freeman smiled affectionately at the memory of their chat about FDR, and he did recall Marte pointing out how the first lady had done so much good, not only for the wartime generation but for everyone, how the guy in the street, like his father, had loved FDR, the man in the wheelchair who had served the longest term, more than thirteen years, of any U.S. president, and who had led America out of the terrible years of the Depression. He had stood up against Hitler and helped save England, despite the pervasive mood of isolationism against him, and had vowed to stop the stomach-turning brutality that was the modus operandi of the marauding empire of Japan. And through it all, Eleanor, like so many uncomplaining wives, had borne her husband's darkness with him and had become indispensable.

Freeman had been Googling the Net for "Eleanor Roosevelt," "French fries," and "big ears" connections all afternoon. By the time the evening news came on, he was getting a headache from staring at the flickering screen. Nothing about any break-in at a military base. He remembered Watergate; that had started to unwind because a B and E had been reported. The story that was grabbing TV headlines this day was another "worm" attack on the Net. Some jerk, working for a big corporation, had left a port open on his laptop and the perpetrator had downloaded the worm into the corporation's mainframes. Once more he went to his laptop, bringing up databases for Eleanor Roosevelt and cross-referencing keywords from them with defense-based links. What he found were "umpteen" entries, as Margaret would have described them if she were still speaking to him.

Eleanor Roosevelt had sure traveled. He Googled "big ears" specifically on the defense contractor linkages. Nothing. There was an "Ears," or rather "Golden Ears" provincial park in Canada not that far north of the big sub base at Bangor on Washington state's Hood Canal, but there were no references indicating a joint U.S.-Canadian armed forces base. But when he saw that this provincial park, the equivalent of a state park in the United States, was landlocked, he thought of a possibility so obvious he was embarrassed that it hadn't occurred to him earlier. Was it possible that there was a navy DARPA base somewhere *inland* in the United States? It didn't make sense, but he ran it. There were only a few, but one of them was in Idaho. Potatoes? French fries? A possibility.

He zoomed in. It was situated on a lake, Pend Oreille, in the Idaho panhandle, thirty-six miles northeast of Spokane.

Spokane itself was east of semi-arid desert country, much of it now irrigated, but Pend Oreille was in a thickly forested valley between the eight-thousand-foot-high Bitterroot Range and the Cabinet Mountains wilderness area which, the general noted, placed the lake between northeastern Washington and northwestern Montana in an area that thousands of years ago had been deeply scoured by glaciers. Then the computer crashed. Why, he had no idea, but it forced him to curb his excitement, having to admit, with a crossword puzzle addict's reluctance, that even if he was correct in his assumption that Idaho was a key to unlocking Marte's message, it was still only *one* of three clues he'd been given, and nothing was making sense. He needed to know more before he could call National Security adviser Eleanor Prenty with his theory that someone was trying to kill a story about a B and E just as someone in the Nixon administration had tried to kill Watergate.

Then, just as suddenly, another connection presented itself. *Eleanor* Prenty and *Eleanor* Roosevelt. He sat back, massaging his neck muscles.

Was there anything more that he could glean from Aussie's conversation? The general had long been a believer, as all who had served under him knew, in Frederick the Great's adage "*L'audace, l'audace, toujours l'audace!*" And it sure as hell was going to take audacity to call his wife in the middle of Linda Rushmein's shower so soon after the verbal firefight over Marte Price. But the damned computer was down and he was impatient. Besides, the fact was that Margaret was fluent in French. He wasn't.

"Hello?" It was Linda Rushmein on the phone.

"Hi. It's Douglas Freeman here. Could I speak to Margaret?"

"I didn't think you two were on speaking terms," replied Linda tartly.

"Could I speak to my wife, please?"

Cold as ice. He could hear women's laughter in the background, but when Margaret came on there wasn't a trace of humor in her voice. "Yes?" It was as if he was a telemarketer interrupting dinner.

"Hi, sweetie," said the general. "How's the party going?"

"Fine. What do you want?"

It felt like he was standing in a force 8 gale without his thermal underwear. "Look, I'm sorry to bother you, Sweetie." *Crawl on your belly, General. Hell hath no fury like a woman scorned.*

"What do you want, Douglas?"

"Well, first I want to apologize. That was thoughtless of me going out earlier to call like that, but you see it was important that I use a landline other than the one in the house. I'm in a phone booth now."

"Is this more secret stuff?" She made it sound seedy.

"It's more secure on an outside landline," he told her. "Anyway, I'm sorry I upset you. I can fully understand how you must have seen it."

"That's big of you," she said icily.

"Look," began Freeman, "this might seem strange, but something very important's come up and I need your help."

"Do you? Isn't Marte smarter?"

He took a deep breath. "No," he answered slowly. "And as far as I know she didn't take French in college, as you did. And you keep it up, right?"

"I read French. I don't speak it—well, hardly at all."

"That's fine."

"What is it?" she asked impatiently. "I have to get back to the party. They're about to give Julia the gifts."

"Right. What does this mean?" He spelled out Pend Oreille.

"I've never heard of a French word 'pend,'" responded Margaret. "But 'oreille' is 'ear.' Why?"

The general was looking down at his tightly folded copy of the TPC—Tactical Pilotage Chart—F-16B. The shape of Lake Pend Oreille could be seen as that of an ear. "Pend" was maybe a hybrid word from the English "pendulous"—long, hanging down. Long ear. The shape of the lake *was* roughly like that of an ear, with a longer than usual lobe. Long ear. Big ear.

"Love you, Margaret."

There was a pause, her voice lowered. "You too, you big oaf."

"See you later, Sweetheart."

"I'll be late."

"Not *too* late, I hope." Margaret heard the excitement in his voice but it seemed to have been aroused more by her translation of "oreille" than by her impending return to Monterey. "I'd like to show you something," Freeman told her. "It's not an ear, but it's long."

"Really, Douglas!" But he could tell the ice had been broken. "I have to go," she told him.

"Bye," he said and, with his heart pounding, quickly dialed information for Vancouver, Canada, and asked for the history department at the University of British Columbia where, several years earlier, he'd taken a "War and Society" course as part of the post-9/11 NORAD—North American Defense Pact—liaison officer exchange program. It had been a course primarily on the history of war and its impact on any number of societies—how Rosie the Riveter had expanded the rights of women during the war, how war had revolutionized technology and vice versa, and how, for the Confederates, the first Battle of Bull Run turned from certain defeat to victory, due in large part to the military's use of railways to rush Southern reinforcements to Bull Run in time to turn the tide for Stonewall Jackson.

The general asked to speak to Dr. Retals. Not there.

Home number? The department secretary was polite, but firm. They couldn't give out home numbers. And so he dialed the regular information number for area code 604 and asked for a David Retals who, if he remembered correctly, lived in or around the university area, out in the Dunbar-Point Grey area. On a Post-it, the general had written, "Big Ears, Eleanor Roosevelt, Idaho."

"Hello?"

"Dr. Retals?"

"Yes?"

"General Douglas Freeman here. I took your course on war and—"

"I remember, General. How are you?"

"Fine, Doc. I need to know something, and I needed it yesterday."

He heard Retals give a short laugh. "You were always in a hurry, General, except, as I remember, with your final paper."

"That should have been an A, Doc," the general charged. "You gave me a B-plus. I was sorely disappointed."

"You were sorely *late*. An hour late, as I recall."

"My damn computer had crashed."

"That's what they all say. How can I help you?" asked the professor congenially, obviously amused by his former student's complaint about receiving a B-plus instead of an A for a late paper—and this coming from the legendary American officer whose standing order was that his officers' mess at breakfast, lunch, and dinner must be closed exactly fifteen minutes after opening so as to punish latecomers and impress upon all the need for punctuality.

"Do you know of any connection, Doctor, between Eleanor Roosevelt and a Lake Pend Oreille?"

"Oh yes. The lake's in Idaho, right?"

"Yes, sir," said Freeman.

"Well," began the historian, "early in the Second World

War, Eleanor Roosevelt was on a flight out west on some business for FDR and, looking down on the Rockies, she saw this astonishingly beautiful lake just west of the Bitterroot Range in Idaho. Anyway, she made a note of it and when she returned to Washington, D.C., she recommended it to FDR, who, at the time, urgently needed a safe inland naval training base that would be well away from the East and West coasts, safe from any possible attack, particularly by the Japanese Navy's air arm. The lake she'd seen turned out to be 'Pend Oreille.' It's around ninety thousand acres, if I remember correctly, and very, very deep, over a thousand feet down in places. Anyway, after training more than a quarter of a million U.S. Navy personnel, mostly submariners in World War Two, this training center on the lake—the navy's second largest training base in the world at the time—was decommissioned in—" The professor paused. "—I think it was sometime in 1946. I'd have to check that. Anyway, though it was decommissioned, it wasn't forgotten. The staff was greatly reduced in size, down to a couple of dozen people at most. I believe the navy turned it into some kind of research station. That's all I know, really."

"Professor, if you were a woman, I'd kiss you."

The professor laughed easily, remembering how the general hadn't been so jolly when he'd received the B-plus.

"Thanks a million, Doc. I owe you one."

"Not at all," said Retals. "May I ask what you're up to?"

"Deter, detect, defend," answered Freeman. It was NORAD's motto, which the professor had mentioned more than once in his course.

"Ah," said the professor. "A word of advice?"

"Shoot," said Freeman.

"Be careful, General. Idaho can get cruelly cold."

"The globe's warming, Professor."

"Not everywhere."

*   *   *

Now that he had something definite, Freeman called Eleanor Prenty again from the 7-Eleven. She was in yet another meeting. He was persistent, insisting that his call was "most urgent," a matter of "the highest national security," and that he had information which, if it got out, could acutely embarrass the administration, particularly in this, its election year.

He was put on hold, his ears assaulted by the most discordant jazz he'd ever heard. Whoever was on the horn sounded as if he were playing underwater and the tape or disk was past its prime, probably scratched. To Freeman, it sounded little better than static. Being on hold was a damn insult. Here he was, able to prove that it had taken him less than twenty-four hours to discover that whichever security agency was trying to keep the lid on the B and E at Pend Oreille wasn't quite up to the job, and what did they do? Put him on hold. It was what Aussie Lewis would call a "piss-poor start."

"Douglas?" The national security adviser sounded polite, but was clearly under a lot of strain, her voice rough with fatigue.

"Eleanor, I've just earned that retainer you pay me and then some."

"How?" she asked impatiently. No doubt he'd dragged her away from yet another of the endless chain of meetings with the president and other *nonretirees*.

"Eleanor, I have a rock-solid source in the press who confirms that a naval research base has been hit. I know where it is. It's landlocked and its name refers to part of the anatomy."

"I know," she said.

"*What?* Son of a—"

"Are you on a landline, Douglas?"

"I may be kept out of the loop," he said testily, "but I'm not stupid. Of course I'm on a landline!"

"Douglas, calm down. I wasn't lying to you when we spoke earlier. I mean, I wasn't giving you the brush-off. The CIA, FBI, and DHS have been sitting on this. It's so explosive they didn't call it through until they thought they'd figured out exactly what had happened. I assume you know how much the president *hates* speculation. He wants hard facts from the agencies when they tell him something has fallen off the rails. Not first impressions, but solid facts. From what we can gather, a computer disk has been stolen, and U.S. forces from the Tenth Mountain Division were seen by some residents in the area riding down toward the base. Defense tells us that the Tenth Mountain Division shouldn't have been anywhere near Pend Oreille."

"Switcheroos!" said Freeman.

"What?"

"Switcheroos, terrorists, infiltrators, wearing the other guys' uniforms. Hell, we've done the same thing in SpecOps for years."

"Well, whatever happened, the disk is gone and apparently it contains *highly* sensitive data. *I'm* not even cleared to that level."

It didn't surprise Freeman, for while he knew that most people would find it difficult, if not impossible, to understand how someone as highly placed as the national security adviser might not be privy to such information, it was often the case. Indeed, in the new Office of Scientific Intelligence the distribution of DARPA files, Freeman knew, was obsessively controlled.

"Look," Freeman advised the national security adviser, "even from what little you've told me and from what I've heard about Homeland Security or whoever it was killing the story after an initial blurb on CNN, this is clearly a no-wait situation. We don't need a lot of suits from either the Intel agencies or Foggy Bottom discussing the options. There's only one thing to do. Go find the pricks who stole the disk. With the right transport I can have my team rendezvous and be on the trail within eight hours." He hurried on, "Hell, one of my men—" He was thinking of Choir Williams. "—lives in the area in question." He said nothing about young Prince, Choir's K-9 dog, who was one of the best trackers he'd ever seen, next to the team itself. "This is what we *do*, Eleanor." Then he added, with some force, "I brought home the bacon from Korea, didn't I?"

"Yes," she agreed, he and his team had successfully carried out a predawn raid on the coast of North Korea, in one of the most hostile military areas in the world, and brought back vital intel. Freeman's team had done precisely what the so-called "U.S. Paratroopers" had done at the DARPA installation on Pend Oreille, except that Freeman and his team hadn't murdered civilians in cold blood. They had fought their own kind—warriors—in the North Korean raid.

Freeman, voice controlled but tight with the tension of expectation, said, "I say again, Eleanor, what we've got to do is go find these people before they get the disk out of the country, right?" Before she could answer, he was asking, "Have your people alerted all ports, airports and—?"

"We have. And we've got hundreds of DHS and FBI agents swarming through every airport in the Northwest. All border personnel have been alerted and are triple-checking every passport. The air force, coast guard, and navy on both coasts are also on alert. That means no plane or vessel is leaving the country until we say so."

"*Time*, Eleanor," the general stressed. "By the time the top brass in the Pentagon get their heads around this, these jokers will be on the West Coast. For Heaven's sake, give me the green light. Let my team go after 'em. We're always ready to go on short notice, you know that. Send in the heavyweight battalions later if I don't get them. But let's go while the trail's still hot. I checked the long-range forecast, and in a few days there's going to be a big snowfall up there. That's not going to help track 'em, Eleanor. It's a wilderness up there—one of the last great wild places in America. And with our regular forces already stretched thin all across the world, what you need is a small, self-sufficient, well-trained ready-to-go group on the ground *now*. Dammit, we can *smell* a terrorist."

Was her sigh one of disbelief or fatigue?

"You all right? he asked.

"Do you fight as fast as you talk, Douglas?"

"Yes, ma'am," he answered good-naturedly, before he was back on the attack, telling her, "We've trained for it, Eleanor. It's what we *do*," he repeated. "When my guys move through the kill house at Fort Bragg, they're not only practicing close quarters combat, they get to use their noses, smell memory. People with different diets give off different-smelling perspiration. My guys use their noses or, by God, I don't pass them." He didn't mention Prince; once that "puppy," as Freeman sometimes called Choir's fully grown dog, got onto a scent he was like a magnet to a fridge. Wouldn't let go.

"Eleanor?"

"Yes?"

"How many of our people were killed up there?"

"I'm not certain as yet," she replied, "but we think around a dozen. Not all the pix have come through from the FBI. It's not like suicide bombers, Douglas. I mean, the sheriff who was first on the scene said nothing much seems disturbed, no butcher-shop massacre, not like the mess suicide bombers leave behind. First photos show one body slumped, sitting on the floor, back to a door. If you didn't look closely and see the body, a man—" She needed a second to regain her composure. "Even the bullet holes aren't messy, at least not in the pictures I saw. It's so—so surreal, as if some of them've just gone to sleep on the floor, except for an older man slumped down by the door. He looks—" She couldn't go on for several more moments.

"He—" began Eleanor, "—the older man, I mean, he—was no older than my dad. It was just so *cruel*, Douglas. They weren't even soldiers, just civilians, scientists, doing their—"

Freeman spoke softly. "I know. These terrorist bastards. They're not warriors. They're vermin." He paused, could hear her breathing. "Eleanor, for God's sake, give me the green light."

"Can you stay on hold for a few minutes?"

"Sure," he answered, without a trace of annoyance. "I like jazz."

While he waited, shifting the receiver from one hand to the other, the jazz static attacked again, this time murdering "Stranger on the Shore." It was only now that Freeman saw the muscular youth, the one he'd seen before, silver stud in his tongue. He'd been waiting impatiently for the phone and was now moving menacingly toward the general. What bothered Freeman most was that he'd been so focused on talking with Eleanor that he'd missed seeing the youth. "I'm going to be awhile here," Freeman told him cordially. "It's an urgent call. You'd be better off to use the phone a couple of blocks from here." What, wondered Freeman, was a kid, even a deadbeat, doing without a cellphone? Did he have anything to do with Pend Oreille or was he a wild card looking for trouble, courting it to fizz up his gray existence where the only certainty was uncertainty?

"Can't use it," said the kid sourly, his jaw jutting in the direction of the phone. "It's busted."

"Listen," said Freeman as politely as time would allow, "I'm sorry, but this is an urgent call, so if you could give me a little space here—"

The youth, more sullen and unkempt up close than he'd appeared earlier in the day, came even closer. Freeman could smell him—sour body odor—and glimpsed soap dripping from a squeegee poking out from behind his waist. "Not much traffic around here," the general commented, while wondering who in hell would use such a deadbeat as HUMINT? Then again . . .

Freeman took a pace toward the youth, who backed off. The phone was dangling.

"Sorry, Eleanor," the general said, picking it up. "Had to get rid of a varmint." But Eleanor wasn't on the line, and he was still in no-man's-land, on hold. He could see the youth returning with an older rube, the latter covered from head to hairy arms in alarming tattoos, his head clean shaven. He held a baseball bat in his right fist. There was more metal hanging from his neck, waist, and wrists than that hung on a Louisiana chain gang.

"You got a problem with muh boy?" the man bellowed.

"No problem," said Freeman. "Just waiting on a long distance call. Federal business."

"I don't give a fuck what business it is," growled the tattooed skinhead. "Now get away from that fucking phone. Let muh boy use it."

The general knew that getting away from the phone was precisely what he should *not* do. The phone cubicle's sides and top meant that the only way Mickey Mantle could get to him with the bat was head-on; either that or the rube would have to stoop low enough to try to get the general's legs, which would put the rube at a momentary disadvantage.

"Get out of the fuckin' booth! Now!" roared the bat-wielding tough. He made as if to get ready for a home run with the bat.

"You ever heard of DARPA?" asked the general.

"Drop that fuckin' *phone*!!"

"DARPA makes good products," the general said calmly, reaching up to his shirt pocket with his free hand, taking out what looked to the tough like a retractable pen, the general holding it toward the man's gut, then clicking it as he would a ballpoint. The bang was so loud Freeman couldn't hear anything for several seconds, his ears ringing, the man grunting, stumbling backward, an astonished look on his face as he fell flat on his butt, his legs jerking spasmodically on the sidewalk like a child's in tantrum, the baseball bat spilling out noisily onto the road. The general unhurriedly retrieved the bat as the man, now flat on his back, groaning, brought his hands to his chest where the hard rubber bullet from the general's nonlethal "pen" had struck him at point-blank range.

The general pointed the bat's handle at the astonished son. "Now you take Daddy home to Mommy. He's gonna need about three pounds of ice on his belly and a change of underpants. And call the police if you want. It'd be my pleasure. Now *scram*!"

As the tattooed man limped slowly off, touchingly assisted by his scruffy offspring, the general returned to the phone that had again been dangling free during the fracas.

"Douglas!" Eleanor was shouting in alarm. "Are you all right? Was that a shot I heard?"

"Car backfiring," said Freeman. There was no point in worrying her. "So what does the Man say?"

"He says go. But there's one thing. We're going to have to release it to the media. That DARPA place is not too far from a little township; the story's bound to get out and the president doesn't want to be caught looking flat-footed. So we're just going to say—if we're asked—that the president has dispatched a Special Forces unit to track these terrorists down." She paused. "When can you leave, Douglas?"

"Soon as you give me one of your High Tails." It was the latest class of Honda Executive jet, small, fast, but big enough to carry the team, their combat backpacks, and Prince.

"Do we have any of those?" asked Eleanor. "In the armed services, I mean."

"Four," Freeman told her. "Two on the West Coast, two on the East." It was obvious to Eleanor that he'd already thought it through. "Aussie Lewis, Salvini, and our multilingual expert, Johnny Lee, can get the Honda out of Andrews Air Force Base in D.C. The rest of us, on this side of the country—myself, Choir, Eddie "Shark" Mervyn, Gomez, and our new guy, Tony Ruth—he's an ex-army Ranger—we can take one of the two Hondas DOD has on the West Coast, the eight of us rendezvousing at Fairchild Air Force Base."

"The big base in Washington state," she proffered.

"Affirmative," answered Freeman. "Forty clicks west southwest of the Ear—I mean Pend Oreille."

All that Eleanor had been told about the region was that it was beautiful and brutally rough terrain. "Be careful, Douglas. The Man will give you forty-eight hours. By then the guys at the Pentagon'll be stirring their battalions and wanting to move in."

"No sweat," replied Freeman. "That's all we need. This hunt was made for my team. Forty-eight hours? We'll corner the bastards in half the time."

"Good hunting then," she said. "Remember, forty-eight hours, Douglas. That's all the lead time we can give you. Any more will be politically as well as militarily untenable once the public starts pressuring whoever the congressperson is for northern Idaho. It could be the election issue of the year."

"Rita Carlisle," said Freeman.

"What?"

"The congresswoman for Idaho," the general told Eleanor, "is Rita Carlisle. Fifty-two and a looker."

"I'll take your word for it but listen, we need to know one thing," Eleanor said. "I've been so busy listening to you I almost forgot. We haven't been briefed as to exactly what has been stolen, I mean what's on the disk. All the Pentagon can tell us is that it's Flow-in-Flight data and that the DARPA scientists at the Navy base were operating above Top Secret level, and Eyes Only. So when you get to the lake, you'd better check with the director of the DARPA installation—or what's left of it. He's on the daytime staff, and the White House'll give him authority to discuss it in more detail with you. We can't figure out what they're going to do with the information they've stolen. After all, the terrorists don't have a navy."

Freeman was surprised by her remark. He put it down to fatigue, for wasn't it obvious what the terrorists were going to do with it? Whatever *it* was DARPA had been testing at the naval base, the terrorists were sure to use it against the United States. "Damn terrorists didn't need a navy to attack the USS *Cole*," Freeman said. "Used a rigid inflatable packed with C4."

"And Douglas?"

"Yes?"

"The Pentagon set up DARPA at Pend Oreille, but apparently not even the Joint Chiefs were told exactly what the scientists were working on. Right now, the Pentagon's highly pissed with the civilian scientists for not requesting full Defcon 1 security for the lake. The Pentagon says that this is what happens when you don't insist on military oversight of DARPA contracts—that civilians, scientists, know squat about security. In all fairness, though, the base is at the end of a lake that's used a lot for recreation and so without moving the base, ironclad security would have been impossible anyhow."

"Don't worry," Freeman assured her. "I'll try not to get in a brawl between anyone, but I'll find out exactly what was on that disk and why they needed such deep water."

"Whatever it is," Eleanor cautioned him, "keep it to yourself. The Man does not want whatever it is going public. It's bad enough a research installation was broken into."

"Of course," Freeman assured her. "I'll keep it strictly within the team."

"Godspeed, Douglas." He could hear the worry in her tone.

When Margaret returned late from the bridal shower for Linda Rushmein's niece, she could smell fresh coffee, but Douglas wasn't there. There was a note:

"Margaret: On SpecFor mission. President's orders. Will contact you ASAP. Be out of touch for a few days. If you need any further explanation, pls ring Eleanor Prenty, national security adviser, at the White House. Her # is in my Rolodex. She'll fill you in, as far as security allows. All my love, Douglas."

Bewildered, she dropped onto the sofa. Unlike her dearly departed sister Catherine, she was not used to coming home to find her husband having left home so abruptly. Where was he? What was he doing? How would she know *when* he'd call? Questions, she knew, that were being asked daily by the loved ones of thousands of U.S. servicemen and servicewomen. But for Margaret, it was far from the norm. Too far, in fact. Was this what her life was going to be like living with "retired" General Douglas Freeman? Glory be, she had thought they would sail congenially together into the golden twilight of retirement. Instead, he was gone. She knew she shouldn't be resentful, but she was.

What could she do? She switched on the TV. If it was this DARPA thing he'd mentioned, whatever it was precisely, if it were *that* important, surely there'd be something on the news by now?

There wasn't. The lead story was about a jailed Enron executive who had presumably been attacked by a fellow inmate, but all he would say was that he'd accidentally tripped, from the second floor, out a window. CNN reported the phone lines were jammed following the story by calls from people who'd been forced out of retirement by Enron's collapse back in 2003–2004, suggesting that he should have "tripped" from the Enron tower instead. The remainder of the news consisted of the day's wrap-ups of the opening barrages in the presidential primaries. A candidate in New Hampshire was running on a platform of getting to the root of the problem of the war on terror by "making friends with the Muslim fundamentalists." Well, at least, Margaret thought, Douglas wasn't home to hear that. His blood pressure was okay but it wasn't *that* good.

CHAPTER THREE

EN ROUTE TO Idaho on one of the East Coast's Hondas, Aussie Lewis's recurring dream about a Special Forces op he'd taken part in in Iraq in 2003, near Karbala, made his sleep restless. More than once, years after the op, his wife Alexsandra had to shake him out of a troubled sleep that had been sabotaged by the same dream. Aussie, generally known for his laid-back attitude, was puzzled, both by the persistence and clarity of the dream. He'd been with a recon group assigned to help a marine corps convoy negotiate the Fedayeen minefields. During a stop to regroup the Hummers after they'd passed through a blinding sandstorm, one of the young marines, a twenty-year-old, the name on the headband of his Kevlar helmet "Wain," had been sent out about twenty yards with his buddy to secure the convoy's right flank. Wain saw a woman in black chador and veil running away from the remains of an artillery-gutted clay-brick house on the city's outskirts and toward the convoy. *"Qiff!"* he shouted. It was the Arabic word for "Halt!" The woman kept coming, one hand frantically waving a dirty white rag, her other hand cradling a baby who could now be heard screaming as the woman, tripping and almost falling in the loose, sandy loam, continued her approach.

"Qiff!" yelled Wain again, his M-16 now shoulder high.

"Give 'er a warning burst," shouted Wain's buddy as

the marine commander walked just ahead of the convoy for a situation report from Aussie and two other scruffy Special Forces types who were pooling their minefield intel. Aussie was now walking out from the convoy, coming up behind Wain and his marine buddy.

"*Qiff*, dammit!" yelled Wain, firing a warning burst, the three rounds kicking up little puffs of dust. The woman stopped, as if only then realizing the American's order.

The whiplike crack from behind startled Wain, who, spinning around, saw that Aussie had fired. The woman stumbled, then fell backwards, her baby spilling onto the sand.

"Jesus, man!" Wain shouted at Aussie.

"Come with me," the dirty-faced Lewis had commanded without breaking stride. "C'mon."

Wain had walked with him toward the body.

"You think that that's a real baby, mate?" asked Lewis.

Wain, though marine hardened, was still in shock. He couldn't think straight; the baby was still crying.

"Don't worry," Aussie had told him. "It *is* a real baby. But look at Mommy here. Ever see an Iraqi woman with such big feet?"

"I—I never noticed," Wain had answered. The baby's screaming was unnerving.

"No," said Lewis, kicking the corpse's shoes. "You weren't meant to. You were supposed to be looking at the baby—and maybe at Mommy's eyes but not her feet." Aussie had bent down and gently pulled the veil aside. "Oh, look, Mommy's got a beard." He stood up. "Friggin' Fedayeen Ba'ath Party thugs."

Wain, his weapon's stock in the sand, bent down to pick up the baby.

"No!" Lewis said, hauling him back by the collar.

"Shit," Wain had objected. "They wouldn't booby-trap

a baby." But the moment he said it he realized he was asking a question.

"How long you been in this hellhole, mate?" Aussie asked him.

"A week," Wain had answered.

"They'll use anything and anyone to get at us," Aussie told him, the baby's screaming rattling Wain further as Aussie, seemingly oblivious to the noise, felt carefully about the baby's clothes, sniffing as he did so like a dog investigating carrion. "Some guys can smell Semtex," he'd told Wain. "I'm one of 'em."

"Semtex?" inquired Wain, trying to maintain his equanimity in front of this SpecFor type who was obviously an experienced warrior. The dead Iraqi was staring at the washed-out blue sky, flies already moving across his bearded chin and mouth. "Semtex. You mean C4 plastique?"

"I do," Aussie had replied, without taking his eyes off the baby whose face by now was crimson, its arms stiff in distress. Gingerly, Aussie ran his fingers down the sides of the infant's covered legs. "Seems okay. Ten to one Mommy's dirty, though. That's why he kept walking." At this point in the dream, "Wain" could always be seen paying particular attention to Aussie's hands which, once removed from his SpecFor combat gloves, moved with the steady, confident deftness of a pickpocket as he frisked the dead Iraqi. "A bomber," Aussie concluded quietly, Wain noting worriedly that the baby's face was turning purple.

"Sticks are around his back," Aussie explained, indicating the dead Iraqi. "From one side to the other, like a corset. I'd say seven of 'em." He looked up at Wain. "Lucky number for the Fedayeen. Seven pillars of wisdom." Aussie grinned with obvious satisfaction at having found the explosive. "You can pick the little guy up now if you like," he told Wain.

Wain was trying to lift the infant carefully but he'd been spooked by the whole thing and fumbled.

"Give him to me," Aussie had said, and, cradling the infant in one arm, unscrewed his belt canteen with his free hand, tilted it slightly, washing his finger, tipped the canteen again and placed his wet fingertip on the baby's parched lips, smiling as the infant sucked off the moisture. Still holding the baby, he walked back with Wain toward a Hummer, Wain's buddy following, maintaining the regulation three-meter gap between himself and Wain.

"What outfit you with?" Wain asked Aussie.

"Get a surgical glove from a corpsman," Aussie had told him. "Fill it with water and prick one of the fingers for a teat. I have to be going—guide you guys through the minefield up yonder, then get back to work."

"What outfit you with?" Wain repeated.

"Head Hunters."

"Where you based?"

"Here and there."

Aussie had been rocking the infant to stop its crying, smiling down at him. "What do do you say we name the little bugger Blue Eyes?" he asked.

Wain and several other marines who had gathered around were grateful for something else to look at other than the heat waves of the desert in which mirages of beige, sun-baked buildings from nearby Karbala shimmered, suspended in the brutal heat.

"Blue Eyes?" said a machine gunner from his port atop a Hummer, the desert goggles on his "Fritz" encrusted with sand. "Since when does an A-rab have blue eyes?"

"Jesus," said Wain, shading his eyes from the sun. "Think the kid's old man coulda been one of our guys?"

"Or a Brit papa," said the machine gunner. "Or an Aussie?"

"Or a Polack," said another.

"Hey, watch it, Ryan," interjected a Polish-American driver in the convoy.

Wain frowned. "Yeah, but I mean, having it off with the *enemy*?"

"With a woman," said Aussie Lewis, winking at Wain. "It's been known to happen."

"Shit," said Wain. "Would you screw a—?"

"If she said *please*," joked Aussie.

There was a burst of laughter from the assembled marines—except for Wain. In the dream his face always clouded over with a brow-creasing frown of disapproval.

Aussie, shading Blue Eyes' sleeping face from the sun, looked over at Wain, opining, "Not all Iraqis are the enemy, mate, though you'd never know that if you watch TV. Uh-oh, little guy's wet himself," he added. "We'd better—"

The crackle of a radio interrupted him and he heard the marines' CO calling out. At this point, Aussie always realized he was in a dream, but was unable to extricate himself.

"Okay, guys," the marines' CO ordered, his voice crackling in the fierce, dry heat, "back in the vehicles. We've got an M1 tank column cutting across from Karbala. They're gonna go ahead of us. Our sappers have confirmed these SpecFor guys' suspicions. We definitely have a minefield two clicks ahead. I say again, minefield two clicks ahead."

Aussie handed Blue Eyes back to Wain. "You know how to change a baby?"

"Into what?" joshed a marine. Aussie had grinned, and there'd been laughter as they climbed into their Hummers.

Wain stood, momentarily abandoned, holding the baby

gingerly out in front of him as if it were a time bomb. "No. Hey, wait!"

"Gotta go, marine," said a driver.

"Shit!" said Wain, rocking Blue Eyes with such intensity that the infant was screaming again.

"Easy," Wain's buddy had said sharply. "You'll rock his brains out. Here, give 'im to me. My sister's got a coupla kids. I'll change 'im in the Humvee. Let's go."

"Well, why the fuck didn't you tell me before?" Wain had reflected with a mixture of relief and irritation.

"I was havin' too much fun watchin' you. Should've seen your face when the SpecFor dropped that Iraqi dead in his tracks."

"So," said Wain, "you tellin' me you weren't surprised it wasn't a woman?"

"Nah—"

"You lying fuck," charged Wain.

As the convoy started off, Wain's buddy told the driver to keep it steady, "No jerking side to side," as he used a khaki T-shirt as a diaper for the little boy.

After the road had been cleared of anti-personnel mines by the seventy-ton M1 behemoths rolling unharmed and contemptuously over them, Aussie had taken Blue Eyes to the Arab Red Cross, the Red Crescent, in Baghdad. As he handed the child to one of the Crescent's nurses, after the boy had been printed and a blood sample taken for the records, the dream, which always presented itself in vivid color, would suddenly and inexplicably change to a stark black and white of the kind Aussie remembered seeing in the film *Sin City*. Aussie enjoined the nurse to take care of him. "He's an orphan."

Aussie had known then that if no one claimed the little boy quickly, rejecting him because he might well be a half-caste Arab, the odds were that he would forever be an outcast as he grew older, and the danger then would be that the only refuge he would find would be in tight-knit terrorist families such as Hamas. There he would learn that as surely as all Christians and Jews were taught that they were descended from Abraham's son Isaac, and that all Muslims were taught that they were descended from Abraham's son Ishmael, he would be taught that his salvation lay in total obedience to Allah's will—as defined by Hamas . . .

Over southern Idaho, a gut-wrenching wind shear slammed into the Honda jet, jerking Aussie violently against his safety H harness. Sitting back hard in his seat, his neck perspiring despite the cool interior of the Honda, Aussie Lewis once again tried to figure out why his particular encounter in the sun-baked Iraqi desert continued to haunt him, and in such tendentious detail. Then again, he reminded himself, he knew that many other vets had recurring dreams from their time in combat too. He shouldn't be surprised.

What would have surprised him, however, was the speed with which the Red Crescent nurse in Baghdad had given the half-caste Blue Eyes to Wadi El-Hage, commander of Hamas's anti-American operations. The corpulent and gimlet-eyed El-Hage saw Blue Eyes' deliverance to Hamas as indeed a gift from Allah, blessed be His name, for the infant's fair skin, if it did not change by the time he was in puberty, would be an invaluable asset to any Hamas agent selected to work against the Americans. Still, El-Hage had no illusions. It was no easy thing training a Hamas agent, for while it was essential in El-Hage's view that the boy receive a good multilingual education in order that he might blend as easily with, say, the Americans as with the Russians, it must be a very carefully managed education so that the student would not become seduced by either Slavic or Western decadence.

CHAPTER FOUR

TWO MONTHS BEFORE the attack on Lake Pend Oreille, three Russian generals who were out of work, out of hope, and out of money—due to the Soviet Union's post-1989 collapse—were invited by two highly placed Ministry of Defense officials from Moscow to a secret meeting. The two officials, rebel officers of the old KGB's Thirteenth Directorate, had chosen Orsk, the Russian city 950 miles southeast of Moscow and fifteen miles from the Russian-Kazakhstan border, for the meet.

Each of these generals, Mikhail Abramov from the Siberian Sixth Armored Corps, Viktor Beria from Infantry, and Sergei Cherkashin from Air Defense, arrived separately at fifteen-minute intervals to be interviewed by the two officials in a smoke-filled booth in Orsk's Hotel Metropole. The two officials, in their mid-fifties, were dressed in ill-fitting suits, as if they hoped to blend in with the thousands of other government officials all over Russia, but both the fatter, red-faced man and his shorter, rotund colleague nevertheless had the air of bristling confidence that so often accompanies the sudden acquisition of money or power. *Shiska*—"Big"—and *Maly*—"Little," as the three generals would subsequently refer to them, ushered Abramov, Beria, and Cherkashin into the opulent, red-velvet-curtained bar on the mezzanine. Big and Little began the meeting by empathizing with each of the generals in turn. They knew what it must be like, they commiserated with the three career officers, to have been rendered *ustarelye*—obsolete—by Yeltsin's "democratic reforms," to be "downsized," as the Americans euphemistically called it. And then to have whatever savings you'd been able to accumulate wiped out, your pension worthless now because the government had failed to rein in inflation and criminal speculators from Moscow to Vladivostok.

"Like so many of your generation," began Big, a cigarette dangling from between his thick lips, "you three generals served your country in the Cold War against the Americans, worked hard all your lives, and—" He paused, extending his arms, palms upward. "—what do you get?" No one answered as he sucked hard on the cigarette, its grayish blue smoke leaking from nose and mouth. "Nothing," he told them, jabbing the cigarette in the air. "You are humiliated. That's what you get."

"In Moscow," added Little, looking at each general in turn, "old soldiers are now packing grocery bags to make ends meet."

"At least," said Abramov, the lean, sharp-featured tank commander, "they *have* jobs. We haven't been paid for two months."

"And," put in army General Viktor Beria, the short, stocky infantry commander, "at least they have some food to put in the bags. The battalion I now command, instead of the regiment it once was, is owed *five* months' pay. *Five months!* It's a wonder there isn't mutiny."

The two officials glanced at each other. "Tell them," Big invited his colleague who, leaning forward on the cracked Formica table, lowered his voice. "Then you haven't heard, Comrades, elements of the Northern Fleet have already done so."

"That damned Gorbachev," said Air Defense's Cherkashin, the oldest of the three, his dull gray hair, as he leaned forward, in striking contrast to the brightness of his bemedaled chest. "Gorbachev started it all. We were once a proud nation until he and his Glasnost fairies ruined everything. They took down the anti-Fascist barricade in Berlin, and now look at what we are. My air defense unit has been scattered to hell and gone. I had six hundred men. Now, since Putin, I'm down to a third of that, and everyone wants to leave for a job with the Arabs."

Neither official interrupted; they couldn't have hoped for a better response as a precursor to their coming offer. Years before, any officer of infantry, air defense, or tank corps, no matter how senior he was, would have immediately been arrested and sent to one of the Siberian gulags for the kind of criticism of the political leadership Cherkashin was making. But now such talk was common amongst officers and other ranks who had seen their careers and livelihoods ruined by what they called the *razval*—the breakup—of the once great Union of Soviet Socialist Republics. Now Russia was surrounded by independent countries, breakaway republics, from the Baltic in the northwest to former Soviet satellite states such as Poland to the south, and flanked by a clutch of Muslim-dominated central Asian republics where the usual resentments between the center and periphery of any country manifested themselves in Siberia's growing challenge to the kind of authority from Moscow that had once decreed that all trains to and from Vladivostok, eleven time zones away, must run on Moscow time.

"Have you been to Leningrad?" Little asked disgustedly.

None of the three generals bothered to remind him that the politically correct name for the great naval base and artistic center was St. Petersburg—as it had been called before the Revolution. "We're going backward instead of forward," he continued.

"Yes," concurred the infantry's Beria, whose beady eyes seemed almost to close as he paused, pouring himself a shot of vodka, his hairy hands and wrestler's build giving him a primitive appearance. He tapped the label of the new Kalashnikov vodka. "You think," he asked grumpily, "Kalashnikov gets royalties for this?" He peered through the cigarette haze at Air Chief Cherkashin and the tank corps' renowned Abramov.

Abramov shrugged.

"Kalashnikov," continued Beria. "He never took a kopeck for the weapon that bears his name. He could have been a billionaire if he'd been a capitalist." Beria now looked hard at the two officials. "You ask if we know what it's like in politically correct St. Petersburg. *I* know, and I ask, what was our Revolution for? Our warships are wasting away. Submarines, battle cruisers, scores of destroyers, all are turning to rust." Beria downed another vodka. "And in Moscow, gangsters are in control. It's like the Americans' Chicago in the thirties, yes?"

Cherkashin, together with the two officials, nodded his agreement. Abramov, the tank commander who, at fifty-five, was the youngest of the three generals, was looking restive, however, an exasperated expression on his face. Big turned to him. "And you, General Abramov. You agree?"

"With what?" asked the steel blue–eyed Abramov, his lean face tight with impatience. "I assume you didn't invite us here to complain about the situation, Comrade. We all know how bad the situation is, how we've been stabbed in the back by *Communist* billionaires and other *democratic* politicians in their lakeside *dachas*. The point is, what can we do about it? How can you help us?"

The corpulent official took another unfiltered Sobranie cigarette from its tin and lit it with a gold Dunhill lighter, a decidedly upmarket item in striking contrast to his shabbily tailored suit. The biting aroma of Turkish tobacco rose voluminously around the booth's thick velvet curtains. "We are not here just to help ourselves, we five here. You misunderstand. We've come here in order to help the entire officer corps; to form a successful economic nucleus to which other disaffected officers might be drawn."

"Quite so," said the smaller official, whose previously impassive face began to crease, his eyes weeping involuntarily under the assault of smoke from the Sobranie.

"Well," mused the infantry's Viktor Beria. "This 'economic nucleus,' whatever it is, will need money. Lots of it. Trucks full of it, if you hope to put things right."

Air Defense's Cherkashin nodded, and Abramov, thoughtfully looking down and flicking away a trace of Sobranie ash that had fallen from the official's cigarette onto the peak of his tank corpsman's cap, said, "No damn rubles. They're worthless."

The big official gave them an enigmatic smile. "You might have to sup with the devil."

"We *will* have to sup with the devil," Little corrected him. "Stalin had to sup with Roosevelt and Churchill to save Mother Russia. Some things have to be done. In '42 Churchill had to kill the French at Oran rather than let their Mediterranean ships fall into Hitler's hands and—"

"Never mind the French," cut in the steely Abramov. "Who's our devil this time?"

"Not Muslims, I hope?" proffered Cherkashin. "Those bastards in Chechnya? Killing our people in the Moscow theater in '02 and all those children in Beslan just two years later."

"We don't know," said the official disingenuously, "whether the Muslims were connected to that."

Cherkashin was outraged. He stood up. "Muslim fanatics *murdered* my nephew. I won't have anything to do with them."

"The Nazis killed twenty million of us, General!" shot back the Sobranic smoker. "We did business with them when it suited us. We got half of Poland; they got the other half. Sit down!" It was said with such unexpected authority that it transformed the atmosphere in the room, Abramov believing that these two officials from Orsk were in fact military men themselves. "We'll be selling equipment capability," the smoker continued, taking another long drag on his cigarette, which was now pointing at the air defense chief. "General Cherkashin, I believe you were a chief negotiator with the Iraqis during the Cold War. How many thousand air defense units did you sell *them*? And you, Abramov, how many of our T-80 tanks did you sell to the Iraqis?"

Sergei Cherkashin made to say something but sat down instead.

"We'd be selling them tanks?" asked Abramov.

"No," interjected the other, smaller, official. "Other equipment capability." He was agitated. "Do you know," he asked intently, looking first at Abramov and Beria, then at Cherkashin, "what our entire military budget was the year after the anti-Fascist wall came down in Berlin in '89?" He didn't wait for an answer. "Four billion U.S. dollars. You know what the U.S.A.'s was?"

"I'll tell them," said his colleague, who now leaned forward to make the point. "The United States' defense budget was not four billion, comrades, but two hundred and sixty billion. Sixty-five times that of the Soviet Union!" His tone and that of his colleague made it obvious to the three generals that they were dealing with more than two senior bureaucrats.

Air Defense's Cherkashin sighed impatiently. "So now

we know how much richer the U.S. is than we are, but why, may I ask, did you choose the three of us—a general from Air Defense, Viktor here from Infantry, and our tank commander, Abramov? Perhaps we are so good-looking?"

Big allowed himself a grin, revealing through the fog-like smoke three gold crowns on on his lower teeth and an extraordinarily expensive crown and bridge in his upper jaw before he resumed his serious tone. "Three reasons, Comrades," he told them, whom he and Little referred to only as A, B, and C. "First," explained Big, "because your exceptional organizational skills have come to our notice. Whether you liked it or not, you were part of Putin's transition team before you were reassigned to your separate commands."

"Exiled," put in Beria bitterly, "a thousand miles from Moscow."

"Secondly," said Big, taking no notice of Beria's comment, "you've all seen combat. In Afghanistan and elsewhere."

"So we three have organizational skills and combat experience," said General Abramov. "What is the third reason?"

"You're very poor," said Big. He looked at each one of them in turn, before exhaling fully, his smoke engulfing them. "None of you can sleep because you don't know how you're going to look after your family in this new *capitalist paradise* of ours." He paused. "You're worried sick, gentlemen." He fixed his gaze on Abramov. "Even you, Mikhail." He inhaled again slowly, deeply, giving them time to realize just how much he might know about them beyond their outward show of braggadocio. As the brownish blue smoke poured forth, he continued, "I know what it's like. Believe me. We now have in Russia the very, very rich and the dirt poor. The rich have reserves to see them through the chaos that's followed Yeltsin, Putin, and their successors. The poor—" He shrugged. "Well, most of them have never known anything else, only now it's worse. But you three—" He was using his cigarette as a pointer again, jabbing it at them. "—Your whole officer class has been raised to enjoy the fruits of your hard work for the party. And now it's all crumbled." He stubbed out his cigarette. "I've seen your medical files. Not your official military medical records, your local—*private*—physician's. Zopiclone?" He left the name of the sleeping pill hanging in the air before adding, "Prozac and Volga!" Volga was the cheapest brand of vodka, and Big gave a sardonic grin, reciting the commercial jingle, "Like the mighty river Volga, it will wash your troubles away!" He leaned forward, the smile gone, shoulders hunched with intensity. "For you, we're offering a way to win back Russia for the party and to earn yourselves some hard cash for your families. It is what the Americans call 'a win-win situation.' Da?" He leaned back and opened his tin of Sobranies, plucking out another cigarette.

"How much money?" asked Air Defense General Cherkashin, his medals clinking as he leaned forward, placing both hands on the table.

"A hundred thousand a month," said Big. "For each of you."

"Rubles?" asked Beria.

"American dollars."

The normally cool, hard-eyed Abramov tried to appear nonchalant, but his face was flushed with excitement and he had to make a conscious effort to sit back and look relaxed, as if he could take it or leave it.

Beria and Cherkashin were stunned.

"Ah, where do we move this equipment, this capability?" asked Cherkashin.

"Where Moscow can't see it," replied the Sobranie smoker. "As far from here in Orsk and from Moscow as possible, in fact. East. You'll be told in due time, if you accept our offer. But once you're given the location, the three of you hold your lives in your hands. We want you to—" Reaching into his pocket, he fished out the gold Dunhill lighter. "We want you to think it over. But quickly. There are plenty of other candidates, disaffected officers like yourselves, but my colleague and I—" He looked at Little. "—have to get back to Moscow. He glanced at his Rolex, asking his smaller partner, "The last plane out of Orsk is at 2100, correct?"

"Yes."

"I'll give you fifteen minutes," Big told the three generals, who were now convinced by the official's use of "2100" that he was a military man. "We'll be down in the foyer," Big added, getting up and gathering his jacket and the tin of Sobranies. "It's either yes or no."

The three generals went out into Orsk's polluted air to talk it over. The road's badly cracked surface was an apt symbol, Mikhail Abramov thought, of the state of Russia. It was the beginning of the end.

"Necessity is the mother of invention," Big had told Abramov, the commander of the grossly understaffed Siberian Sixth Armored Division. It was a phrase that had been quoted many times by the officer corps in the turmoil since the collapse. He himself had had to cannibalize half his tanks just to keep the other half going.

"So?" said Viktor Beria, looking at the leaner Abramov and the taller, gray-haired Cherkashin, the air defense general. "Are you two in? I know I'm sick of constantly scrabbling around to make ends meet."

Abramov had been conjuring up the glory days of the Siberian Sixth; at least the days had been glorious until the humiliating defeat that he, as a young lieutenant, and other tank platoon commanders had suffered in a trap wherein American M1A1 Abrams tanks had duped the

famed Sixth Armored Corps during a winter battle between it and the U.S.-led U.N. peacekeeping force in
Siberia.

"A hundred thousand dollars a month!" said Beria with
a whistle.

"But what is this equipment, this capability, he talks
about?" said Abramov.

"I don't care!" said Beria. "I'm broke."

"I want to know," said Abramov, as the three of them
made their way back into the hotel, "whether this capability is real or not. I at least want to ask him if it's in place,
ready to go, or are we expected to start from scratch? I
need to know that much if I'm to decide."

Abramov posed the questions quietly but without pre-
amble as they met the two officials in the foyer. "What
capability are we talking about? At least give us a rough
idea."

The two officials looked at each other and decided that
a little more bait was necessary to hook the generals.

"A capability," Big answered him, "that is staggering,
General, and which will be ready for full production in
two months if our acquisition of the data is successful.
But beyond that I will discuss it in detail only if you wish
to join our team."

"Whose team is that?"

Little, who had spoken nary a word since the three
generals had returned from outside, suddenly leaned forward, his suit's crease crumpling as he did so. "The old
team," he told Abramov, as if the tank general was a student who'd forgotten his most important lesson, a lesson
which governed all others, "the team which the stupid
Americans think is washed up but is just waiting, as their
George Washington did, to cross the Delaware, to regain
what has been stolen, stolen from our party's grip because
some generals didn't have the balls to overturn all these

ridiculous democratic reforms. Are you with us or not? Do you want to slave away for kopecks in this so-called new democratic Russia or be able to hold your head up again, armed with some real weapons for a change, with something our clients can hit the Americans with, so fast, so utterly, that they'll be pissing themselves in the streets. And which, if successful, if organized correctly, will act as a nucleus to attract more of our comrades to reinvigorate the party. Now, are you with us or not?

Abramov thought for a second. His final humiliation had been having to tell his daughter that she'd have to stop taking her beloved studies in ballet because of the money. He'd stopped her dream. *"Da!"* he told Little. "I'm with you."

And so were Beria and Cherkashin, the air force general asking gleefully, "Now we're in. Tell us, how do we get the Americans pissing their pants?"

Looking at the three generals in turn, Big asked, "Have you ever heard the phrase 'Flow-In-Flight' data?"

None of them had.

CHAPTER FIVE

HIS RECURRING DREAM evicted from consciousness upon his arrival at Fairchild. Aussie, with Freeman and the other six members of the team, was now aboard an oily-smelling Chinook helo heading for the lower, southernmost, end of northwest Idaho's ninety-thousand-acre Lake Pend Oreille. To Choir Williams's extreme discomfort, the team encountered a gut-rolling turbulence as a low-pressure weather system rushing in from the Pacific coast hit a Canadian Express, a stream of freezing air pouring down from the Arctic through British Columbia, a little more than sixty miles to the north of the lake.

As the general studied his Tactical Pilotage map of the rugged 48-mile-wide, 75-mile-long Idaho panhandle that contained both Lake Pend Oreille and Priest Lake, thirty miles north-northwest of Pend Oreille, he shook his head.

"What's up, General?" Aussie shouted over the roar of the Chinook's engines.

Freeman's face was creased by what his team had come to call his George C. Scott look, one of concern and hard focus. It wasn't worry, however. Douglas Freeman tried to spend as little time as he could worrying, a devotee of the man Muslims saw as a holy prophet, and Christians, the Messiah: "Set your mind on God's kingdom and his justice before everything else, and all the rest will come to you as well. *So do not be anxious about tomorrow;*

tomorrow will look after itself. Each day has troubles enough of its own."

Even so, Freeman had to think ahead and Sal, seeing the general's frown of concentration, asked, "Problem?" It was a question that an enlisted man would hardly be expected to ask a general, at least not so casually, but this SpecFor team, with the exception of Tony Ruth, had been in action together before. Besides, the easy familiarity between officers and enlisted men came naturally to such small groups of men who'd been in combat and who'd bivouacked in close quarters.

Freeman's voice thundered over the Chinook's combined rotor slap and engine noise. "No problem, gentlemen. No problem at all." He looked down at Prince, the five-year-old black spaniel whose floppy ears were covered by earmuffs that Choir Williams had made especially for him, and who seemed to perk up as if reading the general's mind.

"The first thing we need to know," the general continued, "is which way those bastards headed off from the DARPA installation at the end of the lake. And for that answer—" He leaned forward and scratched Prince affectionately behind his ears, the dog immediately half closing his eyes in canine ecstasy. "—we need to get Prince here a scent from those terrorist creeps, if we can. That right, fella?" The general's right hand moved from Prince's ears to beneath his chin. Panting happily, Prince eagerly thrust his head forward, asking for more.

From the helo's open door, the slipstream roaring like rushing water against his goggles, Freeman caught a glimpse of the densely forested mountain fastness of the Cabinet Mountain Wilderness Area that flanked Lake Pend Oreille to the east beyond the Idaho-Montana border. To his left, northwest, he could see the six-thousand-foot-high summit of Bald Mountain, and, south of the lake, Cedar Mountain. On the long, ear-shaped lake, which looked to him more like an elongated question mark than an ear, lay several rectangular shapes: DARPA's barge out from the shore, designated DARPA ALPHA on his map; the data hut on the shoreline; and several other storage buildings scattered around the small settlement of Bayview on the ear's lobe, with Coeur d'Alene another twenty miles to the south. Freeman also saw there was only one road leading out from the DARPA installation to Interstate 95, eight miles west of the lake. Prince's nose was at his side, the spaniel's eyes watering from the icy-cold wind that swept over the misty blue mass of the Cabinet Mountains and the Kootenai National Wildlife Refuge beyond the lake where rivulets, born in snow-capped peaks, fed both Lake Pend Oreille and Priest Lake to the northwest.

"Gonna see a grizzly, eh?" Freeman asked Prince, who remained incommunicado as he basked in the extended chin scratch the general was giving him and the back scratch that, now that the turbulence had subsided, Choir was lavishing on him.

"Grizzly?" put in Aussie. "I certainly hope not. Terrorists are one thing, grizzly bears are something else."

"Then," Freeman told the team, "you'd better check your weapons, guys. Make sure you're loaded for bear as well as scumbags."

Salvini had selected a 22.1-pound, 49.2-inch Belgian general-purpose machine gun, or GPMG, a weapon that could fire fifty-round belts of the big 7.62 mm slugs over an effective killing range of three-quarters of a mile, should a "long punch" firefight break out.

For his part, Choir had chosen the German-made Heckler & Koch general-purpose MG36, which was a lighter and shorter machine gun. The MG36, with folding stock and carrying handle, had a transparent thirty-round magazine, fired standard NATO 5.56 mm-caliber rounds, and had a kill reach of more than a third of a mile. In his pre-op briefing at Fairchild, the general had told the other seven men in his eight-man team that while the trail would most likely lead them through thick bush and forest, there would also be open alpine meadows at the higher elevations of the Bitterroot Mountains. In such places, the shorter-range Heckler & Koch's famous MP5 5.6-pound submachine gun was favored by most others in the team. The general's weapon of choice was an AK-74, an updated AK-47 which he'd chosen for its relatively light weight—7.5 pounds—easy maintenance, and greater range than the Heckler & Koch MP5. The general had had his AK-74's original folding metal frame stock replaced with wood so that it could be used as a "door opener" or "skull crusher," should the occasion arise.

As usual in the group, the general had allowed each member of the team, with the exception of Aussie, to select his own weapon. Lieutenant Johnny Lee, the multilinguist, Gomez, and Eddie Mervyn liked the Heckler & Koch MP5 navy version. With its closed bolt action, unlike its open bolt cousin that begins firing when the bolt is "triggered" forward, the navy version fires with the bolt already forward, reducing any aim-altering shoulder bump. And, while weighing only 7.7 pounds, it has an effective kill range of 328 feet firing 9 mm ammo.

It was left to Aussie Lewis, at the general's request, to tote a standard Heckler & Koch G36 assault rifle fitted with an under-barrel launcher that could fire up to ten 40 mm grenades a minute to a distance of approximately 300 yards. The eighth member of the team, Tony Ruth, an ex-Ranger who had stayed in the kind of top physical condition Freeman always demanded of his team members, came along at Aussie's invitation. Tony Ruth had met Aussie Lewis in Iraq, in Karbala. His favorite

weapon was an Italian Franchi eight-round SPAS—
sporting purpose automatic shotgun.

No, Tony Ruth had told the other members of the
SpecWar squad, and anyone who ever challenged him—
and a lot of people had—he wasn't any relation to Babe
Ruth. Yes, he had played in the minors, and worked one
game in the majors. Then Iraq came a year before his retirement. Yes, he sure did intend to go back to North Carolina and play ball, but the example of Pat Tillman, the
twenty-seven-year-old offensive lineman for the Arizona
Cardinals who had walked away from a $3.6-million,
three-year contract in the NFL because he believed it was
time to serve his country and who was killed in action in
a blue-on-blue in Afghanistan in June 2003, had had a
great influence on Tony Ruth, as it had on a lot of other
Americans, and he'd met Douglas Freeman through
Aussie not long after the SpecWar team lost a member on
a SpecWar op off the "Hermit Kingdom"—the North
Korean coast.

"Hey, Tony," Aussie called out, pointing to the Franchi
shotgun, "why not haul a Mossberg instead of taking that
old Italian job? Holds nine rounds instead of eight. You
never know when that extra cartridge—"

"Yeah—" riposted Tony. "But if you've already had to
fire eight rounds of buckshot or door-bashing slugs,
you're in so much trouble you don't need an extra round,
you need a medic. Fast."

"Ah-ha!" said Salvini. "He's got you there, Aussie."

"Oh, shut your face, wop! I'd still bet on a Mossberg."

"You'd bet on anything," said Sal.

"Sal's right," Choir Williams told Tony Ruth. "Last
mission we were on, Aussie was sound asleep aboard the
transport until he heard someone mention a 'bet.'"

"That is correct," chimed in Freeman, always happy to
see such good morale en route to a mission that his gut

instinct told him would stress the nerves and physical fitness of his seven fellow commandos to the max. "Aussie could hear the word 'bet,' " Freeman said, "even if it was whispered at a rock concert."

"I don't go to rock concerts," said Aussie, sniffing. "I'm more cultured than you bastards."

"Oh," said Sal. "How about that cultural movie we saw the other night? That blonde with the big—"

"A question of good photography," said Aussie, affecting a high-minded, dismissive air. "It wasn't the young lady's cleavage that interested me. It was the interpretive angle of the shot and the—ah—subtle arrangement of her wardrobe I was viewing."

"What are you talking about?" said Salvini. "She was naked!"

"Nevertheless," Aussie began, then paused. "Oh, you peasants wouldn't understand."

"Oh?" joshed Ruth. "Well, tell me, *professor*, what would your wife say if *she'd* seen you 'viewing'?"

"Well," Aussie answered slowly, "I think, Mr. Ruth, that she would cut me off for a month!"

Everyone laughed, though Freeman's mirth was restrained by recalling how he might still be in the proverbial doghouse for having to leave *his* wife so abruptly on the mission, especially so soon after their donnybrook vis-à-vis Marte Price.

As the general reached forward to pat Prince once more, he felt the one-shot pen in his pocket. This time it wasn't loaded with a rubber stun bullet but a lethal round. He hoped that all the other equipment in the team's "goodies" packs, provided by DARPA, and the other off-the-shelf wares of war would be as efficient.

"Two minutes!" announced the Chinook's loadmaster as the amber light began flashing.

"Brace!" and each of the eight commandos readied

themselves for a hard landing. Choir held Prince to his chest, the dog, now strapped into his Velcro-hitched hag-var vest, happily licking Choir's face as the Chinook's rear wheels touched down in what sounded like a hail-storm as gravel and sand kicked up by the rotors' fierce downdraft struck the Chinook's fuselage.

Within a minute every man, with his pack, and Prince were on the hard ground of the DARPA base, and Free-man was being greeted by a somber-looking sheriff from Sandpoint, the wilderness resort area of about five thou-sand souls at the top of the lake twenty-seven miles north of the naval research station.

"Bad business," said the sheriff glumly.

"It is," said Freeman. "First thing I need to do is talk to the staff here at DARPA." Away from the exhaust and dust, the general could breathe more deeply, taking in the damp coolness of the mountain lake. Prince had already been doing this, his tongue lolling expectantly, a distinct smile on his face. He loved tracking, though at the mo-ment all he could smell was baking soda, the result of a standing order from Freeman for his men to eschew any deodorant to combat the sweating in armpit and groin. The soda, unlike deodorants, including those that com-mercials boasted were unscented, was neutral and would help absorb the smell of their perspiration.

"We threw up roadblocks," the sheriff assured him, "all around the area north, south, and west of the research sta-tion. And we sent boats across to the eastern side of the lake. All sides covered. But there was nothing. Highway patrols were alerted on the Washington state, Montana, and British Columbia borders, so they didn't get out that way. But they had mountain bikes, you know." He pointed to where his deputy had found the mountain bike tracks up beyond the high hurricane-strength fence. "But they left them behind."

"Which way do you think they're headed, Sheriff? Your best guess?"

"I'd say north—Canada."

"Yep. So would I," said Freeman. The general paused, looking out across the metallic gray lake under the gathering gray stratus. "Everyone's expecting them to be hightailing it in cars or a plane. How about that, Sheriff— a plane?"

"General, we shut down everything. No planes out from Sandpoint except for an emergency airlift of a hiker to Spokane. He broke his leg on one of the islands in Priest Lake farther north of here. Had to bring a float plane for him but he's a local. I know him. 'Sides, I double-checked. Only the pilot and him aboard. Locals— know 'em both."

Freeman slapped the sheriff on the back by way of appreciation. "You've done good work, Sheriff. It'll go in my report."

The sheriff nodded appreciatively, then added grimly, "Ten people murdered in cold blood. Like a family."

"Ten?" queried the general. "I was told there were eleven."

"No, seemed so at first, but one of 'em, Roberta Juarez, a technician, survived. Massive head injuries but she's holding on. With a head injury like that, they no doubt figured she was dead."

"I need to see her," said the general.

"Well, first," the sheriff told him, "you'll need to talk to Grierson, the local M.D. He's a tough nut. Says we can't talk to her for days, maybe weeks, even."

"Choir," Freeman told the Welsh-born American. "Take Prince over to where the paratrooper bikes were abandoned after the raid. Should be good scent there." He suddenly turned back to the sheriff. "You didn't let anyone near the bikes, did you?"

"No, sir. Yellow-taped the area and I've had a deputy there since."

"Good man." Freeman entertained the possibility of the terrorists backpacking out. Next, he called Johnny Lee over. "Sheriff says there's a patient, Roberta Juarez—" Freeman paused and looked back at the sheriff. "—I take it she's Spanish-American, or is that her husband's—"

"She's Mexican."

"Right," said Freeman, and turned to Lee. "You come with me, Johnny. We're going for another helo ride. Quick trip up to Sandpoint. Ten minutes and we'll be there. Let's go." As he strode toward the chopper, he told Aussie Lewis, Salvini, Gomez, Eddie Mervyn, and Tony Ruth to take a break while Choir and Prince were checking out the abandoned mountain bikes that had so successfully been used as props in the terrorists' attack.

CHAPTER SIX

FREEMAN AND LEE moved quickly away from the chopper's downdraft and the exhaust fumes that were polluting the pristine mountain air into the thick antiseptic air of Sandpoint Hospital, their Vibram boots squeaking sharply on the polished linoleum floor.

Through the glass of the intensive care unit, Freeman could see thirty-three-year-old Roberta Juarez lying in a bed, her head in a shroud of bandages. Only her left eye, her lips, and nostrils were visible, giving her an unfortunately ghoulish appearance, an impression reinforced by the fact that her badly bruised right arm was attached to an intravenous drip. It was obvious to Freeman, from his side on view of her neck, that Roberta's hair had been shorn off in the trauma unit. Her left hand was in a cast, the doctor explained, because when she'd been shot, her left hand and arm must have taken the brunt of the fall.

"She conscious?" asked Freeman.

"In and out," replied the young, casually dressed doctor, who, except for his stethoscope, could have passed for a golfer about to go practice his putting. Through the window at the end of the corridor, Freeman glimpsed a menacingly overcast sky. He flexed his wrist and glanced at his watch so that the young doctor would get the message that there was no time to lose. If it started to rain, it would wash away the marauders' scent. There were other ways, of course, to track them—broken twigs and brush—but the best would be for Prince to get the scent from the abandoned bikes and go from there. Since Freeman's call to Eleanor Prenty, the word had gone out to the Department of Homeland Security, FBI, and the Bureau of Land Management in northern Idaho to give "all assistance possible to General Freeman's team."

"Doctor, I need to speak with Ms. Juarez as soon as possible. Find out if she can tell us anything that might—"

"No way," said the athletic-looking doctor, planting himself imperiously in front of the door. "This patient is in critical condition and I—"

"Johnny," the general told his SpecFor translator. "Give me a strip."

Lee whipped out a plastic cuff strip from one of his battle dress uniform's many pockets.

"What the hell—" began the doctor, his face flushed with shock and anger. "Nurse!"

Freeman's face was an inch from the young physician's. "Listen, Grierson, I'm on the trail of terrorists who murdered—I say again, *murdered*—ten Americans because they wanted something that's so classified that I don't even know what it is yet. But I do know one thing, and that is that Roberta Juarez is probably the only person still alive who saw the killers. Anything, *anything* she can tell me could be vital not only to my finding those sons of bitches but to the security of the United States. Now step aside or I'll arrest you under the Patriot Act, Section 11B—'directly or indirectly giving aid and comfort to the enemy.'"

"This is outrageous!" said Grierson. "I'm not moving. *Nurse!*"

Freeman felled him with one blow.

"Cuff him, Johnny!"

The general stepped over the physician, who was gasping for air like a landed fish, and opened the door to Intensive Care. Roberta was moving her head slightly from side to side, moaning. Perhaps the kerfuffle, the general thought, with young Dr. Grierson had brought her around or had disturbed her somnolence sufficiently that she might hear him. He identified himself gently but firmly, not knowing whether she was hearing him. Had she seen anything that might help them identify the killers?

No answer. No response at all.

He pressed the question respectfully but insistently. "The men who attacked you, Ms. Juarez?" Freeman could hear the doctor swearing. Johnny Lee had him cuffed to a hallway chair and told him that if he didn't want to be thumped again he'd better be quiet. A nurse saw them, advanced, stopped, then turned and ran back to her station to call security.

All Roberta could say, her voice cracked and dry, was, "It's spotted." Her dark eyes closed; she seemed to be asleep. Freeman stayed for a moment, gently taking her warm, flaccid wrist, and prayed for her and, if it be God's will, help to catch those who had perpetrated the massacre.

When he emerged from the IC unit, security, a short, overweight woman, perspiring heavily, was warning Johnny Lee that she'd called the sheriff.

"You can come with us, ma'am," Johnny Lee told her as the general emerged from the ICU. "We'll take you to him."

Lee uncuffed the doctor, who was now vigorously massaging his wrists. "You're fucking fascists!" the doctor shouted at both men. The security woman was standing by, openmouthed.

"Get anything?" Johnny asked the general on their way out.

"It's spotted," Freeman told him. "That's all she said."

"One of the terrorists' faces maybe," Johnny ventured, "spotted with psoriasis?"

"Hmm—it's possible."

"You—fucking fascists!"

When they returned from the far end of the lake below Bayview to the DARPA base, the sheriff had mustered the day staff together: seven scientists and their seven technicians who worked on the DARPA "Flow-In-Flight" project. He was told that there were more scientific personnel involved in ARD—Acoustic Research Development—as it related to submarines, but the people Freeman was interested in were those who had been working on the latest deep-water-moored DARPA ALPHA barge and the hut where the terrorists had shot the night staff. They had been added to the Acoustic Research Development complex here only in the years since 2007, when more research money had been freed for homeland-defense-associated projects. The money became a flood following the terrorist attacks in which shoulder-fired anti-aircraft rockets had brought down three American aircraft since 9/11.

"Sorry for your loss," Douglas Freeman told the visibly shaken chief scientist, a Professor Richard Moffat, head of the fourteen-person day shift. "But I need to know precisely what these scumbags stole."

"A disk," said Moffat, a man around Freeman's age.

Though most of the day staff were dressed casually in jeans, like the doctor at the hospital, here in the open they were all wearing either heavy sweaters or Gore-Tex Windbreakers, the temperature having plummeted in the confluency of the Pacific Ocean front that had come barreling in from the northwest, slamming into a warmer Chinook wind driving northward into the Alberta badlands. It was getting cold. Moffat was the only one wearing a white lab coat, stained, it seemed to Freeman, with rust and grease, probably from working near the gantry and cranes of a second green-and-white-striped DARPA ALPHA barge where the staff had to haul in new large-scale test units from the deep, glacier-carved lake.

"I know it's a disk," Freeman told Moffat, "but is there anything more specific than 'Flow-In-Flight' written on it?"

Moffat was finding it difficult to focus, acutely aware that his laissez-faire attitude toward the security of his fellow scientists had been a disastrous mistake.

"Professor," repeated Freeman impatiently, "is the disk labeled in any other way?"

Moffat was staring across the lake at the cold-looking mountains. Freeman knew that his SpecWar team had probably a half hour of reasonable weather before the churning gray clouds gave way to rain.

"Professor, I know it's tough on you at the moment, but time's of the essence here."

"What—oh, sorry, General. The disk was simply labeled 'DARPA ALPHA Flow-In-Flight.'"

"What kind of data were on the disk?"

Moffat had the zombie look of someone in shock. "That's highly sensitive material, General."

Freeman shook his head in disbelief. Murphy's Law was on the loose. Hadn't Eleanor Prenty gotten through to Moffat and cleared the general of any D.S.R.—document search restriction? Or perhaps Eleanor *had* gotten through but Moffat couldn't remember in the state he was in.

"All right, now listen to me, Professor. I want you to focus. Your highly sensitive material has been stolen by terrorists, and my team is going to have to know exactly what to look for." For a moment the chief scientist stared at Freeman as if he had no idea who the general was.

"We need to focus," Freeman reiterated.

The professor's eyes shifted from Freeman again out to the slate gray waters of the lake. "It's a lot of diagrams and formulas, like so much technical literature. I don't see how anyone without a degree in—"

"Doc!" cut in Freeman. "I've been sent by the president."

"Yes." He paused. "I've been told that."

"So what's on the fucking disk? Is there a diagram, something we can key onto should we see it?"

Moffat thought for a moment. "Doreen?" he called out, and a thin woman in her twenties, chestnut curls wreathing her face, walked over from the gaggle of DARPA ALPHA scientists who were talking to the FBI and DHS agents. Moffat introduced her as Dr. Wyman and told her what the general wanted, assuring her that Freeman was "cleared to the max."

"Well," she told the general, "we've been recording data from trials of a super-cavitating, that is, super-spinning, torpedo. These super torpedoes were originally pioneered by the Russians. One of them, a Shkval class, could run at two hundred miles an hour and was aboard the Russian *Kursk*."

Freeman told her he remembered the *Kursk*, an Oscar II class sub that sank in the Barents Sea in the summer of 2000.

"It was because of the presence of this super-spin torpedo on board," Doreen explained, "that the Russians refused offers of help from other countries to rescue the *Kursk*. They were afraid that either we or the Brits would get our hands on the technology." Doreen paused, glancing about to make sure that no DHS or FBI agents could overhear. "Our intelligence community got it anyway," she told Freeman. "And we've solved problems the Russians couldn't because since Russia went belly-up, we've outpaced anything the Russians had. We've gotten up to super-cavitation at a mile a second."

Freeman was impressed, but Moffat's downcast look was that of a man who knew his career was over unless his scientific brilliance could trump his appalling failure in security. He stared out at the lake again as Doreen asked him whether she could tell Freeman about "the Torshell."

"Yes," said Moffat softly.

Quietly, her face strained because even with her boss's permission she was still reluctant to explain the enormity of what America had lost, Doreen explained the secret. "A Torshell," she told him, "is a super-cavitating—that is, super-spinning—fifty-caliber torpedo-shaped rifle round that we've developed from our research on the super-cavitating torpedoes. We've drilled a wire-thin hole through the bullet. Think of the thin wire in one of those bag ties you pick up at the grocery store to twist-lock a plastic bag of vegetables or bread rolls, stuff like that."

"Will this take long?" the general asked, glancing up at an increasingly morose sky and flicking up the leather cover of his watch.

"No," Doreen said, "it won't take long but you need to understand how it's very new, this technology. Revolutionary, in fact."

"Go on," said Freeman, trying to contain the legendary impatience that had ironically also led to some of his greatest military breakthroughs.

"Well, as I said, because of the research here, we've been able to apply super-cavitating, super-spinning technology to what has been the usual fifty-caliber ammunition rounds. What we've done is drill into a tungsten-core bullet a nano-thin lining of incendiary chemicals. The bullet, as in the case of the much larger torpedo, cavitates or spins at super speed because a gas shoots out in front as the chemical inside morphs from a solid to a gas because of the heat from the torpedo's, or in this case the bullet's, propellant. This jet of gas shooting out the front forms a protective bubble around the bullet in air—or in water, in the case of the torpedo—and so the bullet or torpedo has next to no resistance."

Freeman had understood five minutes ago. "You've developed a super-fast bullet."

"Faster," said Doreen, "than anything ever produced—except, of course, the speed of light."

"How fast?"

"Well, the Russians, with their Shkval torpedo, have reached two hundred miles per hour in water. Slow compared to what we've been able to do. It's largely a matter of who has the best computer-governed lathes. The tolerances are incredibly small."

"So," asked the general. "What speed has DARPA ALPHA been able to reach?"

"NUWAC," Doreen told him, "our Naval Underseas Warfare Center, has already broken the sound barrier with a torpedo."

"At DARPA ALPHA," added Moffat in a voice so lifeless he might as well have been doing nothing more than giving Freeman the time of day, "we've developed a projectile, a bullet if you like, that's reached Mach 10."

"Son of—" exclaimed the general. "You've got my attention!"

"That's more than eleven thousand feet a second," Moffat continued in his monotone. "Faster than anything in the history of warfare."

"Inside the usual cupronickel," Doreen Wyman added, referring to a normal round's copper-nickel jacket, "the bullet would melt and break up, even with the gas bubble reducing most of the drag. But in conjunction with NUWAC, we've developed a metal-carbon resin jacket that will remain intact until point of impact."

Freeman instantly recognized the enormous implications, how such a round developed by DARPA ALPHA in this long, landlocked lake more than a thousand feet deep would change warfare forever. They were at a turning point. At Mach 10, such a round could penetrate a tank, the bullet's superheated molten jet raising the temperature so high inside the tank it would explode.

"How long would it take," asked Freeman, "to manufacture this supersonic round?"

"*Hyper*sonic," Moffat corrected him. "Mach 1 to Mach 5 is supersonic. We're talking hypersonic, General."

"All right, how long would it take to lathe a hypersonic prototype of one of these rounds?"

Doreen Wyman, Freeman could see, was going to take the Fifth on this one.

"Professor Moffat?" Freeman pressed. "How long?"

"A week—if you had the right state-of-the-art computer-controlled lathes, et cetera."

"And the disk!"

"Yes," admitted Moffat sheepishly, looking out at the slate gray water again.

"Do you agree," Freeman asked Doreen Wyman, "that they could have prototypes in a week?"

"From the time they get the disk, yes. A week."

It was time to move out.

Prince had gotten a good scent from the abandoned bikes and had led the team to a large jetty, farther down from the DARPA ALPHA shore, from where it was assumed the terrorists had escaped by boat. But which way? The lake was twenty-five miles long and five miles wide. Freeman stuck with his and the sheriff's Canada-bound idea. With all road and air corridors closed, there simply weren't that many ways out, and Canada, sixty-four miles to the north beyond Lake Pend Oreille and Priest Lake, seemed not only the best escape route because the rugged, heavily forested terrain would provide great cover but because there was always the added enticement of Canada's long, undefined border, and the fact that Canada simply didn't have the manpower to field effective patrols.

The sheriff, overwhelmed by the catastrophe, walked forlornly down to the jetty.

"Any leads at all?" asked Freeman.

"Nothing very concrete," replied the sheriff. "Dr. Moffat has asked the navy to send up one of their Hawkeye aircraft to help you with communications in this area. And an FBI guy told me a blood-soaked note was found in one of the victims' hands."

"A note?" mused Aussie. "What'd it say?"

"Hard to tell," the sheriff replied. "One of the DHS guys told me all they could make out was a few letters— looked like 'RAM' and 'SCARUND,' whatever the hell that means." He spelled it out for them, and Aussie wrote it down.

"RAM. Computer capacity: random access memory?" ventured Freeman.

"Or people's names?" suggested Johnny Lee.

"Perhaps," said Freeman, recalling his visit to Roberta Juarez at the hospital, "the words have something to do with Roberta saying, 'It was spotted.' " No one could see any connection whatsoever.

"All right," said the general. "No leads but Prince's nose at the moment. We have to assume the terrorists have had ample time to reach the northern end of Pend Oreille, where they'd have to leave their boat and hoof it up to Priest Lake. And if the bastards know what they're doing, which it seems they do, they'll be avoiding any known back roads because the sheriff's boys are out in full force. So, let's see if Prince here can regain the scent up at the north end of Pend Oreille." The general knelt down, the team doing likewise, Prince sitting as if waiting for his best in show ribbon. "Dear Lord," began Freeman, "we praise You, we thank You for this world, and we here ask that You watch over us, guide us, so that we may do Your will in the battle against evil."

"Amen," they said in unison, and a group of DHS and FBI agents looked variously astonished, embarrassed, and humbled. Prince panted in anticipation of the hunt.

The general, Aussie, Sal, Choir, Ruth, Lee, Gomez, and Mervyn grabbed their weapons and MOLLEs and boarded the Chinook. Already Freeman could see the Hawkeye that Moffat had requested. If the terrorists, with their head start, reached Priest Lake forty-six miles north of DARPA ALPHA, following the general direction of secondary logging roads through the deep forest, they would have a straight twenty-five-mile south-to-north run up the full length of Priest, where they could then pass through a two-and-a-half-mile-wide connecting channel to another three-mile stretch of water. Had they planted a boat? The map showed that along the edge of Priest Lake's primeval forest there was a smattering of "Mom-and-Pop"-type cottages and a tiny marina, but not much else.

Aussie Lewis, seat harness on, using his MOLLE as a footrest, wondered aloud, and loudly, "Hope we're not heading in the wrong fucking direction."

It was unlike Aussie to start the game with a pessimistic prognosis, and the general wanted to counter it immediately. For most of the team, Aussie's question was nothing more than that, but Freeman, knowing Tony Ruth was a relative newcomer to the team, wanted to stanch any possible pessimism. "Sometimes," he shouted to Aussie over the noise of the Chinook's rotor slap, "the most obvious route is the correct one. The scumbags who stole that disk'll be in a hurry to get that information back to their masters in the Mideast, Chechnya, wherever."

"They don't have to do it in person," said Johnny Lee.

"How about them using a landline? With a computer and modem they could set up and transmit the disk's contents from anywhere they like."

The general shook his head, and Prince looked concerned. "Sheriff and DHS have all the landlines, public phone booths, et cetera, covered," answered Freeman. "Besides, now the story's out, the terrorists are going to know that anyone seen using public landlines with a modem and the like is acting suspiciously and should be reported. Anyway, NSA is going to be picking up all private transmissions."

"How about satellite phone?" asked Eddie Mervyn.

"Too insecure," Freeman replied. NSA'd be all over it like the measles. No, the scumbags are heading for the Canadian border; I know it in my gut. Somewhere along the line where there's minimal surveillance, manpower problems. Canada's a huge country, bigger than the U.S., and the whole country's population is only equivalent to California's. It's as if every other state in the union were empty." The general grabbed Prince affectionately by the ears and spoke to him as if the dog understood every word. "Prince, you tell Aussie here that you and I know. Right? We just feel it in our bones, don't we, boy? Those bastards are headed for British Columbia, and we've got to get them before they reach it. 'Course you and I know by now they're no doubt in civilian garb. Probably look like a bunch of Greenpeacers out to see the flora and fauna."

"They better watch out," said Sal, as Prince, sitting up close to Choir, looked on, "otherwise a grizzly'll bite them on the ass."

"*You* be careful," joshed Aussie, "otherwise—"

"General?" It was the Chinook's loadmaster sergeant. "Radio call for you from a Richard Moffat."

For a second, Freeman was wearing what Aussie had long ago dubbed his Patton frown. He took the phone, cupping the mouthpiece. "Richard *who*?"

"Chief scientist," Choir reminded him. "Richard Moffat."

"Hello, Doctor. Freeman here."

"General, we think we might have an answer for you regarding Dr. Juarez's 'It's spotted' comment."

"Oh yes," answered Freeman.

"First, I should tell you Roberta Juarez didn't survive."

"Oh, shit!"

Prince's head shot up, worried by the general's sharp tone.

"I'm sorry to hear that," Freeman told him.

"Thank you, General," Moffat acknowledged.

"Anyway," continued Moffat, "about her 'it's spotted' comment. Apparently, for security reasons, only one person—who I found out was off sick today—knew about an arrangement that was insisted upon by the chief of naval operations—"

"Yes?" said Freeman, fighting the temptation to say that it was a damned pity that the CNO or somebody else hadn't paid more attention to damned perimeter security in the first place.

"Well," continued Moffat, "the arrangement, which was deliberately withheld from DARPA directors—as an added security measure should a director ever be taken hostage and interrogated under duress—was that two scientists here at DARPA ALPHA, one on the day shift, one on the night—the night shift person being Roberta—had agreed to 'spot' the disk."

"Yes?"

"Well, what was meant by 'spotting' was that at the end of their respective shifts, these two people would take the disk, and I'm talking here about a three-and-a-half-inch floppy, faster than a CD-ROM but larger than a USB memory device, and for security they'd place a very small circular NDE (non-data-erasing) battery within the reverse—hollow—side of the metal hub so that—"

"So it would transmit a tracking signal," Freeman said excitedly, anticipating Moffat, "in case it was stolen!"

"Yes. Normally the disk's battery has a ten-second delay so it won't be activated while the disk is put in its jewel case at the end of the day."

"I get it," said Freeman. "But if somebody steals it without its jewel case, its battery would be activated. A beeper!"

"Correct. I've passed this on to Pacific Coast Command and the E-2C Hawkeye out of Whidbey Naval Station. It's festooned with electronic eyes and ears, and it's going to patch you into its radio net as soon as it picks up any signal from the disk."

"Brilliant!" said the general, using the declarative adjective he'd picked up from his sojourns with Britain's SAS regiment. "Absolutely brilliant!"

"Ah, General, there are a couple of other things you ought to know about."

"Shoot!"

"Dr. Grierson—the physician—"

"Yes," said Freeman. "Mr. Cool. The doctor who was looking after Roberta."

"Yes. Ah, well, the word's out that he and the hospital are suing you as being complicit in, ah, Roberta's death. I thought you ought to—"

"Fuck 'im!" said Freeman, his face reddening, the phone in one hand, the other holding a grab bar against the turbulence they were encountering. "Fuck 'im! But thanks for giving me the heads-up, Doc."

"You're welcome."

"That prick physician," Freeman told Johnny Lee,

"who I had you arrest at the hospital? He's suing me! Poor woman's dead and he's got a lawyer on my case."

"Ah," said Aussie disgustedly. "These guys've got attorneys comin' out their ass."

Prince was worried, backing up against the team's two Zodiacs as if looking for protection. Choir reassured him that the general's anger had nothing to do with him.

"*But*," Freeman announced, "good news. That disk the pricks stole—"

"Has a beeper!" cut in Aussie.

"You've been listening in on my phone conversations," charged Freeman, with mock severity.

"I have." Everyone laughed.

"I ought to have you arrested!"

"General Freeman." It was the helo pilot's voice. "We're descending to the Priest Lake turnoff."

"Hold on!" cut in Freeman. "Don't land here. I've just heard from Moffat that the terrorists are carrying a beeper, so I want to contact the Hawkeye to see whether they can get a fix on the bastards."

"Roger," answered the Chinook's pilot. "We'll take you back upstairs for a while."

The general, allowing for Murphy's Law, expected it to take much longer than it did to contact the Hawkeye but in fact they were exchanging info within five minutes. One of the electronic warfare officers aboard the Hawkeye was seeing a dot pulsing on his screen with the urgency of a boil about to burst. The E.W.O., one of the "moles" aboard the essentially windowless aircraft, sat beneath the rotating, spiral-painted rotodome. He routed his call through the "box," and the binary codes of zeroes and ones sorted themselves out into a military frequency that could be heard on Freeman's modular infantry radio, informing the general that the E-2C Hawkeye was picking up a clearly identifiable beep from Priest Lake. To underscore the sound, the electronic warfare officer brought the "beep" sound on line so that all the team members could hear it via their MIR's earpiece. The Hawkeye informed Freeman that the plane would loiter on station to provide GPS-assisted intel.

"Thank you, Lieutenant," Freeman told the E.W.O. "But I urge you to stay beyond MANPAD range."

"Appreciate your advice, General, but I hardly think the terrorists would bother adding shoulder-fired rockets to their load."

The general signed off and wasted no time informing his pilot that the Chinook's new landing zone would have to be as close as possible to the beep point the Hawkeye was reporting. The signal put their prey two miles west of an island in the southwest corner of Priest Lake. The island itself was about a mile offshore.

"I love that fucking beeper," said Aussie. "The fuckers are hoist by their own petard."

"What's a petard?" inquired Salvini, who was tightening the webbing that held the helo's two Zodiacs firmly against the bulkhead.

"Johnny?" called out Aussie as he busied himself checking out his HK G36 assault rifle's under-barrel grenade tube, the grenades festooned about him. "You're our linguist. Tell this ignorant savage from Brooklyn what a friggin' petard is."

"I don't know," said Johnny Lee, the skin over his high cheekbones tightening with concern; for all his knowledge of Asian, Mideastern, Slavic, and Romance languages, he didn't know what a petard was.

"It's an explosive device," Freeman explained, "formerly used to bust through walls. To be hoist by your own petard means you screw up your own plans by your own actions. What Aussie means is that the very thing those scumbags stole is giving them away." He allowed himself a smile despite the serious business they were embarked on.

"Serves the bastards right," said Tony Ruth, with grunts of approval from Gomez and Eddie Mervyn, who were tightening the slings on their navy rig Heckler & Koch submachine guns.

"And," said Choir, "if those swine haven't picked up the Hawkeye's transmit to us, they won't know. It'll be one big surprise when we suddenly appear on top of 'em." He turned to his beloved spaniel. "That right, boy?" Prince's tail was wagging affectionately as Choir adjusted the Velcro tabs on the dog's hagvar bulletproof, anti-shrapnel vest. Prince had easily passed the long, hard training for a tracker at Lackland Air Force Base in San Antonio, Texas, but he had never liked the vest, for while it protected his body in the area between his head and hindquarters, it was heavy.

"Don't let's get ahead of ourselves," Freeman cautioned Choir. "These swine are clever dicks, otherwise they wouldn't have been able to pull off this attack. They've obviously been planning for it for a long time. I checked with the FBI and DHS guys and they say that Tenth Mountain Division has had no reports of theft vis-à-vis their Paratrooper mountain bikes or uniforms. That tells me," added Freeman, his voice rising above the noise of the Chinook, "that these terrorists planned their op down to the last detail—" He paused, holding his left hand up for silence, his right hand gripping the roll bar as he listened to the beeper. Damn! It had ceased, which told him that his quarry might be in a "dead zone," physical barriers blocking transmission, or—

"Maybe the terrorists know they've got a beeper," cut in Johnny Lee.

"Well," said Freeman, "the best we can do is keep our eyes and ears open." His left hand indicated the southwest quadrant of his navigational pilotage chart. "We'll land here, two miles west of this island, the last reported beeper contact. We'll move in the bush along the west side of this old logging road that runs south-north parallel to the lake. We'll follow Prince and our own noses but—and I can't stress this too much—there are isolated cabins, not many, but some with a boat launch for hunters and fishermen. So remember, even if we get a beep right on top of one of them, *identify* before engaging. These scumbags—twelve of 'em by the bicycle count—may have commandeered a civilian vehicle to save travel time between Pend Oreille and Priest Lake. For them there'll be no need to worry about identifying friend or foe. Everyone is now their foe, so they'll be quick on the trigger. I'll try to stay in contact with the Hawkeye and in whisper contact with you via your MIRs." The general paused. "Questions?"

"We have any idea what they look like?" asked Salvini. "They could still be in U.S. battle dress."

"They could," the general agreed. "But my guess, Sal, is that they've gone civilian. The media will have the story out by now, or at least their version of it. Reporters can be sat on for a day, maybe, but there's no way that the murder of ten American scientists and a security guard in a small community can be hushed up for much longer. So, Sal, my answer has to be that the creeps could still be in our battle dress uniform or hunting gear. But not many hunters use automatic weapons, which I presume they're carrying."

"True," said Aussie, "though I know some so-called sportsmen who hunt deer with AK-47s and M-16s." He shook his head in disgust.

During the remainder of the flight, Freeman and his team did a quick study of the list of cabins and of ten people who, the sheriff had told him, had fled civilization to live year-round by the now storm-caged lake.

*   *   *

Jake McCairn, sixty-five, had a bad back from too much stress, he thought, and had retreated from the world into his wild, primeval domain. He enjoyed not having to shave or wear his dentures. He liked animals more than people, and when he saw this army guy coming out of the forest at the edge of the lake and calling out, "Mornin'!" Jake ignored him and continued checking the float-lines he'd set for rainbow and Dolly Varden trout.

"You Jake?"

"Eh?" Jake checked another of the lines—nothing.

"You're Jake McCairn, right?"

"What of it?"

"Signs on the way up from Sandpoint on Pend Oreille say you've got a boat for rent."

"Sometimes. Why?"

"My name's Ramon. My squad and I need a boat to go up the lake for a while."

"Should've brought your own boat. What d'ya expect, big marinas with neons flashing?"

"We had a boat, a Zodiac, but it got ripped up by a bear or something up—"

Jake McCairn emitted a guttural cough that was a stand-in for a laugh. It could be heard by Ramon's men thirty feet away in the woods fronting the lake. Low nimbostratus was coming lower, gray mist leaking from it and wreathing the lake in banks of bone-chilling fog.

"So," said Ramon, producing a wad of fifty-dollar bills. "Could you let us use your boat for a bit?"

"Nope. Going out to the island soon. Gonna get me a wolf skin." With that, Jake turned his back on the stranger and went back to his line casts.

Jake heard Ramon's footfall behind him and turned to see about ten or twelve men approaching him from the marshy edge of the lake, and heard the unmistakable sound of an approaching helicopter. He looked up, could see nothing but gray cloud no more than five hundred feet above a gray sheen on the lake, a sign that the sun still existed and was trying to get through here and there.

Ramon grabbed him in a hammerlock, and now the other men were running across the marshy margin between the woods and lakeshore, McCairn protesting violently until one of the men punched him so hard McCairn could hear his jawbone crack.

"Now," asked Ramon, dark brown eyes appearing almost black in the weak daylight, "where's your fucking boat, before we break your—"

Jake tried to spit at them but only bloody dribble came out, running down onto his beard-stubbled chin.

"Break his leg," ordered Ramon, glancing anxiously at the leaden sky for the helo.

Jake attempted to speak but couldn't, the pain of his broken jaw so intense it came out as "Boa's . . . up 'bou' three hundred yar'."

"Get him to his feet!" Ramon ordered. "Rashid!"

"Naam!"

"Speak English!" Ramon snapped. "You and Omar deal with the helo if it looks like it's going to land."

"Yes, Captain."

"C'mon!" Ramon told Jake, jabbing him hard with a Heckler & Koch 9 mm sidearm. "Take us to the boat and fast or we *will* break your leg." He jabbed the old man again. "Think I'm kidding, Mr. McCairn?"

Jake stumbled along through the reeds and fist-sized rocks, and in his hurting fury managed to ask, "You 'mericans?"

The soldier ignored him. When they found the boat, two of Ramon's men brought the outboard from their torn

Zodiac. Then they cut his throat. They started the out-board, a gray wolf howled, and Ramon realized that the dead man's boat could carry only six men.

There was no argument as to who would go and who would stay behind. Ramon's commandos from GUPIX, the Government of Palestine in Exile as they called it, al-ways knew that such difficult tactical situations might arise. The four of them, including the two American citi-zens from one of the vehement anti-federalist Idaho mili-tias who had helped them in their mission against the U.S. government, had trained long and hard, and each man un-derstood what he might be called upon to do in order that those with the disk could escape. And so morale remained high as Ramon told five of his men that he would go with them and the disk in the boat, while the other six men would stay behind.

The sound of the helicopter had now shifted from being eastward, near Montana, back toward them in the thick soup of nimbostratus. Ramon took comfort in the knowl-edge of how stressed the pilots must be. It would be tough enough on a clear day, flying in the tight airspace in the mist and cloud-shrouded amphitheater of the Rocky Mountains and surrounding hills, but this must be a night-mare. It was nothing like the Iraqi desert, Ramon mused, and he was struck by the sweet irony that in Iraq, in the desert, the terrain had favored the infidels' infiltration, whereas here America's rugged terrain helped by inhibit-ing a helo's maneuvers.

"Son of a bitch!" shouted Tony Ruth, who, struck by the loudness of the strong, resurrected "beep" being am-plified over the Chinook's internal bay speaker, declared, "We must be on top of the mothers!"

"We are!" confirmed the loadmaster.

"Gonna be tricky!" opined Aussie, looking down at the

wide, marshy margin between the lake proper and the edge of the woods.

"That's what we *do*," riposted Freeman. "We do tricky." He glanced down at Prince, who was panting, sensing the excitement and hearing the soft stream of defensive flares that the Chinook was dropping prior to landing. "That right, Prince?" said Freeman. "We do tricky, right?" Prince's tail was thumping a bulkhead.

"When we land," began Freeman, "I want every—" He glimpsed a bluish tail of exhaust at the edge of the woods.

"Missile!" yelled the pilot.

They felt the helo jink sharply right, then—

The explosion was earsplitting, and for several moments neither the general nor the rest of the team, who were slammed hard against the fuselage in their H-straps, could hear anything. Then the high whine of the rear rotors' portside engine took over the world, screaming as it fought to compensate for the loss of power from the knocked-out starboard engine.

"Going down!" yelled the loadmaster.

Nothing sounded or smelled right anymore, the usually loud but reassuring sounds and odors of a Chinook in steady flight now replaced by decidedly out-of-whack noises and the nauseating smell of leaking hydraulics as pilot and copilot fought to get the machine under control, flares still popping through gray stratus and mist. For a moment the big helo rose promisingly against a violent wind shear, but then they began to plummet.

"Hard landing!" shouted the loadmaster, and Choir, holding the spaniel close to him, could hear Prince whine.

They were out of the gray world, the metallic sheen of the lake sliding downhill, the helo's nose rattling like crazy and rising insanely, the forward rotor spinning, the rear blades slowing arthritically before stopping altogether, fuselage gyrating in the pilot's unequal battle with gravity; then they saw a long streak of dark woods west of them along the shoreline now seeming to run uphill. An eagle was glimpsed, then a darker, softer green than the woods was racing up at them, getting bigger, then WHUMP!—walls of reed-scummy water erupted all around and a sound like hail as a downpour of dead stalks and other lakeside detritus struck the Chinook's skin.

They had come down about a quarter mile from the shore in five feet of water, marsh to the left, open lake to their right.

Young Prince was whimpering like a puppy, but no one said a word. Every one of the eight-man team had braced for a tailbone-smashing crash, but the water and marshy margin of the lake here on the southwestern end afforded them if not a soft landing, then at least a less violent one than they had any right to expect.

Tony Ruth looked the most shaken. Prince's bright and alarmed eyes were looking up at Choir for reassurance. The pilot and copilot were shouting to each other above the noise as they shut down all ancillary systems that could quickly catch fire if the gas tanks had been perforated. In addition, there were still some of the supposedly anti-missile flares aboard, and they too posed a fire hazard.

"What happened with those damned flares?" Freeman demanded.

The pilot and copilot glared at the general. They had managed, against extraordinary odds, to bring the Chinook to a crash landing in marshland about fifty yards east of the dark line of thick woods, no one seemed badly hurt, and what was Freeman saying? Not "thank you, boys," but what happened to the fucking flares?

"How do we know!" said the helo captain. "They're supposed to sucker missiles into thinking they're our exhaust, but something went wrong. Sure as hell wasn't our flying—sir!"

"Sorry, gentlemen. You did a great job, but we all nearly bought it because—"

"Captain," cut in the copilot, "we're still getting the radio signal from that beeper. It's up ahead of us about three clicks, on the lake. They're definitely on the water, General."

"You hear that, guys?" Freeman shouted to the team, who had already dislodged the two six-man Zodiacs from the webbing and were ready to slide them down the rear-door ramp out to the marsh, from which cold mist was blowing into the helo like smoke. "Their beeper puts them about three clicks from here on the lake, so let's—" Rounds were thudding into the side of the helo, and through the open ramp door, Aussie could see winks of light coming from the woods about two hundred yards from their position.

"Damn!" said Freeman, "they must have split up. We can't use the Zodiacs on the lake. They'll pick us off like flies. Captain," he enjoined the chopper pilot, "can you stay here and give us their bearing for as long as possible?"

"Will do."

"Good man. Aussie, you and Sal have got the longest-range weapons. Stay with the two pilots. Hunker down, return fire. We're going to have to wade through the marsh to the shoreline, get through the woods to that road, and hit those bastards from the rear. No other way."

"I'll radio for reinforcements," said the pilot, "if the helo's box is still working."

"Good," said Freeman, who then ordered everyone to lighten their packs. The copilot informed him that while the radar was still functional, the chopper's radio was out. The best the pilots could do was keep Aussie and Sal informed of the getaway boat's position so that as well as being able to return fire with their longer-range weapons, the SpecFor commandos could notify the rest of Freeman's team via their MIR headsets.

"Good enough," said Freeman. "So, Aussie, you and Sal are CNN."

"Roger that," confirmed Sal.

The volume of incoming fire zipping above their heads and tearing into the fuselage was increasing and, despite his enthusiasm, Freeman realized that there was no way he could have his team wade through the marsh and expect any of them to be alive by the time they reached the shore, let alone the edge of the woods.

"We'll use the Zodiacs after all," he told them. "Aussie, you and Sal get ready to throw everything you can at that bunch in the woods. The rest of us'll drive the Zodiacs across the marsh toward the line of woods. Reeds'll screw up the outboards' props, but they should get us there." The reeds, Freeman hoped, would also dampen the outboards' noise.

The general shifted his AK-74 to his left hand and grabbed hold of the Zodiac's pull cord, as Choir, with Prince at his side, came over the gunwale. Ruth, Johnny Lee, Gomez, and Eddie Mervyn were already in the second Zodiac. The best they could hope for was to use the body of the helo for cover, keeping it between them and the enemy's position as they headed for shore.

Aussie reached for his G36 and Sal positioned his heavy-hitting machine gun with his sling.

"Go!" yelled the general. Aussie and Sal opened up, aiming at the winks of the enemy's small-arms fire coming from about two hundred yards away to the northwest, the hot gases from Aussie and Sal's weapons bending the reeds close to the helo, the two Zodiacs, on full power, speeding across the fifty yards of thigh-deep marsh between the downed chopper and the line of pine, fir, and golden-yellow larch. Aussie and Sal's fire was not only loud but accurate, and in the melee of return fire, Aussie's "Fritz" was almost knocked off by a ricochet caught in the helo's rotor. He and Sal heard a cry as one of the enemy "winks" was suddenly eclipsed.

Aussie and Sal's enfilade wasn't the wild, sweeping cover fire seen in movies, where it seems the good guys have an endless supply of ammunition. Instead it was concentrated, well-aimed fire not meant to simply keep the enemy's heads down but to take them out.

By the time the opposition—Aussie and Sal guesstimated there must be a group of five or six of them—had taken cover from the two SpecFors' on-target fire, Zodiacs 1 and 2 were in thick reeds only ten yards from the woods. Freeman, the other five men, and Prince were ashore, but by now the terrorists had recovered from the surprise of Sal's and Aussie's heavy and accurate bursts of fire and raked the Zodiacs, putting both out of action. Prince was growling.

Freeman could see the boat first detected on the helo's radar disappearing from view about two to three miles up the lake, close in to the northwestern shore. And he knew that with the sound of the crash, even the relatively few people who had cabins near or around the lake would raise an alarm which, he hoped, would bring police reinforcements and local reservists from Sandpoint. But the town was fifty miles away by road, and by the time any reinforcements might arrive, the terrorists in the boat would have gotten beyond the lake proper and entered the two-and-a-half-mile-long channel that would take them into Priest Lake. All of which rapidly brought Freeman to the conclusion that there was only one thing to do. His six-man squad would have to do a marathon—minimal-ration, ammunition pack, forty pounds to a man—along the lone fifteen-mile section of the secondary road, an old logging trail that ran more or less parallel to the lake at a distance of a quarter of a mile in places, four miles in others, from the water. There was no chance that he and his five could outrun the terrorists fleeing in a boat, but he might be able to reach another boat or vehicle to catch up with them or head them off.

The general hoped that meantime the Hawkeye would be frequency scanning, and, while he would be unable to make contact with the helo any longer, that it would keep him updated via his modular infantry radio. Freeman had one asset that would save some time: Prince. With the terrorists' scent firmly impressed upon his olfactory sense, he should be able to help them avoid any time-consuming, deadly ambushes by the five or so rearguard terrorists who had been firing from the edge of the woods at the helo. These scumbags would almost certainly cut back through the dense woods and rush to the road. Then Freeman suddenly realized his advantage. If he, Choir, Ruth, Gomez, Johnny Lee, and Eddie Mervyn could run to the secondary road a mile and a quarter to the west of where they were at present, they might be able to beat these rearguard terrorists who, he saw on his tactical map, were at the foot of a densely forested slope. The terrorists were three miles from the secondary road rather than the one mile his team had to cover before reaching it.

"Right," said Freeman quickly. "We go. Fast!" Adding, "Now we'll see who's been spending too much time with Mommy!" Freeman thought of Margaret, but immediately pushed her out of his mind. Gomez, Eddie Mervyn, and Tony Ruth exchanged grins.

The team headed off, Freeman on point, through the thick woods and the ubiquitous salal brush, its green, mist-polished leaves pushing against them at shoulder height with the same kind of determination, it seemed, as the plant used whenever it invaded a new area, crowding out all other vegetation in its way. They were violating the

first rule of the Special Forces: be quiet. The salal in particular, while not prickly, had leaves that were rigid
enough to resist a mere brushing aside as one could do
with sword ferns and the like, and the six men and dog
created so much noise that it sounded to Choir as if a tank
was moving through. But Choir knew that the general
knew when to break the rules, and besides, Prince was
nearby, ready to stop and stiffen at the merest whiff of a
terrorist's scent.

Then they got a break. They had reached a hiker's trail,
presumably one that linked the secondary road and the
lakeshore through the forbidding woods. A hard, pushing
slog suddenly became a run, and someone's camelback
was sloshing, for which, at the appropriate time, Freeman
would ream out the offender in no uncertain terms. Running, it made no difference, but if and when they were
forced to close on the enemy quickly, silently, even the
greenest cadet knew that the smallest sound could give
him away.

It wasn't the fastest mile in history, but for men weighed
down with arms, ammo, and essential war wares, it was
exemplary. In another five minutes they saw the road and
slowed, senses on high alert. They walked quickly, quietly now, until they could see that the road was clear, then
split into two teams: the general, Johnny Lee, and Choir,
with Prince leading, on the eastern side of the northbound
road, Ruth, Eddie Mervyn, and Gomez on the opposite,
western, side. They were running again, resolute in their
intention to bypass the terrorist group that had been firing
on them and to keep going until they found a cabin or one
of the few small marinas scattered around the lake's
seventy-mile-long shoreline. With luck, they could get either a boat or a vehicle in which to hightail it to the northern end of the lake before the "disk" party disembarked
into the woods and followed one of the creek beds on the

twenty- to thirty-mile hike to the border and the equally
wild country of the Canadian forests.

Prince, panting, growled at a rush of sound that suddenly burst from the bush, sending all six men to ground
until they realized the noise was that of squirrels, not
men. Prince stopped to look back at them with what seemed
to Freeman an expression of mild contempt for their unwarranted belly flops.

They were running again, and from their GPSs they
knew that soon they would be adjacent to the general area
from which the rearguard terrorist squad had been firing.

CHAPTER SEVEN

A WORLD AWAY, the White House was learning just how important, indeed critical, it was to recover the DARPA ALPHA disk. The prospect of any country, even the tried-and-true allies Great Britain and Australia, having possession of America's revolutionary Flow-In-Flight technology was, as Eleanor Prenty told the president, sending shock waves through the Pentagon. She placed an 8½-by-11-inch scaled-down drawing of the "gas in nose cone" torpedo before him. "It's downright traumatizing the chief of naval operations. It would mean a sub having the ability to fire at an enemy ship two hundred miles away. The DARPA ALPHA people say there would be no wake, no warning."

"Wouldn't the targeted ship hear it?" posed the president. "I mean, on its sonar?"

"At a mile a second, it would be like—" She consulted the notes she'd taken from the CNO. "DARPA ALPHA scientists tell us that—" She had to turn several pages, her hand trembling. After being on her feet this long, and stoked with coffee since the crisis broke, she was beyond exhaustion. "The scientists say that at ten miles, for example, the sonar noise from the super-cavitating torpedo would last no longer than a quick jab on a door buzzer. But if you think the CNO's in near-coronary mode, you should read the stuff I've been getting from the Joint Chiefs. The army is piss—sorry, sir. I mean—"

"The army's pissed that they hadn't heard of DARPA ALPHA until today?"

"Yes, Mr. President." Eleanor moved her laptop so he could see the map of Washington state's Kitsap Peninsula. "The army knew about DARPA's Division of Naval Surface Warfare up here at Bayview and about the Keyport testing lab and torpedo range on the Kitsap perimeter. But DARPA ALPHA was—is—completely different in intent and in staffing from the DARPA installation we knew back in 2006."

The president shrugged. "Can't blame them. These things have to be run on a strictly need-to-know basis. Black ops. We can't all know what everybody else is doing."

"Well, the army's particular worry is that they see the super-cavitation technology in a smaller, bullet-sized projectile that could pierce the armor of the Abrams M1. More important, it could penetrate the armor of our new lighter, faster Stryker vehicles, which have gained so much favor in the Pentagon after the army brass realized just how—'constipated' is the word General Freeman once used—the big M-1 is when trying to travel on non-American roads. The tank weighs in at seventy tons, and on any other highway system than our own or on the German Autobahns, it becomes a dinosaur, no matter how well armored and upgunned it is. Which is why we need to get that disk back. And quickly."

"How's Freeman's team doing?"

"FBI says that the sheriff at Sandpoint has told them that there've been reports of a helo going down in the area, possibly brought down by a MANPAD shoulder-fired missile, but—" She paused, exhausted, so much so she asked the president if she might sit for a moment.

"What—oh, of course." But Eleanor had no sooner sat, her feet resting on the border of the plush round blue oval carpet that bore the Great Seal of the United States, than the president was asking, "Freeman's team okay? Functional?"

"Yes, sir," Eleanor replied, catching her breath. "The moment the Navy's Hawkeye lost contact with the helo and tracked its down position, the local sheriffs and air rescue in Coeur d'Alene were alerted. Then Freeman's team came through on their infantry radios. Freeman says it's well in hand, and he doesn't want more troops in there confusing the issue. Says it's a case of 'too many cooks spoil the broth.' Says he's closing in on the beeper via the radar contact the downed helo still has with the beeper that was planted in the disk."

"Okay," said the president. "I'd prefer to send in more men, but Freeman's the man on the ground. If he feels he's closing, there's no point in us getting in his way." The president turned to the large map of the Idaho panhandle that had been wheeled into his office. "I can see Freeman's point. Must be some of the densest part of the country up there. Even so, I want the nearest army battalion on standby just in case he needs a last-minute assist."

"That's already been taken care of," said Eleanor.

The president turned from the map to her. "Next thing, Eleanor, is for you to be driven home and not come back here for twelve hours. That's an *order*. Got it?"

"Yes, sir," she said gratefully, but not without a feeling of guilt that she should stay.

"Go on now," he ordered. "Scram."

"Yes, Mr. President."

CHAPTER EIGHT

EVERYONE ON THE team—Choir, Johnny Lee, and Freeman on the eastern side of the road, Tony Ruth, Gomez, and Murphy on the western side—saw Prince stop short, pine cones flying in front of his paws. The weight of his armored vest was starting to tell, his panting more rapid than it had been when they left the helo, but the rest of him was rigid. He was pointing. They froze. Freeman knelt on the soft earth and fallen leaves on the road's shoulder, and Tony Ruth could see the general's gloved right hand switch his AK-74 from the "off" position. Everybody else had done the same.

The disquieting noise of their controlled breathing could be heard above the stillness of the forest from which a white mist bled. Prince was pointing into the woods from the road at a barely discernible opening in the wall of trees and brush only a few yards from the road's shoulder. Had the terrorists' rear guard anticipated his move, wondered Freeman, and also raced through the woods from the lakeside to reach the road? Both sections of Freeman's team had automatically adopted CAF, covering arcs of fire, so that they could engage the enemy and guard each other.

He saw the silhouette of an AK-47's front sight above the trail and fired. Both of his sections opened up, using the falling corpse, a U.S. Army uniform, as their central

aiming point. The air was ripped apart by the sudden fury
of the firefight, but it was all one-way, the enfilade from
Freemen's men having the crucial advantage. Anyone behind the first man they'd killed would be unable to get
past him easily on the narrow trail and forced to ground
amid timber and brush that was now the recipient of concentrated fire, 7.62 mm and 5.56 mm rounds pouring into
the woods in a narrow cone. If the screams and Arabic
curses of the dying were anything to go by, all six of the
terrorists were either down, dead, or badly wounded,
Prince growling ferociously at the mere gall of the inter-
lopers.

"Johnny, Tony, Choir!" Freeman shouted. "Come with
me." He then told Eddie Mervyn and Gomez to "clean up
then catch up," as he and the other three, with Prince leading, continued their forced march north on the deserted
road. Freeman, on point as usual, spotted a faint gleam of
metal in the woods off to his left. It was a downpipe from
a creeper-covered cabin set well back, about a hundred
feet, in the forest. The general led his men in through
shoulder-high salal that formed the perimeter of a small
clearing, mist enveloping the surrounding timber like
malevolent layers of swamp gas. A thin, lazy plume of
smoke issued from the cabin's stone chimney. A beat-up
Ford Explorer, its left rear fender badly rusted and strips
of duct tape holding in a rectangle of transparent plastic
that had replaced the back window, stood forlornly a few
yards from the rear of the cabin, its tires' tracks disappearing into the overcast green of salal.

Freeman extracted one of DARPA's "products"—or
"goodies," as the Special Forces called them. It was a
matchbox-size scanner-remote-key that, upon activation
with one push of a man's thumb, scans for the solenoid
opening frequency of a vehicle and unlocks it. A more
civil approach, knocking on the cabin door, explaining

the dire need for the vehicle to catch up with the terrorists, to overtake them, had occurred to the general, but the very thought of the disk being in enemy hands was chilling enough, the possibility of Americans being attacked by such weapons evicting any idea of social niceties.

A woman inside the cabin was screaming and a man in a tie-dyed nightshirt came running out with a baseball bat.

"Stop!" yelled Freeman. "U.S. Army Special Forces. We need your vehicle. We'll pay you compensation. Give me the keys."

"What the—"

"The keys! Quickly!"

The man, dropping the bat, ran back into the dimly lit cabin, followed by Freeman. The general watched him go past a potbellied stove to a small table by a creeper-covered window. "Here!" He tossed the SUV's keys to Freeman.

"Thank you, sir," said Freeman as they came out. "Stay inside. Bad day to be out."

"You're as bad as the guys you're after!"

Freeman lobbed the keys to Choir, and glanced back at the man. "What other guys?"

"Guys who done the same as you to Mick Sutter."

"When?

The man's sense of outrage was increasing. " 'Bout twenty minutes ago. Busted into his shed, stole his car. Tried to call the cops but they'd cut his line. Smashed his cell too. Just charged in like you guys."

"If his phones were taken out, how come you know about it?"

"He walked down the road a ways to a neighbor's. He called us."

"You have any description?" Freeman asked him, adding, "We're on your side."

"Huh," said the man derisively. "Funny way of showin'

it." But Freeman could tell the man believed him. "They was dressed like you guys. Battle gear. Dark eyes, Mick's wife said. Middle Eastern guys. Like A-rabs. They looked wet—like they'd been out on the lake."

"What kind of car did they take?" asked the general.

"Gray—old Dodge Colt."

"License?"

"Canadian. Sutters are Canadian—stay all summer and fall. Thelma," he called back to the woman in the cabin, "you got that license plate number Mick gave you?"

"It's RCV —" said the woman, timidly emerging from the cabin with a piece of paper, her hands shaking, pulling jerkily at her bath robe. "— RCV 625."

Choir backed the Explorer out quickly, throwing gravel. Freeman made contact with Sal and Aussie via their headsets. "You still have a beep?"

"Affirmative. It's coming from what's indicated on the Tac Nav chart as a campground, a new one—Melson Campground—near the top of the lake. Possible they're changing into civilian—" There was the crackle of static, and then Aussie and Sal could hear Freeman telling them that now that the rearguard action was over they should wait at the helo until further notice. The general had no sooner finished talking with Aussie and Sal than he heard Eddie Mervyn coming in on his MIR line informing him that, as suspected, all the rearguard terrorists—six of them—were dead. Freeman thanked Eddie and Gomez, telling them that he, Ruth, Choir, and Johnny Lee were only a quarter mile up the road, they had an SUV, and would pick them up within a few minutes.

After Mervyn and Gomez were in the SUV, the team headed north on the lone road. The Ford Explorer was doing a maximum of thirty miles per hour, Ruth on the passenger-side running board, the general on the driver's-side running board, both looking ahead for any sign of an improvised booby trap. The Explorer's defroster was on the fritz, so Choir had to use his free hand to wipe the condensation from the windshield. Thirty miles per hour on the straightaway was Choir's compromise between getting there quickly but still having time to jam on the brakes, should anything suspicious appear on the road that was now funneling into a dark tunnel of trees.

Freeman figured Choir's speed was a bit overcautious, but one anti-personnel mine on the road could rupture a tire and bring everything to a screeching halt.

There was no mine, but an all-but-invisible cable strung tautly across the road.

"Brake!" yelled Ruth, Choir shouting, "Heads down!" Choir's controlled skid saved the Explorer from taking the impact full-on, its right side slamming against the cable. Ruth, caught by the cable, was lifted up by it, his helmet flying off, his severed head rolling along the road's shoulder in a flurry of dead leaves, his torso gushing blood. The nose-clogging smell of burnt rubber wafted over the others as the SUV stopped, everyone in utter shock, their obscenities rending the air. Recovering first, Douglas Freeman said, "God watch him," then "Put him in the back! *MOVE!*" As they did so, the pungent odor of burnt rubber hung about the vehicle like a funeral pall.

Choir was as white as a sheet. It had been Ruth yelling, "Brake!" but it had been Choir who made the mistake of swinging the wheel instead of letting the vehicle hit the wire full-on, in which case it would likely have twanged over the roof without touching either Ruth or Freeman. Freeman ordered Choir to get back in and drive. Again Freeman took his position on the driver's-side running board. "Go!" To prevent them from hearing the head rolling around, Johnny Lee, in the back, almost sick to his stomach, wrapped it up in a bunch of old clothing the owner had obviously dumped in the backseat, and stuffed it into a corner. No one spoke save Freeman, who, riding the driver's-side running board, bellowed into the window against the slipstream, his eyes on the road all the time, "Stay focused! We can't do anything to help Ruth now. But we *can* make those bastards pay for every—" Freeman's body lurched forward, his left wrist jammed against the driver's-side mirror as Choir braked hard, a swirl of leaves rising from the road's shoulder under the impact of the skid temporarily blocking Freeman's view.

"Mines!" screamed Choir.

"Six of them, right?" said Johnny Lee.

"Yes!"

Now Freeman saw them: six small, black objects, no more than a hand's span wide, placed, staggered, across the road so that it would be impossible for a vehicle to pass without making contact with at least one of them.

"Back up," he ordered Choir, "till we're at least fifty yards away."

Choir had no sooner stopped the Explorer than the general, regretting that neither Sal nor Aussie's longer-range weapons were at hand, ordered Gomez and Eddie Mervyn to concentrate on two targets apiece while he, Freeman, would deal with the remaining two. Choir turned the SUV's engine off. The ensuing silence was eerie. They could smell the rain in the air. An ominous deep green color curdled the sky, promising heavy snow to the north along Idaho's border with B.C. Leaves scuttled across the road with unnerving urgency. Although superbly trained, Gomez and Eddie Mervyn were showing signs of stress, Mervyn unusually jumpy, Eddie breathing rapidly. Still, their aim was true, and through the roar of the submachine guns Freeman could see the targets disintegrating. But something was wrong. There were no explosions.

"What the—" began Johnny Lee.

"All right," said the general. "Let's go." He told Choir to

stop momentarily by the targets then quickly stepped down from the driver's-side running board and retrieved part of what they had thought were mines. "Son of a bitch!"

"What is it, General?" pressed Choir as Prince, on high alert, cocked his head inquiringly, Gomez glancing anxiously at his watch, figuring that at the speed they were going they were less than six miles from the campground. Eddie Mervyn and Johnny Lee were watching the road intently through a shower of ice-cold rain.

"China!" said the general. "Saucers. They put six damn saucers upside down across the road!"

"Probably got 'em from the cabin they busted into," Eddie Murphy suggested.

Choir wasn't interested. All right, so they were cunning. But right now, hunched tight over the wheel, eyes straining, the SpecFor veteran was preoccupied, watching the rain-slicked road, the calf of his right leg a tense bundle of nerves and muscle, ready to stab the brake at the first sign of another wire, the terrible, dull thud and thwack of Ruth's decapitation burned into his memory forever.

The general guesstimated that they were about five miles—around seven minutes—from Melson Campground, and he knew that the terrorist he was after, this "Ram," if that was what he was called, was infuriatingly smart, almost, the general allowed, as smart as he was. Well, hell, the general told himself, one thing that he and the team weren't going to do was drive pell-mell into the campground. It was early fall, and though he doubted there would be many campers, if any, after the Labor Day weekend, he'd have to be careful not to get any more civilians involved. They'd stop the Explorer a quarter mile before the objective and go in for the kill on foot.

Approaching the campground on the run, Prince, on point, was panting so loudly, Freeman thought, that he could be heard a hundred feet away on the narrow, pot-holed road that led through a tunnel of trees to the camp-ground. It was hoped that Prince still had the scent and that the eager spaniel could lead the general and his four-man team to exactly where the terrorists were, or to what hiking trail they'd selected to take them northward to the Canadian border fourteen miles due north.

Freeman's SpecFors halted fifty yards from the camp-ground. They could see bodies strewn by the entrance where a bullet-ridden Winnebago stood facing them. Its driver, a woman, her door open, was slumped over the wheel. Two children, seven, possibly eight years old, were lying very still on the ground, the nearby grass so green it contrasted vividly with the pools of blood. The children's faces were horribly disfigured, abdomens disemboweled. Prince became rigid and pointed. Several gray wolves, tails down, were slinking away on the off side of the camper, one of them baring its blood-smeared canines at the intru-sion on what obviously, from the gruesome state of one of the children's bodies, had been the predators' meal.

Freeman signaled Choir to put Prince back to work to find the enemy's scent, which Prince did quickly despite the rain, leading them to a trailhead a hundred yards be-yond the campground by one of the creeks. They fol-lowed Prince along the Dodge Colt's tracks, which could be easily seen where the gravel ended and the grass be-gan. Eddie Mervyn was mouthing obscenities. The car, Canadian plates RCV 625, had been nosed into heavy brush. There were a lot of pine needles around it; the nee-dles had probably showered down when the doors, now shut, had been opened. None of the team thought there was an ambush set up; that would be an unwarranted loss of time for the terrorists. But none of the team expected to walk past the Dodge scot-free. The car was probably "rigged for red"—ready to blow via trip wire.

Ten minutes later they knew there were no trip wires, and that they had wasted ten minutes. And they no longer had the "beep." It wasn't their modern infantry radios that had been jammed. Rather, the thunderous collision of two big storm fronts, whose electric-blue strikes were dancing neurotically amid the Selkirk Mountains that bordered Idaho and the Canadian province of British Columbia, had temporarily scrambled all radio communication. Prince, having led them to the Dodge, was now sneezing so hard and frequently that the team wondered if the terrorists had used black pepper or some other equally confusing compound to throw the dog off.

Don't panic, Freeman told himself, as if addressing the other members of his team. Stay calm. Go back to the campground's entrance, look for boot marks, get *your* sense of sight working, and working hard.

But it was no use. The heavy rain had obliterated any footprints or enemy smell for Prince to work with. The spaniel looked up and the general could have sworn the dog's eyes were saying "Sorry."

"It's all right, Bud," said Freeman, kneeling, catching his breath. "You've worked hard." As the general patted Prince, he glanced back at the murdered woman in the Winnebago and the bodies of her children, which neither Johnny Lee nor Choir wanted to deal with.

Freeman called in on the sheriff's Sandpoint police frequency. A message machine answered. He gave the team's location and told them, "We're in trouble. Send in whoever you can. We'll try to pick up the scumbags' trail and we'll secure the campground perimeter just in case."

It was a mark of his leadership—to know that he was beaten and not let pride prevent him from calling in the bigger, albeit slower moving, search and rescue elements. With no scent, no beep, and heavy rain, tracking the bad guys was virtually hopeless. But just because he'd failed on his quick dash by helo to Priest Lake, there was no reason now to prevent the bigger battalions from coming in. Until it occurred to him—the most unexpected scenario of all—that because each tent and trailer-home site was so secluded in this heavily forested area, the terrorists could be hiding *in* the campsite itself. Freeman could not give himself or his team a reason why the terrorists should do this, but he did know that a good leader examines all the possibilities.

Freeman, Choir, Gomez, Lee, and Eddie Mervyn began doing a search, moving swiftly yet cautiously from one site to another. It was bad enough to have lost a man already, and Freeman didn't want any more casualties in this— so far, at least—futile mission. Prince was doing his all, between bouts of sneezing that jangled their nerves. It took all of Choir's concentration not to say, "Bless you," to the dog each time, so close was his bond with Prince. He could see that Prince was becoming increasingly uncomfortable under the weight of the protective vest. Now and then the spaniel would stop and paw at it, to no avail.

Johnny Lee saw the strand and screamed, "Down!" Everyone did so, including Prince, but he'd already tripped the wire that had been strung a few inches above the apron of soggy ground. The bang of the claymore mine and the whistling of its seven hundred steel balls temporarily blocked out the sound of the rain. They were all hit with ricochets coming off the surrounding trees, but their hagvar helmets, vests, and high-collared battle dress uniforms had saved them from any incapacitating injury, though Choir's right thigh would be badly bruised from one ricochet. Prince, however, had not been so lucky. Having caught part of the blast on the part of his hindquarters not covered by his hagvar coat, he now lay yelping in a tangle of wire dangling from the exploded mine's carcass. Choir limped to his spaniel's side, Freeman already calling in search and rescue in Coeur d'Alene via Sandpoint for an evac helo. Eddie Mervyn, Gomez, and Johnny Lee went into T.D.P.—triangular defensive position—to cover the general. The delay, they all knew, meant more gained ground for the terrorists, who the team now believed must be escaping on one of the many trails that wove their way farther from the campground into the wilderness of the Idaho–British Columbia border.

"Hang on, old boy," Choir whispered to Prince, unbuckling the bloodied rear strap of Prince's armored vest. "Hang on."

A half an hour later, as they waited for the SAR helo that they could hear beating the air somewhere above them in the torrential downpour, their fatigue, the loss of Tony, and now, possibly, of Prince, sat upon them like a heavy, gray sheet of metal. Freeman knew that they had lost too much time to catch the terrorists before they crossed the border into Canada. By now, the regular army forces had had time to assemble and, under presidential orders, were taking over the search. The general, Gomez, Mervyn, Choir, and Johnny Lee all tried to hide their bitter disappointment as they regrouped, waiting for a lift back to Sandpoint, but the plain fact was that the terrorists, despite having lost half their number in the fiercely fought rearguard action at the lake, had soundly defeated Freeman's team.

In the next twenty-four hours, as a few grim locals put it, "the hills were alive with the sound of curses," as battalions of army reservists and army rangers, guided by forest rangers, scoured the high wilderness areas west, north, and east of Priest Lake, pressing ever farther into the mountainous fastness of Idaho's panhandle. Only one thing of any relevance was found, and that by a ranger corporal. It was a manila envelope with "General D. Freeman—*Personal*" written on it. The envelope had been placed inside a large, transparent plastic Ziploc bag together with what looked like black marble-sized pieces of bubble plastic. The bag itself had been attached to a tree at the side of one of the many hiking trails that crisscrossed the border. The area was inaccessible by vehicle and, for this reason, was frequently used by drug mules carrying prized "B.C. Bud"—marijuana—across into the United States.

There was very little conversation as Douglas Freeman and his reunited team were heloed back to Sandpoint, where, as Freeman was tersely issuing instructions for the transfer of Tony Ruth's remains back to Arlington, a major delivered the Ziploc bag. The general held it up against the gunmetal sky, examining it carefully for any sign of booby traps, though the fact that it had been forwarded to him by army rangers without anything untoward happening was reasonably good assurance that it hadn't been rigged. Still, this was the post-9/11 world, and there could be anthrax or some other equally lethal powder in the manila envelope inside the Ziploc. It didn't take much to kill you. The general walked downwind, away from his team, the black melted plastic bits sliding back and forth in the bag like popcorn. He carefully removed the envelope from the bag, slipped out his twelve-inch Cold Steel blade from its scabbard and, holding the envelope downwind at arm's length, slit it and waited. No powder. Next, he carefully opened the yellow, folded, letter-sized sheet of paper: "AMERICANS SUCK."

The general, the sole passenger aboard the DOD's West Coast Learjet en route back to Monterey, was handed an encoded e-mail by the copilot. It was from DARPA's General Charles at the Pentagon, and confirmed what

Freeman had feared most, that the black blobs of plastic in the Ziploc bag had once been a computer disk. The sickening implication was that the terrorists must have downloaded and transmitted the super-cavitation data via hilltop line-of-sight modem—and that with apparently no copies at DARPA ALPHA, America now had no record of the data, shifting the balance of power dramatically, and terrifyingly, from the West to the terrorists.

The general's concomitant fear was that already the precious data was being fed into the brains of computer-controlled lathes that could turn the requisite hard carbon and steel composites into weaponry and ammunition with hitherto undreamed-of accuracy and destructive power.

Eleanor Prenty handled the news networks with typical aplomb. She allowed Marte Price to interview her on this evening's *Prime Time* to state that classified material had indeed been stolen from a DOD installation at Lake Pend Oreille.

"What kind of material?" asked Marte Price.

"Personnel files."

The look of incredulity from Marte Price was seen by millions of viewers. "Secretary Prenty, are you telling me that—" She glanced down at her notes. "—ten, no, *eleven*, Americans have been murdered by terrorists because they wanted *personnel files*?"

Prenty's Washington-honed expression gave away nothing.

CHAPTER NINE

"SO!" THE PRESIDENT growled at Eleanor Prenty, who was standing respectfully behind him on the Oval Office's carpet as the chief executive of the United States, hands clasped behind him, gazed out through the bullet-proof glass into the Rose Garden. "The hard drive's been destroyed and the *backup* disk stolen. And now we have the possibility—indeed the probability—that some terrorist cell, who knows where, will throw it back at us in the form of a prototype bullet, torpedo, or missile, a technology which we don't know how to counter because we've had the damn technological data stolen."

"Mr. President," said Eleanor, in what was almost certainly the understatement of her career, "I know it looks bad." She paused. "It *is* bad, but Chief Scientist Moffat has e-mailed me that it's only the very latest C.P.L. equipment—"

"For God's sake, Eleanor, speak English!"

"Sorry, sir. That's computer precision lathing equipment that would be needed to tool up for the extraordinarily small tolerances required to produce the super-cavitation hardware. I've alerted every one of our embassies, consulates, cultural, and trade liaison offices to keep their eyes peeled for any shipments of such ultra-high-quality equipment to any big or small-arms manufacturers throughout the world. And for all we know,

Roberta Juarez—" She saw that the president was trying to put a name to a face and explained, "She was one of the senior scientists working on this super-cavitation stuff."

"Yes," replied the president. "I remember now."

"She was the one," continued Eleanor, "who alerted us to the fact that the floppy backup disk had a battery transmitter in its hub before she died. Another of the dead scientists had a note in his hand with 'RAM' and 'SCARUND' written on it."

"My God, you think that's that sarin—nerve gas?"

"No," said Eleanor, "but, given it was presumably the last thing he wrote, we presume it's the name of the terrorist leader or that of one of the other terrorists."

"Huh! Probably the one who left Freeman that note." The president turned around to face her. "That must have hurt. Filthy insult like that."

"I'm sure it did," said Eleanor. "It upset me." She took a sheet of paper from her briefcase. "This is the forensics report on the envelope and the discarded shoulder-fired rocket launcher the terrorists used to down the Chinook."

"What have we got?" the president asked glumly. His reelection desk calendar reminded him that tomorrow he was to give a progress report on the war against terrorism.

(1) TRACES OF THIOKOL TX-657 REDUCED-SMOKE SOLID FUEL WITH DISTINCTIVE SULFUR CONTENT, AS SUSPECTED BY GENERAL FREEMAN WHO WITNESSED THE MANPAD LAUNCH. SPECTROMETER ANALYSIS OF SULFUR LOCATION SPECIFIC.

(2) ELECTRON MICROSCOPE AND SPECTROMETER ANALYSES OF BROWN ENVELOPE, WHICH IS CHINESE, AND YELLOW PAPER NOTE ADDRESSED TO GENERAL FREEMAN AND PLACED INSIDE TRANSPARENT PLASTIC ZIPLOC BAG

REVEAL PULP ACID USED TO MANUFACTURE PAPER
NORTHEASTERN CHINA. ALSO YELLOW PAPER IS 21 CM ×
29.7 CM, A STANDARD CHINESE SHEET, WHILE OURS IS
21.5 CM × 27.9 CM. SEVERAL MICROSCOPIC GRAINS OF SOIL
DETRITUS FOUND IN DISCARDED U.S. UNIFORMS ON
CANADA SIDE OF IDAHO-CANADA BORDER REVEAL LO-
CALIZED IDAHO–BRITISH COLUMBIA DEPOSITS. GRAINS
OF SOIL AND GRASSES FROM BOOTS' SOLES AND INTERI-
ORS WERE ALSO SPECTROMETERED AND REVEALED SOIL
INDIGENOUS NOT ONLY TO PACIFIC NORTHWEST BUT TO
AREAS OF NORTHEASTERN CHINA AND RUSSIAN FAR
EAST IN LAND ADJACENT TO AND INCLUDING LARGE
WILD BIRD SANCTUARY IN AND AROUND LAKE KHANKA.
DEPOSITS OF CRUSHED BIRD EGGSHELL AND DISPROPOR-
TIONATE AMOUNT OF GUANO WERE FOUND DEEP IN THE
SOLES OF SOME OF THE BOOTS, THE GUANO'S COMPOSI-
TION POINTING TO TANCHO AND SEVERAL SPECIES THAT
NORMALLY CLUSTER NEAR OR ON LARGE BODIES OF
FRESH WATER, SUCH AS LAKE KHANKA. INSIDE THE
BOOTS SEVERAL MICROSCOPIC SPECKS OF ANT REMAINS
DETECTED, ALSO INDIGENOUS TO LAKE KHANKA AREA.

"So, Eleanor," asked the president, "what's your take
on this soil stuff? A wild bird sanctuary? You think any
of this has anything to do with the attack on DARPA
ALPHA?"

Eleanor shrugged. "CIA has used soil forensics to locate terrorist training areas in the past. The director of national intel is more interested in how we can stop the
manufacture of DARPA ALPHA's hypersonic technology. As I did, he's also alerted the State Department,
which has sent an Immediate/Urgent Defcon 3 to all U.S.
embassies' military attachés to be on the lookout for the
movement of any high-precision computer-slaved lathing
equipment needed to tool up for everything from torpedo

and artillery nose cones to small-arms 7.62 mm rounds. CIA and DARPA ALPHA's General Charles concur that in two months at the latest, one damned terrorist with a rifle will be able to take out anything, from an M1 Abrams tank to our billion-dollar Joint Strike Fighters to any commercial aircraft or any other vehicle."

The president unleashed a train of obscenities, several of which Eleanor hadn't heard since 9/11.

"Let's pray, Eleanor, that someone somewhere can get a handle on this. Do we have current SATPIX of this Lake—" He looked down at the DHS report. "—Khanka?"

"CIA courier is bringing over a package." She glanced at her watch. It was almost time for the next press briefing. Right now she wanted to quit the White House, get out from all the pressure, go home, and be with her daughter Jennifer, go shopping, play Scrabble. No, that would take too much energy. Why not go to bed—pull the covers up, go into a cave, do anything but face a hostile Washington press corps? She imagined that this was how Condi Rice must have felt when confronted by the European press scrums, whose members had relentlessly pushed for details about the CIA's POW "rendition" policy, in which Al Qaeda suspects were spirited away to secret prisons in eastern Europe. If the press even suspected what was on the DARPA ALPHA so-called "personnel files" disk, and that no backup had been found, it could sink the presidency. *Didn't the press know,* Eleanor asked herself, *that scientists were human too, that yes, maybe Roberta Juarez, God rest her soul, should have had a backup of the backup, but how much backup do you have for your own computer? C'mon, people, give us a break. We're doing the best we can.*

"Eleanor?"

"Oh, sorry, Mr. President."

"You okay?"

"Yes, yes, I'm fine. I was just wondering whether Roberta Juarez had another backup disk somewhere. So far there's no sign of one."

"Great," said the president, his tone one of utter exasperation. "So not only have the terrorists destroyed the damn disk, probably downloaded to their HQ by now, but we have no record of what it is they've stolen. And those people who did know what was on the disk are all dead. God help us. We need a miracle. I mean it." He looked up as if startled. "Those men who were on Freeman's team. They're out of the picture now, but are we confident they'll keep their mouths shut?"

"Absolutely," Eleanor assured him. "Freeman had Fairchild—the air base near Spokane—disperse them back to their homes. Fairchild used six different planes, Special Forces, so no names were given out. At least the press understands something about the need for privacy when—"

"That won't keep the tabloids quiet for long."

"No, it won't," she replied.

"The Pentagon, I suppose, is unloading on Freeman."

"Everyone's unloading on Freeman, Mr. President. Success has a hundred fathers, but failure—"

"—is an orphan," said the president. "Are *we* unloading on him?" It was an election-year question, ends justifying the means. If you win the election you can do a lot for the country but you need to win.

"I don't think *we* should," she answered. "He mightn't be as fast as he was, an old warhorse, but a warhorse nonetheless. Among the older guys his leadership and soldiering in that Far Eastern U.N. command is still legendary."

The president nodded knowingly, recalling the feat of arms in the taiga. Freeman's famous U-turn! He paused for what seemed a long time to Eleanor, then confessed to her, "I'm sorry for even posing the question. Of course I'm disappointed as hell that he never bagged those terrorist bastards, but he was fast off the mark."

"And," added Eleanor, "if we do pick up their trail again, his team might be useful."

"If we don't pick up something, it'll cost me the presidency."

Eleanor Prenty knew he was right, and it wasn't her habit to throw him a soft pitch. The Iranian hostage crisis *had* cost Jimmy Carter the presidency. And though you couldn't put a price on American lives, she knew that the loss of the top secret data from DARPA ALPHA, and the fact that no backup disk was in sight, would in the long run be much more punishing for the country. His opponent knew it; everyone knew it.

"I'll have to put it to rest," he said solemnly.

Eleanor was alarmed. Did he mean he would have to absorb the loss politically, as Carter had done after the attempted rescue of American hostages by the American commando force had crashed and burned in the desert night, holding the administration up to more ridicule by the Iranian revolutionaries? "You mean, Mr. President, that we'd have to eat it?"

"No, no. By putting it to rest I meant we'll have to run it down, go after the terrorists no matter where they go. No matter what people say about Bush going into Afghanistan and Iraq, it showed the world that we'll go in anywhere *and* go in *unilaterally* if we have to. We're not letting people come into this country, murder our people, and think they can ever find safe haven."

Eleanor Prenty was visibly relieved, but only temporarily, because both she and the president knew that all the tough talk in the world was nothing more than rhetoric unless the intelligence community could locate the receiver and the specific location of the stolen property. No one in America wanted another wild-goose chase for WMDs that didn't exist. That had been a monumental intel disaster. What had Colin Powell and then three-star General Freeman called it? "The mother of all intel screwups!"

"The problem then," the president reminded Eleanor, "was that we didn't have enough agents on the ground, relied too much on high-tech, satellite photos, et cetera. It takes years to build up the kind of HUMINT networks like Al Qaeda had." The Rose Garden's sharp, unforgiving thorns suddenly appeared to him as ill omens. He turned away from the garden, and Eleanor saw that his hands were clasped so tightly that they were bone white, drained of blood. And National Security Adviser Eleanor Prenty knew that unless, in the parlance of the media, something broke, and soon, not only the presidency but the fate of the entire country would be in terrorist hands. The country's chief executive and commander in chief looked across the Oval Office at Frederic Remington's bronze sculpture, "The Bronco Buster," alive with furious action.

"We've alerted all carrier groups, right?"

"Yes." It was what all presidents had done in times of crisis, to extend the country's reach and allow it to strike back if possible. But where?

"Would you want to involve Freeman again?" Eleanor asked.

"Yes. He may have lost them but he was Johnny-on-the-spot. And because he's already been up against them, he might know something, deduce something, that we can't."

"I agree. We owe it to him."

"No," the president said. "We don't owe him anything. He volunteered. We owe the man he lost and those who were murdered."

An aide entered with the latest intel report. The president scanned it. "Nothing," he concluded, dropping the file on the desk. "Not even a possible recipient of the info. Can you believe that?"

"Well," Eleanor told the president, "I'm not at all surprised."

The president looked haggard, defeated. "Well, all we can do right now is pray. Pray for a miracle."

CHAPTER TEN

Monterey

"ARE THEY GOING?" Margaret asked, closing the book she had hoped might distract her from the media circus outside their house.

"Not yet," answered Douglas Freeman. He felt foolish, standing in his robe by the living room's rose red drapes, peering through a narrow slit in the curtains. "I think they're just moving cables, lights, and stuff around. Difficult to tell in the glare. Dozens of lights. Like we're on *Oprah*."

"We are," Margaret said tartly. "We're the sensation of the moment."

Douglas looked around at her. "Well, Mrs. Freeman, you *are* sensational."

A smile escaped. "You're not bad yourself, General."

He returned the smile. "Why don't you go off to bed, Sweetheart? Might as well get some rest."

She sighed. "No point. I couldn't possibly doze off with that mob camped outside. Could you?"

"Yes. A soldier learns to sleep anywhere he's not needed for the moment. He might have to go days if the balloon goes up."

"Then you should rest now. No point in staying up."

The red drapes turned pink as a beam of light swept the length of the room.

"What on earth was that?"

"A damned searchlight. You'd think we were in a POW camp."

"We *are* prisoners," Margaret said resentfully.

The general, hands thrust hard into his pockets, walked over to the living room sofa against which his wife's face looked even paler than Tony Ruth's had in the moments after the cable had beheaded the SpecFor warrior.

Douglas took his wife's hand. It felt remarkably warm. "I'm sorry you've had to get caught up in all this."

"I'm a soldier's wife now. You told me once that it comes with the territory. With command."

"It does, but usually you can keep family out of it. I shouldn't have come home, should've stayed away . . ."

She lifted her free hand, slipped it around his waist, and nuzzled into him. "Some of them were here, camped outside the house, before you even arrived at the airport."

"They'll go away," he told her, "soon as the next story breaks."

"Don't worry about it," she said. "We've got enough provisions. We can stay holed up in here for—" She shrugged. "—as long as it takes."

"You mean," Douglas added, forcing a grin, "until the milk runs out!"

Margaret didn't ask for much, but one of the first things Douglas had found out—the first night of their honeymoon—was that Margaret had a sacrosanct ritual. At 10:30 she would shower, prepare her bowl of cereal, pour the milk, and scan the "funnies" as she ate, finishing before the news at eleven. Sex was nonnegotiable until the weather forecast was over and the sports report threatened. But this night the general knew there was no chance of any conjugal enjoyment. Like many another soldier, postcombat coitus came in second only to slaking your thirst. But defeat, failure on the scale of the DARPA ALPHA murders and the nation-threatening theft that came with them, could rob a man, especially a commander, of any emotion other than self-punishing regret, the awful, accusatory postmortems of "what ifs" and "if onlys" that undermined self-confidence in the field and the bedroom. What he needed, he knew, was a win, a victory, a *chance* at a victory, to redeem himself in his own eyes and the team's.

"They'll go away," Margaret told him. "They have the attention span of a newt."

"A what?"

"A newt."

Freeman laughed. "You nit!"

And that started her off giggling, "nit" and "newt" shooting back and forth between them like fireflies in the gloom, a burst of manic energy, as inexplicable as it was unexpected, fueling the exchange, then vanishing as quickly as it had appeared.

"Dammit," said the general, getting up, walking over to the drapes for a brief reconnaissance, then to the kitchen. "I should have choppered the team ahead of where we were getting the bip from the transmitter on the disk. Gone ahead and set up an ambush."

Margaret knew little if anything about military tactics, but she intuitively sensed a spouse's duty to support whatever decision the other had made, unless there was something to be gained by a useful suggestion. What would that be? she wondered. She tried to recollect what he'd told her about the "op" on his return, but she simply found it too tiring to keep up with all the details, some of which she realized she had probably picked up from Marte Price's *Newsbreaks* on CNN.

"Why *didn't* you go ahead on the trail and—" Good

grief, she hadn't meant to say that, but it was what his musing had suggested to her, and besides, wasn't he asking himself the very same question?

"I didn't do it," he bellowed from the kitchen, "because there's not just *one* trail up there! It's rugged mountain country. Wild country. Trappers've been going through those forests for hundreds of years. *One trail!* Son of a bitch, there's a hundred trails, all hidden in the forest. I had to move fast, Margaret—with only seven men!"

"Well, then," she said sharply, "you did your best. And that's all anyone can do." She paused. "Anyway, what's done is done." There was an edge to her voice that was a caution, a yellow light for this conversation to end, not to cry over spilt milk. She couldn't stand it if there was even a hint of self-pity.

"Where's the damn decaf?" he bawled.

"Where it always is. Right cupboard above the sink. *Men!*"

"What?"

"I said, '*Men*.' You never know where anything is."

"I would if this cupboard was organized. Goddamned jumble in here. Dark as Hades!"

"Turn on the light!" she admonished.

He stood grumpily by the kettle, ordering the water to boil faster, until he realized he hadn't depressed the "on" switch. As the water began roiling, its subdued sound like the far-off rumble of artillery, the cold kettle of a few minutes ago grew warm and shuddered slightly as if it were coming to life. "Would you like a cup?"

"Decaf?" she said. "Sure." His offer, her acceptance, constituted a cease-fire.

"Sorry," he said, as he handed her the white mug, his second favorite, with the Brits' Special Air Service insignia and motto "Who Dares, Wins."

"Sorry for what?" she said, affecting surprise.

"Being so damned egotistical." He sat down carefully in his TV command chair. "Must have seemed that I'm more concerned about my reputation than about my team."

Margaret smiled diplomatically. "Ego's first cousin to morale."

He looked at her pensively. "Was that a shot?"

"An observation," she replied coyly. "Do you know a general without an ego?"

He was about to answer when they heard a rumble outside and the rose red drapes were once again swept by lights.

"They're moving," she said, more out of hope than conviction. Douglas listened intently. Like the nuclear subs that kept a library of ships' sounds and "noise shorts" in their sonar libraries, he had, over his years as a man who had soldiered all over the world, compiled an impressive sound library of his own. Blindfolded, he could tell precisely what kind of tank or armored personnel vehicle was approaching, friend or foe.

"Nothing new out there," he concluded.

"Then what's all the noise about?"

"Warming up," he said. "Ready to leave. Or just repositioning." He got up quickly and went to the slit in the drapes. "Flashlights moving about," he said. "Fog's thicker. If I didn't know better, I'd say they were laying smoke to hide in."

"We're the ones hiding," said Margaret.

"I have a feeling," he mused, "I don't know why." He paused. "Do you ever have that feeling," he asked her, "deep inside you, a premonition almost, that something you wouldn't normally expect—"

"Déjà vu?"

"No . . ." He turned away from the drapes and she

could see the expectation in his eyes. "I mean that you just know something is going to come along to help you out of a tight spot."

"Intuition," said Margaret.

"Yes. Intuition."

"Do you remember," he continued, "when Patton was in the doghouse with Ike over slapping that soldier in Sicily?"

"No."

"Well, for a while Patton thought he would be locked out of the D-Day invasion." Freeman, still trying to ascertain whether more media were arriving, withdrawing, or repositioning, turned around and looked at Margaret. "He said, 'God will not allow it. I must fulfill my destiny.'" Douglas Freeman paused, as if expecting his wife to agree that he, Douglas Freeman, would, like Patton, end up fulfilling his destiny, end up victorious despite the slough of despondency in which he now found himself. He could see, had known in fact for a long time, that while Margaret would comfort and support him for better or for worse, she would not lie to him.

"I wouldn't know," she told him. "I don't have such premonitions."

"I feel it," he told her, turning back to spy on the media. "I know, Margaret. I'll—my team'll—get another chance to run those scumbags to ground!"

It was precisely at that moment, eleven minutes after three in the morning, that the phone rang. Margaret answered, and though sure that it was yet one more reporter, tried to sound civil. "Freeman residence." It was a woman's voice, saying that she was calling from the Pentagon and inquiring as to whether General Freeman would be available to take a call in ten minutes from the CNO—chief of naval operations?

"Yes," Margaret answered her, hung up, and relayed the message to Freeman.

"Ah," said Freeman. "The CNO."

"What's the navy got to do with it?" Margaret asked.

Douglas smiled at her. It wasn't a husband-to-wife expression but rather that of a patient adult to a child. "Big navy chief," said Freeman. "Boss of DARPA ALPHA. It's a naval base—not army."

"I'm not that dumb, Douglas."

"What—" He paused, seeing his reflection in the wall mirror. He looked like Patton, with Ike about to reinstate him. "Did I sound patronizing?" he asked Margaret.

"Yes," she said. "Perhaps you might try being a little less sure of yourself when this naval person calls. Pride goeth before a fall!"

"Naval person!" he joshed. Her naïveté regarding military ranks, indeed regarding all things military, at once amused and pleased him. It meant he could always tell her something new about American defense, about a soldier's life, discuss a fresh topic over dinner instead of sitting there boring her. Mundane table talk, and its sheer repetition, he believed, could finally be every bit as damaging to a marriage as an affair.

"How long did the operator say?" Douglas asked. "Ten minutes?"

"Yes," said Margaret. "Don't be impatient. You know how people are. Ten minutes could mean half an hour."

Tired of pacing back and forth past the light-suffused drapes in the living room, he decided to go to his study, switched on the computer, and called up his team's e-mail addresses—all except Ruth's. Margaret brought in his coffee, and the general could see that despite her overall cooler demeanor, his wife was excited, too, but worried. Hoping for him that, like Patton, he would get another chance to track down his enemies, but worried, like so many military spouses who never got used to seeing their loved ones going into harm's way.

The phone rang, startling her, Douglas indicating that she take the call—a little psychology in order, he thought.

"Freeman residence."

A demanding voice asked, "Do you use grain-fed beef and organic vegetables?"

For a second Margaret hesitated. Was it Aussie Lewis? she wondered. Was it code? "To whom would you like to speak?"

"What—is this the Dim Sum Restaurant?"

By then Douglas was on the line. "*No*," he said emphatically. "You've got the wrong number."

There was a click and the hum of the line.

"What a rude person," said Margaret. "The least he could have done was apologize."

"Is Dim Sum open twenty-four hours?" asked Douglas.

"Yes. I think our number must be very similar. Why, is there something wrong?"

"No," said Douglas tentatively, thinking it over, then more assertively, "No. But this whole business about the terrorists, I mean, puts you on edge."

Margaret concurred. "Everyone's on edge. Have been since we found out our own government has been listening in on all our calls."

When the phone rang two minutes later, Douglas took it. It was a Pentagon operator, presumably the same one who had called Margaret. She apologized to the general, but the CNO had been delayed. He would be calling shortly, however. Douglas said that was fine and thanked her for calling. He put the phone down.

"Godammit! He's delayed!"

Margaret could see that he was worried that the delay might mean he was out of the running.

"Don't fret," she told him.

Freeman nodded amicably. "You're right. You know why?" Before she could answer, he told her, "It's because

I still have that intuition. This is no courtesy call at—" He glanced at his watch. "— 0330."

"You're right," Margaret said, "unless the chief of naval operations wants to order takeout!"

They both laughed. Margaret decided she'd now have a cup of Evening Star herbal tea. It was said to calm the nerves, creating an ambience of tranquility, an ambience that was shattered by the shrill ring of the kitchen phone. Not wishing to seem too eager, Freeman hesitated for a moment as he took the receiver from his wife, giving her a wink and a smile. She was pleased. He was ready. How often had he told her that luck is no more than being packed, ready to act on a moment's notice?

"General!" The drawl of hard consonants was unmistakable.

"Aussie?"

"The one and only, General. Sorry for calling so early but I wanted to give you a heads-up before the media get to you."

"Well, mate," replied Freeman, "you're a bit late. They've parked outside—en masse."

"So you've heard already?"

"Heard what?" Freeman asked impatiently.

"The scumbags," said Aussie. "They've bought it."

Margaret was straining to hear what Aussie was saying, her face muscles tightening as she tried to make sense of it. Douglas, she saw, looked stricken.

"Where?" Freeman asked Aussie.

"On the Canadian side. Apparently the RCMP were called. Funny thing, though—I mean funny peculiar, not funny ha-ha—was that it was a coupla civilians who tipped the Mounties."

For Freeman the image of a scarlet-tuniced Mountie with the distinctive peaked hat, brown leather riding boots, and yellow-striped riding britches leapt to mind, even though the general knew that this was the ceremonial garb of the Royal Canadian Mounted Police and not the more utilitarian khaki, yellow-banded cap, and yellow-striped navy trousers that constituted the workaday uniform of Canada's famed federal police.

"A firefight?" he asked Aussie.

"No," Aussie replied. "Not a shot fired from what I was told. They went off the road into a great bloody ravine, snowing like crazy."

"Who told you this, dammit?" pressed Freeman, who was anxiously awaiting the CNO's call and growing more tense by the second with the knowledge that because Margaret had declined to pay extra for call waiting, the CNO was probably trying to get through right now.

"Mate o' mine in our Mountain Division told me," Aussie explained. "Gave me a bell."

"Bell" was British and Aussie slang for someone phoning you. Freeman was struck anew by how cellphone communication had revolutionized life. In this case it had allowed Aussie Lewis's buddy in the field to effortlessly transmit the news before official channels.

"So you're telling me," said the general, "that the terrorists are confirmed dead?"

"Yeah. Thought I'd give you a bell before Marte Price and the jackals hit you with it out of the blue."

"Can you call your buddy back and get more details?"

"I tried, General—knew you'd want more info, but I can't reach the bugger." Aussie momentarily lost his accent as he affected the neutral tone of the ubiquitous cellphone operator: "The customer you have dialed is away from the phone or temporarily out of the fucking service area. Please try again."

"Do you know where the ravine is?" the general asked Aussie.

"Somewhere near Ripple Mountain, Mike said, just

north nor'west of the border corner area between Idaho and British Columbia. Mike—my buddy—said the Mounties had to chopper in to retrieve the bodies."

"An accident?" said Freeman.

"Looks like it. Minibus they were in went off the road on a curve. Black ice all over, apparently. The weather channel's been telling people to stay off the roads up there. Hell, General, they are—*were*—towelheads. Desert guys. It's a sure bet that they knew squat 'bout driving in snow."

"Towelheads," said Freeman. "All of them?"

"Not all. Two were Brit Muslims, I think. You know, British citizens."

"You sure about that?"

"Well, that's what Mike told me. His Mountain Division company was sent up to help the Mounties. Intel section took mug shots. Bingo! For every one of the pricks there was a match either on Interpol's or our Homeland Security's wanted-terrorist list."

Freeman sat down hard at the kitchen table, holding the phone in a peculiarly disembodied way, as if he'd had the wind punched out of him. By now Margaret had the gist of Aussie's call, and whereas her husband seemed undone by the news of the terrorists' demise, Margaret struggled to contain her delight. He wouldn't have to leave her, or put himself in harm's way, now, if she had heard correctly, that the DARPA ALPHA murderers were dead. She heard her husband's urgent, almost desperate, tone as he pressed Aussie Lewis, "Are you positive that they're all dead? Did your buddy, Mike, actually see them in the ravine?"

For the first time Margaret thought she detected a hesitancy in Aussie's voice and strained to hear, helped by the fact that Aussie's voice was loud to begin with. "Well, General, I'm not sure whether he personally saw the scumbags, but he's a trustworthy bloke. Doesn't bullshit. Anyway, the jackals'll soon know, I guess. Marte Price and her wannabes in the press will be in a race to get it on the air. Big story. I reckon they'll be coming to you for your reaction anytime now."

"Thanks for the heads-up, Aussie. I 'preciate it."

Freeman gently returned the phone to its cradle, and sat in silence. He could hear the kitchen clock. He dropped a lump of sugar into his black coffee, stirring it for what to Margaret seemed like an inordinately long time until she couldn't bear it any longer. "What are you worrying about now?"

"Have you ever heard or read a news story that got all the facts straight? I haven't. They always get something wrong, particularly body counts." He sipped the coffee while looking through the living room at the drapes. It seemed as if the glare had abated. He turned to Margaret. "Do you remember 9/11? How the number of dead was always wrong? Incomplete? And that big mine disaster in '06, down in West Virginia? CNN said all the church bells were ringing, all the miners safe. Then we heard, no, there had been a mix-up in communications. They were all dead except one man who survived."

"Douglas, you seem disappointed they were found. I mean, I would have thought that grisly as it all is, you must be—" She stopped, unsure of what word she should use.

"Happy," he said, "that they've been found? I suppose so, but that note the creeps left for me makes it personal. Besides, Aussie's information isn't something I'd take to the bank. It's secondhand info that Aussie's buddy in the Mountain Division got from somebody else, and where did they get it from? First thing you learn in this trade, Margaret, is that the first reports are invariably wrong."

"I take it then that you think there's a possibility that not all of those horrible people are dead?"

"Yes, and what irks me—" He was interrupted by the guttural sound of trucks and vans starting up outside, headlight beams lighting up the kitchen blinds.

Margaret walked over to her husband. "Douglas, I don't want you to be irked by anyone. The disk those people stole has been destroyed, hasn't it? I mean CNN is saying what you said, that the terrorists must have transmitted the information via hilltop modem, or whatever those things are called, and then the disk was smashed."

"So?" he asked sharply.

"Then they've won, haven't they?" She regretted her words the moment she'd uttered them. "I mean," she added quickly, "you did your best, darling, and it's over."

"That, Margaret, is what sticks in my craw. Can't you understand?"

"So it's a matter of hubris," she retorted.

"And murder," he shot back. "Cold, premeditated murder of Americans. Civilians."

"My point is, Douglas, what can you do? The damage has already been—"

The phone rang and the CNO, having no way of knowing that General Freeman had been informally briefed by Aussie Lewis, informed Freeman that the Royal Canadian Mounted Police had retrieved bodies thought to be those of the terrorists from a ravine not far from the U.S.-Canadian border.

Douglas now understood why all the media vans and satellite dish trucks were leaving. For the media it *was* over, the gaggle of reporters no longer interested in Freeman's thoughts on the subject. He asked the CNO how many bodies had been found.

"There's some confusion about that," the CNO replied. "As there often is in these kinds of situations, General. If it's one thing I've learned, it's to be circumspect about giving out precise numbers. Mounties inform me the snow was deep, some of the bodies almost entirely buried in the drifts. I think it'll take a day or two to know for certain. They were all in U.S. Army uniforms, though, and no dog tags, so there's no doubt about them being the terrorists. I'd say it was a lucky break for us except that I think we have to assume the DARPA ALPHA data have been transmitted. I've forwarded the information you got up there from your interview with Dr.—"

Freeman heard the rustle of paper, then the clack of computer keys on the other end, and guessed that the CNO was trying to retrieve the head scientist's name.

"Moffat," Freeman suggested. "Richard Moffat."

"Yes, that's it. I've sent the information to the DI." He meant the director of intelligence. "Meanwhile the bodies are being flown to Vancouver to see whether we can get any leads from them: Who they were, where they were from, et cetera. I'll let you know. I apologize for calling you at such an ungodly hour, but I wanted to thank you for your—" There was an awkward pause. "Ah—for your getting right onto it."

Freeman thanked him for his courtesy.

"You did your best," Margaret told him. Her comfort did nothing to assuage his feeling that he'd failed. If only he and the team had caught the bastards before they had a chance to burst-transmit the data. If only the prick's vehicle had plunged into a ravine before they'd had a chance to transmit the information that would change the world. If only. Ah, he was thinking too much about himself. By way of an antidote for his futile brooding, he e-mailed Choir Williams about Prince. That beloved spaniel was the best damn tracker dog in America. In the world!

At dawn his computer signaled he had mail. Prince was dead.

That was the most savage, the single most demoralizing hit he'd taken in the whole business. It wasn't that he was uncaring about Tony Ruth's death. The decapitation of anyone was as grim a sight as any combat soldier has to look at, but human beings bore their own responsibility, and in this case Tony had gone willingly, like his team members, following the general as they had before into what Freeman's soldiers knew, despite what the relativist moralists of academe might say, were crucial battles against evil. A job for which they volunteered. Not so the likes of Prince, Freeman mused, an animal that had no choice but that was nevertheless with them in harm's way. And anyone who thought a canine wasn't conscious of fear was a fool. And while there was no animal-human bond stronger than that between Choir and Prince, it would affect the whole team. In a moment of self-doubt, Douglas Freeman wondered whether they would ever volunteer to follow him again. Of course they would, and he jettisoned the doubt almost as quickly as it had assailed him, kicked it out in disgust, for it was nothing more than self-pity in disguise. There was no room for self-pity in a world in which hundreds of thousands of children perished each year of starvation and preventable diseases, and where there were breeding grounds for teenagers who would blow themselves up in the insane terrorism waged against the West.

He recalled what Margaret had said regarding the futility of worrying about the possibility that one of the terrorists might still be on the loose. The data—she was right—were almost certainly in the hands of whoever had paid enough to get them who had financed the attack.

The phone rang. "Hello," said Margaret in her usual courteous manner, then suddenly her tone turned icy. Covering the mouthpiece, she hissed, "It's that tart of yours."

Marte wanted to know if the general had any comments vis-à-vis the discovery of the bodies in the ravine.

"No comment," he told her.

"Huh, that's unlike you, General. I've never found you lost for words."

"I'm not lost. There's nothing to say."

"There are a lot of people in Washington questioning Eleanor Prenty giving you the assignment."

"I was ready," he told her. "That's all. My intention was to get into the area quickly, hopefully to slow them down while our regular forces had time to get in there. With so many of our SpecForces in the Middle East I had one reserve team ready to go. It's as simple as that."

"Hmm. What would you advise the president to do now—if your opinion was sought?"

"I haven't been asked, and besides, it's not my place to advise the White House."

"Oh crap, Douglas. You were trying to run this thing from Day One. Don't go all humble on me. What would you do now?"

He knew what Marte was up to. She was trying to get a good fight going between the guy who blew it and the administration, a quick, feisty sound bite that would rile the White House in an election year.

"I have no comment, Marte."

"Okay, but off the record. Do you think we're in trouble with this one?

"CNN?"

"No, us—you, me, America."

Shit. Obviously she didn't know about the pieces of melted black plastic in the Ziploc bag, the melted plastic that had been the DARPA ALPHA disk.

He was too slow to reply. With the intuition of a top-notch reporter, she sensed something was wrong, something was being held back.

"C'mon, Douglas. You know I've never violated a confidence. Tell me, is this big?"

"No comment."

Replacing the receiver, Douglas met Margaret's jealous stare full-on. "You can come with me if you like, but I've got to give her a more honest answer than that, Margaret."

"Why didn't you tell her—"

"Not here," he cut in. "Not with the possibility of NSA and Homeland Security ears listening in. All the other stuff, the CNO, Aussie—that's all right. NSA probably already knows all that, but they don't know what I think."

Margaret saw that his intensity wouldn't brook her jealousy of the tart, not now. "I'll get my coat. The fog's bound to be chilly."

And it was in the fog on the way to the 7-Eleven that she asked him just how bad he thought the situation was.

"For me? I'm in the doghouse." Dog—he thought of Prince. You could see the wonderful devotion in a dog's eyes. He liked cats too, but dogs better. They needed you.

"No," Margaret said. "I know how bad it is for you. You look tortured tonight. I mean, tell me honestly, just how bad is it for the country?"

"It's bad, Sweetheart." He slipped his arm about her warmth, her perfume reminding him of the Hawaiian islands, the corny love songs he'd heard coming from around Fort DeRussy's outside bar next to the Hilton, the pink flamingoes. "Hypersonic is unbelievably fast," he told her. "A hypersonic torpedo, nuclear warhead, could be fired at a U.S. port from a trawler hundreds of miles offshore. We'd have no chance of an intercept."

Margaret felt a shiver and leaned closer to him and very quietly asked him, "Who do you think sent those killers to steal it from us?"

"I don't know. It could be any of half a dozen countries, from Iran to China."

"Good Lord," she said, her voice a whisper in the fog, the sound of the sea muffled behind its curtain. "Could we *do* anything if we knew?"

"Hell, yes. We've got carrier groups all over the globe. We could launch a—" He stopped, two figures emerging out of the thick fog no more than ten feet in front of them. They turned out to be young lovers, the man nodding at them. "Good evening."

"Evening," Freeman replied, and a few seconds later, said, "It's killing me, Margaret."

"I know," she said. Every muscle in his body was tense. "What are you going to tell—"

"Marte? The truth. That if they, whoever they are, have time to tool up, we'll be sitting ducks. So that if we do find out who they are, we'll have to move fast. There's nothing like getting the press behind you. Cuts a lot of red tape, really gets things moving."

"Let's pray," she said.

"I already have."

His conversation with Marte was devoid of warm-up, in part because he was tired and needed rest; in part because, as a matter of courtesy to Margaret, he didn't want it to be a long, sit-down, old-times kind of conversation.

"What," Marte asked, "might happen if we don't contest this?"

"Catastrophe for world stability."

"By which you mean all of us in the West? You don't have to be politically correct with me, Douglas."

"That's why I wanted to talk. Most reporters are afraid to just come out and say that for all our faults, the West is still the best, and you and I know that as well as the Muslim terrorists. The runaway train coming at us is China."

"You think Beijing's behind these murders?"

"No, but anyone who hasn't had their head in the toilet for the last ten years knows that there's going to be an East-West war. When China's insatiable appetite for oil, coal, bauxite, and so on can't be satisfied by legitimate means, then push is shove, and the arms dealer is a kingmaker."

"So the United States has to go wherever this leads us and get the technology back."

"Right. Or if they have the machinery set up, ready to turn out prototype rounds, we'll have to go in and destroy it."

"Like Iran and the enriched uranium."

"Yes, and here's where I get blunt, Marte."

"Gee, that'll be a change." He heard her laugh. "Shoot," she said.

"We need the media to say what I've said, to *stress* the importance of us being willing to go where we have to to get it back." He paused to look out at Margaret and give her a wave. She smiled, blew him a kiss—as if they were newlyweds. Marriage was the one good thing when your job has just run off the road.

"That's a tough one, Douglas," he heard Marte say. "I mean, the administration doesn't want to look like it's incompetent—dropped the—what is it, Flow-In-Flight?"

"Yes."

"On the other hand," said Marte, "the White House has to sell the truth, which I assume you're telling me, to the public in order to win support for any unilateral kick-ass we might have to do, if we know where it is."

"Exactly," said the general. "Big problem, though, is—was—Iraq in '05. No WMDs found, so why should anyone believe the government's perceived need to go in—wherever—to stop them using what we shouldn't have lost in the first place. Checkmate, right?"

"The bodies, Douglas."

"Say again?"

"The Americans who were murdered. WMDs are concepts, apparitions. But here we have the pictures of the murdered scientists, and the old guy up by that lake, the name of which none of us can pronounce."

Douglas pronounced it phonetically, as if it had been

written in English. "Lake Pond-Oh-Ray. The worst," he continued, "the absolute worst, were the children."

"Children?"

"At the campsite." Somehow she hadn't heard all the details. He told her the essentials, of the bloody, indiscriminate trail that the terrorists had left from DARPA ALPHA to Priest Lake.

"That's good; that's better than any WMDs. Children— people hate that. They'll want to go after the bastards, and never mind the 'no extradition treaty' bullshit. America will go anywhere after scum who murder children." He could hear the soft tap of keys on a laptop.

"Any other details?" she asked. He hesitated. "One of the children was unrecognizable." He told her about the wolves. He said he had to go, and told her it'd be nice if CNN could help the family survivors, if there were any.

When he came out of the booth, the ocean flooded his senses and he took a deep draft of sea air, something he'd always loved since the moment he'd first sniffed the sea a thousand years ago when his dad had taken him on camping trips. No campers then—just a small pup tent, a Coleman stove, condensed milk, two fishing rods, and the world was simple.

Margaret hadn't said anything yet about the conversation with Marte Price, but felt she should say something to show it didn't bother her, for it *did* bother her. "Say what you wanted?"

"Yes," he said. "I did."

"Feel better?"

"I feel like a shower."

She was nonplussed.

"What's that special bath the Jews have?"

"I don't know. A bath's a bath."

"No," said Douglas. "A rabbi told me about it once, when you take everything off that separates you from

God, from the purity of the water. Women have to take off all makeup, eye shadow, false nails—everything—so that they can get clean again."

"You don't feel clean?" she asked.

"Doesn't matter how you deal with this scum. Some of it inevitably rubs off."

"Oh, Douglas, you can't really mean that?"

"I do right now."

"You're tired."

As they returned home the fog was thicker and Freeman, despite his usual disparagement of anything smacking of superstition, took the worsening of the weather as an omen that the world, that time itself, was closing in on him. It wasn't self-pity but it was a glass-half-empty moment, and on the evidence of the DARPA ALPHA debacle, he felt it was a realistic assessment.

"I've been thinking about that note you got," said Margaret as they entered the house. "What a horrible thing to read. But that man's pride will be his undoing, Douglas." She shook her head, tight-lipped and censorious as she took off her coat and headed off to unload the dishwasher.

Freeman felt distinctly uncomfortable, remembering the flashes of immodesty after his famous U-turn against the Russians.

"Yes," Margaret declared, "that horrid note of his might yet haunt him."

"If he isn't already dead," said the general.

"I shouldn't say it, I suppose—I mean, it's not very Christian—but I hope he's dead."

"So do I," said Freeman, but it sounded to Margaret more like an obligatory response than a fervent wish. She straightened up from the dishwasher and fixed him with her gaze. "No," she charged. "Not truly. You'd prefer—I mean, you'd *like* to chase him down."

The general said nothing, topping up his coffee.

"Douglas?"

"What?"

"You like it, don't you?"

"What do you mean, woman?"

"I mean, you men. You like fighting, don't you?"

"Well, if that isn't a blatant sexist remark I don't know what is. If I said anything like that about women, Linda Rushmein and her night riders'd have me in irons."

She ignored his comment. "Douglas!"

He met her stare but couldn't sustain his look of hurt surprise. He blinked first, shifting his gaze to the small, triangular pane of glass high in the kitchen door, out into the darkness. "I love it," he said gently. "God forgive me, but I do." He faced her again. "To fight for the right. I suppose that sounds pompous, naïve even, but I believe there is evil in the world, Margaret. And what they did up there was evil to the core. Even if I didn't like the sting of battle, I'd have a duty to pursue them if I could."

"You did your best, Douglas."

He was afraid that she might be right. "I'm dog tired," he told Margaret. "I'm going to grab some shut-eye."

"Dawn is breaking."

"So, I'm tired. Aren't you?"

"Yes, but—"

"It's not against the law," Freeman cut in.

"I merely said—," she began.

"You've got this Anglo-Saxon hang-up about sleeping during the day. Goddammit, half the country—"

"Don't be blasphemous."

"Then don't be so damn pious. You have these damn silly rules. Because your folks were farmers doesn't mean it's a sin to do things differently."

"I was merely surprised at someone who—"

"Don't be. I've had just about all the surprises I can deal with at the moment."

"It isn't my fault, *General*, that you didn't run those—those monsters to ground."

"Never said it was."

"You know, Douglas, you're right. You *do* need sleep. A lot of it."

"You're a Republican!"

That did it. They burst out laughing at their childishness, a dam of anxiety broken, the tension swept away in a torrent of running giggles, adult normalcy returning only when the full measure of the terrorist attack on DARPA ALPHA was reiterated, albeit reluctantly, in a terse news report they watched on TV, National Security Adviser Prenty having to admit under persistent questioning that not all of the "murderers," in the administration's phrase, had been accounted for.

"How many are still at large?"

"One," she replied tersely.

"Is that hard intel?" pressed a correspondent from Fox. "Or soft intel?"

Eleanor kept her composure. It was a question born of the media's skepticism following the Iraqi WMD fiasco. "It's hard intel," she said. "From the D.N.I."

"There's something else," said Douglas, his arm around Margaret's shoulder, holding her close.

"What do you mean?" Margaret asked.

"Something's wrong. I can smell it. They know something else. I've known Eleanor Prenty for donkey's years and she's got something else on her mind. She's keeping something back."

"Well, I would think," Margaret said tartly, "in that case she would have the common courtesy to let you know exactly what's going on."

Douglas Freeman agreed. Margaret had a point, and a strong one at that. Even if the White House didn't want to inform him, as a matter of courtesy hadn't it occurred to them that he might still have something to offer by further debriefing?

Belying his present low expectation of the administration, a call came twenty minutes later during the only bathroom break Douglas Freeman had taken all morning, and so it was that the general took one of the most important calls of his life and in the history of the Republic while sitting on the can, the exhaust fan purring softly in the background and he afraid to flush as he listened to the White House operator instructing him that a Homeland Security agent in Monterey was en route, as she spoke, to deliver a packet to the general by hand. After reading it he was to call National Security Adviser Prenty, but not from his home number.

"Well?" Margaret asked, as Freeman, with a preoccupied air, zipped up and buckled his belt, the puzzled expression still with him.

"The White House," he explained, "is sending me something." He looked at his wife, who, after handing him his cellphone, had lingered outside the bathroom door. "What in damnation's so important that she couldn't tell me on the phone? Whole country knows by now what happened."

"Perhaps they've found the missing terrorist in hiding or something, and don't want it made public. It could alert him."

"Huh, he's already been alerted. Rest of his gang found dead. No, it's probably something—" The front door chimes sounded, their mellifluous notes in marked contrast to the tension both Douglas and Margaret felt.

It was the DHS agent, a tall African American clad in a dark blue suit. His striped DHS identity card was clearly visible through the front door peephole.

"That was quick," observed Freeman, venturing a smile, which wasn't reciprocated. The whole world seemed tense.

The full forensic report was twenty-one pages of graphs

and columns galore—all measurements from microns to centimeters, weights in milligrams. His eyes raced over the information, stopping at the written summary that covered the last two pages. For Douglas Freeman, one of the most important nuggets of information was a brief footnote that mentioned that the rocket used against them on the helo at Pend Oreille was made in either Poland or China, given the composition and ratio of aluminum to steel. A splinter sample from the wooden grip of the shoulder-fired rocket launcher showed that it had at one time been infested with pine beetle, bore holes visible during examination, the insects' secretions showing that this species of pine beetle was found in the Russian taiga.

The paper on which "AMERICANS SUCK" had been written was of Chinese manufacture, the ink used very definitely "China black," a high-quality calligraphic ink compound manufactured almost exclusively in Harbin in China's far northeastern province of Heilongjiang, whose Heilong River (Amur to the Russians) bordered Russia's Far East, the river once the site of fierce Sino-Soviet clashes during the latter half of the twentieth century. This was Freeman's country, where he'd fought against the Siberian Sixth.

Debris from the punctured fuselage of the downed Chinook from Priest Lake had been run through the spectrometer, where the traces of sulfur used in the warhead registered. The structure of the sulfur was typical of that found in what used to be called the "Manchurian mines," that is, northeastern China.

Margaret saw her husband's brow furrowed with such intense concentration that she barely recognized him. She knew it was said of him that, like so many good leaders, he was a "quick study" and could home in on a vital piece of wheat amid the chaff of countless reports that used to flood his desk. And though he was retired, his was an administrative skill which he had kept honed daily, skimming through the plethora of newspapers, blogs, and magazines and journals from *The Economist* to *Foreign Affairs*. And so the e-mail he was about to send to an old friend, Charles Riser, who was presently U.S. cultural attaché in Beijing, was markedly short and to the point. And because the general was not privy to the present official ciphers or codes, the message was transmitted in plain language. Using the forensic report's mention of the *tancho* as the vital clue for Riser, the e-mail, subject "Ornithologists' Destination," read "Group wishes to visit migratory bird sanctuary for *tancho*. Can you suggest prime location?"

Charles Riser, despite his prodigious knowledge of Oriental culture, did not know what *tancho* meant, and asked Bill Heinz, the embassy's military attaché.

"Japanese crane," replied Bill. "You've probably seen lots of 'em on postcards, Japanese watercolors. They're a big deal in Japan."

Now that Riser knew what *tancho* meant, his China hand's knowledge came into play. "Well, one of the biggest sanctuaries would be Lake Khanka, the one up beyond Harbin. I think it straddles the Sino-Russian border."

Riser e-mailed a coffee-quaffing Douglas Freeman about Lake Khanka. It was a huge four-thousand-square-kilometer body of water and marshland, ninety kilometers long and in places seventy kilometers wide, that constitutes one of the largest bird sanctuaries in the world. The wetlands and lake are fed by the upper course of the Ussuri River in a large depression where terrible forest fires over thousands of years had apparently rendered an area which should have been thick, boreal forest now only sparsely treed, leaving meadows and some copses of Mongolian oak. It was also reputed to be the last great refuge of the endangered far eastern leopard and Siberian tiger, and a vital refuge for hundreds of thousands of migrating birds, including the *tancho*. He also added, courtesy of Bill Heinz's files, that there had been repeated complaints by Chinese "enviro nuts" about some kind of armament testing in the area adjacent to the lake.

In their computer-cum-music room Freeman forced himself to contain his excitement as, having quickly scanned Charlie Riser's e-mail, he called up his meticulously cross-referenced military-industrial files, which he was confident were better than the Pentagon's intel. "Lake Khanka" had rung a distant bell in his memory about Sino-Soviet border disputes, and its significance fairly jumped out at him from the monitor: Lake Khanka, at latitude 44 degrees, five minutes north, longitude 132 degrees east, on the far eastern Russia-China border, was less than fifty kilometers north of the Deng Jiang sulfur mine, sulfur being essential for any armaments, including the newer Man Portable Air Defense rockets of the kind that had downed his SpecOps Chinook at Priest Lake. Calling Margaret over, he pointed to the area map he had called up, zooming in on the area, highlighting a place southwest of the lake called Gayvoron, noting that it must be the railhead.

"Oh no," said Margaret as she saw him snatch a light Windbreaker from the hallway. "Surely you can call from home."

"Not this one, sweetie," the general replied, grabbing his cap, giving her a peck on the cheek. "Sweetheart, Murphy is always hanging around. Get sloppy on security just once and it's like leaving your car unlocked."

From the repaired phone booth down by the 7-Eleven, Freeman dialed the White House and this time was immediately put through to Eleanor Prenty.

She got right to it. "You've read the summary, Douglas?"

"Yes. And I've deduced that everything points to those scumbags' camp definitely being situated around a place called Lake Khanka. It's situated in—"

"Yes, we know," Eleanor cut in impatiently.

"What?" He was stunned. *"You* know it's Lake Khanka?"

He heard a sigh that conveyed to him a sense of patient resignation on the other end. "Douglas, I think you're one of the most brilliant military commanders this country's ever had, your failure to catch these terrorists notwithstanding. But you—" She was sighing again, really pissing him off. "Like us all, I guess, you have some surprising blind spots."

"Such as?" he asked grumpily. "My *failure* to catch these terrorists notwithstanding."

"Don't be childish, General. I haven't got the time. None of us have. Remember, you and all other senior officers, active and retired, supported the Patriot Act."

Now, as Aussie Lewis might have said, the penny dropped in Freeman's brain. "Son of a—you've been tracking my Internet inquiries."

"I have not. NSA has. Surely you must know that their computers are surfing the Net 24/7. As soon as certain phrases or terms pop up, the computers automatically tag and record them. Hell, Douglas, they do the same with me. You might not realize it, but some terrorist cells have staged random break-and-enters so they can use a citizen's computer. That way any backtracking of the terrorists' METAs to that ordinary citizen's line is futile."

"METAs?"

"Messages to activate," explained Eleanor. "It's an NSA acronym."

Freeman's brain was racing, despite his acute fatigue.

"So you knew? I mean, NSA put the forensic analysis together with my computer files on Lake Khanka and Gayvoron?"

"It was your sulfur mine around which all the forensic stuff jelled," Eleanor told him.

"Then it's a matter for our air force," said Douglas. "I expect Moscow'll be as pleased as we are to take out a terrorist camp." He was thinking of how the CIA and KGB had joined forces and worked so well together to prevent a planeload of Russian nuclear scientists from leaving Russia for Iran.

"It's not as easy as that," cautioned Eleanor. "The president's been in contact with the Russian premier. There's no way Moscow will allow a bombing mission on Russian soil. Besides, even if they did, we'd need much more precise targets than Lake Khanka and environs. Do you know how big that place is?"

"Of course, you're right," commented Freeman, embarrassed by not having seen such an obvious problem. He sure as hell needed some sleep.

"Plus," continued Eleanor, "once it gets out that we want to go after them by bombing, there'll be an outcry from every environmental group in the world. Can you imagine it, Douglas? Americans bombing a hallowed bird sanctuary? We're hated enough already around the world, without every bird lover and Audubon Society on earth screaming bloody murder!"

"So what's the best they'll allow us?" pressed Freeman. "What kind of force can we mobilize?"

"Moscow'll allow an MEU to be ferried in by air and for us to hit the terrorists' camp. But we've only got twenty-four hours, max."

The general was rapidly estimating how much time it would take for a SOC MEU, a special-operations-capable Marine Expeditionary Unit, of two thousand men to be dispatched, fight a winter battle, win, and withdraw. "That's hardly enough time to—"

"Well, that's all the time they've given us, Douglas. It's nonnegotiable. Moscow wants to clean up its backyard terrorists as much as we do ours. But even with all the goodwill we've engendered between us since the end of the Cold War, they're still very prickly about the whole thing. It's a political minefield for the guys in the Kremlin. We're damned lucky they'll let us in. Thank God for the KGB-CIA joint venture against the nuclear scientists trying to hightail it to Iran. At least that's set a precedent."

"Well, do we have any HUMINT on the area?"

"We have several agents out of Harbin. Taiwanese sleepers. CIA has asked them to send out burst intel transmits to the Seventh Fleet in the Taiwanese straits. Our MEU attached to the fleet will be going in from the *Yorktown*."

"Well, that's the best news I've heard so far." Freeman's last SpecOp, into North Korea, had gone in from *Yorktown*. It was a 45,000-ton Wasp-class LHD-26B landing-helicopter-dock ship, part of the U.S. Marines' "Gator Navy," so-called because of the potent amphibian force the marines had proved to be in the victorious but bloody landings from Guadalcanal to Saipan. It was complete with forty-five assorted choppers, several of the hybrid Ospreys, two V/STOL—Vertical or Short Takeoff or Landing planes—Joint Strike Fighters, and three LCACs, which were hovercraft landing craft.

"We have another piece of information," Eleanor told him. "Our military attaché in Berlin has received HUMINT from Germany that nanotech high-precision lathes are on the move east. Anyway, the president wanted me to seek your counsel."

"I don't know," mused Freeman. "It'll be a very tricky operation, any which way you look at it."

"That's why," said Eleanor, "the president wants you to lead it. Will you?"

The moment he hung up, Margaret knew. "*Surely* you didn't accept it?" she asked. Freeman said nothing. "Oh, Douglas! I'm no politician, but can't you see what this is?"

"An honor."

"*Honor?* It's—oh, Douglas—"

"I wish you'd stop saying, 'Oh, Douglas.' Anybody'd think I'd robbed a goddamn bank!"

But she wouldn't be deterred. "I'm no military expert, Lord knows, but I can see a trap when it's staring me in the face. I haven't spent *all* my time going to bridal showers with Linda Rushmein."

"Margaret!" he said sharply. "It's obvious why I was chosen. I'm the only goddamned general who's—"

"Don't use that language, please!"

"I'm the *only* general," he said, looking for all the world like Patton uncaged, "who's had firsthand experience in the taiga, in the U.N. mission I led. I mean, my whole *team* has firsthand experience of the terrain, and—"

"Douglas, Douglas, do you honestly believe that you were the first choice?"

He said nothing, but the tension could have been cut with a knife.

"It's a trap, dear, a political trap. Even I can see that. No one who cares about his career would dare volunteer. Can't you see they're using you? What do they care? They're appealing to your ego, Douglas."

He gave her a long, hard look and turned sharply about, snatching up the TV remote. "It's a matter of honor. The president asked. The president of the United States of America has asked *me* to finish the job that *I* started. He's obviously got more confidence in me than—" He strode off into the living room to get the latest update.

Margaret sat, or rather slumped, down in her lounge chair. After a long silence, she asked, very carefully, "Does the president have any idea of how many terrorists are in this wretched camp near—"

"Lake Khanka," he said quietly. "No, no one knows. It could be a small outfit or a big complex. We'll have to wait for a recon report from HUMINT."

"From what?"

"People on the ground. In the area. Spies," he said irritably. "Informers."

She had her arms folded tightly below her breasts, the normally soft features of her face hardened in her fear for him. She remembered how Catherine used to pray for him every night he was away. "You could be killed."

"If their base, if those people, get a chance to tool up for hypersonic weaponry, Margaret, a lot of people, including a lot of Americans, are going to get killed."

To make matters even worse for Margaret, CNN's Marte Price, in an exclusive from Washington, D.C., was confirming that the die had been cast. As she spoke a retaliatory U.S. force was being readied for an attack on the terrorists' camp at some as yet undisclosed location overseas. CNN's Pentagon correspondent reported that the force would most likely be deployed from one of the United States' carrier battle groups. Such a group would most likely consist of a carrier, two frigates, two guided-missile Aegis cruisers, four destroyers, a replenishment vessel, and two nuclear attack submarines, all in the service of protecting a Wasp-class helo carrier transport carrying 2,100 combat troops of a Marine Expeditionary Unit under the command of a "full-bird" colonel. It was not known, she told her viewers, who would lead the assault, but it was rumored by confidential sources within the administration and the Pentagon that several of the armed services' highest-ranking field commanders had strenuously objected to any precipitous action, citing the unmitigated disaster that was President Carter's attempt in 1980 to rescue American hostages in Iran in a similar "in-out" lightning strike. It seemed that no one who valued their career prospects wanted anything to do with what Marte Price was characterizing as a "high-risk undertaking."

"Did you hear *that*?" Margaret asked her husband.

He pretended not to hear. Closing his eyes, he recalled the last known positions of the U.S. Navy's carrier battle groups, and deduced that unless there had been a radical shift in their combat patrol areas, it would be Admiral Crowley's Seventh Fleet CBG which would be closest to Lake Khanka. If this were the case, the MEU he was to lead would be that of Colonel Jack Tibbet aboard the *Yorktown*, one of Admiral Crowley's twelve-vessels. Scuttlebutt had it that because the navy, as were the other branches of the American armed forces, was dangerously overextended, it might well be that Crowley, who used to be captain of the carrier *McCain* as well as overall admiral of the fleet, would have to serve as captain of *Yorktown* as well as admiral of the fleet for the duration of this mission.

"I mean, Douglas," Margaret pressed him, "aren't you getting too old for . . ." It was the worst possible thing she could have said.

CHAPTER ELEVEN

FOR DOMESTIC CONSUMPTION, the Russian president, in his distinctive baritone, vociferously objected to any "interventionist plan" against Russia by the United States or any other country. The truth, however, was that the Russian president's dire warning, wildly greeted by crowds from St. Petersburg to Vladivostok, was strictly pro forma. For the fact was that within the Kremlin from which Putin and his successors had tried to govern following the collapse of the Soviet Union after the Cold War, there was growing alarm at the rash of rebel commanders who, having been suborned by bagmen into becoming rapacious capitalist arms dealers, viewed Moscow as nothing more than an impediment to their rapidly growing fortunes. In this test of wills, there were those in the Kremlin who harbored a hope that the Americans could be used to help redress the imbalance of power in Russia, wresting control away from Moscow and transferring it to powerful regional rebel groups.

Such a group was the triumvirate in Russia's far east dubbed by Big and Little, two veteran English-speaking rebel officers of the old KGB's Thirteenth Directorate, as the "ABC," a cabal of three generals, Mikhail Abramov of the Siberian Sixth Armored Division, Viktor Beria of the Siberian Third Infantry Division, and Sergei Cherkashin of the Siberian Air Defense Arm. FSB, the Russian security service, the new KGB, knew that ABC, jointly financed by Muscovite gangsters and fundamentalist Arab groups in the Middle East in open defiance of Moscow, had concentrated and arrayed their forces around Lake Khanka and were considered to be amongst the best dug in of any of the breakaway rebel units. ABC had been careful to funnel the initial money provided by their backers into securing the best frontline troops available to defend the Lake Khanka perimeter and the railhead in the town of Gayvoron, from which armaments by the ton were being delivered to the port of Vladivostok 150 miles to the southeast. FSB reported that ABC had in effect built a private military economic zone in the far east wherein they could manufacture and export armaments well beyond Moscow's reach.

The idea of trying to oust the ABC risked a civil war in the area, and the very suggestion of yet another civil war in Russia and yet another breakaway territory like Chechnya was as unpalatable to Moscow's ruling elite as it was to the civilian population at large. And so, in one of those strange, upside-down ironies that violated all the tenets of the Cold War, the Kremlin, while vigorously objecting to the U.S. plan in public, simultaneously saw it as the best chance of ridding Moscow of the ABC, whose so-called business practices, *Pravda* declared, were "even worse than Enron's."

Yet Moscow knew that the risk the Americans would be taking was enormous. Lake Khanka was 120 miles inland from Vladivostok. Moscow knew the Americans, led by this so-called American legend, General Freeman, would have to not only contend with a vicious ring of sophisticated anti-aircraft weaponry, including MANPADs and emplacements of four SAMs of the type that had downed the American Scott Brady's fighter over Bosnia, but also fight against paid-off rebellious elements of the Russian navy.

CHAPTER TWELVE

ALERTED BY THEIR coast watchers and unable to move their lucrative weapons complex, ABC was waiting. And ready. For the hundreds of men of the ad hoc Russian Regiment, everything was at stake, survival and money in amounts that the three disgruntled ex-Soviet generals had never dreamed they would be within striking distance of. The markup on Igla, Vanguard, and pirated Stinger-design MANPADs alone was 218 percent. Production costs had fallen drastically, with Lake Khanka providing a guaranteed supply of water for coolant. Productivity was also spurred on by bonuses for the fast loading of ABC's ship-container-sized cargoes of twenty missiles per RORO—Roll-On, Roll-Off—load. Mideast sales tripled in the first six months of operation, bonuses for overtime so coveted that the soldiers from Abramov's tank company, Beria's infantry, and Chekashin's air defense ground crews assembling the delicate guidance heads and 8 percent sulfur solid propellant were breaking all civilian productivity rates set in the go-slow environment of the old Soviet regime. And now they had in their possession the U.S.'s super-cavitating technology. More bonuses. As bonuses increased, so did expectations, the men wanting even more overtime. Indeed, a strict duty roster had to be enforced as some soldiers, particularly from Beria's infantry battalions, had been skipping regular perimeter security duty so as to put in overtime on the assembly lines. When General Beria first heard from Big and Little in Moscow that an attack by the American ATFOR—American Anti-terrorism Force—was a possibility, he immediately tightened up all "perimeter skipping" by instituting the death penalty for any Russian absentee on the grounds that shirking this duty was desertion. It had a salutary effect, as those who wanted to make more money selling more missiles to Hamas and others were only too willing to inform on comrades whose executions created a vacancy and hence more lucrative overtime on the already lucrative assembly line.

"You won't have to worry about the Americans," Abramov assured Beria and Cherkashin. "My T-90s'll take the bastards out before they get a chance to get out of their helicopter seats."

"Bullshit!" announced Beria. "My infantry'll be the force that'll settle the matter. You'll see." He slapped Cherkashin on the shoulder. "Your air defense missiles and tank rounds can't take out every individual, Sergei. I tell you, my lads'll be onto whoever survives their drop."

"Drop?" said Abramov brusquely. "They're not crazy enough to try parachuting their force in. Besides, bad weather is coming. It will be like duck shooting for our men. No, General, the Americans'll be ferrying them in by helicopter." Abramov then turned to Cherkashin. "Your missile batteries should find them easily."

"Not a problem, Comrade. We'll blow them out of the sky. It'll be raining Americans. Dead Americans."

They all laughed. While none of the three believed it would be a cakewalk, it was obvious that the American MEU force of two-thousand-plus marines had no chance of surprising ABC when it had to move in from the Sea of Japan before unleashing any attack. Even so, the three rebel Russian generals were determined not to burden themselves with any time-wasting formalities that would slow down ABC's production lines. Accordingly, the triumvirate phoned each of the company's commanders, pointing out to them that insofar as everyone's financial future, from general to private, was on the line, there'd be no time to implement what they called the "restraints" of the Geneva Convention. There would be no American prisoners taken.

"Should we issue a written directive?" posited Beria.

"Why?" said Abramov, shrugging at the infantry general's question. "Then it's on paper. You're not in the party anymore, Viktor." He paused, then added, "Remember what happened at the Wannsee Conference?"

Viktor and Sergei Cherkashin nodded. It had been the meeting convened by Reinhard Heydrich at Wannsee in Berlin where the final solution of the so-called Jewish Question was settled, of which no copies were to be kept, but one copy *was*, and because of this copy Adolph Eichmann and others paid the price. At the beginning of ABC's formation they had rationalized their willingness to sell their souls to a terrorist clientele as a decision that was really based on an intention to rebuild and reassert Soviet might. But Putin and others hadn't been able to get a handle on the Chechen terrorists, and so ABC had adopted the oldest rationale for corruption in mankind's history: If you can't lick 'em, join 'em. And when they realized the enormous profits to be made selling hitherto stockpiled Soviet weaponry to terrorists, the crisp sound of newly printed currency soon drowned the conscience of any lingering party loyalist. Besides, there was no turning back. The dream of making a bundle, retiring to a dacha on the Black Sea, held them in its thrall. There would be swimming pools, caviar by the bowlful, your own private security as you lay in the hot Caspian sun. And flunkie lawyers arranging for you to go legitimate by investing in the big American pipeline being built through the Stans, the seven countries that before Gorbachev had been Soviet republics, kept in line by the kind of iron discipline the three generals had used to establish and maintain order at the Lake Khanka complex.

"Any sight of them yet?" Cherkashin, the most impatient of the three, asked his duty officer, who was monitoring the big screen of the air defense radar.

"No, sir. But we'll know the second they take off from that helo carrier, the *Yorktown*."

"You sure?" pressed Abramov.

"Yes, General. We have people on the coast."

Abramov was now looking down to the right of the radar console at the situation table of the kind used by Royal Air Force controllers during the crucial Battle of Britain, contemplating the cutout silhouettes of the twelve American vessels. His old-fashioned reliance on the blackboard amused the younger computer-age duty officer. But all three of the Russian generals had seen what had happened to Saddam Hussein's air force when the Americans had taken out the Iraqis' early warning radar with Stealths. The Iraqis, with their sophisticated radar knocked out and without a "situation table" of the kind Abramov was now studying, were literally working in the dark and rapidly losing control of their dire situation.

"Question is," pressed Abramov, "whether the Americans will launch fighters from the *McCain*."

"No," said Cherkashin confidently. "Moscow might turn a blind eye to a quick insertion of U.S. troops on our soil. After all, we accepted Allied intervention in 1917 in Archangel, but Moscow's pride'll draw the line at permitting foreign fighters in Russian airspace."

"What I don't understand," said Abramov, is how American intelligence found its way to us."

"Luck," proffered Beria. "Pure, stupid American luck."

"Whatever it was," put in Cherkashin, "we should make damn sure we get this Freeman. He's a cunning bastard. He's like that Patton. And this'll be the second time he's been here. We don't want to have to deal with him again."

On this there was unanimous agreement.

"Well," said Beria, "last I heard, our Arab friends were working with someone in Hamas." He paused. "Or perhaps it was the Abu Haf's al-Masri Martyr Brigades. Some youngster who has lived in America, studied there."

"A bomber, you mean?" said Cherkashin.

"Perhaps," said Beria.

"I don't know," said Cherkashin. "If the Americans see anyone coming near them they'll shoot first and ask questions later. They've learned in Iraq what we learned in Afghanistan. Arabs have used kids as bombers."

"Do *we* have such people?" inquired Beria.

"No," answered Abramov. "But Beria has a point. Last time I was in Palestine, closing the deal for what will be our first batch of the super-cavitating MANPADs, I also came across one of Hamas's leaders, an Iranian officer with the Abu Haf's al-Masri Martyr Brigades who had been given the job of mentoring a young boy with jet-black hair and blue eyes. He was about eleven, maybe twelve years old. Orphaned as a baby in the Iraq War. A true little Muslim fanatic who, the officer told me, had been schooled for a time in America—immersed in the enemy's culture."

"So?" said Cherkashin who, despite his brilliance as an air defense commander, lacked the kind of forward-looking imagination Abramov possessed.

"Ah, too young," said Beria dismissively.

"Exactly!" said Abramov, warming to his own logic. "That's precisely my point."

Beria nodded approvingly, eager to show that he was as

quick as Abramov, and certainly quicker than Cherkashin in seeing where the tank general was going. "Yes, a blue-eyed kid. Clever." He paused, his forehead creased in concentration as he sought to extrapolate from Abramov's, or rather, the terrorists', idea. "The boy could appear injured, perhaps caught between us and the Americans."

Cherkashin was mulling it over. "But they'd search him for weapons."

"Yes," said Abramov. "But that wouldn't be our problem. All that's necessary is to have him found by the Americans—wandering, dazed, frightened. The Americans are suckers for a lost kid."

"But," Cherkashin cautioned, "all this presupposes Freeman will be here, that he won't be directing operations aboard *York City*."

"*York*town," Abramov corrected him, adding, "I hope your knowledge of our air defense ring, Sergei, is better than your knowledge of General Freeman. Like Patton, he's always with his men. He'll come, believe me. He'll lead them in."

"The kid you saw," pressed Beria. "This blue-eyed American-hater. You say he's been to America?"

"Yes, yes," said Abramov. "Of course. Probably sent him in with illegals. Across the Canadian border. For how long, I don't know, but he's now back in Pakistan, at one of their "holy-war" madrassa schools. I saw him briefly in Islamabad when I did the last arms sale."

"You think it might be possible," asked Beria, "for Hamas to get him here in, say, the next twenty-four hours?"

"Of course," said Abramov sharply. "If we offer to help them kill an American legend, the Arabs will send him on a flying carpet. Don't worry, we'll get him. One way or the other. Which reminds me, have all platoon commanders been shown that photo of him on the Net?"

"Every infantryman has the photo," Beria assured the

tank commander. "And I've personally put a bonus of ten thousand dollars on his head."

Abramov, pleasantly surprised, gave one of his rare smiles. "And your men, Commander?" he asked Cherkashin.

"My men have also been promised high bonuses." He thought of his brother, grimacing with the memory of the day he was killed in combat against the U.S.-led U.N. peacekeeping action in *Sibir*. A 120 mm Sabot round from one of Freeman's Abrams tanks had hit the T-80. Cherkashin looked as if he could see straight through the thick cement walls of the subterranean bunker. There had been nothing left. His brother had been vaporized.

"If my men capture him," Beria told Cherkashin, "I'll make sure they hand him over to you."

"And my men," Abramov assured him, "will do the same."

It was near dusk, and before it got too dark, Abramov wanted to inspect the Sixth's tank commanders and make sure everyone was maintaining high alert. And with Cherkashin's mention of tank ammunition, he wanted to quiz the gunners to make certain that in addition to HE rounds, they would have enough armor-piercing Sabot rounds with which to repel the Americans who, because of ABC's first-rate camouflage, would be coming in blind, if they'd be coming at all. Many at ABC's Lake Khanka complex believed that after all the huffing and puffing in Washington was over, there would be no attack, that the Americans were all talk. As Abramov walked outside, as expected he couldn't see any tanks, and the marshland waters were turning golden in the fading sun.

CHAPTER THIRTEEN

ON THE LOWER decks of the Wasp-class helo-carrier-transport *Yorktown*, the Marine Expeditionary Unit, under the command of Colonel Jack Tibbet, was being assembled. The air was thick with the smell of oil and the shuddering roar of engines and giant exhaust fans as Tibbet's marines reviewed last-minute details prior to going topside to hear the mission commander, General Freeman, give his pre-op address. There was an understandable expectation that the general, if not being outright contrite after the humiliation of losing the terrorists' trail, would at least be apologetic about having to put the MEU in harm's way because of his foul-up at Priest Lake back home. In both the foreign anti-American press and the left-of-center liberal press at home, he was being portrayed, despite his earlier accomplishments and battle honors, as a "loser."

As he slowly, reluctantly, shuffled his way in the confusion of the lower deck toward the elevator, young Peter Norton, the son of Robert Norton, Freeman's former second-in-command from his Russia days, was one of those marines who weren't looking forward to what must be the general's mea culpa. To have the terrorists' "AMERICANS SUCK" note flashed around the world by Al Jazeera was bad enough, but to have the man who had failed the mission bare himself in front of the men and women he was now expected to lead fearlessly into battle was something that no marine wanted to either hear or witness. It was a violation of strict marine tradition to go into a battle zone under anyone but their own, even if Freeman was an ex–full general of the army.

But if there was one thing that the American-led war against terrorism all over the world had taught the marines and every other branch of the armed services, it was that traditional ways of doing things often had to be overruled in the interest of expediency. *Yorktown* was the nearest MEU ready to go; it had been as simple as that.

There was a somber mood throughout the ship and little of the light banter that normally preceded an MEU op. Everyone knew that Freeman's foray into this rebel-held Russian territory could be Freeman's *Folly* if what was euphemistically referred to as "unsettled weather" conspired with the crack Russian defenders whose forebears, in their ubiquitous T-34s, had stopped the German Panzers in the terrible massed winter battles of 1943 and 1944.

Peter Norton, harboring the chilling possibility of having to drive his 6,000-pound cargo-carrying Hummer in the vicinity of the rebel Russian tanks, was in the grip of an ice-cold fear. Having been demoted from full-combat-marine status to combat driver, he was depressed enough already without having to think about being thrust into or anywhere near a heavily defended enemy position. He had begun experiencing the chest-gripping, profuse-sweating, "I'm going to die" anxiety attacks a few months before. Out of concern for his own well-being and as a machine gunner aboard one of the MEU's ground team's armored Hummers, he had dutifully reported to sick bay, and the panic attacks had quickly been brought under control by a daily dose of ten milligrams of the anti-anxiety medication Paxil. But he had not been sufficiently alert to the fact that the navy, into whose organization the

marines were integrated, remains the most tradition-
bound of the armed services. As well as being the most
"senior" service, it remains deeply suspicious of "shrinks,"
whether they be psychologists or psychiatrists. In Peter
Norton's case, the navy was even more rattled by the
acronym PIUS—possible instability under stress.

Peter hadn't told any of his marine buddies about his
connection with Freeman. Nor had he tried to use his father or Freeman, who it was unlikely even knew he was
on the *Yorktown,* to pull strings to overturn the damning
psychological profile that he was sure had cost him pro-
motion and a reduction in pay. When he heard the criticism of Freeman aboard *Yorktown*, Peter was even more
convinced that he had done the right thing in not owning
up to any connection to the man whom most of Peter's
marine buddies resented having been placed in overall
command of the MEU. But he did regret reporting the
panic attacks. Though nothing was said to him directly,
Norton found his responsibilities further decreased, and
when the mission was announced, his official designation
was no longer combat driver but standby support driver.
And the only reason he had been assigned this job as a
food-supply driver in Colonel Tibbet's battalion HQ was
that the armed forces were spread so thinly in the far-
flung world war against terrorism that all trained personnel, including drivers, were scarce.

In the tightly packed, claustrophobic, fuel-laden atmosphere on the vehicle decks he was finding it difficult to
breathe. He felt the old, chest-gripping fear rising in him
and, as a psychological diversionary tactic, began checking his stack of dark brown, plastic-wrapped MAMEs,
marine meals, which, as cold rations designed out of the
marine battle lab in Quantico, Virginia, were far superior
to the usual MREs, meals ready-to-eat, which troops frequently threw away because what the MREs provided in

nutrients, they lacked in taste. Colonel Tibbet passed by, the tall, lean marine commanding officer, nodding to Norton on his way. Then he stopped and turned on his heel. "Norton? Peter Norton? Right?"

"Yes, sir," answered Peter, with some timidity.

"You were the guy who suggested we stock up on— what was it, Mars bars, for the next combat ration?"

"Yessir," replied Peter obediently, then typically added, "but it wasn't my idea, sir. It was General Freeman's."

"Freeman's?" said Tibbet with obvious surprise. "You know General Freeman?"

"No, sir. Well, not personally, but he sent a memo to the quartermaster general after he'd found out how the Brits on the ships during the Falklands War passed on all their rations and went instead for Mars bars."

Tibbet was nodding knowingly. "Huh—sugar surge, I guess. Makes sense. But General Freeman should've recommended Hershey bars."

"Yes, sir."

Tibbet moved on toward the TOW anti-tank-missile-loaded Humvees that would be airlifted by one of the *Yorktown*'s Super Stallions, unless there was interference in the assemblage of the air force from the *Yorktown* by foreign aircraft. In such a case the *Yorktown*'s marine V-STOL Harriers would provide a potent protective screen for the MEU force. The Harriers were tasked with going in to destroy what the MEU S-2 intel chief had been convinced by *McCain*'s signal exploitation space and by HUMINT routed to the *McCain* by the U.S. Embassy in Beijing and the Shanghai trade office was a Russian complex near Lake Khanka and its marshlands.

There was a problem, however, with the SATPIX. It showed an H-shaped building but no anti-aircraft emplacements, and a mobile AA battery was everyone's nightmare on such an op—that is, *one* of the nightmares.

It was General Freeman's comment about the unusual number of airborne birds cluttering the satellite images of the area that had first aroused the MEU's intel chief's interest. Freeman had pointed out to him that the fact of the birds *constantly* rising, circling, and landing on the lake—"neurotically," Freeman had said—pointed to a terrestrial anomaly that "must be frightening the shit out of the cranes, et cetera," causing them to take flight much more often than what an ornithological report confirmed was normal. If there was an earthquake, Freeman had told the officers' mess on *Yorktown*, the entire area would liquefy.

"It's liquefied already, General."

"True. What I meant, Captain, was that even the wooded areas that we might rely on would simply become a vast slurry. Awful for armor." What spooked the marines' intel officer most was the sheer volume of bird traffic being monitored in the "blue tile country," the blue-tiled inner sanctum of the U.S.S. *McCain*'s signal exploitation space compared to what was normal. "Neurotic," he decided, was an apt description of the avian activity.

Now Colonel Tibbet was inspecting the line of Stinger-mounted Humvees. Two swivel-mounted boxes on each one of the ten vehicles contained four anti-aircraft missiles, eight Stingers in all, a potent defense system by any measure. After a quick inspection of these units, he walked quickly past the supply Humvees which, because his mission was not an amphibious-landing op as such, would have to be delivered, together with extra fuel bladders, by helo sling and would have to carry the total supply load, from prepackaged meals to gas masks, a job usually shared by the marines' five-ton trucks which the *Yorktown*'s big landing craft ferried ashore after the troops disembarked. But this KITDO, or kick-in-the-door operation, as the troops called it, to Lake Khanka was to be confined to airlift only. Tibbet was about to leave the vehicle deck and walk up one of the many internal ramps between decks to the big hangar, when he paused and called back to Peter Norton, "How'd you know it was General Freeman who sent that memo?"

"My dad told me, sir."

"Your *dad*?"

"Yes, sir. He used to be the general's 2IC."

"Huh!" said Tibbet, wondering why the son of a G-2 hadn't risen any higher than a driver. No shame in it, but not what you'd expect.

General Freeman's stentorian voice coming on the *Yorktown*'s public address system sounded as if it was coming from on high, its tone brooking neither interruption nor contradiction.

"Shit," opined one marine. "Sounds like Moses."

This is no apology, Peter Norton told himself. This was an old blood 'n' guts Georgie Patton speech. And what made it doubly impressive or eerie, depending on the audience of two thousand marines scattered throughout the ship, was Freeman's likeness on the monitors to the controversial World War II general.

"Reincarnation," said a machine gunner.

"Bullshit," responded another. "What d'you think, Norton?"

Peter shrugged. "Don't know."

"It's going around *town*," boomed the general, "that I'm a 'tired old horse'! Now, I take umbrage at that. I've been a horse's ass, but I've never been 'old'!" There was a smattering of laughter 'tween decks and on the *Yorktown*'s roof, where the flight crews in the preemptory ballet of war were busily parking the first five of the helo carrier's fifteen big Super Stallions, the choppers in takeoff line, rotors still, folded like the wings of enormous, sleeping dragonflies. "What makes it worse," continued

Freeman, "is that the joker who said I'm a horse's ass was a liberal Monday-morning quarterbacking son of a bitch who wouldn't know a condom from a balloon."

The marines roared their approval, getting into it now. Marine Commander Tibbet, high up on the island's bridge, was shaking his head as he stared down at Freeman who, he saw, had climbed atop one of the big Super Stallion's cockpits, even as its deck crew fit-tested the helo's cargo hook and banana-shaped sling.

"That comment about liberals'll be on CNN in about five minutes," Tibbet complained to *Yorktown*'s diminutive Captain Crowley. "The man's got no sense of —I don't know—"

Why, Lord, why, Crowley petitioned Heaven, did he have to have George Patton reincarnated on *his* boat? A naval captain, like anyone else, abhorred controversy. Technically, Crowley mused, as long as Freeman's on my boat, he's under my command. *Technically*.

"Now," continued Freeman, "I want to tell you men and women that if I were you, I'd be a mite teed off at suddenly being under the command of a horse's ass!" A roar of laughter erupted 'tween decks, flowing up from the vehicle and hangar deck over the ramps, spilling out onto the flight deck. "But I'm here to tell you that I've seen my share of combat, and I've still got some ideas about how to deal with scumbags. And—" He was interrupted by another roar, this one of such anger that it startled *Yorktown*'s captain but turned Colonel Tibbet's frown into a knowing smile: Their blood was up. "—And I want to tell you," thundered the general, "that I and my team of veterans are here to work *with* you, not *over* you. This is from first to last Colonel Tibbet's show. I'm here in an advisory capacity only, but you'll see me around—" He paused. "—not sitting like a horse's ass, but galloping in with your Super Stallions. And—"

There was clapping and cries of "Way to go, General!"

"And," continued Freeman, arms akimbo, his camouflaged Fritz with its airborne strap cupping his chin, "I intend to shit all over those comrades who give our enemies the means to kill our children. *Are you ready?*"

"Hoo-ha!" came the guttural marine response.

"God bless you all," Freeman told them, "and God bless America!"

The cheers of the marines were now interrupted by the coughing, spitting noise of the helicopter engines starting in unison, their collective roar amid the choking exhaust fumes drowning out the war cries of the first wave of 750 marines to embark on the mission which Freeman had suggested should be called Operation Bird Rescue. The president had thought it a brilliant choice, so politically astute that he had sent a short thank-you note.

The heavily laden marines filed up from the cavernous recesses of the *Yorktown*, moving antlike along the flight deck and disappearing into the bellies of the Super Stallions, whose giant rotors threw circles of dazzling, transparent sunlight, signaling that each of the choppers' titanium-forged blades had now joined one of the earsplitting concerts of war.

In *Yorktown*'s landing force operations center, deep within the O2 deck, Freeman, like Tibbet, loaded for bear, was going over their joint plan of attack. Like all good plans in life and in battle, it was simple in concept. Of course the devil, as always, was in the details. First, *Yorktown*'s Cobra gunships would ride shotgun on both the northern and southern flanks of *Yorktown*'s helo stream. Second, the Cobras, fed SATPIX intel, would soften up all of the rebel AA defenses, leaving Tibbet's first wave of infantry to go in and gut the ABC complex. HUMINT assets believed the two two-story structures, connected at their midpoints by a two-story ferro cement walkway and surrounded by a virtually treeless one-square-mile perimeter, comprised the central cog in ABC's operation. The complex was believed to be the place where the manufacture of terrorist weapons had made what the Pentagon's practitioners of the "dismal science" of economics referred to as a "quantum leap in economies of scale." All of which was pretentious Pentagon jargon for the fact that terrorist weapons manufactured in the ABC complex had shifted from the garages of the Middle East to high-efficiency American-style assembly lines.

Moscow, Freeman understood, had still not given official permission for the American helos to enter Russian airspace, it being accepted by Washington that on advice from the United Nations there would be an outraged denunciation of the U.S. choppers' presence, led by the Russian delegate Petrov and supported by the French. This was also accepted by the White House as necessary to make the Russian president look tough even while it offered him a chance to be rid of the rebel ABC without having to commit regular Russian troops to fight Russians. What the Russian president had not clarified, however, was whether American fighters or bombers would be permitted to enter Russian airspace. But he had reiterated to Washington that he would be able to restrain regular Russian air force and naval units from becoming embroiled with the MEU for only a maximum of twenty-four hours. Douglas Freeman assured Colonel Tibbet and *Yorktown*'s Crowley that as titular head of the MEU's operation, he would take full responsibility for releasing *Yorktown*'s Harriers and *McCain*'s Joint Strike Fighters against the ABC complex at Lake Khanka should a Russian air attack threaten American lives.

"Fleet won't go for this," *Yorktown*'s Captain Crowley warned Freeman and Tibbet.

Freeman's jaws tightened. "Let's get one thing straight,

gentlemen. I've been personally tapped by the president of the United States to be the senior-ranking officer to command the operation. As such, it's not my intention to go running around the damn fleet getting permission slips so I can leave the room and go to the toilet. Is that understood?"

Tibbet was noncommittal. The *Yorktown*'s skipper, however, was not so sanguine about Freeman's willingness to act independently of him as admiral of the fleet.

"General," the *Yorktown* skipper informed him, "a quick, enciphered e-mail to the White House could clear this up."

"With all due respect, sir," Freeman replied, "by the time they fart around in that situation room down in that Washington basement—hell, I mean half of those jokers down there don't know where Baltimore is, let alone this damned lake—it'll be hours before we get the green light. That time lost could cost us marine lives—a lot of lives. And now that our chief source of real-time intel, CNN, has blabbed it all over that we're about to go in after this ABC complex, the enemy'll be dug in even more than usual, securing their defensive perimeter like there's no tomorrow. And let's hope there's no goddamned armor about," Freeman added. "I say let's quit pig-frigging around with e-mails to the White House. Release your Harriers upon request by either the colonel or me. I told you I'll take the rap."

"You can afford to," retorted Crowley, "you're retired." He immediately wished he hadn't said it. Tibbet was watching the general and he saw Freeman's face redden in controlled anger.

"Retired or not," retorted Freeman, "I have the little matter of my reputation at stake. You gentlemen know how it goes. In our business you're as good as your last op. Like a damn movie star: one big flop and you're in the doghouse. Priest Lake's my doghouse, and I want out. Badly. But I'm not going into this just because I want to save my ass or get my picture on the cover of *Time*. I'm doing this for those poor bastards, law-abiding Americans, who were just sitting there working one moment and were blown to smithereens the next by those scumbags."

Tibbet had no difficulty in imagining fire coming from the general's nostrils. "Anyway," the general continued, "if our helos don't take at least one round from Russian ground defenses, I'll eat my hat. And if they do, that'll justify release of the Harriers."

Crowley hoped the Russians wouldn't violate the twenty-four-hour agreement with Washington, but if they did, the fighter-bombers would certainly come in handy.

"Admiral?" It was his duty officer. A few minutes later Crowley informed Freeman, "My D.O. tells me there's been a leak. We're being inundated with e-mail requests about Bird Rescue. Some correspondents, including a gal from *Newsweek*, are saying the name the Pentagon gave to this mission is a cynical ploy to win over the environmentalist lobby in support of yet another unilateral U.S. invasion. Would you comment?"

"Invasion!" Freeman said angrily. "This is an operation to chase down a bunch of goddamn murderers. You can tell them from me that—"

"Wait a second, General," said Crowley, who instructed one of his computer operators to take down Freeman's comment verbatim.

"Tell them," said Freeman, "that the list of endangered species on Lake Khanka is as long as your goddamned arm. The one to give to the media is the *Grus japonensus*. Half those liberal bastards might even be able to spell it. It's a very rare, endangered species of red-crowned crane, and there's a critter called the sheathfish endemic to the region." Freeman turned to Colonel Tibbet. "I like giving the bastards that one, Jack. Just watch and wait for one of the TV anchors to keep a straight face with 'sheath.'"

"Ah," Crowley told the computer operator, "I suggest you clean that up a little before you send it. Okay with you, Douglas?"

Colonel Tibbet grinned, welcoming a flash of levity to the occasion, and Freeman readily agreed. There was no point in deliberately riling them up. It reminded him of Marte Price and his deal with her to give her first crack at an exclusive in return for her having come clean about the government's initial and futile attempt to keep the attack on DARPA ALPHA under wraps.

They could all hear the mounting thunder on the roof, and the appearance of Tibbet's S-2, the marines' intel chief, confirmed the MEU was ready to "rock'n'roll."

"Look," Freeman told Tibbet and Crowley. "If we can knock these bastards out at Khanka, it won't be just them and the terrorists' stockpile we'll be taking out, gentlemen. It'll be a lesson to any other ragtag damn terrorists that no matter what it takes, when you kill Americans, we'll come after you—in your own damn country, if need be. So that Captain Crowley here might even release his Harriers."

"I'll put the Harriers on standby," said Crowley. "That's as far as I'll go for now."

Freeman shook his hand.

"Maybe," cut in Tibbet, trying to help his old naval colleague Crowley stand his ground against Douglas Freeman's well-intentioned but relentless charge, "you tried to reach Washington to get 'weapons-free' for the Harriers, but your encrypting program temporarily crashed?"

Freeman winked at Tibbet. "I like it!"

Crowley kept a straight face. "I'll take that under advisement."

John Cuso, the executive officer who had been seconded from *McCain* to *Yorktown* to assist Crowley, had seen his share of helo assaults launched from the ship, but it was always a new and exciting experience for him. From Vultures' Row, high in the control island, Cuso looked down at the frantic, yet endlessly rehearsed, preparations for combat. He could see the fifteen Super Stallions and Tibbet and Freeman crouching low as each was hurried aboard his respective chopper, a lead Super Stallion for Freeman, his six-man SpecOp team, mortar squad, and other marines aboard, a command Huey for Tibbet. Cuso wondered how many would return. What had Hitler said? Making war was like grabbing a gun and walking into a pitch-black room—anything could happen.

Each of the fifteen Super Stallions in *Yorktown*'s thirty-two-helo force would be carrying fifty fully loaded marines, which meant putting 750 marines in the target zone in the first assault wave—providing there was no interference en route. Each of the big Stallions had three .50-caliber machine guns, one located in the forward starboard crew door and two on pivot mounts for open-ramp firing, all three weapons fed by linked-belt .50-caliber ammunition. As the air armada rose above a blue, choppy sea, two-thirds of the total marine MEU combat force was en route toward the rugged coast of Russia's far east, which was already in sight as a dark squiggle on the horizon.

Aboard his Huey, Colonel Tibbet was double-checking the landing area selected from the SATPIX where two Super Stallions were to deposit their sling-carried fifteen-thousand-pound bladders of aviation fuel for both helos and Harriers, should it become necessary to call for the

Harriers to provide close air support and enough loiter time over the target. During the vital refueling, squads of marines would rush to form a defensive perimeter screen, though it was not anticipated that much ground fire at all would be encountered, given the absence of troops on SIGINT and SATPIX intel.

Though clouds appeared to be thickening and were clustering ominously along the coast, forming a line of ragged gray ahead of them, the rising of the thirty-two-aircraft armada made an impressive sight. An able force, if ever he'd seen one, thought Tibbet, whose high morale had been duly noted by Peter Norton who, in an attempt to contain his rising fear before the mission, had closed his eyes, trying to concentrate on the happiest, most relaxing times of his youth—picnicking and swimming in the James River to beat the awful, humid heat of August.

As the low-flying MEU approached the coast, a Russian fisherman-cum-coastwatcher, Alexander Rostovich, whose great grandfather had been killed as an adviser to Ho Chi Minh's legions against the Americans in Vietnam, was awakened to the choppers' sound. Grabbing his binoculars, he glimpsed a white U.S. star with a white bar either side of it on one of the incoming helos of the U.S. air armada. Racing into his fishing hut, where he kept an old but reliable 8 mm Mauser that was always loaded for the sharks that bothered his nets when he was fishing off Timpevay Bay or for bears that could wipe out a year's carefully tended vegetable patch in a few seconds, Rostovich raised the weapon and let fly a round at the armada, pulled back the bolt, swearing as he did so, rammed another round home, and fired again. By sheer dumb luck, this round hit the cockpit of a Stallion, spiderwebbing the copilot's window screen and narrowly missing his head.

"Ground fire!" the copilot reported. "Three o'clock, from

that hut down by that garden. Anyone see it? Along the cliff edge."

"I've got it, Stallion. He's mine," came a voice, the violation of radio silence no serious thing, given the number of helos that were airborne and clearly visible to isolated settlements along the coast. In addition, the ABC, thanks to CNN, Al Jazeera, and all the others, clearly knew that the strike was imminent. One of the SuperCobras, feared by and known to Saddam's soldiers as the "Skinny Birds," peeled off into a steep, 180 m.p.h. dive, the helo firing its three-barrel rotary chin-mounted chain gun, the one-in-five red tracers dancing crazily about the hut. The hut collapsed, as did Rostovich. There was no fire or explosion, nothing more than a cloud of dust rising above the imploded hut, the coastwatcher lying spread-eagled in a garden of collapsed trellises. Little chance he was still alive. In any event, the target had been "neutralized." Even so, Jack Tibbet did a one-eighty and called for the six Harriers. There was no way he could know how much ground fire was about to open up, and, with Crowley's blessing, decided that he'd rather be called overcautious than unnecessarily risk his marines on the coast before they reached the target.

"Blackbirds go!" ordered Crowley, and within minutes the Harriers, electing to make their short takeoff over the vertical lift to conserve fuel, were aloft, Freeman simultaneously requesting *McCain*'s vertical takeoff Joint Strike Fighters to assist in suppression of hostile ground fire, "should it become necessary," the latter phrase a qualifier indicating that the American aircraft would not fire unless fired upon, a political fiction that might qualify as an acceptable order in the Byzantine business of the military's post-op inquiries. All that was known in the fleet was that a Super Stallion had taken a *hit*, and "no," the copilot rudely informed Tibbet's G-2, "it was *not* a fucking bird.

It was a fucking *round*, a fucking 7.62 mm rolling around in the damn cabin." For all anyone, including Freeman and Tibbet, whose lead helos had already passed well beyond the fisherman's hut, knew, the entire helo armada might be coming under ground fire. All everyone had heard for certain was that radio silence had been broken because a Super Stallion had come under ground fire. The Stallion had taken a "direct hit." Soon the rumor amongst the fully laden combat troops, wedged uncomfortably between their web-seats and the fuselage, was that a Stallion had gone down.

"Anyone get out?"

"Don't know."

"Shit!"

In Aussie Lewis's wry assessment, the usual fuckups had begun.

"Where are those friggin' Blackbirds?" asked the Stallion's copilot, who had narrowly missed being killed.

"On the way," his pilot told him. Relax."

"Yeah, right."

"Relax, Evers," repeated the pilot more sternly. "I know this is your first hot mission, but we've a ways to go. Freeman and Tibbet know what they're doing."

"Yeah. Sorry."

"It's okay. I know it's hard, Dave, but you've been trained by the best. You'll be fine."

But there was trouble aboard the Stallion. It was coming from a hoarse-voiced general, Douglas Freeman, who, by sheer accident during a chat with a mortar crewman, discovered that the marine, indeed the entire mortar crew and one of its M40A1-marine-trained snipers aboard the Stallion, had by some oversight been through marine Colonel Cobb Martens' weapons training battalion—made famous by Colonel Michael Nance—without having been given an AK-47 or AK-74 familiarization course. Freeman told the pilot to radio Tibbet, who, red-faced, sent an encrypted fast-blast message to *Yorktown* to the effect that anyone waiting in the second wave who was not familiar with firing either the AK-47 or AK-74 must be so instructed. Immediately.

There was a problem. There were no AK-47s or AK-74s on the *Yorktown*. It was an American ship, for crying out loud.

"What?" was the general's thunderous reply. He couldn't believe that in the twelve vessels that constituted the Seventh Fleet there wasn't a single AK-47 in any of the ship's armories. It seemed particularly improbable, given the popularity of the virtually indestructible Russian weapon among British and American Special Ops teams like his.

"I know where there're some," Aussie Lewis assured him. "Unofficial, of course. They've got 'em stashed in *McCain*'s armory. There's an ex-marine captain there with special arms training. He was wounded in Iraq. He's now working in *McCain*'s Blue Tile. He's, ah, what you might call a 'collector.'"

"Is he?" said Freeman who, turning to Lieutenant Terry Chester, one of Jack Tibbet's platoon commanders, ordered, "Message *Yorktown* that Colonel Tibbet and I expect every marine to know how to fire and strip an AK-47 before our Stallions return to pick them up. If we get into a logistics screwup and anyone runs short of ammo, an AK-47 snatched off a dead Russian might be the thing that turns the tide."

On the *Yorktown*, the general's "turn the tide" phrase was met with skepticism, but not, as one might have expected, by the veterans, who knew how an extra clip of ammo could save your hide. The skepticism came more from those young Leathernecks who hadn't been in action before, whose number comprised about seven hundred of the MEU's total sixteen hundred personnel. Some of them, such as young Peter Norton, who, though he had never met Freeman, knew something of him, understood that he was fanatical about logistical details, one of his ruling adages being "For want of a nail, the shoe was lost, for want of a shoe, the horse was lost, for want of a horse, the kingdom was lost." And had they known Freeman, skeptics would also have known that Douglas Freeman's attention to logistical detail had been justified by every hostile engagement he'd been part of.

"How far to target?" Aussie asked the Stallion's burly crew chief.

"A hundred and forty-seven miles," said the chief.

"That by road?" Aussie asked, leaning forward expectantly, elbows pressing down hard on his pack. Sal and Gomez were watching intently.

"As the crow flies," answered the crew chief.

"Well," said Aussie, "I'm not a fucking crow!" and sat back, visibly more relaxed. So were the other team members. It was a curious "good luck" ritual for Aussie, normally the least superstitious of men. At some point at the beginning of a mission he would always ask the crew chief, "How far to target?" and hold his breath. If the reply was so many miles or clicks, Aussie would ask, "That by road?" and the reply, common enough in the airborne services, was usually "As the crow flies." As long as the crew chief's answer had "crow" in it, it was a sign to Aussie that the mission would be successful.

"Ya hear that, boys?" he shouted at his team. "As the fucking crow flies."

"What?—" said Sal absently, checking his weapon. "Oh yeah, crow—right."

"Gonna be a piece o' cake!" said Aussie.

"No problem," said Freeman, who was keen to maintain high morale, but he and Tibbet had pored over the logistics of "the devil's domain" and knew the crucial element on this mission was not surprise—that had been lost because of CNN—but *rapid* resupply. Otherwise, as the general and colonel concurred, it could be a monumental balls-up, the general's second Priest Lake.

What the general hadn't told Aussie or the team—had never told them—was that he made it his business before every mission to give the crew chief aboard their helo or landing craft a heads-up about Aussie's "crow." In a team where there were few, if any, secrets, this was an exception that the general had made.

No matter how close he and his men had become over the years, he believed that for each member there had to be a moat across which neither friend nor foe should venture, an inviolable port that was the private preserve of secrets which only men and their Maker knew, the terrible memories of comrades lost, like Bone Brady, the fatally wounded SpecOp soldier whom, years before, Douglas Freeman had shot at point-blank range. It was the man's face, head flung back, eyes rolling comically and all the more grotesquely for that, bloodied teeth, bottom jaw sliding from side to side, that haunted the general. No matter that Brady had begged to be put out of his misery, the face would rise up in the gut-tightening minutes before deployment.

For a moment, Douglas Freeman's head slumped in shame, but he sat up quickly, ramrod straight, and made as if to clear his eye of grit, always a problem with so many men and things aboard, packed tightly together.

"Know that fella Orwell?" he shouted at Johnny Lee. "Limey who wrote that *Animal Farm*?"

"Read it in school," said Johnny, straining for his naturally high-pitched voice to rise above the roar of the helo's three big turboshafts.

"Yeah," said Freeman, pushing Bone Brady's face out of range, turning his attention to maintaining morale. "Well, Orwell said that he sometimes thought life was a constant battle against dirt." Freeman wiped his eye with his sleeve, hoping that their brownish green camouflage uniforms wouldn't stand out too starkly against the ice. In frozen marshland the camouflage would be perfect, but not against the white sheet of a frozen lake. "Aussie!" he called out.

"Sir!" shouted Aussie obediently, like a good marine, that is, more formally than he would have had only the team members been present.

"Joke," ordered the general.

They hit an air pocket.

"Choir barfing?" asked Aussie.

"Not yet," said Salvini. "Is that the joke?"

There was laughter now in the dark, stuffy, dimly lit interior.

Choir smiled and doffed his Fritz to Aussie as if his horse had just won the Triple Crown. "*Do*," said Choir, raising his voice, imitating an upper-class snob, "tell us your amusement."

"My *amusement*?" said Aussie, head back in mock surprise. "Screwing."

"Screwing *what*?" shouted a marine, name tag "Picard."

"Anything that moves!" shouted Salvini.

"Birds," said Aussie, feigning indignation, using the Australian slang for young women. "Nice-looking birds."

"How 'bout one of those protected—" began a marine,

name tag "Jackson, K.," who was nursing a squad automatic weapon, "—What d'you call those birds?"

"Cranes," said Marine Picard. "Yeah, would you screw a crane, Aussie?"

"He'd have to stand very still," Aussie answered. "I wouldn't chase the bugger!"

Catcalls and raucous laughter broke out so noisily that they momentarily drowned out the "whoomp whoomp" of the Stallion.

"Fussy," said Choir, now adopting a cockney accent that made his pronunciation sound like "pussy."

Aussie was suddenly alert. "Pussy? Where?"

The entire marine platoon was laughing and chortling at the silly banter, Marine Jackson, who'd initiated the exchange with Aussie, now being referred to as "Pussy," a name that he knew as a marine would stick to him as long as he was in the corps—or dead.

"Joke!" another marine insisted. "That Aussie isn't quitting on us, is he?"

"No way!" replied Aussie.

"Keep it clean," said Freeman. "Women aboard."

Aussie's head shot up. "*Where? Show me where!*"

A lone hand was raised. She was an African American, Melissa Thomas, Tibbet's MEU's first woman combatant.

"No problem," said Aussie. "It's as clean as a whistle."

"Stand up!" someone ordered Aussie.

"For the lady, sure," said Aussie. "I don't mind—"

"No," shouted a SAW gunner. "So we can fuckin' shoot you if it isn't funny." That got a big laugh, one of the loudest coming from the general who, as much as any of them, probably wouldn't have laughed at this nonsense during stand-down time but whose unspoken anxiety about going into combat would lead him to grasp on to anything that would offer temporary relief.

"Well," said Aussie, "this young married couple, both marines—"

"Hey!" shouted someone. "No same-sex marriage in the corps bullshit. Right, Thomas?"

"Right!" Melissa shouted.

"Let him finish," said a gunny, one of those sergeants who ran the corps.

"Right," said Aussie, raising his voice to a near shout. "Can you hear me?"

"Yeah, yeah, get on with it!"

"So," began Aussie, "this couple are arguin' about who should get up to make coffee every morning, and the guy says to his wife, 'I think you should be the one to brew the coffee. You're the woman of the house,' and she says, 'Don't give me that crap. We're both working, so I don't see why you can't get up and brew the coffee.' So this argument goes on about who should brew the friggin' coffee an' she sees it's going nowhere so she says, 'Will you take scriptural authority on this?' The guy says, 'Scriptural?—You mean the Bible?' She says, 'Yeah.' He thinks for a mo, then says, 'Okay. Bring it out.' And there it was in the New Testament: '*He*-brews.'"

There was a concerted groan within the Super Stallion. "Shoot 'im!" someone shouted, but still they liked it. The joke had done just what Freeman had wanted it to do, channeling the precombat jitters, especially amongst those, such as Melissa Thomas, who Tibbet had told Freeman had been too young for the war in Afghanistan and Iraq and for whom "Operation Bird Rescue" was their first real mission.

"That," the general told Aussie, "is the corniest damn joke I've ever heard."

"I like it!" shouted Choir.

"Yeah, you would," said Aussie, "you Bible-thumping Welsh turd."

"Thank you," riposted Choir, "very much."

Freeman was grinning, but Melissa Thomas, sitting at the rear of the starboard row of canvas-webbed seats by the Stallion's door, wasn't. She envied the ease with which each member of Freeman's six-man SpecWar team enjoyed one another's humor. She still couldn't get that kind of response from her rifle squad, no matter that ever since she'd responded to the commercial on TV that showed marines fast-roping down from a haze-gray helicopter, freeze-framed as they raced into action from the helo, she'd done all that was required of her. "Can you do it?" the commercial's narrator had challenged. "If you can, you're one of the best."

Her brother Danny "dissed" the ad as elitist, and that's precisely what appealed to her—that and the stirring background rendition of John Philip Sousa's "The Stars and Stripes Forever!" It was an old story: the military as the African American's way out of the ghetto. If you couldn't dribble and sink a basketball in her Detroit ghetto or get a scholarship to college, your horizons were very limited. The Marine Corps, after a dogged battle against Congress, had finally been forced to yield, and women were in. But that was only half the battle. Female marines had not been allowed in ground combat units. Being assigned to Operation Bird Rescue meant that Melissa Thomas was the first female marine in history to be purposely put in harm's way rather than in a supportive capacity aboard ship. Melissa had learned much, particularly about self-reliance, the corps having the lowest officer-to-personnel ratio in any of the United States Armed Forces, and she said a prayer asking God to help her to be strong, conscious of the fact that she was a trailblazer, not only as an African American but as the first female marine to be in combat on the ground. She thought of the bus journey to Parris Island along the lonely, two-lane elevated road over the swamps and the ebb and flow of the salt marshes of South Carolina's Port Royal Sound, recalling the moment when she'd first come to stand in the painted yellow footprints in front of the receiving shed, knowing that there were drill instructors who wanted her to fail.

Ever since she was a young girl in Detroit she had always wanted to be part of a shipboard marine contingent, her uncle explaining how a marine's original role in the English navy was to go aloft, high into the rigging, so as to snipe the enemy and to enforce the captain's discipline on their own ship. With images of raising Old Glory on Iwo Jima dancing in her head during the hard, unforgiving physical and mental conditioning of Parris now behind her, she had become the first ever female marine combatant to be assigned to an amphibious unit aboard the floating military airbase called *Yorktown*. But with few exceptions, Melissa had been only grudgingly accepted by her fellow marines, an outsider informally assigned to little more than "swab deck" status aboard *Yorktown*, no matter that she had qualified in everything they threw at her. She'd run the marine gauntlet from the recruits' "fright night" in her "Forming Phase" to Phase I's backbreaking, sinew-sapping PT to Phase II's mastery of the M16A2 5.56mm combat rifle to North Carolina's Camp Lejeune as the first female recruit ever to attend the School of Infantry, hitherto the sole preserve of male recruits. And finally, there was graduation day when her DI presented her with the coveted eagle-topped globe and anchor emblem of the United State Marine Corps, and for Melissa the special moment when she introduced her dad, now frail with age and eyes brimming with tears of pride, to DI Morgana Schmidt. Schmidt, a black belt–level martial arts drill instructor of the Fourth Recruit Training Battalion, had overseen recruit Thomas and the other 69 recruits in the platoon all the way from Pick-Up briefing to graduation, carefully, at times roughly, guiding Melissa through the morphing of yet another civilian into a United States Marine.

As the Super Stallion hit a series of sharp wind shears, she felt a wave of nausea pass through her, something she had not felt since experiencing what her DI had introduced as a "visit to the pool," a gross understatement, if Melissa had ever heard one, of the terrifying requirement of each marine to float in full battle dress and boots in the dreaded water-training facility.

Even now, the memory of impending drowning and the palpable dread one experienced on approaching the hated drop boards over the water which she, like any other recruit, had to master, still haunted her dreams, and now, as the Stallion continued to buck, she prayed to God, as she had prayed with the *Yorktown*'s padre, that she would not find herself in deep water in combat.

As they approached the gray, socked-in coastline of Russia's wild and lonely far eastern coast, turbulence struck the Super Stallions.

"Need a bag?" Sal asked Choir.

"How 'bout a bucket?" proffered Aussie.

Choir's expression segued from mild anxiety into a broad smile. "I'm feeling great."

The Stallion dropped again, the G-force lifting many of the marines off the web-seats to clearly voiced expressions of disapproval from the men and Melissa who, on this helo alone, formed a third of the MEU's Bravo rifle company which, in turn, constituted one of the three rifle companies of what would be the MEU's battalion landing team.

Freeman saw the alarm on Melissa's face, but it vanished as quickly as it had appeared, marine discipline arresting any potential show of alarm. For her to have complained or even sworn would have immediately been seen as a typical "skirt" reaction. The parent in Freeman wanted to reassure her that the turbulence would probably subside as soon as they passed over the coastal mountains between Glazkovka and Cape Titova on the air route that he and Tibbet had selected through the valleys between the Kiyevka and Ussuri rivers. But the officer in him told him not to single her out; it would only reinforce her marginalization, which he'd sensed, albeit subtly, during liftoff from *Yorktown*. Still—

"Well," announced the Stallion's crew chief, "we're well past Cape Titova!" Hoots and laughter followed.

"Bring it on!" yelled someone.

Freeman saw Melissa Thomas smile, trying to be one of the boys, and he empathized with her sense of being an outsider—everyone had such moments—and thought about how he might help her to feel included in the team. He asked a marine in the mortar squad, a loader, about Thomas's classification.

"She's an E-2, S/S, sir."

"Ah," said Freeman, the designation telling him she was a private first class with sniping credentials. Impressive.

"Yes, sir," continued the loader. "She's a good shot."

A "good shot" was an understatement. S/S told the general that this marine with the shy, dark eyes had been tough enough to have graduated from Parris with not only a high score in marksmanship but also the designation "Scout/Sniper." It was an outstanding achievement, but for a woman in a man's world, it was yet another way of moving herself, albeit unwittingly, further from her fellow marines. The rifle with the big scope told Freeman that Melissa must have been able to *repeatedly* hit a man-sized target in the head at ranges greater than half a mile. You didn't have to be a giant to do that occasionally, but

to do it consistently meant you had to be strong and have
iron nerves. "Nerves of iron," Freeman used to tell his recruits, "not nerves of steel, because steel springs back at
you. No, you need iron will to lie there for hours in your
hide, not moving so much as a hair. Waiting, controlling
your bladder sphincter through sheer will. You might
have the luxury of a scope spotter to share the mission
with you, or you might be alone." It was Douglas Freeman's intention, as had always been his inclination, to
make the outsider feel at home.

A collective groan greeted another sudden gut-
plummeting drop in an air pocket, Aussie catching a
glimpse out of one of the Super Stallion's starboard windows of a white squiggle of river which he guessed must
be the Kiyevka, and farther west, ragged fragments of
mountain mist above woods that in parts obliterated the
sliver of another river cutting through forests as thick and
dark as anything he'd seen on the other side of the world
at Priest Lake.

The general too had seen the black forests and detected
a heightened tone of urgency rushing back from the Stallion's cockpit into the forty or so pack-laden marines of
Bravo rifle company. For a millisecond Eddie Mervyn
and interpreter Johnny Lee saw what looked like a marine
Harrier diving through the gray stratus, and detected an
acrid smell invading the cabin.

"Hold tight!" yelled the crew chief. "Evasive action."

"Another fucking fisherman?" said Aussie.

"More than one," said the crew chief unsmilingly.

The Stallion was bucking and yawing violently amid a
black, pock-scarred sky, the pilot battling the yoke, fighting to evade the AA fire.

"Oh, shit!" said a marine, one of the few who had a
clear view through one of the square windows over the

helo's stubby portside wing. A loud ripping noise cut through the vibrating roar of the Stallion's three engines and the deep thumping of its rotors as the helo's gunners opened up, hot shell casings momentarily glinting golden in a sudden sunbeam that quickly disappeared into the stratus. The Stallion was on instrument flying, the copilot thanking God for the upgrade that had finally given the CH-53Es the forward-looking infrared and radar.

"Eight o'clock! Eight o'clock! AA!" The ramp's right-side rear gunner was shouting to alert his ramp and crew-door colleagues. Aussie was able to glimpse only part of the helo's two arcs of red tracer that were streaming earthward as they sought to silence the two anti-aircraft batteries manned by gunners who from this height looked no bigger than toys.

"More at six!" bellowed Eddie Mervyn.

"I see 'em!" acknowledged the crew-door gunner. This was followed by long, concerted bursts from the Stallion's gunners, the interior of the "fuse," the Stallion's long troop cabin, filling with cough-inducing cordite fumes together with the smell of perspiring bodies, the heat having been turned way up to counteract the freezing rush of the slipstream through the open ramp and front crew door. Aussie saw Freeman talking animatedly on the radio phone and then caught sight of the Harrier, its 25 mm GAU cannon obliquely spitting devastating white fire into both AA batteries, knocking them out.

Several marines were being sick without time to grab the thick, brown paper "lunch bags" issued earlier by the crew chief. Over the noise of machine-gun fire, the rotors' whoomp whoomp, and engines roaring, there was now a series of almost inaudible, soft, popping noises as the Stallion released its flares in hopes of drawing any anti-aircraft missiles to them rather than to the helo. Upon entering Russian airspace, everyone with the Bird Rescue armada had been worrying about SAMs, the big Russian surface-to-air missiles that had taken such a heavy toll of the B-52s and other American aircraft in 'Nam. Freeman, however, with the Priest Lake catastrophe fresh in mind, was more worried about the smaller, deadly Igla and other shoulder-fired MANPADs at this relatively low altitude. Iglas had a range of more than two miles. He was praying that the AA gunfire was all the flak that would come the helos' way. The general checked the Super Stallion's airspeed indicator: 167 m.p.h. With the Stallion's engines on maximum power, they should be over the site soon, unless more AA batteries were waiting in ambush down the valley.

A marine lurched forward, his insides blown across the aisle. There was a tremendous flapping noise as ragged aluminum edging from the fist-sized hole that had been shot out of the Stallion's starboard side trembled violently like a flag in a stiff gale. There was panic, half a dozen marines covered in entrails and blood, one of the most disgusting sights Freeman and his team had ever seen. The crew chief, though, had witnessed it before, and with astonishing agility, given the crazy gyrations of the Stallion as its pilots fought to regain control after the impact, he had produced two large khaki plastic bags, which he dumped at the feet of those covered in the blood and entrails which, moments before, had been their buddy, Private First Class James Cartwright.

"This bag," yelled the crew chief, opening one, "has clean rags in it. The other is for the dirty rags. Got it?"

One marine, his face splattered with his dead comrade's blood and other unidentifiable pieces of flesh and bone, couldn't respond, his eyes frozen, his body rigid with fear. The crew chief shook him hard by the shoulder, the chief's canvas glove immediately soaking up blood. "Hey!" shouted the chief, his right hand grabbing the marine's chin. "You hear me, Marine?" He said it with a DI's command voice, an undisguised call to duty, a tone born and bred daily by the corps, in the corps, for the corps. The marine answered the crew chief by assuring him that he was okay.

Freeman glimpsed a marine beside him. It was Melissa Thomas, down on her knees by the dead marine, placing a red gelatinous lump of something she picked up into the dump bag. The AA fire was already past, but no one noticed for several seconds. Freeman's team had seen dead and dying from Southeast Asia to Iraq, but several of the marines were traumatized by the sight of one of their comrades with his entrails blasted out of him. Aussie assured the traumatized marine, "You'll be right, mate. Hang on." Unable to find his "lunch bag" in time, the marine was throwing up violently into his helmet. He fumbled for his canteen.

"Nah," said Aussie, giving the marine his own sick bag and taking the man's helmet from him. Aussie turned to the crew chief. "Got some extra water, Chief?"

"Right with you," said the chief, and went back to his seat under which he had a four-gallon plastic drum of distilled water, which he passed to Aussie. The SpecFor man dumped the helmet's contents into the big plastic "out" bag. The cloying stench of sick mixing with the smell of aviation exhaust was enough to make several others feel ill, including Johnny Lee and Choir. Aussie washed out the sick marine's helmet, and gave it back to him. His name patch read "R. Kegg."

"Listen," Aussie lied to the grateful young marine, who looked no older than sixteen, "combat'll be easier than this."

The marine nodded. "Thank you, sir."

"Anytime, mate." Aussie could see, however, that the young marine was abnormally strung out with anxiety.

"Listen, press your tongue hard up against your palate. It forces you to breathe deeply. You'll relax." Aussie paused. "They teach you that at Parris?"

"I wasn't at Parris, sir," the youngster said, almost apologetically.

"Oh," said Aussie. "So you must live west of the ole Mississippi. "You were trained at Point Loma then?"

"Yes, sir. I'm a—I'm a 'Hollywood Marine.'" He tried to smile.

"So, did they teach you that trick?"

"What—oh, about pressing—"

"Yeah, pressing your tongue against the roof of your mouth?"

"No, sir."

"Well, what the fuck *did* they teach you?" said Aussie, smiling. He turned to Melissa Thomas, who was helping to clean up the mess. "Did you learn that at Parris?"

"I'm not sure," she answered, embarrassed by the sudden attention.

"Not sure? Hey!" Aussie yelled so loudly he startled young Kegg. "You marines! Listen up. A tip from Uncle Lewis. On long op flights, or short ones, in any sticky situation, you press your tongue hard up against your palate. You *will* get more oxygen. It helps, believe me!"

"Who are you?" demanded a marine.

"Grandstander!" offered another.

Aussie ignored them and winked at Melissa, who was helping him and who, unlike some of the others, understood that Aussie Lewis was only trying to boost morale, distracting them from the horror that had been visited upon them by the anti-aircraft fire.

"You've seen this stuff before," Aussie told Melissa.

"I was a nurse's helper in an ER for a while," she replied. "Before I joined the corps."

"Good for you, marine," said Aussie.

Melissa returned the smile which, given the bloody circumstances aboard the Super Stallion, struck some of the marines as disrespectful at best, at worst, obscene, in the presence of the dead marine. But Melissa couldn't help her response to Aussie; it was the first time since Parris that a man, and a renowned SpecWar warrior at that, had said something so warmly to her.

"Thank you," she said.

"He made a pass at you?" taunted one sullen marine as Melissa returned to her seat at the rear of the helo and buckled up.

"No," she replied. "He said something nice to me."

"I'll bet."

"Hey, Thomas," asked a marine who was nursing a SAW. "This Aussie. Isn't he the guy who coldcocked that A-rab fanatic?"

"All A-rabs are fanatics," proffered a mortar squad loader.

"Bullshit!" said another marine.

"Whatever he used," said the SAW marine, "that's him. Right? *That's* Aussie Lewis?"

"Yes," said Melissa. "That's him."

"My old man told me 'bout that convoy," put in another marine. "The A-rab was belted and was using a baby as cover, tryin' to blow up the whole fuckin' convoy when Thomas's boyfriend here wasted the fucker. So, technically, he didn't coldcock him. He used a shotgun."

"Horseshit!" argued another. "The Aussie took him out with a piece."

"I heard the crazy bomber was a woman," said the mortar loader.

"Whatever he used," repeated the SAW marine, "that's him. That's Aussie Lewis."

"What happened to the baby?" another marine inquired.

"Who knows?"

"Probably died," concluded the loader. "Either that or he's a martyr by now, ready for all those virgins."

Melissa saw something move up forward in the semi-darkness and instinctively gripped her rifle. It was the crew chief checking his watch against the speed indicator, his sudden movement unnerving her, everyone on edge. "Twenty minutes to amber," the chief announced.

"Twenty *minutes*?" growled one of the SAW gunners. "Feels like we've been up here twenty *hours*."

Choir Williams was looking pale again. The fact that he had never complained about his motion sickness was one of the things Freeman admired most about the warrior.

The general moved down the lines, chatting with the marines. It was hard physical work talking against the racket of the three engines, the rotors, and the bone-juddering vibrations that followed the AA fire. But he kept at it, exuding confidence and strength, talking casually to the troops about anything, surprising them with his grasp of detail, as when he passed Melissa Thomas, explaining to her how the end of the Cold War had spawned two Russias: On the one hand there was the affluent, technically savvy Russia, and on the other, the outmoded but still politically powerful Communist Russia. They were in fierce opposition, jockeying for who would rule in the twenty-first century. "The Russians, like us," he pointed out, "like any sensible army, don't go into a fight advertising who their officers are. Hell, their Spetsnaz—SpecWar troops—don't wear any insignia at all. But you can tell who's in charge." The general looked at Melissa and her squad. "Anyone know how?"

"Because," said a loader, "they're the ones yelling at everybody."

Freeman laughed easily. "Maybe, but the surest sign is that they're the best dressed. Lot of them are still like the

British officers in past wars. If they can afford it, they have their combat fatigues as well as full-dress uniforms made on Nevsky Prospect."

"Where's that, sir?"

"St. Petersburg," said Freeman, glancing at the airspeed indicator. The Super Stallions were capable of around 170 m.p.h. but with a load of fifty marines and because fragments of the AA hit had bled off some hydraulic lines, they were down to 141 m.p.h. Even so, the warning amber light would be coming on soon. Someone asked Freeman how it was that the terrorist H-block had been missed by satellite surveillance for so long.

"It's cold," Melissa Thomas ventured. "Wouldn't show up on the infrared?"

"No," said Freeman. "Buffalo's cold in winter too, but SATPIX'll pick up any building in Buffalo because of all the heating vents. They show up beautifully on the IR cameras. So our best intel guess is that the terrorist tech wizards have designed a thermoslike roof shield so that the H-building shows up as a thermos, without giving us any idea of what's inside." The moment he said this, Douglas Freeman felt an ice-cold tremor run through him. What if the soil analyses, et cetera, were wrong, and the damn place was an empty shell, a trap? He was determined to keep the possibility to himself. His job now was to keep morale as high as possible. "So," he told Melissa and every other marksman, which, given the marines' standard, meant every man on the helo, "you should look for the bastards with the best-pressed battle fatigues and shoot *them* first. I hope you notice that I, on the other hand, am no better dressed than any of you. I'm indistinguishable from any of you, 'cept for my big mouth." More laughter, more confidence-building after the bloody disaster that had just taken place aboard this, the marines' second helo. Huey One, carrying Tibbet and his HQ communications group, was a half-mile ahead.

"Ten to amber!" came the crew chief's voice. Freeman was wondering what had happened when the Harriers dove on the AA position. Had it been completely destroyed, its guns as well as its crew? Or would it be re-crewed and play havoc with the second wave? As so often happened, those in the middle of the action were the least able to discern exactly what was transpiring. He thought of Hitler again and the dark room. The Nazi Führer had been right about that.

CHAPTER FOURTEEN

THE LOUD "BOOM" that reverberated across the frozen marshlands and savannahs and through the woodland of Lake Khanka was unmistakably that of an anti-personnel mine exploding. Normally neither Abramov, Beria, nor Cherkashin would have bothered even looking up from their respective offices in the H-block, but this morning was different. With a marine expeditionary unit known to be en route to the complex, the detonation caused each general to immediately check the computer-controlled security display on his monitor. The half-mile-wide perimeter that ran around the ABC complex was mined and patrolled by Beria's motorized rifle company's amphibious BMPs, Boyevaya Mashina Pekhoty, infantry fighting vehicles. The BMPs, traveling between dug-in squads of eight men, maintained a 24/7 perimeter watch, while a mobile "Animal Squad" on standby was ready to dash out from the H-complex and replace any of the mines. There was eager competition for the night shift because deer were the most probable trespassers, and the commanding officers, for all their missile-made money, couldn't get a steady supply of venison due to past overhunting either by the Chinese, who worked the rice fields west of the lake, or by the Russian population east of Lungwangmia.

The phone jangled on Beria's desk, he being responsible for perimeter defense.

"Da?"

"Major Kermansky here, General. It was a *Vulpes vulpes.*"

Beria was gruff. "Don't show off, Kermansky. What the hell is that?"

"A red fox, sir. Very rare nowadays."

"Fur any good?" asked the general brusquely. Normally Beria didn't care a fig about what animal or bird it was, but red fox was an endangered species, and a fox-fur collar would make an exciting gift for his mistress in Avdoyevka, twenty miles east of the complex. ABC had put it under curfew.

"I doubt it," said Captain Kermansky, one of those recruited with bonus bait from the naval infantry battalion south in Vladivostok and a man who, though he had sold out to ABC, insisted on wearing his old unit's badged beret and blue-striped T-shirt beneath his battle smock.

"Is none of it salvageable?" asked Beria. Kermansky could be lying, saving the prized red fur for himself.

"No, sir. Sometimes they only get a foot blown off but he was blown to hell."

If the anti-personnel mine had blown the fox to hell, wondered Beria, how come Kermansky could tell it had been a male?

"I'll bury it deep," said Kermansky, as if he was doing the general a personal favor instead of doing what every man in Beria's infantry company had been told to do in order to prevent any enviro crazy hearing about it on the bush telegraph.

But this time Beria surprised him. "Bring it to me. Maybe I can get a collar out of it."

"But sir—"

"Bring it to me!" snapped Beria. "Or you won't see a bonus this week." With that, the general slammed the phone down. The call, intercepted like all other Russian or Chinese radio traffic by the operators in *McCain*'s cutting-edge signal exploitation space, was duly logged by the duty officer as a useless piece of information, along with all the other intercepts of nonenciphered Russian and local Chinese military traffic.

"What was that all about?" asked Landing Signals Officer Ray Lynch, bored now that *McCain* had launched its quad of Joint Strike Fighters, on radio silence, to catch up with the Harriers who, in response to news of the anti-aircraft fire against the Super Stallions, were now following the south bank of the Ussuri River.

"Mr. B of ABC," the translator reported to Lynch, "wants the coat of a red fox that blew itself up on a mine. Says he'd like a collar made from it but his comrade—" The operator paused and called back the intercept note on his monitor. "Some guy called Kermansky, sounded like an officer, he says the fox was blown to pieces. High intel, huh?"

The SES's officer of the watch shrugged, but nevertheless reminded the translator that any ABC intercepts were to be forwarded to Freeman or Colonel Tibbet. "Maybe they can make something of it."

"What the hell's a dead fox gonna tell them?"

"That the perimeter's mined," put in Ray Lynch.

The SES team resented Lynch being in the SES. The Blue-tile Area, because of the ultrasecret status of its advanced supercomputers, was strictly off-limits to all but designated ship's officers and the captain. Though Lynch had clearance, he had no real business there. SES called him "Lizard Lynch" because he was always lounging around in SES like a lizard in the sun and looking over their shoulders.

"Well," the CPO countered Lynch, "General Freeman already knows the perimeter's mined, so we don't have to tell him that. But our SATPIX have picked up a number of heat splotches where there's a temperature differential between undisturbed frozen ground and the ground that's been dug for a mine. That'll give him specific locations of mines."

The message, sent from the surreal quiet of the Blue-tile room to the thunder of the Super Stallions, was being deciphered by the copilot, who jotted it down on his sidearm computer. He tore off the two-inch-wide printout: "A red fox has been killed. Stepped on a mine."

"You're joking," said the pilot.

"No sirree. *McCain*'s SES is sending us a fucking intercept about a fucking fox. A red fox."

"Oh, well, then," said the pilot, his voice dripping with sarcasm, "A *red* fox. A Commie fox. This could be very important, Dave. Better give it to the crew chief right now."

The copilot summoned the crew chief. "Big intel coup, Chief. Better tell the general. And tell our fellow marines that amber warning'll be in five."

"Amber in five," acknowledged the chief, "and red fox to the general. Got it." The crew chief read the message, shaking his head. He, Freeman, and the marines were about to deplane and the enemy knew they were coming, even if they didn't know the precise landing zones, and here was SES wasting everyone's time. A red fox was kaput. Big deal.

The PA crackled as Freeman took the message.

"Oh shit!" It was the copilot. "Hold on, marines. We have several blips up ahead, chopper speed, but they aren't friendlies. Our fighter jocks should take care of 'em, but we'll be popping flares and may have to take evasive maneuvers."

Freeman was alarmed and tried not to show it. The blips, he assumed, were probably ABC helos coming to attack but he was confident that the Harriers and four JSFs could deal with them. The red fox, however, worried him. "Chart?" he asked his SpecOp team interpreter.

Lieutenant Johnny Lee brought it up on his laptop and showed him the SATPIX's mines, a veritable moat of explosives around ABC, each mine indicated by a tiny "x." From the angle Freeman was looking at them, they resembled a graveyard—hundreds of crosses.

CHAPTER FIFTEEN

"WHAT'S UP, SIR?" Aussie asked the general, who didn't hear him at first. The amber light came on. Ten minutes to green, and the air armada's marines were gripping their weapons tightly, checking that their C-4 was safely packed, and doing deals with God. Senses were so strained that the stink of the scared soldiers, an oil drip from a leaking line, and vomit was overwhelming.

"General?" Aussie asked again.

"Damn fox," said Freeman, his face tight with concern. "Killed on one of their mines. An SES intercept."

Aussie's brain was racing to keep up with Freeman, but sometimes that just wasn't possible, given the breadth and depth of the general's experience.

"A fox, wolf," he told Aussie, "whatever, would never deliberately walk on a mine. They can smell anything that's been handled by a human for months. Besides, carnivores've been hunted to damn near extinction, so they know better than to go anywhere near that H-block with all its odors. Which means it was well out on the perimeter."

"Animal'd still smell it out there," challenged Aussie.

"Yes," conceded the general. "But there's one thing, however, that'll override human scent—any scent—so that even a fox with its nose to the ground'll miss it."

"Snow!" said Choir.

"Ten minutes to green!" shouted the crew chief.

"Snow!" said Freeman in disgust. "And we're in NATO khaki green."

"Shit!" said Aussie. "Must've fallen this morning."

"And still falling," said Freeman. "I'm going up to see the pilot. Bad enough we should have to try landing in snow, let alone sticking out like a whore's tit once we deplane. Might as well paint targets on our ass." He jabbed a finger at the laptop. "Our LZ is by a wood near this marshland. We could find cover in these woods outside the H-block perimeter."

"Five minutes to green!" warned the crew chief. "Lock it up!" It was a new order occasioned by upgraded lock-in pins that secured the webbed shoulder and waist harnesses in the event of a hard landing.

"Maybe no snow's fallen on the LZ," said Aussie hopefully. "I mean maybe that was just a sick old fox. Couldn't smell worth a damn, even though there was no snow to cover the mine?"

"Too many maybes," said Freeman, but as he glanced down at the vastness of eastern Siberia he couldn't see any snow, only the sheen of the lake. It was enormous. The marines heard a gut-punching thud as the hydraulics began alternately bleeding and gorging with fluid that would fully extend the helo's huge rear ramp door. An enormous Russian sky stretched before them, but it came to an end farther west in what the SES had warned was a "significantly bruised line of L-3s," thunderheads, stretching north to south like malevolent ships of the line. The Stallion, flying at 150 m.p.h. with a tailwind, was soon out of the mountainous and hilly country east of the lake, which they could see was completely frozen. Then they were descending over flatter, lower ground ten miles west of the lake, the land here a mere sixty-five yards above sea level, frozen but still no snow. Aussie could be right, the fox having detonated the mine not because snow had smothered the scent of it but because, quite simply, foxes, like humans, Aussie pointed out, aren't always at the top of their game.

"Fact remains," Freeman told Aussie, "I should have insisted on arctic white coveralls just in case." He signaled the crew chief and asked him to check with the pilot for any sign on radar of snow clouds. The answer was that he couldn't be sure but the line of L-3s was moving east toward them. Freeman turned his attention back to the dots—too slow for fighters, slow enough for helos— and a concomitant mass of smaller dots, as if a mass of iridescent pepper had been shaken on the screen.

"What do you think?" Freeman pressed the pilot. "Helos dropping chaff?" By "chaff" he meant strips of aluminum foil that would confuse enemy radar. In this case it would be impossible for the helos of the approaching MEU to get an accurate idea of the helo force approaching.

"That's my guess, General," the copilot said while feeding the larger dots on the radar screen into the computer's memory to see whether there was a match between the radar signatures of the large dots and the known radar signatures of enemy aircraft types. The monitor's orange-striped matchup bar was flashing the accompanying text: "Hind Mi-24," a kind of attack helo.

"Bandit. Six miles and one o'clock." In the Stallion's cabin the red light was pulsing.

"Three minutes," announced the chief. "Eight miles." And Freeman knew that if the first wave faltered, failing either to keep the defenders inside the H-block's perimeter or destroying the H-block itself, Moscow might summon the troops believed to be based in Kamen Rybolov, nine miles south of the ABC complex, to join the rebels. For a split second, Freeman recalled Patton telling the troops of Third Army that "Americans love a winner and will not tolerate a loser," and Freeman's 2IC, Robert Norton, saying that Russians liked to win just as much as Americans.

"It's not snowing, sir," the chief informed him, "but it looks like one mother of a rainstorm up ahead, another arctic blast coming in over China's Wanda Shan Mountains."

"Good," said Freeman, which surprised Melissa Thomas. "Rain we can use."

"One minute."

"Bandit. Two miles! Evasive action."

The radio seemed to explode in multichannel chaos, the Stallion descending, Cobra gunships and Mi-24s mixing it up. "Watch him, watch him! Lock him up, lock him up! Good kill!"

The general rose, grabbing the PA mike, grumpily brushing the flexi-cord away from his face. Melissa remembered how Kegg had told her, "The old man's a dead ringer for George C. Scott." She didn't know who George C. Scott could be, but the phrase "dead ringer" bothered her, and in the midst of the din all around, she had the strangest premonition, stronger than any she'd ever had, that while Douglas Freeman might win this battle and pass into legend, it would be his last, that though victorious, he would, like Admiral Lord Nelson, die at the moment of his greatest triumph. She immediately told herself it was nothing more than a figment of her imagination, but the stark image of him falling in this, his last battle, gripped her like no other premonition ever had.

"Holy shit!" someone yelled, the big Stallion rising higher and higher, popping flares, orange blossoms in a mad rain; then the Stallion descended once more.

"Marines!" Freeman shouted, to the accompaniment of rain drumming with such intensity against the Stallion that even the general had to shout in his command voice to be heard. "You're marines. Half fish. Remember, weather is not neutral. Use this to your advantage. *Use it!*" The red light was steady, ten seconds till touchdown.

In the cockpit pilot and copilot were sweating profusely. What they'd assumed to be frozen ground or marshland below was obscured by a furious rush of hail that was hitting the Stallion's rotors and fuselage like a mad sower throwing bullets instead of grain.

"Brace!" came the pilot's warning.

A jolt, and the off-center touchdown was of such force that against all intent, weapons flew from the hands of several marines only milliseconds before the huge helo's front wheels took the full weight of men and matériel, the noise of the big rotors in the downpour sounding like an enormous car wash. Freeman, his team, and the forty marines of Bravo Company's First Platoon ran down the ramp, its zebra-painted edges a blur as they deployed into waist-high reeds and a cold rush of unfamiliar odors. From somewhere on their left flank, how far away it was difficult to tell, there came the deafening noise of other rotors scything through the downpour and the sounds of battle already under way. The rain had reduced visibility to zero, the urgent throbbing and roar of Cobra gunships and marine Harriers mixing it up overhead adding to the ceaseless crackling of small-arms fire and the distinctive *swoosh* of air-defense missiles, heard but unseen overhead, all combining with the frantic screeching of thousands upon thousands of birds and other wildlife, creating an ear-ringing cacophony and confusion that was enough to unnerve even the most hardened veteran.

Their Stallion was lifting off for the 170-mile return journey to patch, repair, refuel, and repack for a second wave of 750 marines from Tibbet's battalion, waiting aboard *Yorktown*. All of which meant it would be an hour and a half at the earliest before any reinforcements might arrive for the men deplaning and unslinging the Hummers, mortars, and other weapons that were vital to any offensive against the ABC complex.

A tremendous, ear-punching boom was followed by a huge, roiling orange-black ball of flame rising several hundred feet above them through the rain. Two Cobra gunships had collided. Their burning debris fell slowly through the downpour, momentarily illuminating a small wood on their left flank. To his dismay, Freeman saw snowy ground and ice-encrusted marsh ahead, a mass of ice-sheathed reeds looming and fleetingly turning orange in the fire's light, the reeds, some instantly dried by the heat, rattling furiously in the explosion's aftermath.

Beyond the marsh they could see the gray of rain and nothing more, no H-block or any other structure. The most they could hope for in that moment was that the marines of Bravo Company's second and third platoons and the assault force's four Stallion-ferried anti-tank Hummers and six light fast-attack vehicles had been put down close by. A quick GPS check by platoon leader Lieutenant Terry Chester confirmed that the Super Stallion had delivered his marines and the general's SpecOps team to within a quarter mile of the LZ's center, a prodigious feat of flying, given the atrocious weather.

"Down!" shouted Freeman upon hearing the peculiarly rushing, shuffling noise of incoming, the Russian 122 mm round exploding in the woods in a yellow crash and sending white-hot fragments singing and ripping into a small stand of trees, shrapnel whizzing into and out of the wood.

"I'm hit!" cried a marine.

"Corpsman!" shouted the platoon sergeant, but the marine medic was already there. The young marine who'd been struck in the head by wood splinters was bleeding profusely. Stunned, he sat up and looked at his M-16 with a puzzled expression. The corpsman shouted at him to keep his hands away from his face. Thick smoke almost completely obliterated the marsh directly ahead, only about sixty yards away. It looked as if swamp gas was rising until its whiteness suggested a smoke-making round had landed there.

"Keep your eyes open," Freeman ordered unnecessarily, as everyone was straining to see, anxious to link up with fellow marines from Bravo Company on either flank, and simultaneously fearing the danger of blue on blue, what correspondents, such as Marte Price and her ilk, would call friendly fire.

"BTR, two o'clock!" yelled Aussie Lewis, crouching down by the wood, pointing at the vehicle's presence no more than a hundred yards away. One of the most brutish of the Soviet-designed troop transports, the Bronetransporter was a huge, eight-wheeled armored personnel carrier, its two armor-lidded front eye slits, boatlike hull, sloping sides, and tortoiseshell-like top giving it the appearance of some lumbering, metallic reptile from another age. That, however, as Lieutenant Chester knew, was an illusion.

"Freeze!" he ordered. "Javelin only."

The BTR, a type 60, Freeman thought, by the looks of it, would probably be carrying twelve troops inside, each soldier most likely armed with the new AKS-74U, a weapon that Freeman had chosen for himself. A shorter-barreled, folding-stock version of the AK-47, it was designed for easier use in the confined space that was the rear troop section. This meant the twelve Russian troops' weapon would have a shorter range than most of the weaponry the marines carried. But he also knew the AK-74 had more whack per cartridge than most regular submachine guns.

By now, Freeman, like Chester, was wondering whether the Russians had spotted the platoon, both the general and Chester, in unconscious unison, training their binoculars on the enemy war wagon, Freeman quickly tapping the digital focus button for as sharp an image as possible through the curtain of rain. The BTR's turret, with its heavy 14.5 mm and lighter coaxial 7.62 mm machine guns, was slewing left to right like a trap shooter unsure of which sector he should be watching.

"Amateurs," Aussie told Freeman. "They don't know where the hell they're going. In panic mode—maybe here, maybe there."

"Kegg?" called out Lieutenant Chester.

From long battle experience, Freeman's vision, unlike that of Kegg and most of the marines, wasn't held captive by the BTR. Instead he was scanning through a full 360 while taking care not to show himself above the reeds at the edge of the marsh that fringed this western sector of the vast lake. Mines were much less likely to be buried here because of the glutinous mud. He glimpsed a marine. It was Kegg, moving smartly forward with the Javelin anti-tank unit. But Freeman was more interested in looking beyond at the rising clouds of steamy vapor of the kind that he'd seen rising from the hot pools of New Zealand and Yellowstone. He could smell animal excrement, which struck him as odd, given that the ground was frozen. Perhaps he had stepped in a fresh pile of it.

Adjusting his throat mike and popping the digital earpiece from the matchbox-sized collar unit into his ear, the general made contact with Lieutenant Chester. Chester's voice sounded scratchy, the platoon commander having just inhaled a pungent odor.

"Captain, something weird going on here. That vapor up ahead. You see any hot springs on the chart pre-op?"

"No, sir. Could be swamp gas."

"Could be," acknowledged Freeman, "but I've got a gut feeling we ought to stay put."

Chester agreed, if for no other reason than he, like Colonel Tibbet and the others now under Freeman, knew that much of the general's legendary reputation rested upon one simple fact: He was a meticulous observer. It was something first noted by Bob Norton, his old 2IC in Third Army. Norton, in a lecture at the Army Staff College, pointed out that most women could tell you the eye color of their close friends and acquaintances. Most men could not. Freeman could. There was something about the vapor he'd seen that bothered him. There was an eruption of marines' small-arms fire off to their left, maybe 150 yards, at what was probably the first Russian they had seen in the marshes so far. The BTR's turret immediately slewed in the direction of the firing, the BTR itself growling, exuding a coal black plume of diesel exhaust into the rain.

"C'mon, Kegg," Aussie hissed. "Fire the fucking thing!"

The marine was using a tree at the edge of the woods to steady the weapon. It had been only twenty, thirty seconds at the most since Lieutenant Chester had summoned Kegg, but the BTR was picking up speed across the frozen marsh where shoulder-high stalks of ice-sheathed grass were starting to bend as the rain deiced them.

Suddenly the Russian behemoth foundered, its slanting chin breaking through the plate-thick ice. It was only a momentary pause, however, and the amphibian, its exhaust and bilge jet spouting up high at the rear, continued crashing forward in the marsh, deep enough now that the BTR was afloat, looking to Kegg like a mechanical hippopotamus moving inexorably toward the marines.

Young Kegg, having snapped the Javelin's launch unit to the disposable launch tube and steadying the fire-and-forget fifty-pound weapon assembly against an aged Mongolian oak tree, looked through the four-power scope, centered the hulking BTR in the green and black of his infrared world, and fired. The kick motor flared, with minimal backblast for Kegg, then the one-two punch of the missile hit the BTR, the Javelin's initial charge blasting down through the topmost layers of the BTR's roof, the second, shaped charge piercing the armor proper. The BTR was now a crematorium. The vehicle stopped, its wake of dark, chocolate-colored diesel and exhaust-blown reeds pushing forward over it like a flood. Freeman saw the rear door open and heard the feral screams of rage and terror as two, perhaps three, Russian soldiers—it was difficult to tell how many in the fiery swirl of bodies and debris—came splashing out. One man was afire, trying futilely to swim toward the splintered and icy edge of the marsh, when the BTR's munitions blew, making it look as if a cyclonic fire had hit.

Melissa Thomas felt her heart pounding in her chest, half in fear, half in—God help her!—empathy for the enemy as marine rifle fire ended the swimmer's misery.

"Hold fire!" It was Freeman bellowing above the other nearby sounds of battle. "Follow me!" The general, breaking cover, Eddie Mervyn at his side, was running hard toward the lake but skirting its icy perimeter as Sal, Choir, Aussie, Johnny Lee, and the forty-man platoon followed.

"Good shooting, marine!" Chester told Kegg, and, seeing how shaken the boy was by what he'd done, knowing that there were eight, possibly nine, men cooked alive inside the BTR, added, "DARPA ALPHA, Kegg! *Good shooting, marine!*"

Kegg had difficulty hearing the lieutenant because of the noise off on their left flank where, he guessed, Colonel Tibbet's HQ section must be engaging the Russians. And what the hell, wondered Kegg, was the general up to, running pell-mell, leading the first two squads of Chester's four-squad platoon?

Kegg started in fright as Freeman's team, closer to the lake with Chester's first two squads, opened up on a five-ton Russian truck that came roaring through the steamy vapor, packed with helmeted troops and heading straight for the drowning BTR. An officer on the running board was shouting and waving his AK-47 at Freeman's team and the lead marines. But neither the officer nor his troops in the back of the truck had seen Chester's other two squads now emerging from the tall grass by the wood, the truck coming under such an enfilade of fire from these marines' M-16s, SAWs, and H & K submachine guns and Chester's burst of six rounds in half a second, that it had no hope. Out of control, the vehicle started sliding at speed toward Freeman and his team, striking a hard clump of stunted and wind-knotted reeds by the lake's edge with such force that it flipped and rolled. Bloodied bodies were strewn across the ice, weapons, mostly AK-47s, slithering, some of them sliding so far that they disappeared into the rain-freckled water of the marsh where the BTR was sinking, the tip of its whip aerial just visible, which told the ever-observant Freeman that the lake here was about ten feet deep.

Several of the Russians, still able to function, scrambled frantically on the ice, trying to retrieve their weapons, but Freeman's team and Chester's first squad of ten marines gave ABC's troops little chance of recovery. Only one man from the truck survived the marines' storm of depleted uranium. The ice seemed to come alive as frozen chips, some red with blood, flew into the air.

Then, suddenly, a head popped to the surface, followed by a pair of thrashing arms; a BTR crewman had survived. Though gasping frantically for air and dog-paddling furiously, the Russian plunged his right hand back into the water and came up firing his 9 mm pistol at Aussie, who dealt with the interruption with a burst from his H & K. "Silly prick!"

"Look after these two," ordered Freeman, indicating a forlorn and soaking-wet duo. One of them, rescued by

Freeman, who had extended his unloaded AK-74 to the floundering man, was the only survivor of the BTR, the other, though slightly wounded, was the only trooper from the truck who had not been killed in the short but furious exchange. While Aussie, whose right calf had been nicked by one of the truck-borne soldiers, was having it attended to by the corpsman, it took Johnny Lee, the team's interpreter, only five minutes, with the help of a grim-looking Eddie Mervyn, to conclude that neither of the two prisoners knew anything about the H-complex other than that they had been summoned for perimeter defense as part of some reciprocal arrangement between ABC's H-block commanders.

What worried Freeman was that most of the dead soldiers were wearing blue-striped T-shirts beneath their sandy green battle jackets. Naval infantry. Together with Spetsnaz, SpecOps, and airborne infantry, these naval troops were the best the Russians had, and Freeman knew that despite the massive drawdown of military assets following Putin's ascendancy to Boris Yeltsin's throne amid the ruble's nosedive, the naval infantry remained an elite fighting force.

"He keeps saying," said Johnny Lee, pointing to one of the two prisoners, a thin, wiry type who had a bad burn on his left arm and was cradling it with his right, "that he and his comrade are POWs, says they're—" Lee had to shout against the rattle of small-arms fire and the ear-ringing explosions of nearby battle. "—entitled to protection under the Geneva Convention."

"Geneva *what*?" opined Aussie, smarting under the corpsman's alcohol swab. "Tell 'im I haven't seen that film."

"No joking, Aussie," Lee replied. "He's claiming they're regular troops called to secure the ABC perimeter, and as such—"

"And as such," cut in Aussie, "they're aiding and abetting fucking terrorists. If they're regular troops, they shouldn't fucking be here. Even Moscow's declared ABC persona non grata. Right, General?"

"Correct," said Freeman, adding quietly to Aussie, "at least for twenty-four hours." The general then turned to Lee. "If I thought they knew anything more than the route out from ABC, Johnny, I'd shoot 'em if they didn't cooperate."

Chester, having managed to make radio contact with Tibbet's HQ group so that close-in hand signals in the near-zero visibility were no longer needed, ordered nine of his ten four-man teams to spread out.

"Captain," Freeman called to Chester, "I'd like my team to concentrate on finding entry. Those truck tracks should be visible for a while. I'll call you the moment we get in."

"You betcha," acknowledged the marine lieutenant. "Stay well."

"I'll try," said Freeman, turning over the two prisoners to Chester. Then he addressed his six team members. "Okay, guys. Everyone marine ID'd?"

They were, with small, infrared diamond shapes on the fronts and backs of their helmets and camouflage battle jackets.

It began snowing. "Aw, shit!" announced Sal. "That's all we need."

The four marines of the tenth fire team, ordered by Chester to stay behind to provide a perimeter defense for the arrival of the second wave of Stallions, if they'd *come* in zero visibility, plastic-stripped the two Russians. A corpsman, having given the burn victim a shot of morphine, assisted the team's sniper in unlacing the Russians' boots. And with a hastily invented sign language, they told the two POWs they'd be shot if they tried to run. The two navy infantry comrades nodded their heads vigorously. They understood.

"D'you think," began one of the marines in a voice barely audible amid the increasingly confused sounds of the battle farther in, "the general was kidding about shooting these guys if he thought they knew more—you know, just shoot them?"

"Geneva Convention!" interjected the burn victim anxiously.

"Hey, you know English."

"Little bit."

"Yeah, well you know what shut the fuck up means?"

"Da!"

"The Geneva Convention," said the sniper authoritatively, "does not apply to masked terrorists and those who aid and abet terrorists in any way." The other three marines were impressed, more by their buddy's matter-of-fact delivery than by the answer. After all, they knew how marines had viewed terrorists and fellow travelers in Iraq.

As Freeman led his team along the edge of the lake's frozen western marsh, he could feel the pressure of the twenty-four-hour deadline mounting. Could the first wave hold long enough for the second wave, which would have to fly in on instruments alone, to land in the increasing foul weather? And could he find traces of the truck's tires on the frozen ground before the snow hid them, showing him and his team the way back to ABC through the minefield that surrounded the H-block? And he of U-turn fame had brought in the first wave *sans* white coveralls. He had rolled dice with the meteorological officer's report and lost. But his team was moving in the harmony that comes only with practice, with knowing how each man operates, with being able to recognize one another, even in the dark, by footfall alone. Everything was starting to look white, the rattle of machine guns sounding farther west now, away from the edge of the lake itself but still in the marshy area. The team could hear shouts, in English and in another language that Johnny Lee told Freeman was neither Russian nor Chinese. So far as Freeman knew, his team had been landed in the right grid, but he'd sensed from his short radio communications with Tibbet that while the colonel had been careful not to give coordinates, he had indicated, via slang, that his HQ platoon was on Freeman's left, as it should be, but more than half a mile farther west, while Chester's fire teams were spread out a hundred yards to Freeman's right. Murphy, he of Murphy's Law, was always waiting in the wings, as Freeman and his team had found out at Priest Lake, but despite everyone not landing precisely where he should, it sounded as if the first wave was at least moving in the direction of the terrorists' H-block.

Passing through waist-high reeds, checking his wrist GPS, the general estimated that the outer limit of the half-mile-deep minefield that surrounded the ABC complex and from which Terry Chester had surmised swamp gas was rising was no more than fifty feet away to the right of Bravo Company's line of advance. Douglas Freeman sniffed the snowy air, whiffs of cordite coming downwind in what was now a heavy, swirling snowfall. The general held up his hand and everyone stopped as he knelt in the cold, still marsh grass that was now shoulder high and completely hid him and the team from view, and saw tire tracks impressed in the frozen earth not yet completely covered by the snow because of a tree bough. He glanced back and saw Eddie Mervyn and Gomez only a few paces behind him, Sal, Choir, Johnny Lee, and Aussie farther back with the marines. Something which he couldn't articulate at that moment cautioned him not to raise his voice, for while the snow-muffled thumps of the

Russian mortars sounded about a mile off, the general's experience of winter battles told him that the Russians were only half that distance away.

Then he realized why his sense of smell was giving his brain a flashing red signal: marsh gas stank. The marines who'd done their training in the intertidal swamps around Parris Island would know that too. Rotting vegetation gave off the rotten-egg smell of hydrogen sulfide. There was no off-putting odor to this vapor. Maybe he'd been right all along and it was a hot spring. He gestured for Eddie and Gomez to come closer, and spoke softly. "See that vapor rising? About fifteen yards off by that clump of woods?" Both had seen it, assuming, as Lieutenant Chester had, that it was swamp gas. "It's got no smell," Freeman told them. "Watch the ground directly in front of you as well as our flanks." Both men acknowledged his advice, knowing how easy it was not to do this when one was walking. Freeman, in the same low tone in which he'd instructed Gomez and Eddie to come with him, pointed to yet another wood on their left flank and instructed Aussie and the marines, "I want you to head over to *that* wood on our left flank." The area he indicated was on high ground. It was about two acres in size, with brush and trees that would afford them good cover.

Aussie gave him a thumbs-up farther back at the head of the column, while Freeman, drawing his AK-74 bayonet, with Eddie Mervyn covering him with his shotgun and Gomez as Tail End Charlie for the three of them, approached the area where the vapor was coming from and which his GPS told him must be just a foot or two beyond the outer limit of the mined perimeter, while Aussie, Choir, Johnny Lee, and Sal, the two POWs, and Chester's marines moved to the wood Freeman had indicated. The reeds were shoulder high, but as they walked farther and passed a small copse of wizened Mongolian oak, the ground underfoot was becoming higher, and quickly the reeds became shorter, so that in another fifteen feet they passed from shoulder- to knee-high reeds.

Suddenly something enormous burst out of the reeds. Eddie Mervyn was so startled he stepped back and fell, detonating a mine. The explosion ripped into his buttocks and groin, the mine's detonation further terrifying any wildlife in the reeds, like the huge bird that had broken cover.

"Don't move!" Freeman shouted at Gomez. Even as he was getting up, snow and earth were still raining down on him. Eddie was hemorrhaging severely, and the second wave's relief choppers were at least one and a half hours away, if they made it. Freeman could have called in a high-priority Mayday, but that would have imperiled the entire team. He knew, as did Eddie, that in this situation the best that could be done was first aid and pumping him full of morphine so that, though he was already in violent spasm, the pain would be diminished.

Gomez, shaken despite all his SpecWar training, fumbled at first, almost dropping his helmet, before he managed to pull out his Ringer packet of four-inch, foam-gel-impregnated gauze pads. Freeman grabbed the packet, ripped open the waterproof seal, and used the six pads as one compress on the gaping wound between Eddie's legs, the gauze becoming one with the wound and, under the pressure of Freeman's hand, stanching the hemorrhaging, as Gomez, recovering his wits, injected Eddie with 10 cc of morphine for the pain.

"It's all right, Eddie," Gomez told him. "We're getting you medevaced. You'll be out of here in—"

"Lying son of a—oh, God, God, help me!"

Aussie was getting Johnny Lee, Choir, Sal, and the marines ready for a rescue squad, but knew that Freeman wouldn't request it, as it would put more lives at risk in a possible minefield. All Aussie could do for the present was to form a C-section defense on the perimeter of the wood, should the Russians send out anyone to investigate. "Bastards aren't gonna find a fucking fox next time they come nosin' around here!"

No one but Choir, who'd been sitting next to Aussie in the helo and heard Freeman and the helo's crew chief talking about the fox, knew what he meant. Choir flicked his H & K's safety to off as the general and Gomez carried Eddie back to the shelter of the copse of Mongolian oak.

As if the enemy had heard Aussie's comment, the team and marines heard the guttural roar of a big diesel. This time it wasn't a BTR or truck that showed up but a BMD, a fighting infantry vehicle. Another amphibian, but this one a post-Putin top-of-the-line, air-transportable BMD-3. For a tracked monster, it was moving fast, at forty miles per hour, its metal treads throwing up a high wake of powder snow as it skirted the ice along the edge of the lake before slowing and then entering the marsh reeds. Then it stopped a hundred yards from where the mine had exploded and began to hose the reeds across a fifty-yard front with its 30 mm anti-aircraft cannon and its coaxial 7.62 mm machine gun. In the copse of oak, where Freeman and Gomez lay protecting either side of Eddie, Gomez checked Eddie's vital signs. They were all bad. Amid the wood-chopping racket of the BMD strafing the reeds and firing in the general direction of the wood where Aussie and the marines were hunkered down, Eddie's voice faded to a weak rasp and he uttered a desperate plea for his mother.

Freeman turned sharply to Eddie. "Leave your mother out of this and stop whining. You'll be fine. A new flexidick and you'll be pushing pussy in no time. That son of yours, the four-year-old, what's his name? Foster?"

"Yeah," Eddie managed to groan.

"Well, hang on to that. You're gonna go bowling with him." He took off his Fritz and handed it to Gomez. "Another gel pack. Quickly."

"What's your girl's name, Eddie?" Freeman asked, even though he knew it.

"I—what—Melanie. I need medevac."

"Don't we all!" joshed Freeman. "You'll be fine. Just keep thinking about bowling with young Foster. We'll get you out on the second wave."

Eddie was rolling from side to side in pain.

"Stay still, Eddie."

"They're gone!" he moaned. "My balls've been—"

"They're fine," Freeman lied. "Just a bit mussed up."

"Oh God," Eddie moaned. "Give me a shot of morphine for crying out—"

"We just did."

Freeman glimpsed a straight white vapor trail that streaked from the wood through the falling snow, saw the BMD buck and its right track unravel off its steel wheels. The explosion of the BMD's magazine was so violent that it sent a searing wind through the trees, whipping up dead branches and flinging them against the denuded trunks and the log behind which Freeman, Gomez, and Eddie Mervyn had sought shelter.

"Payback One to Payback Two," Freeman whispered hoarsely. "You receive?"

"Loud but sliced," came Aussie's reply, which meant that Freeman's transmission was segmented.

"Are you receiving?" asked the general, his speech more deliberate.

"Loud and clear now."

"Eddie's gonna make it," Freeman said, more for Eddie's morale than from conviction. Gomez and the general had stopped the bleeding, but Eddie's chances were fifty-fifty unless they could get some lactate into him and stabilize. For that they needed saline. The general quickly considered the options. He and Gomez could carry Eddie to Choir, who had the saline, or Choir could bring it to them. Freeman decided while it might seem more logical for Choir to come to Mervyn, that Choir, Aussie, Lee, and the others in the wood were in a more sheltered and thus safer area in which to *treat* Eddie than by the log. Besides, if Choir were to be shot down trying to reach them, then Freeman's SpecFor team would be without saline. Still, as he helped heave Eddie onto Gomez's back, he knew it was a gamble. ABC, with its apparently unlimited resources, was no doubt listening in to field communications, and despite the best efforts of *McCain*'s SES to jam the Russians, it would take less than a minute for any state-of-the-art Russian computer radio-frequency scanner to zero in on the American sources of transmission.

"Let's go!" Freeman told Gomez, who was still shaken by the horror of Eddie's wound. Eddie had confessed his fear of just such a wound, the one most feared by men, during the days when he was Gomez's swim buddy at SEAL school in Coronado.

A surge of small-arms firing, at least platoon-sized, could be heard erupting farther west of the lake where the bulk of Tibbet's marines had landed, closer to the Zapadnyy Siniy Mountains than planned. While Freeman and Tibbet's HQ group were also west of the lake, they were closest to it and to the H-block, which no one had yet reported seeing in the foul weather. Indeed, the one thing Freeman, Terry Chester, Colonel Tibbet, and their men were certain of was that there was no certainty about the disposition of units in this first wave of more than six hundred troops, and no clear picture of the emerging battlefield. It was impossible to discern meaningful patterns from the mélange of radio traffic that included orders, some frantic, from both the Russians and the Americans, whose transmissions were often jumbled in the frequency-jumping of both sides. It was always the same—not knowing where everybody was and the concomitant worry about the possibility of blue on blue.

This time when Freeman, with Gomez carrying Eddie, retraced their earlier path through the reeds, following their now barely discernible footprints in the falling snow, the general made sure that neither he nor Gomez wandered off the path lest they too detonate a rogue mine.

The vapor the general had been on his way to investigate was still rising from a multitude of tennis-ball-sized bubbles breaking open through the cracked ice that had fissured at the base of the reeds on the high ground where he, Eddie Mervyn, and Gomez had been walking when an enormous gray bird had shattered the ice-polished reeds, flying up into the swirling whiteness of vapor and snow that hung over the marshland. Perhaps, thought Freeman, the Komissarov River, fed by runoff from the Zapadnyy Siniy Mountains, was a conduit of hot spring water pouring into the lake. But there was still no smell emitted by the vapor, which here and there created ballpark-sized areas of dense fog next to areas where there was no vapor rising and where visibility improved up to twenty feet.

It was Gomez who first heard the freight-train shuffles of approaching artillery—122 mms, Freeman guessed—and while the rest of the team immediately fell flat to the ground, the circular rubberized nose cone of the Predator tube that Aussie had slung on his back swung around hard, hitting him in the nose and starting a bleed. While all the marines in the area also hit the dirt, Freeman told Gomez not to move. To remain standing was counterintuitive, but it was better than moving off the path through the reeds and risking detonating a mine.

The two screaming shells fell short with a tremendous

"whoomp!" their explosions sending huge shards of ice whooshing through the air. One of the surfboard-sized splinters slammed into a copse of pines and disintegrated into smaller pieces that tumbled down like broken glass around Freeman, Gomez, and Eddie. It told Freeman two things: one, that the Russian terrorists were definitely scanning, and, two, that they'd reacted far more quickly than he'd anticipated on the basis of hearing a simple transmit, sending out their state-of-the-art BMD-3 to investigate the tripping of the anti-personnel mine. Were their inner defenses so much weaker inside the perimeter, Freeman wondered, that they worried about one measly anti-personnel mine going off? There had to be another reason, the general concluded, for the panicky response of trying to kill a few soldiers with artillery.

"You all right?" Freeman asked Gomez who, despite being in A-1 physical condition, was straining under the weight of his comatose friend.

"Yeah," answered Gomez. "It'll be better once we get moving."

As Freeman took point, his right hand, from force of habit, reached for his radio mike, then he checked himself. The best he could hope for was that Aussie, Sal, Choir, and Johnny Lee would see him and Gomez, carrying Eddie, making their way over the two hundred yards to the protection of the wood. As fast as caution allowed, Freeman, followed by Gomez, began to move out through the tall reeds, hearing gunfire closing in from the west, with more artillery rounds screaming in, exploding in and around the position they'd just vacated. Freeman's ability to retrace their steps out of the reeds with surprising speed, given the bad weather, was due to the general's photographic memory. His skill in noting and remembering minute details along the way was less innate than learned in battles all over the world, from featureless deserts, where windstorms could obliterate telltale tracks, to Arctic storms, where falling snow threatened to do the same. And Gomez's ability to keep up a good pace, despite having to bear his wounded comrade on his back, was mute testimony to the extraordinary level of physical fitness Freeman's SpecWar warriors habitually maintained.

As Freeman and Gomez broke out of the tall marsh reeds below the vapor-covered mound that was the local high ground, they could hear more incoming. The eerie shuffling sound was much closer now, becoming a scream, the rounds' explosions shaking the ground beneath them, geysers of earth, dirty snow, and reeds shooting high into the frigid air then raining down on the mound twenty yards behind them where there were more eruptions as anti-personnel mines were detonated by the concussion.

In his determination to reach the protection of the wood and the two Russian prisoners, the general, always cognizant of a potential blue on blue in the confusion of combat, especially here in fog and snow, raised his AK-74, the "stay-where-you-are" signal, in the direction of the wood where he hoped Aussie, Sal, Choir, and Johnny Lee were still waiting for him to arrive.

Suddenly Gomez stopped. "Hold up, General." Then, "You hear that?"

"Yes," acknowledged Freeman. "There must be hundreds of them over there."

Gomez, tiring quickly now, realized that the general had mistaken his question. Freeman was talking about the scores of birds gathered in another section of the vaporous marsh. "No," said Gomez, Eddie's weight getting to him now. "I mean the Hummer." It had stopped at the wood now only thirty yards away. The Hummer was topped with two four-tube canisters of TOW anti-tank missiles.

"Where the fuck were they earlier when we needed

them?" Aussie challenged. Still, he was glad to see the vehicle. Everybody was glad to see it.

A marine corporal had stepped out of the Hummer, followed by two other marines dressed in "snow whites," one of whom was Kegg.

"Where'd you get those?" Freeman asked.

"Dead Russians," one of them said, grinning, until he saw how badly Eddie was injured. Quickly, Kegg helped Gomez, the general asking for saline from the Hummer's kit.

"Good man," said Freeman, as Kegg's marine buddy handed him the pack. Choir also brought a saline pouch. Freeman now turned to the four marines in the fire team nearest the wood's perimeter. "Where are the two pricks?"

"The prisoners?" said a marine. "We tied 'em up over there behind that brush, General."

A marine corporal glanced uneasily at the other three marines in his fire squad as the general strode toward the two Russians. They were sitting forlornly in the wood under cover of a huge, snow-laden fir, its branches gnarled and deformed over the years from the bitter, grit-laden westerlies that came sweeping down from the Wanda Shan in China and on through the nearby foothills of Zapadnyy Siniy before howling, bansheelike, across the thirty-five-mile-wide expanse of the lake, on whose closer shore ABC had built its Stalinesque H-block, which at the moment lay hidden by the blizzard that had made a mockery of *McCain*'s optimistic weather forecast.

"I'm tired of this damn weather," Freeman opined formally to no one in particular, but his tone alerted his teammates that the general, in the manner of George Patton, was about to voice a direct request to the Almighty to intercede on behalf of Operation Bird Rescue. Before this, however, Freeman gave instructions for Gomez and a marine corpsman to do what was possible as soon as possible for Eddie Mervyn who, despite having received an infusion of saline, seemed to have slipped further into coma. Freeman prayed they could keep Eddie alive long enough for the SpecWar warrior to be medevaced out by one of the choppers in the second wave.

Both Russian captives were visibly alarmed when the American general, whom Abramov, Beria, and Cherkashin had described as a madman, suddenly took off his helmet and, holding it under his left arm, his AK-74 cradled in the other, bowed his head. The Russian duo were clearly alarmed by the general's body language. Was it the prelude to executing prisoners?

While the four marines, including the corpsman who was helping Gomez with Eddie, exchanged uneasy glances, the general's SpecWar team, with an ease obviously born of practice, formed a protective square around their general who, amid the sounds of intermittent gunfire far and near, began his prayer, his hair turning white with the snow that showed no sign of abating.

"Almighty God, we beseech Thee in this battle to afford us better weather so that we might vanquish our terrorist foes and destroy their evil here and forevermore. Amen."

With this, Freeman put his helmet back on and turned to Salvini. "Sal, cut 'em loose."

As Sal drew his SAS knife, the younger of the two ABC Russians, a lean, short man in his early thirties who didn't speak English, stiffened in fright, looking imploringly at his comrade, who did know some English, for an explanation of what was happening. Had the mad American's prayer been for his prisoners? A last rite before he executed them?

"General!"

It was Gomez in shock, his face crumbling, his shoulders

shaking in a futile effort to dam his emotions, so that the moment he'd called the general, every man present knew that Eddie Mervyn was dead. Freeman's eyes were turned intently upon the two prisoners, not wildly ablaze with anger but with an unblinking cold rage. It was the kind of rage they'd seen in the eyes of Comrade General Abramov, the commander of the tank and armored company, when Abramov had been told that one of their terrorist clients had tried a double cross on a big payment for a railcar full of Igla shoulder-fired MANPADs shipped from the nearby railhead at Kamen Rybolov and across the wooden bridges of the marshes to the south. There was no pity in the comrade general's eyes. Instinctively, the two Russians, still sitting on the ground, moved their backs against the trunk of the big fir tree, as if it might give them some protection from what the American might do. They watched nervously as the Americans' general got down on one knee, looking at the dead American who had been his comrade in arms. As inconspicuously as possible, the two prisoners looked at the marines and the rest of Freeman's team for any expression or body language that might convey what the prevailing mood might be amongst them, whether the grief would turn to anger, both prisoners knowing what *they* would do had the situation been reversed. The edict from Abramov, Beria, and Cherkashin had been unequivocal: All of the American "gangsters" were to be summarily executed. And the edict wasn't confined to the Americans, as demonstrated by ABC's ruthless "cleansing" of those "elements" in the civilian population around the lake who had had the temerity to protest ABC's takeover. Dozens of corpses had been dumped in the vast, surrounding marshlands.

As Freeman, handing his AK-74 to a marine, looked down at Eddie Mervyn's boyish face, he was also seeing the faces of the dead, the murdered at DARPA ALPHA, and the smoking funeral pyre of the thousands at Ground Zero. Taking off his gloves, he closed Eddie's eyes, but the eyelid muscle retracted the lids, and Aussie Lewis handed Freeman two small stones that did the job, Freeman having been as insistent as any DI on Parris Island that his men not carry any change into combat.

Freeman rose quickly from the snowy ground of the wood and then, with an abruptness that belied the gentleness he'd shown kneeling by Eddie, he asked Aussie Lewis whether the wood's perimeter had been secured.

"Yes, sir."

"Where are the bastards now?"

"Don't know for sure, General, but most of the noise is coming from the north of us, about two miles away. I'd say they're giving Tibbet hell."

The general didn't respond, but turned abruptly toward the prisoners, and Aussie Lewis saw in his eyes the metamorphosis from soldier to avenger of all those Americans murdered since 9/11. "Which one of you speaks English? *A little!*" This phrase was said with such menace that the Russian who spoke English was reluctant to admit to the fact, but he remembered that it was one of this man's soldiers whom he had told, "I speak a little." He raised his hand so tentatively, "I do, sir," that he might have been a schoolboy terrified of his teacher.

"Now you listen to me, you son of a bitch!" The general was taking his sidearm from its holster. "You understand 'son of a bitch'?" he asked the Russian.

The prisoner nodded, the cold fury in this American's face so obvious that the Russian's throat constricted, rendering him temporarily unable to speak, and he could feel his skin now itching like crazy.

"Sir," interrupted the marine.

"What?"

"Sir, I think I hear armor 'bout a quarter of a mile away to the west."

This only added to the general's sense of urgency. He was still glaring at the hapless Russian. "Do you understand—"

More freight-train-like rushes came shuffling through the pristine air, the rounds exploding with a roar which, though muffled by the snow, nevertheless was still deafening, and left the general's ears ringing.

"Stand up!" Freeman ordered them. "You know why I asked you to stand?"

The smaller of the two whey-faced prisoners looked imploringly at his English-speaking partner. What was going on?

"You want us to stand," said the English speaker. "We stand."

"You're standing," Freeman told them, "because I do not shoot men when they are sitting. You understand that, you terrorist turd?"

It was clear to Chester that while the Russian didn't cotton on to every word, he understood readily enough and was terrified.

"Now, you told us you came from the H-block, from the building, but you know nothing *about* the building. Correct?"

The Russian nodded, his Adam's apple bobbing nervously. "Correct, Admiral."

Chester bit his lip to stop himself from smiling. He could see that the Russian was far too terrified to even try making a joke.

"I am a general," Freeman told them unsmilingly. "And you have murdered thousands of innocent men, women, and children."

The English-speaking Russian found voice to tell his comrade what had transpired.

"Nyet, nyet!" the Russian speaker was repeating.

"Da!" retorted Freeman, with such resounding authority both men fell silent. He fixed his stare on the English speaker. "Your name?"

"My name?"

"Yes, goddammit. Your *name*!"

"Ilya. My comrade's name is Boris."

"Ilya, you and your comrade know more about ABC's setup than you've told us."

Ilya was shaking his head as vigorously as Boris had. "We have not been inside much. I swear on mother's grave."

It was never good practice to talk too much to prisoners, Freeman knew. Their names and conversation lent humanity to their otherwise sullen or scared faces. But Freeman, as Colonel Tibbet had told his marines, kept in mind the sight of the seemingly endless funeral processions after the terrorist attacks on America since 9/11, and the bravery of the victims, the people on Flight 93 and the scientist at DARPA ALPHA with "RAM" and "SCARUND" written on the note in his hand.

"You steal our plans," said Freeman, slowly and deliberately, ignoring the cacophony of battle just a mile south and west of him down by the rail line, "then sell them to other terrorists who kill our children. *You* help them. *You* are as guilty as they are. You're *not* prisoners of war, you're opportunists, outlawed by your own people in Moscow. You're co-murderers. Terrorists!"

The Russian prisoners didn't understand "co," but "murderers" and "terrorists" they did understand, and now looked grim in addition to being scared. They didn't whimper. They were, after all, opportunists who had been trained as soldiers. Outlawed by their country as terrorists, regular soldiers turned bad, and they'd been told by Abramov, Beria, and Cherkashin to expect no mercy from Moscow or the "American intervention-ists" if they were caught. They had crossed the line, be-coming fantastically wealthy by Russian standards, their MANPAD bonuses alone catapulting their lifestyle into another world, way above that of the average Russian.

"Koreans," burst out Ilya. "We are not only people in-volved. Koreans are helping."

Freeman was nonplussed. He could hear more incom-ing. What was this Ilya telling him about Koreans? "Tell me more," Freeman urged.

The other Russian, Boris, couldn't conceal his surprise at Ilya having mentioned the Koreans, who Freeman quickly surmised must be either one of ABC's best customers—or joint manufacturers?

"Tell me more," Freeman pressed.

"Nyet!" cautioned Boris, and Freeman shot him dead, Ilya jumping sideways in fright.

"Holy shit!" It was the Hummer corporal.

"Be quiet!" ordered Freeman, and turned the gun on Ilya. "Tell me about the Koreans. *Quickly!*"

Ilya's hands shot up in mute surrender, the body of his dead comrade spread-eagled in the scant snowfall that had penetrated the thick branches of the fir tree like clumps of icing sugar on the dead man's chest, his eyes wide open, his expression grotesque, as if his dentist had just asked him to open wide.

Ilya was trembling. "Believe me, Admiral, I have not much been in ABC. It is not a lie."

"What about the Koreans, dammit?!"

"They are—" He couldn't think of the word.

"General." It had taken a lot of guts for the marine cor-poral to speak after being expressly told by Freeman not to, but the sound of the armor was getting closer.

"What?"

"Tank, sir. Getting closer. Can't see 'em yet in the fog, but—"

"Then go find them and take them out. Do your job, man."

"Yessir." The corporal's right hand circled in a "rev up" motion and the other two marines, who'd given the white overalls they'd taken from the dead Russians to two of the four fire team marines, jumped back into the Hummer, Chester telling Melissa Thomas to join them. The corporal called back to the fire team. "There'll probably be infantry behind this fucker when we see it, so you boys be ready to give us an assist when we nose out of these trees to fire."

"You've got it, Corp."

Ilya was perspiring, babbling something, but neither Freeman nor Johnny Lee could understand him, the Russian in such a state of emotional turmoil that words wouldn't come to him, and so he made as if he was shoveling.

"That better not be bullshit," the general snapped without a trace of humor, never more serious in his life. "What do you mean? Trenches?"

Ilya was in a frantic charade, and he, like Freeman, had never been more serious in his life.

"Don't try to think of the word," Lee told Ilya. "It'll only go farther away." But apparently the thought of what the *admiral* would do to him if he didn't make it clear only heightened the prisoner's anxiety in his search for the English word. In desperation, he ceased his shoveling motion, and instead gave Lee the word in Russian. *"Fonar."*

"Flashlight?" said Lee.

"Da!" said Ilya, making as if he was walking through a—

"Tunnel!" said Freeman.

"Da! Tunnels! Yes, Admiral. Tunnels."

"How many?"

"Three."

"Incoming!" warned Aussie. A tremendous crash of steel ripping into timber followed. Everyone was down for cover except Freeman, grabbing Ilya by the lapel. "Where are the tunnels? Mother of—" He remembered the vapor coming from the high ground, vapor that had no smell. Heating vents! ABC's weapons were being made underground!

Freeman pointed his H & K 9 mm sidearm down at the ground. "Down there, yes?"

"Yes."

"Entrances?" Freeman asked next. "Johnny, ask him if there's one entrance, two, how many? An entrance for each tunnel?"

Ilya, realizing that information was his only salvation, was now speaking at such a rate that Lee had to slow him down.

"He says that for security reasons there's only one main entrance for all three tunnels, and this is deep under the H-block, under the administration offices."

"Is it North Koreans who are building the tunnels?" Freeman asked.

"Da, General." With Boris supine beside him in the snow, Ilya was suddenly a gold mine of information. The gist of what he was saying was that the North Korean Communists who, as Freeman and anyone with even a passing acquaintance with North Korea knew, had watched American air supremacy over Korea in awe during the war of 1950–53, had also realized that in future wars, the only way for industry of any kind to survive American air-power would be to do as their North Vietnamese comrades had done in Cu Chi, that is, to burrow underground, deep underground, so deep that their military garrisons and factories couldn't be penetrated by the American bunker-busters that had laid waste to Saddam Insane's regime. What Ilya was also explaining was that in exchange for desperately needed foreign currency, the North Koreans' tunnelers extraordinaire had been engaged by ABC to do the dirty "hard yakka" labor, as Aussie would have called it, of burrowing deep into one of the rock spars that speared out into the marshes from the base of the nearby Zapadnyy Siniy Mountains, the deep missile assembly and storage plant located ninety feet underground and heated by harnessing the hot spring conduits that vented in and about Lake Khanka's marshes.

The crash of artillery rounds from the creeping, rather than target-specific, barrage had now passed beyond the wood, but had the enemy armor done the same?

"Can you hear any armor?" the general asked Lee, aware that his own hearing was deficient in what he had described to Margaret as the high, birdsong "trill and squeak range."

"No, sir," answered Lee. "I don't know what's going on."

Freeman's intuition told him something particularly troubling was afoot. Was ABC's rebel infantry following the tank? And had they now spread out, moving stealthily through the sea of reeds toward the last radio spot? If so, this meant the Russians would have to pass by the wood before they reached the SOT farther west from which he had radioed Aussie in the wood.

For now, despite all his impatience to find the tunnels—if Ilya was telling the truth—the general knew they would have to find the tank. In the event of a second wave, a tank could destroy as many helos as it had rounds, killing a hovering Stallion with one shot from its main gun, its coaxial 12.7 mm heavy machine gun obliterating any of the troop carrier's surviving marines.

"Damn!" said Freeman. He whipped out a small notebook from his thigh pocket and a small, flexi-grip indelible pencil that was firm enough to make a note with but not hard enough to be a deadly piece of shrapnel, as hard plastic or alloyed ballpoint pens were prone to become when their owners were hit. In Iraq, on the day Aussie had shot the bomb-belted "woman" running at him with little Blue Eyes, Aussie had seen a Brit sapper who'd lost an eye because a plastic ballpoint pen had disintegrated when he'd been nicked at chest level by a round from a terrorist's AK-47. The plastic pen had shattered, but its "ball" had perforated the Brit's eyeball, also taking out the optic nerve.

"Draw me a picture of the entrance," Freeman told Ilya. "Any lie, you understand—propaganda bullshit—and you die, Ilya. Understand?"

Johnny Lee told Ilya the same thing in Russian, just to make sure.

The Russian, left hand trembling, though less now than it had been when the general had shot Boris, began drawing a diagram of the H-block building, telling Freeman that it was very cold inside it. "No warming," Ilya told them, "so it does not show on satellites."

"Ah," Freeman said, "that's why it doesn't give off a heat signature for the satellites' IR lens."

"Everyone in the tunnels," said Ilya, "wears down-filled Gore-Tex. You know Gore-Tex?"

"Everyone knows Gore-Tex," said Freeman. "Show me something I don't know. Show me where the tunnel entrance is."

"Okay, Ad—General. I'm telling you truth now. No propaganda bullshit."

"You'd better be, son, or you can join Boris."

If the Russian thought the conversation between his

captor and himself was going to produce any kind of Stockholm effect, his captor coming around to understanding why he and Boris, in the chaos of post–Cold War Russia, had thrown in their lot with ABC and helped kill innocent Americans for money, it wasn't going to happen. There was no room in Freeman's mind for these slaughterers of civilians. Freeman glanced through the white blobs of snow-covered bush at the wood's perimeter out at the fog-blanketed whiteness of the reeds, anxious to see Melissa Thomas and the three other marines returning in the Hummer. Either that or the sweet-sounding swish of a TOW missile en route to enemy armor.

He glanced back down at Ilya's drawing, showing three tunnels ninety feet below the surface accessed by elevator from the H-block. At the base of the elevator there was a large open area from which the tunnels branched and which was sealed off from the elevator shaft by large double doors. The tunnels themselves were about ten feet in diameter and six feet apart and ran parallel to one another for a distance of about three hundred feet. Thruways that connected the tunnels were spaced at fifty-foot intervals.

"Ask him," Freeman told Lee impatiently, "what the arrangement is in each tunnel. What's being made?"

Ilya, sensing the general's agitated mood, responded quickly. He labeled the three tunnels "A, B, C," for Abramov, Beria, and Cherkashin respectively, explaining to Lee that one was for installing missile motors, the second for electronics, anti-infrared guidance, et cetera, and the third tunnel was for the installation of warheads.

"Where's the exit?" asked Freeman.

"Entrance is also exit."

"That's dumb. You go ninety feet underground and the tunnels run for three hundred feet. What if there's fire?"

"Exit still being dug by Koreans here." Ilya pointed to the end of the three fingerlike tunnels where they converged in a fifty-foot-diameter area. "Same size as the entrance."

"Is it finished?"

"Almost. One more month. Maybe less. There is much blasting by the Koreans but this delays assembly and our three big bosses in ABC—" He indicated the H-block he'd crudely drawn sitting ninety feet above where the tunnels began. "—They are not so interested in making exit for workers, only making more missiles to sell."

"To sell to *terrorists*!" Freeman charged.

"Yes," said Ilya, looking more chagrined than sorry. The Russian moved his map of the three tunnels around for Johnny Lee to get a better view, thus affirming his cooperative spirit.

"He's telling us," Lee told Freeman, "that many of the parts for the weaponry are stacked in the interconnecting tunnels, and no smoking is allowed in any of the tunnels."

"Now," Freeman told Ilya softly, his tone nevertheless pregnant with authority, "draw the way in through the minefield. You'll be in the front vehicle, comrade!"

Ilya flinched, so did Freeman, as another arty battery opened up, sending more freight train rounds on their mission to kill U.S. marines. Freeman glanced at his watch. If Thomas, Kegg, and the other two marines, including the corporal, didn't return in ten minutes, he was going to break cover and go after ABC's armor. Unless the tank was disabled, the second helo wave, as well as his and Tibbet's marines already on the ground, was doomed. Like so many plans he'd seen in civilian and military life, everything, as the academics at staff college sometimes said, "was in a state of flux" or, as Aussie succinctly put it, "everything was going to rat shit."

*   *   *

The snow was falling even more heavily now and there was still no sign of Melissa Thomas, Kegg, the other marine, and the corporal, or enemy armor. It was as if everything had been swallowed up in what was now a full-blown blizzard, the wood as silent as a tomb, Freeman's team and Chester's marines statuelike in the swirling whiteness. Even the sound of the small-arms fire and the occasional scream of Russian MANPADs, which the Russians were using as ground-to-ground munitions in the absence of any discernible radar signatures in the air, were muted. Many of Colonel Tibbet's men had still failed to link up due to the erratically spaced landings the big Stallions had been forced to make due to the Cobras' sudden midair collision. To further discombobulate the Americans, the Russians had affixed a small, thimble-sized Stuka screamer to their artillery rounds and some of their missiles, designed, as had been the Nazi prototype, to instill ice-cold terror into their potential victims. The first time he heard it, Freeman immediately recalled the stories of his great-grandfather, who had served as a liaison officer in the American International Brigade during the Spanish Civil War of 1936–39, about how the inhabitants of Guernica had been the first nonmilitary target in history to be flattened by the Luftwaffe, Goering's air force, practicing on the unarmed civilians of the town as a curtain raiser to the Nazis' blitzkrieg—lightning war—that began World War II.

The sound of a broad front battle had dropped off from the more or less sustained ripping noise of machine gun fire, guttural roars of big Triple A, and the high-pitched screaming of the heat-seeking MANPADs, to pockets of noise. These erupted spasmodically from what Freeman guessed were isolated squads of infantry and four-man fire teams, the backbone of the MEU, engaging Russian patrols and gun emplacements, all of which the snow would be covering, helping to camouflage the terrorists' positions against the attacking marines. Those not engaged in these isolated clashes were in a physical state reminiscent of suspended animation, each marine's body wound up like an alarm clock, the alarm due to go off at any moment, but no one knowing quite when. Every marine, as well as Freeman's team, was praying for the arrival of the second wave, but every one of them knew it would be a hard thing for Tibbet to have to send the enciphered message to "come on down," the old quiz shows' phrase a current favorite of marine slang, though Melissa Thomas was more often than not the recipient of Oprah Winfrey's ubiquitous "You go, girl!" a double-edged encouragement thrown at her as she'd struggled to stay afloat in Parris Island's Water Facility.

While one marine and the marine corporal remained in the Hummer, Thomas and Kegg were kneeling in a natural blind of shoulder-high reeds whose formerly frost-stiffened stalks were now starting to yield to the weight of snow as pea-sized powder crystals gave way to bigger, sloppier flakes that adhered and quickly accumulated on the stalks. Melissa knew that if she and her fire-team buddy Kegg didn't move soon, the reeds would be bent over by the weight of snow to knee height and lower, and both marines knew that the prone position, in what was now a four- to five-inch snow cover, some drifts back at the wood more than a foot deep, was not the position from which to do any useful recon. Everything in this sector, less than a mile west of the lake, had become unnervingly quiet since the as-yet-unseen tank could no longer be heard.

Marine Thomas, moving her right arm with glacial slowness, had managed to squirt a shot of "defrost" on her rifle's long thermal-imaging Nite-Sight scope, and knew she had one of the mag's five 7.62 mm Match

Grade rounds already chambered, and the rifle's trigger weight set for a three- instead of a five-pound pull. She knew that even in good weather a quick shot was often difficult to get off in time, and that in these near-zero-visibility conditions it would be impossible, were it not for the scope's infrared capacity. All she needed was a heat bleed, a man's head moving, a blurry-edged white spot against a green background. But she'd never before fired at another human being, and not from five hundred yards. In the abstract, she had no doubt, but now, here, her heart pounding under the stress, the cold, it was the same feeling she'd experienced when first she stood on the edge of the water tank on Parris Island. And choked. "Remember," Kegg had told her as they'd alighted from the Hummer into the reeds, "the terrorist assholes we'll be hunting will be trying to take us out before our guys can consolidate and go looking for the H-block. And, shit, it's their home ground."

He was right, but she reminded herself the marines had gone over the 3-D computer-generated SATPIX maps of the area ad nauseam, so that, despite the all-but-featureless expanse of the reeds here, west of the lake and less than five miles north of the railhead at Kamen Rybolov, each marine, with his GPS wristwatch, should know where he was.

Though not speaking, Melissa, Kegg, and the two others, by carefully studying their thigh-pocket charts, had estimated that they were less than two miles from the H-block, whose vague outline had shown up on SATPIX, and that the tank they had heard must have stopped, for even given the sound-suppressing quality of snow, the nails-on-chalkboard-like screech of steel treads on steel wheels should have been audible.

Then Melissa heard movement, slight yet distinct, about twenty feet off at two o'clock. Was it a bird, like

the one who'd spooked that guy in the reeds who in turn
had triggered the anti-personnel mine? Or was it someone
moving? And if so, friend or foe? Kegg heard it too, and
froze, ready with his M4 5.6mm carbine. This shortened
M16, with grenade launcher attached, was more easily
handled in the reeds than an M-10, and Melissa saw the
tip of his trigger finger ready to either unleash a 40mm
grenade or fire a flush-out burst of 5.56mm rounds. But
the same questions dogged him: Was it a man or an animal? A mistake could cost you your life or the haunting-
till-you-die agony of having initiated a blue-on-blue.
Melissa wanted to raise her sniper's rifle for a quick look
through the scope, but that'd be like waving a flag, besides which even the slightest movement would cause
the reeds to move. She heard a hissed, *"Ga ja!"* Kegg
saw reeds shivering, and fired, not a profligate hosing of
ammo but a marine-style burst, into the middle of the rustle. Melissa fired from the hip, seeing green-white reeds
exploding in burnt-brown fragments as her heavy 7.62
mm round tore its path through the vegetation in a nanosec-
ond. For her, however, time morphed into that strange
slow motion that danger decrees, when time for those
involved irrationally stands still.

Then screaming and chaos as a firefight erupted. Melissa,
punched backward, saw three figures, heard, *"Ga ja! Ga
ja!"* again, Kegg lobbing a grenade and dropping down
next to her, a mad rushing like a bull charging amid the
crash and flame of the grenade, and more feral screaming.

The Hummer broke cover from the shoulder-high reeds
twenty yards back, the corporal driving hard into the reeds,
the other marine manning the front-right-door machine
gun, its red tracer cutting through the snow-bent stalks in a
segmented red line ending where he'd seen the trouble, the
corporal careful to steer east of the GPS vector that marked

the edge of the mined moat of frozen marsh around the H-block, the latter still unseen but supposedly there, SATPIX verified.

Three terrorists were down, all dead from what Kegg could make out, but his marine training had instilled in him the caution needed when approaching a downed enemy. Terrorists, more than any other combatants marines had encountered, except perhaps for the South Seas detachment of the Japanese Army in 1941–45, were known to booby-trap their dead *and* themselves, lying on a grenade, pin pulled, the weight of their body holding down the spring lever. You rolled them over at your peril. Melissa found it excruciating to breathe; the impact from the terrorist's AK-47 burst, or rather from the one shot that had hit her in the chest, although having been stopped by her flak jacket, had caused an enormous and painful welt on her left breast, the shock of the hit having penetrated deep into her chest, and, she suspected, broken a rib. But there was no way she was going to complain and become the whining bitch. If she did so, it'd be in e-mails home from *Yorktown*—if they got out of this mess. She could imagine the leads: "Congressman Calls for End to Female Combatants"; "'A Woman's Place Is in the Home, Not on the Battlefield,' Say Southern Baptist Bishops."

"You okay?" asked Kegg, who, while he kept his eyes on the three bodies, stood up slowly, his M4's clip-on launcher having another grenade up the spout just in case.

"Yeah," she told him.

Kegg moved off to the right to avoid being in her line of fire. "Cover me," he told her.

The terrorists looked dead, from head shots and grenade shrapnel, but he knew he had to be sure, feel the wrist pulse. Melissa, the fifteen pounds of her M40A1 sniper rifle feeling like a ton, covered him, the pain in her rib cage feeling like someone twisting an ice-cold knife inside, every intake of air an act of will.

There was no pulse in any of them. He wasn't going to turn them over. Even so, he and Melissa could see they were two Caucasian terrorists and an Asian—Chinese or Korean. They reported this to the Hummer corporal whose vehicle's roof-mounted TOW radar was sweeping the snowy expanse for the tank that had disappeared, the corporal as well as Kegg and Melissa hypothesizing that the earlier squeaking noises they'd heard had been armor *retreating* from a defilade position beyond the wood.

"Should search them for intel," Melissa Thomas said, trying not to grimace with her pain, but Kegg noticed anyway and, seeing her flak jacket perforated, asked, "You bleeding?"

"No. Just a bit of indigestion. That slug winded me."

"Damn lucky it wasn't higher," the Hummer corporal said. "You'd have a tracheotomy you didn't ask for."

She grinned manfully, asking him again, "Should we check them for intel?" She knew it was paramount in this kind of operation, especially given the minefield. SATPIX had indicated temperature differential spots where earth had been disturbed, dug up, but snow covering the ground made it difficult to pinpoint the mines while you were being shot at.

The corporal had a lariat, formed with the rope from the Hummer's front bumper. He tossed the loop over the dead Asian. "I'll haul him over in case he's lying on a 'pine cone.'"

"I like that better," said Kegg, who wanted no part of frisking anyone lying facedown.

"Let's get out of here," said the other marine, manning the front-door gun. "I've got dots on the radar. Big ones."

"Second wave?" asked Kegg.

"Due north," said the Hummer's front-door gunner, doubling as radar nerd.

"So?" pressed Kegg. "What's the problem?"

"Problem, marine," cut in the marine corporal, "is that our second wave would be coming from the southeast, maybe due east, not out of the north."

"Oh," said a disappointed Kegg as the Hummer reversed, taking up the rope's slack at the front, the door gunner enjoining his fellow marines quietly but urgently to get aboard as he watched the radar dots grow. "Let's get going. If they're voodoos, we're too exposed."

Melissa Thomas smiled for the first time since her chat on the Stallion with Freeman. "Exposed." Maybe, she thought, in the sense they were out on the frozen expanse of marsh, but the snow was falling so heavily, visibility was now only twenty feet at best. That was as much a defense as a hindrance.

The snow-dotted body rolled over. The Hummer advanced and reversed twice more. There was no sign of a booby trap on either of the other two bodies; the three terrorists probably hadn't time to do anything more than get off a few rounds in the direction of Melissa and Kegg before Kegg felled them.

As the marine corporal quickly recoiled the rope, Melissa, with a great effort and the stink of the Hummer's diesel exhaust temporarily shutting down her nose, knelt down and started frisking the Asian while Kegg and the corporal who'd finished with the rope began searching the two Caucasian terrorists.

"Bingo!" said Melissa.

The corporal and Kegg turned toward her, the Hummer's gunner repeatedly making a 360-degree sweep, urging them to hurry up. "Let's go! I don't like it."

"What've we got, Thomas?" the corporal asked, watching her unrolling a scroll she'd found inside the Asian's jacket.

"Some kind of map," Melissa answered.

"C'mon, guys!" said the gunner.

Melissa flattened it out quickly. The map was the size of a man's handkerchief. She and Kegg glanced at it, then she rapidly rolled it up, tucking it inside her helmet against the liner. "We'll give it to Freeman. That SpecWar guy of his—the lieutenant—"

"Lee," said the gunner. "Yeah, Lieutenant Lee. Hey, that tank's gotta be 'round here somewhere."

"Relax," the corporal told him. "You see it on the radar?"

"No," said the gunner, "but those fuckin' bogeys are moving in."

"Maybe they're UFOs!" joshed the corporal.

"You a fucking comedian?"

"How many bogeys you got, Pete?"

"Looks like nine," the gunner answered. "Three threes."

"What was that?" the corporal asked Melissa as they walked to the Hummer. "The printing on that guy's map? Arabic?"

"Korean, I think," said Melissa. "Anyway, that Lee guy's multilingual. He should know." She looked back at Kegg. "Might know what *'Ga ja!'* means too."

"Maybe it's his grocery list," joked Kegg.

"For cryin' out loud," said the machine gunner, looking anxiously over the reeds and stealing a glance at the radar. "What the fuck's going on with you guys? Let's *go!*"

A nervous rifleman on the wood's perimeter squeezed off a three-round burst before Freeman and Aussie saw the Hummer's whip aerial and its TOW missile housing through the falling snow. The Hummer was hit "midships," as described by the enraged corporal who had been driving, and who was now tearing the proverbial strip off a young marine whose first live fire in combat was to hit the Hummer. Freeman kept out of it. The marine's humiliation was punishment enough. Besides, the general, more conscious than anyone in the wood of time slipping by and the twenty-four-hour deadline bearing down on him, turned his attention to the scroll found by Melissa Thomas on the dead Asian terrorist. As the general unrolled the scroll, saw the dotted lines and elaborately styled calligraphy, he realized that the map was more or less a duplicate of Ilya's more roughly drawn sketch. But whereas Ilya had said the entrance to and the exit from the tunnels were the same, the dead Korean's map, his nationality confirmed by Johnny Lee's examination of the black-inked characters, showed an exit tunnel.

"The characters written here," Lee told Freeman, "indicate it's a tunnel wide enough for two men."

"How does the exit tunnel connect up to the three tunnels?" asked Freeman. He was having trouble reading the drawing overlaid with characters. "Does it go up from the fifty-foot area Ilya mentioned?"

"Yes," confirmed Lee.

"Not a trap is it, Johnny?" pressed Freeman, brushing big, sloppy flakes of snow off the map. "I mean that dead son of a bitch Kegg and Marine Thomas wasted violated every military code, carrying around detail like that. Could it be a plant? Sucker us in?" Memories of "AMERICANS SUCK" were lit large in the general's mind.

"No," Lee replied confidently. "I don't think so." He turned to Melissa Thomas. "Was this terrorist you got the map from in Russian fatigues?"

It was a crucial question, but neither Melissa, Kegg, nor the corporal could vouch for the answer. He'd been pretty well covered in snow, and the Hummer with the rope had turned him over several times, but—maybe the two Caucasians had been dressed a little differently from the Korean, but the truth was that in the confusion and speed of the firefight none of the three marines could be certain. They'd all been looking at the dead men's faces when the Hummer's rope turned them over.

"I'm not sure," said Melissa. "I'm sorry, General."

"No problem. You did well."

"Thank you, sir," said Melissa. "Why's it important about how he was dressed? The Korean, I mean?"

The general glanced over at Ilya. "Because my friend Ilya here tells me there've been a lot of Koreans working up here. So if the Korean terrorist you marines took out was a civil engineer, not an army type who wouldn't or shouldn't carry maps of the system, that'd lend credence to this scroll you found. It'd make sense for an engineer, army or not, to have this with him. It'd be like our tac maps." He meant the tactical maps Colonel Tibbet, himself, and selected company commanders had to have. The general paused and, as casually as he could, asked Johnny Lee, "Any date on it?" And he watched Ilya, whose eyes were avoiding the general's with such ill-disguised purpose that Freeman became more convinced that Lee's answer would be critical.

"Yep," said Johnny Lee. "It's got intended and completion dates marked near all the separate tunnel stuff."

"Hmm," murmured the general. While the others were looking down at the map, he was watching Ilya again. "Any date on the exit tunnel, Johnny?"

"Yep. It's dated—" Johnny turned the map around, placing it on a stump under cover of the fir's branches, using two H & K 9 mm mags to weight it down. "His calligraphy's ornate, flowery, but it's not really very neat."

They could all hear the first "wokka-wokka" and

"whoop-whoop" noises of approaching helos. Russian or American, no one knew; radio silence was complete.

"It—" began Lieutenant Johnny Lee, "I mean the exit tunnel is marked as having been completed two months ago!"

"That a fact?" said Freeman urbanely, his left hand accommodating an itchy spot beneath his Fritz, his right returning his 9 mm to its holster. "Funny," he continued, hearing the approaching din of aircraft, and looking up high through the fir's snow-packed branches at the invisible racket thundering directly overhead. The heavy pulsing in the snow-thick air told every one of the first wave's marines spread out higgledy-piggledy in the landing snafu that they were either being reinforced by *Yorktown*'s second wave or attacked by gunships.

Johnny Lee's answer that the exit tunnel had been completed months ago was followed by such a cacophony from the helos that Freeman's instruction to Ilya had to be delivered in his full command voice. "You were leading my men into a trap. We go in the entrance and your comrades—your *comrades*," shouted Freeman, "would be in there, lights out, waiting for us. A trap, you cunning son of a bitch!"

"No, no, General," pleaded Ilya. "I didn't know. No—"

Freeman slung the AK-74 over his left arm, jabbing his finger at Ilya. "You told me, you terrorist son of a bitch, that there was no exit yet, that it wasn't completed!"

Ilya's eyes told the general he'd run out of excuses. He was asking for mercy, having prevaricated with just enough of the truth to set up the trap that would have annihilated the Americans. Suddenly Ilya lunged at Freeman, pulling the general's KA-BAR, bringing the knife up with such speed that Freeman, putting his hand on the pistol's grip, ready to draw, had only a split second to "up" the holster, the gun still in it, and fire, the parabellum round exiting the canvas holster and striking the Russian in the chest, punching him back. He fell, staggered to his feet, taking Freeman's second shot in the throat. His carotid artery, punctured, gushed blood, giving Freeman time for the third shot, the 9 mm slug ending the business in a flurry of snow as the Russian fell back onto the fir's snow-laden branches, his blood staining the clumps of virgin snow that suddenly cascaded down from the tree's branches, a denuded branch, relieved of its burden, springing up, rising another foot or two above the ground.

Now, in addition to the headache-inducing din of the armada of helos, Freeman's team and Chester's marines could hear another sound, which Melissa Thomas and Kegg recognized as the loud, ripping noise of machine-gun fire. It was coming from the helos above, which were invisible except as blips on the Hummer's radar, and identified as enemy craft by Freeman's and Chester's infrared friend-or-foe helmet patches. The Hummer's helo-experienced corporal identified the craft as Black Shark Kamov 50 attack helos and Hind transporters.

The Black Sharks and Hind transports were arriving head-on with the second wave of Joint Strike Fighter–escorted Super Stallions. No one thought it was anything but a rather deliberate, tactical ploy by the air force general, Cherkashin.

"He's a hard son of a bitch," pronounced Kegg.

"Who?" asked the Hummer corporal. What the hell was Kegg on about? "Do you mean Freeman, or the son of a bitch who sent his choppers in to fuck up our second wave? Cher—what's his name? Cherkov?"

"Cherkashin," Kegg corrected him. "No, I mean Freeman's the hard-ass. Shooting POWs like that."

"POWs, my ass," cut in Aussie. "They were friggin'

terrorists. They'd sell their sister for two bits. Fuckin' mercenaries. All of 'em."

"So?" interjected the corporal. "Who made you Pope?"

"Listen, Sonny," Aussie shot back, "you would've had your sorry ass in a trap if Thomas here hadn't found that map."

"What makes you think we're not in one now?" said Kegg. "Maybe the map's a trap."

"Hey," put in the front-door gunner, "map's a trap. That's a rap."

"They'll wrap your ass if I'm right," said Kegg.

The front-door gunner had no response, or if he did, he left it unsaid. Everyone's attention was drawn to the claustrophobic throbbing in the sky.

Despite the danger presented to him by the presence of the enemy helos, as a soldier Freeman had to admire Cherkashin's strategy. With many of the inferior Russian radars whited out by snow and therefore posing a high risk of blue on blue amongst the Russian helos, Cherkashin, like Rommel in the France of '44, had clearly decided that he must engage the Americans—in the air, in this case—before they had a chance to land in force and link up with the first wave. Much of the surprise Cherkashin was creating with this helo attack was due to sheer luck in obtaining an "unofficial loan" of the elite helos from the Siberian Sixth Armored's air wing located just east of Spassk-Dalni, fifteen miles east of the lake's southeastern shore. In fact, the air battle now under way had begun north of the lake as the MEU's second wave of Stallions tried an end run around the northwestern half of the lake, hoping to come up behind the Russians that the *McCain*'s SES had picked up even given the blizzard conditions over the lake. Cherkashin's Black Shark helos, which NATO Commander Roger Hawkins had nicknamed "Werewolves," had proved how good they were in tight turns of 3.5 Gs and dive speeds of 200 and more miles per hour with their 50T thermal imagers. The joint Russian-Israeli-built Erdogan version, with its pilot and copilot sitting in a NATO-weapons-compatible cockpit encased in 12.7 mm-proof armor plating and equipped with the world's first operational helo rocket-assisted ejection system, was particularly deadly. One Super Stallion had already been shot down by an Erdogan's rapid-firing 2A42 30 mm cannon, its pilot eschewing high-fragmentation rounds in favor of armor-piercing rounds. The gun's virtuoso performance owed much to the shark-shaped helo having a coaxial rotor but no tail rotor, enabling it to perform a flat turn, its gun free to move through either an unrestricted vertical or horizontal circle as the Shark climbed and dived. With its two 2,200 horsepower, side-mounted turboshaft engines, the helo performed maneuvers that would have seemed impossible to an earlier generation of chopper pilots.

As Freeman often told his team, everything has its limitations, and the swarm of nine Black Sharks was no match for the four American vertical takeoff and landing Joint Strike Fighters led by *McCain*'s Chipper Armstrong. Each of the big 247-pound, 27 mm gas-operated revolver guns was so deadly that, slaved to the JSF's avionics, it outshot the Black Sharks' best in close air battle. And because the Americans' radar was 87 percent more effective than that of the nine Black Sharks, the thirty American gunners in this second wave of fifteen Super Stallions were able to take their copilot's voice feed directly from his heads-up radar display without any intermediate step, which gave them a two- to three-second advantage.

Johnny Lee, listening in to radio voices in the frantic chaos and urgency of the air battle, repeatedly heard the American helos being referred to as "Freeman's Birds."

"Shit," said one of Chester's marines, "they think you're running the show, General."

No one contradicted him, because now that Freeman had the map, it seemed as if he was certainly the man best informed to run the show, given that Tibbet was still pre-occupied trying to gather in the disparate units of the first wave.

"Johnny—" Freeman began.

"Down!" shouted Gomez, who was kneeling beside Eddie Mervyn's rigid body when they heard a swishing sound overhead, the heat generated by the flight of the missile creating a tumbling roll of warm air that swept the wood like a prairie Chinook, sending large plops of snow falling from tree and bush.

"That was close," said the Hummer corporal. "I thought—" He was silenced by the Hummer's gunner, who said he thought he'd heard the squeak of a tracked vehicle several seconds before, but had since lost all trace of it in the din of more than twenty-four helos diving, hovering, landing, and all of them seemingly firing at once. Some of the errant rounds ripped into the frozen marsh and reeds skirting the lake. Freeman now heard the second wave being put down only a mile and a quarter west of the ABC complex, as planned, but over a mile north of the first wave's scattered troops. This meant Tibbet would lose valuable time, having to hustle if he was to have his second wave join the first.

What neither Tibbet nor Freeman knew was that by calling in every IOU they had, as well as offering U.S. currency bonuses on the spot, Mikhail Abramov, Viktor Beria, and Sergei Cherkashin had obtained an ad hoc force of 480 troops, which were being ferried in by four high-T-tailed Ilyushin-P transports, each of the planes' four big D-30 KP engines controlled by updated computer avionics, so that landing on the relatively short

ABC runway was virtually hands-off despite the snow-fall.

In much the same way, for the first time in out-of-country operations, two of the Marine Expeditionary Unit's JSFs, the first fighter piloted by *McCain*'s Chipper Armstrong, the other by Rhino Manowski, set down as instructed by Tibbet's enciphered ground-to-air communication once radio silence had been broken in the Russian helo attack. While Armstrong's JSF put down on a slab of frozen marsh by Freeman's wood, Manowski landed his plane by another "wood island," as it were, nearer Tibbet, who had now reached cover just outside the perimeter where a platoon of second-wave marines were coming under sustained rocket-propelled-grenade, heavy machine gun, and AK-47 fire. But in the whiteout, this enfilade from the unseen Russian defenders was more smoke than fire, with only a small percentage of the Russian infantry defenders having the use of IR scopes and sights, the weather forecasters having disappointed them as well as the Americans. Amid the cacophony of rotor slap and battle, Freeman was writing quickly on his knee pad, sketching out a plan of attack using Ilya's map, gambling on his hunch that Ilya's map of a route through the minefield would be accurate because it had clearly been Ilya's intention to lure all of the Americans into the tunnel at one end and bottle them up in a killing zone.

"Johnny," Freeman called out to Lee. "Encrypt this and send to Jack Tibbet: 'ABC H-block—'"

"Hang on, General," cut in Lee, uncharacteristic alarm in his voice. Freeman recognized it as Lee's "computer down" tone, as Johnny's ungloved hands tapped the fold-out keypad again with the same results. "Nothing's going through, sir. Like it's frozen."

"Maybe it is," said Choir, his voice all but lost to a sudden surge of fighting all down the line.

"All right," said Freeman, obviously annoyed but un-
fazed, writing quickly on his blood-spattered knee pad.
"Johnny, try the encrypted function again." Lee did, and
it didn't work. "We only have PL, General."

"All right, dammit, plain language'll have to do. Contact Tibbet's HQ and explain about the tunnels' approximate location. But obviously we can't give him any
tactical information and we haven't much time. So while
you're messaging his HQ, Johnny, I'll see what I can
do—dig up a trick or two from the old days—in a follow-
up PL message."

In all his time with Douglas Freeman, Aussie had never
seen the general's hands move so fast—like a Vegas
dealer's—and within five minutes, during which time Lee
was radioing Tibbet's HQ, the general tore off a message
sheet, telling Johnny, "Send the following."

WYFWBAANGHARIUNNEOENOLTDDVONKMLIIWME-
DYEMNIIRRLOEEOTPPDUUGBTEEEICROOHNTTD-
KEOTITHEGFCDHTRERAOETOEAMRMRIOFXNOOBUVGUIC
USLSEOSTETEEA.

The din of the battle soon reached an apogee, then dramatically fell off, the snow drifting, piling up, under a
bone-freezing wind that was howling down from the Zapadnyy Siniy only a few miles to the west.

"Are we going in, General?" Aussie asked.

"No option," pronounced Freeman firmly. "We attack."
He had one eye on Johnny Lee who, though the biting
wind was freezing his hands, was forcing himself to focus so as not to screw up the burst message to Tibbet. Any
pause by Johnny would count as a "space" in the train of
letters; a missing 0 or 1 in a binary message would jumble the sequence and thus scramble the message.

"Signature?" Lee asked the general.

Freeman thought of his favorite president, Franklin Delano Roosevelt: "All we have to fear is fear itself. We'll use FDR," he told Lee.

Johnny was blowing on his fingers and flexing them. "Signature within or without, sir?" he asked Freeman.

"Within."

"Very well. All set to—" They heard the unmistakable whoosh of a fuel air explosive, the FAE bomb sending an enormous flash of orange through the snow that immediately turned to steam then to sheets of filigreed ice that cracked on the frozen marsh like shattered glass.

"All set to send burst transmission," Lee informed Freeman.

"Send."

"It's gone, sir," said Johnny, but he looked worried. Any transmission was easy to intercept. Cracking the code?

"Listen up!" Freeman told his fellow soldiers. "We've got the best outfit possible here, my team, a Hummer with four TOWs loaded and four in the rack, and a fire team par excellence, with Terrible Thomas and Killer Kegg." There was a snort of laughter.

"What more could we ask for?" continued Freeman. "Soon as I get acknowledgment of this message, we find our way back to where Eddie got it, *but* we keep strictly *this* side of the GPS mine line. The snow will've buried any sign of booby traps, so even with this map showing where the exit from the three tunnels is we're going to have to move slowly till we find the exit door. From the terrorist's map, the door is like one of those used on an old house's coal chute. The exit itself appears to be a steeply graded stairwell about eighty feet or more long, and it's barely wide enough, if Johnny's interpretation of this map is correct, for two men abreast." He paused. "Though in this damn refrigerator I wouldn't mind being next to a breast myself."

"Hoo ha!" came the marine reply. Melissa Thomas's smile was tired and patient, the smile of a woman who had heard much more gauche comments from grown-up boys.

Freeman became serious again. "This isn't going to be a cakewalk but I'm confident we'll be able to reach that exit door if this map is right, and remember the approach to it won't be mined, otherwise it wouldn't be a damned exit! Questions?"

Aussie asked about the entrance to the tunnel. If Freeman attacked the exit, wouldn't ABC's technicians be able to escape back out the entrance?

"Doesn't matter if they do," replied Freeman. "Right now we're after the machinery more than the men." He paused, checking that everyone was ready. "Right," he said, "check your weapons. Remember, condoms on the barrels so snow doesn't get up the spout and freeze the rifling. Got it?"

"Got it."

"Good."

With the chaotic roar of the helos fading as quickly as it had begun, Freeman's force moved off in the relative silence, broken here and there only by sporadic "blind man's firing," as Freeman called it. A hundred yards out, the marine corporal, sitting in the Hummer, could have sworn he heard a squeaking sound. He also knew hearing it was like watching clouds; you often see the image that the mind projects, and sometimes you hear noises that aren't there, sounds born of imagination and the circumstances of the kind the corporal was encountering now in the conditions of war with the Russian terrorists, of whom he'd seen very few, except for those in the ill-fated BTR and the truck, wanting to kill every American they could find. The damp air all around was thick with the pungent smell of burning gasoline and high-explosive fumes rising slowly from those places in the minefield moat where more than forty Americans, their transport Stallion thrown off course by the Black Sharks, had perished as it hit the ground, its huge rotors cartwheeling and breaking up, the fuselage suddenly bursting into flame.

CHAPTER SIXTEEN

ABRAMOV HAD BEEN holding back his twenty T-90s behind the protection of the minefield that skirted ABC's H-block and the thicket of Cherkashin's anti-aircraft defenses until the weather abated and visibility improved enough to unleash his armor and make devastating use of his laser and infrared targeting. But he suspected now that he had made an error and waited too long. Initial reports coming into the H-block from Beria's lone-sniper observers in reed hides at the edge of the minefield indicated that "white bears" now outnumbered "brown," which told Abramov, Beria, and Cherkashin that not only had a second wave of Americans arrived but that these new American arrivals were equipped with "snow whites," or winter uniforms.

Then suddenly, and completely unexpectedly, Beria burst into Abramov's office, waving a piece of yellow paper of the size ABC had given Ramon, who had so successfully led ABC's Spetsnaz commando group in the attack on the American's DARPA ALPHA base.

"God exists!" Beria bellowed to a startled Abramov. "Mikhail, I bring you a gift!"

"What in hell are you talking about?" asked the tank commander, looking up grumpily at the diminutive Beria, whose chin seemed barely to clear the top of Abramov's huge metal desk.

"Where's Cherkashin?" Beria inquired loudly, looking about the map room adjoining Abramov's office.

"He's busy," said Abramov brusquely, clearly irritated by Beria's exuberance, which was in marked contrast to his own bad mood and anger at himself for not having committed his tanks earlier. It had been his dream to avenge the one humiliating defeat his Siberian Sixth had suffered.

Abramov had been smart enough this time around, or so he had told himself, to not let his tanks loose when Bird Rescue's Cobra gunships had shown up in the first wave. His intel group had assured him the Cobra attack helos would not return in the terrible weather. The gunships simply were not equipped with sufficiently good avionics, given the distance between the U.S. fleet and Lake Khanka. Furthermore, his perimeter snipers had been told that *if* the Cobras did risk a second wave, they would, like any other helo, be vulnerable when refueling from bladders dropped by the cargo-hauling Stallions. Any in-flight refueling was deemed to be "out of the question" during the blizzard. Cherkashin's air defense had assured Abramov that such a delicate maneuver required visuals as well as outstanding instrument flying by the Cobra's two-man crew and the tanker's pilot in what the Russians referred to as a "Tit and Sucker" maneuver. But Abramov's G-2, his intelligence chief, had confirmed that there were reports by coastwatchers of American helos refueling in the air.

Beria had placed the yellow sheet of paper, which was also the color used for radio intercepts, on Abramov's desk, waving his hand side to side as if to clear the room of the smoke from the ultraexpensive Diplomaticos No. 2 cigar, one of which Abramov always had on the go, ever since ABC's massive profits had enabled the tank commander to buy the very best Havana cigars.

"What's this?" Abramov asked, picking up the yellow intercept strip unenthusiastically. Beria strode to the window, momentarily struggling with the latch, and letting in a draft of the frigid air, glancing at Abramov's snow-covered main battle tanks surrounded by Cherkashin's twelve multibarreled ZSU anti-aircraft units and a score of Igla MANPAD teams. Beria thanked his lucky stars, that, as much as Moscow wanted ABC destroyed, the Russian president simply could not allow any foreigners, *especially* Americans, to bomb Russian soil, rebel or otherwise. For the Russian president to allow anyone, especially Americans, to bomb would risk enraging even those Russians who, though opposed to the terrorist activities of ABC, could not tolerate foreign bombs falling on the Motherland. It was a visceral reaction born of the collective trauma of Hitler's Operation Barbarossa, the massive and savage invasion of Mother Russia, when Hitler's Luftwaffe had sent in the Nazis' Screaming Stuka dive-bombers to pulverize Russian defenses and terrify the civilian population.

Looking out the window as Abramov scanned the yellow page, an excited Beria was reveling in ABC's double good fortune. First, in how Moscow, by securing a "no-bombing" agreement with the U.S. president in dealing with ABC, had in effect rendered ABC's H-block and minefield off-limits to American aircraft and now ABC's second lucky break, which had come in the form of an intercepted transcript of a message between the American General Freeman and the marine commander, Colonel Tibbet.

"The Americans," said Beria, coming back to the desk, his finger tapping the yellow sheet of paper, "think they are the only ones with state-of-the-art computer scanners?"

"So," said Abramov, still not convinced, "you have intercepted a line of letters. What's it mean?"

"Our intel boys are working as fast as they can. They think it's a letter-for-letter code. You know, each letter stands in for another letter. So when you put 'B' it could be 'A' or 'C.' We're running the parameters now."

"Why isn't it encrypted?" asked Abramov brusquely. Digitized?"

Beria shrugged. "Not every squad carries an encrypter. Maybe their encrypter wasn't working."

"Huh," said Abramov. "It looks too easy."

"Well, then," countered Beria. "What does it say?"

"I don't know," admitted Abramov, taking a long, clenched-teeth drag on his Diplomaticos. "I've just seen it this second, haven't I?"

"Our boys'll crack it," said Beria confidently, taking back the yellow strip.

"Leave it," Abramov told the infantry general. "I'll peruse it as well. Meanwhile our met officer says this snow's going to turn to rain. A layer of mist'll be moving from north of the lake down toward us, but it should be clear enough that I'll be able to go out and attack with my armor. Americans'll have nothing comparable. Biggest things they can haul under those Super Stallions of theirs are Hummers and light howitzers, and the most they're ferrying in are two of the howitzers, otherwise they couldn't have carried the required troops' weight to make up the second wave.

"Don't worry, Mikhail," Beria said. "Your T-90's'll eat those marines alive once the weather—"

"I know that!" snapped Abramov, his tobacco-stained teeth in a snarl. "The point is to let my boys loose when the worst of the weather lifts but there's still enough mist to give us cover as we speed through our minefield's exits. We'll have to move fast before the Americans rush the minefield exit, which isn't visible now but will be once they backtrack our tread marks. I want your infantry to be ready, Viktor, to watch my flanks."

"Ready? They've *been* ready, waiting all around the perimeter, dug in until they can move en masse. My God, haven't you heard them firing?"

"I've heard a lot of noise," retorted Abramov. "But we're still frozen in position. We'll see who's been firing *accurately* when we can see what the hell's going on. We're still in the fog of battle, Viktor. Same as the Americans."

"Don't complain about the snow, Mikhail. It's what's buying us time against the American force. Once your armor rolls out we'll flush them out for you. Grease your treads with their guts."

Abramov had no doubt he'd mash the Americans, though he might lose a few of his T-90s and 122 mm mobile missile launchers. These were still firing spasmodically at very low altitude to sweep the snow-filled air of any American helo caught in the critically vulnerable hovering position, disgorging men and matériel. Abramov looked down again at the long string of letters on the yellow sheet.

"Don't worry," Beria assured him. "Our intel comrades are working the permutations and combinations now. They'll crack it soon."

" 'Soon,' " said Abramov, "better be before the weather clears."

"They'll crack it," Beria promised.

Abramov looked at his watch. "Rain is predicted in thirty minutes. Then it tapers to showers."

"Ah, you can't always trust those weather people, Mikhail," opined Beria. "Look how it was supposed to be low overcast, maybe showers, then what do we get dumped on us? Tons of snow. A veritable blizzard, Comrade."

"That's because we're so near the mountains," Abramov told him. "You know how quickly things change."

Beria wasn't convinced, though as he left Abramov's office he recalled how, contrary to public opinion, weather forecasting was now 87.8 percent accurate, even in seaports as far away as Vladivostok and Vancouver. And so, when he found Cherkashin in the map room, he told him that Mikhail was probably right about the optimistic weather forecast. But the normally garrulous air force commander was in no mood for optimism. He was furious that the snow had effectively grounded the two MiG-29s promised him by his brother-in-law in Spassk-Dalni East.

"Sergei," Beria assured him, "you won't need the two Fulcrums. You've given us good anti-aircraft fire already. Now it's our turn."

Cherkashin, his white mane in disarray, stared at Beria. The infantry commander's optimism annoyed him. War was so unpredictable that few of those in it had any clear idea of how it would turn out.

CHAPTER SEVENTEEN

AS THE HELO, Marine One, descended gracefully to the south lawn of the White House, the president of the United States confessed to National Security Adviser Prenty and his press secretary that he'd made a mistake in agreeing to come back from Camp David. The line of protestors was much longer than Marte Price had reported. "They bus them in," said the press secretary.

"Who," asked Eleanor Prenty, "buses in protestors against us tracking down terrorists?"

"Those people," replied the press secretary, "who don't think America should make unilateral decisions about sending our armed forces into other countries."

The president felt the gentle touchdown. "And what do you think?" the president asked his press secretary.

"I think you did the right thing, Mr. President. So long as terrorists think they can hit us and run to sanctuary, we have to go into the sanctuaries."

"Well said."

The president stepped down from the chopper, returned the marine's salute, and, slipping his tie back under his suit jacket, felt the hardness of the bulletproof vest beneath. He gave a presidential wave to both the protesters and those, including a group from Idaho, who were holding signs up supporting the "Bird Rescue" intervention.

"Mr. President," said Eleanor Prenty, walking beside

him, "by my count, the supporters outnumber the pro-testers."

"Good," the president told her. "But if Freeman and Colonel Tibbet don't pull this Bird Rescue off and de-stroy that damn terrorist complex, we'll tank in the polls. Excuse me being such a hard-ass, but I can't do what I want to do in this country unless I'm reelected, and I sure as hell won't be if Freeman and Tibbet blow it."

He had no sooner entered the Oval Office than the white phone, the direct line from Moscow, rang.

The Russian president wanted the American anti-terrorist force out of Lake Khanka before the twenty-four hours were up. He was taking a great amount of flak from the opposition in the newly elected Duma, the Russian parliament.

The president of the United States told his Russian counterpart that he understood, and would have the Penta-gon give Freeman the timeline. "But please, Mr. President, don't let any of your enemies know. In fact, I suggest it would be better if you didn't mention it to any—"

"I am not an idiot," retorted the Russian president. "Then there would be added pressure on me as well as on your General Freeman. But tell this Freeman to hurry up. He wins or loses when the twenty-four hours have passed, and it is getting late. Otherwise I cannot hold the hotheads at bay. It *could* be general war."

Freeman couldn't receive the White House message, however, because his team's encrypter was out of com-mission.

Tibbet had received Freeman's transmit and acknowl-edged the same, but since then there had been no reply from the general. "Still nothing on encrypt?" Tibbet asked his second in command.

"No, sir. Not on encrypt. Thought he might have fixed it by now or picked up another decoder from another platoon in his sector, but I guess everyone's lying low till the snow—"

"Not Freeman," cut in Tibbet, who was looking at his marines strung out on either side of him, lying down behind the escarpment that his platoon was using as protective high ground beyond one of the small, acre-sized woods that stood like islands in the sea of marshlands that bordered, and in some places spread out for miles from, the lake. The escarpment was only a few feet high, but with the piling up of snowdrifts it had grown to nearly twice that height, Tibbet reminding his men that they must lie low until he received Freeman's situation report. If the general's "Go" or "Yankee" call couldn't be sent because the general's encrypter-decoder machine was down, then his "Yankee" call would come either by Hummer, runner, or in plain language, but not before Freeman judged his team ready for a joint attack against ABC.

"What direction for the attack, sir?" inquired Bravo Company's Major Hoyt.

Tibbet grimaced in the snowfall. Though the snow was easing off, it was still bitterly cold. He kept flexing his gloved hands to keep his blood moving.

He gave the major the coordinates for the planned attack. "But keep them to yourself until we—if we—get that "go" call from Freeman. I don't want it going through the company if, God forbid, one of our guys is captured and tells them that we know where the tunnel's entrance and exit are. Remember, that time they got one of our guys in Iraq and—"

"Arty!" someone shouted, and Tibbet's group of seven and two fire teams kissed the snow again. The shell sounded like a 220 mm, one of the Russians' thermobaric rockets. It slammed into a rise of marshland scrub several hundred yards to Tibbet's left, the shock wave sweeping over Tibbet's marines like a furnace blast.

"We'll be in trouble when the weather clears," said Major Hoyt. "Those TOSs have a cant sensor and computerized fire control. Once they can pick us up visually they—"

"I *know* that," said Tibbet. The Russian TOSs were big, ugly boxes of thirty rockets set on a T-72 chassis. He felt anxious and looked at his watch while taking care not to express any more signs of anxiety in front of his HQ group. He estimated that there were now more than 1,200 marines landed, consolidating the line. It was a very thin line, given the huge area of the lake and environs. The 1,200 had sounded like a lot, however, to the marine quartermaster back on board *Yorktown*, who had to find every item needed, from the "snow whites" he'd sent with the second wave to each of the Marine force's thirty Land Warrior Micro Air Vehicle Systems. Each LAWMAVS was no bigger than a child's rubber-band-and-balsa-wood glider, and had a transparent fuselage containing a laser range finder, video camera, and computer. The hair-thin spars of its tiny tail and wings were transmitter antennae. But now, like Chipper Armstrong's and Manowski's JSFs, the LAWMAVS, one issued to each forty-one-man platoon in the MEU, were grounded by the atrocious weather.

Jack Tibbet ordered his communications operator, "If we don't get a 'Yankee call' in ten minutes, I want you to send a plain language to Freeman. Get your pad."

"I'll punch it in now, sir, and save."

"No, to hell with it. Send it now."

"Right, sir," replied Jimmy.

Tibbet frowned in concentration. "PL message is as follows:

AIRSEYRAENAKDEYE.

Tibbet paused, remembering the emergency keys he and Freeman had agreed on. The first plain-language transmit from Freeman would contain a BIRTE—built-in reverse target (error) with a *three*-letter key at the end of the message to open it, the three-letter key being any three-letter initials of a U.S. president: HST for Harry Truman, or JFK, LBJ, GWB, et cetera. Tibbet's reply, also with a built-in reverse target error, was to be signed off with the *two*-letter initials of a president, such as AL for Abraham Lincoln, JC for Jimmy Carter, et cetera.

"Sign it HT," said Tibbet. "It's a hurry-up for Freeman," he explained to his radio operator. "We can't broadcast the fact that we've had a twenty-four-hour deadline placed on us. The terrorists here at Lake Khanka would love to know that. We might have to go in sooner than we thought."

"Message sent, sir."

"Very well," acknowledged Tibbet.

"Snow is easing," said Hoyt encouragingly.

"Not fast enough," said Tibbet. "We can't even use our MAVs. They were supposed to relay back good pix to us."

Jimmy, Tibbet's radio operator, had been monitoring the weather forecasts. "Sir, they say the weather's changeable around the lake here. And with those mountains nearby, everything can change in a jiffy."

"*They* say," Tibbet said. "Who are *they*, Jimmy? *Farmer's Almanac*?"

"No, CNN, sir. That Marte Price woman. She's covering the op."

Tibbet muttered an obscenity. As Tibbet's radio operator, Jimmy Vanes was one of the few marines authorized to "dial up" CNN pix on a cell, because no commander wanted his troops second-guessing themselves in the midst of a battle because of some talking face five thousand miles away in Atlanta, like those "embedded" correspondents who had reported every hit the U.S. Army took and every terrorist hostage murdered, creating the impression that U.S. and Coalition forces were on the ropes.

"Turn that damn CNN phone off, Jimmy."

"Yessir. Sorry, I—sir! Reply coming in. Plain language reads: YGAONOKDETEOEGSOTJ. Last two letters 'TJ.'"

"Thomas Jefferson?" proffered Tibbet.

Jimmy was already breaking the message, minus the two signature letters "TJ," into two lines. It read:

YANKEEES
GOODTOGO.

"Very well," said Tibbet. "Pass the word."

In ABC's H-block, Sergei Cherkashin rushed in, thumping the snow from his fur hat and gloves. "What a break, huh?" he said, smiling, the frosty air issuing from his breath rising up to mix with Abramov's cigar smoke.

"What are you talking about?" asked Abramov tersely, still feeling that his armor in its hidden revetment areas could be bombed once the snow stopped and their engines started up, giving off infrared signatures of the kind his two big TOS tracked rocket launchers were looking out for in the American lines along the perimeter.

"They cracked the code of that Freeman to Tibbet message?" Beria asked hopefully.

"No, no, Comrades," said Cherkashin, stomping his snow-laden boots, "I mean the message from Moscow. My assembly line captain—who, I might add, gentlemen, is keeping the three tunnels working as we speak—heard it not more than five minutes ago."

Beria and Abramov said nothing. ABC's assembly line captains were *supposed* to keep the production lines moving 24/7 no matter what. Did Cherkashin think the U.S. Marine Corps took a day off in battle?

"Well," Cherkashin began, pouring himself coffee, relishing the moment, despite knowing how much his petty drama annoyed his comrades, "this captain heard it on the 'banned' Chechen terrorist radio network. It appears that fourteen hours before the Chechen network heard of it, our glorious Comrade President issued the Americans a twenty-four-hour deadline. *Twenty-four hours?* And," Cherkashin glanced up at the old pendulum clock, a museum piece in the sparse, brutal Stalinesque architecture of the H-block, "that means by now these boys the Americans have sent to do a man's job have only four hours to do us any damage. So, my comrades in arms, this shit Freeman is in a box. *Our* box. We've got more men than he has, plus your twenty T-90s, Mikhail. All we have to do is keep him away from the tunnels for another—"

"He knows about the tunnels." It was Abramov, hands forming a chin rest, the smoke rising from his head as if he was on fire. "Your stupid computers, Viktor," he told Beria. "While they've been, what did you call it, crunching the numbers, I've worked it out with pen and paper." With that, the tank commander of the Siberian Sixth turned around the notepad he'd been working on and fixed his eyes on Beria who, frowning, stared down through the Havana's bluish brown haze.

Abramov sat back in his chair. "Well, Viktor, you've been crunching numbers, with all your permutations and—what d'you call them—combinations, but they're all wrong. You haven't got the message, have you?" Abramov didn't wait for a reply. "Because you assumed the key, the signature key, in that plain-language message that your experts intercepted is FDR. These three initials were given at the end, so you thought, 'Ah, it's a three-line message.' In fact, it's a *nine*-line message, arrived at by the sum of the number of letters in Roosevelt, nine. Obviously the key for their message was the initials of any American president, so the three letters 'FDR' are just to tell them which American president's name to use. It could have been an American actor or something, but the prearranged key between Freeman and Tibbet was presidential initials."

Viktor Beria gazed down noncommitally at Mikhail Abramov's jottings. There was no doubt that Abramov had indeed cleverly broken the long line of 129 letters in the plain-language string down to nine lines of fourteen letters each, so that the plain language text revealed Freeman's message to Tibbet as:

WHENYOURECEIVE
YANKEEGOODTOGO
FROMMEBOTHOFUS
WILLNOTHITEXIT
BUTHITENTRANCE
ANDWIPETHEMOUT
ANDMRPETERROSE
NEVERDIDGAMBLE
GOODLUCKFORUSA

Beria picked up the yellow sheet and sat down in one of the six ugly but functional metal chairs that lined the room's walls.

Abramov was sitting back now, allowing himself a victorious smile. "So, Viktor, you're right. We do have a gift." Abramov drew in a full draft of the dense cigar smoke. "We know that when Freeman radios 'Yankee good to go' to the colonel, Tibbet, the Americans are going to attack the entrance. And, thanks to the Chechen radio report, we now know Freeman and Tibbet have to attack effectively in the next few hours to allow for any hope of success and—" Abramov paused for effect. "—it will give us ample time in which to evacuate the tunnels."

"Beautiful!" said Beria approvingly, his arms spread out like an angel's wings. "We get all our technicians out and set one big fuck of an explosion at the entrance. Blow his— what do the Americans call those marines, leathernecks? Yes, Comrades. We'll blow Freeman and his leathernecks sky high. The snow will be red with American blood."

"I like it," said Cherkashin, the mood in Abramov's office so upbeat it was all but palpable. Cherkashin was beaming. He looked at both the infantry and the tank general. "We've got him, Comrades, in the box. Once he's in, we'll close the lid. He's finished."

Abramov exhaled, the usually taciturn, no-nonsense commander of the Siberian Sixth allowing himself the visceral excitement of anticipated revenge. "Yes," he agreed. "It's payback time for our nemesis, gentlemen, but a word of caution. Close the entrance's two blast doors, but don't leave the outer door unguarded or he might suspect a trap. We'll load the space between the outer and inner security doors with explosives. We can destroy the enemy without destroying the equipment." Abramov looked at Viktor Beria. "How big is the outer door, Viktor?"

"Five meters high, ten meters wide."

Abramov nodded. "And the depth of the space between the entrance's outer door and its inner blast door?"

"One meter," said Beria. "Maybe more."

Abramov sat quietly, thinking. None of the three bothered to go down to the tunnels much; once you'd seen the technicians assemble one MANPAD, torpedo, or missile on the tunnel's production line, there wasn't much more to see, and the air, despite the constant roar of the high ventilation shafts, was dank, heavy with the sour smell of perspiration. Abramov, Beria, and Cherkashin preferred

being in the ABC H-block, down in its palatially fur-
nished bunker, if necessary, taking care of the consor-
tium's business, which had never been better since the
fundamentalist Muslim terrorists' decision to carry out
bin Laden's promise to destroy America.

"You know," boasted Beria, "these boys of mine,
guarding the entrance, they might stop Freeman by themselves, without the need for any explosive."

"Is that a wish or a question?" Abramov shot back as he
simultaneously grabbed his landline phone to call the duty
officer in charge of the guards at the entrance to the tunnels, asking Beria, "Are you worried about them, Viktor?"

Abramov punched in the duty officer's number, while
answering his own question to Beria. "I wouldn't concern
myself, Viktor. They get their bonuses, same as everyone
else here. But look, if they can't hold, we'll blow them up
with the American bastards. We can't afford a disruption
of production. Ramon and his friends have been unequivocal on this point. And for what his clients pay for our
merchandise, you can't blame him. The Arabs especially
are constantly pushing him for product. They want to be
the first to use it against the U.S. in the U.S. That's why
they sent El-Hage up here."

"Yes," added Cherkashin, "with his blue-eyed boy."

"Who El Hage sleeps with," Abramov countered, "is
not our concern."

The duty officer was sorry he'd kept Abramov on hold;
he'd been in the bathroom. Abramov fined him a hundred
dollars on the spot for not having arranged for someone to
man the phone during his absence. "Now," Abramov continued, "be sure that you seal that second door. Switch off
the air flow that's sucked down from the surface to feed
the tunnels. Just have enough air coming in from the intake shafts we have hidden in the reeds around the exit."

Abramov saw Cherkashin glancing agitatedly at his

watch. "I know what I'm doing, Sergei. You look after your anti-aircraft batteries. If this snow stops, you might be busy for a while. The Americans'll try to use any gunships they managed to put down around the lake. We've had BMD patrolling there, but remember the lake is four thousand square kilometers. We've been shelling the woods sector in hopes of hitting anything hidden in them, but the snowdrifts have created a lot of hiding places that normally wouldn't be there on the flats." Abramov turned to Cherkashin. "Viktor's right. With such a time limit on them, the Americans are in a box." He paused, asking his two comrades, "How do the Americans say it? Shooting fish in a barrel?"

Before either man could respond, Abramov advised Cherkashin, "So, Sergei, have your men ready with their MANPADs. Al Jazeera will love it. It'll be the best commercial we could have wished for. But be thorough. We don't want to take chances. Seal the exit doors as well in the unlikely event that a few of the bastards escape the explosion in the entrance and manage to make it through the tunnels to the exit shaft."

"Good," said Beria.

"Yes," replied Abramov, "we'll play it safe." He couldn't suppress a smile. "Can you imagine, Comrades, CNN has another special coming up and doesn't even know it! This'll be bigger than Katrina."

"Will there be enough air sucked in from the exit ventilators for our guys in the tunnels?" asked Beria. "I'd say pull them out, but you're correct. We've got a backlog of Al Qaeda and Hezbollah orders."

"And," added Cherkashin, "we have Wadi El-Hage here from Hamas, with his blue-eyed boy."

"What's the deal with El-Hage?" asked Beria.

Abramov didn't respond, busying himself with consulting his *rukovoditel vzryvchika*—blaster's manual—for the correct amount of RDX with a detonation of 26,000 feet per second in order to annihilate the Americans.

"What's the deal?" repeated Beria.

"Don't you read my memos?" responded Cherkashin, miffed that Beria didn't recall all the work he and Abramov had put into securing the deal between ABC and Hamas. "Our agreement with El-Hage is to give him a hundred Igla and Vanguard MANPADs in return for him having Hamas kill the infidel American general."

"That was a contingency plan," Beria conceded, "when we first heard that Freeman had been assigned to track down Ramon and his team."

Cherkashin's tone was terse with sarcasm. "Well, Viktor, I'd say having Freeman in our backyard is a fucking *contingency*!"

"All right, all right," answered the infantry commander. "I just left it up to Mikhail."

"You always do," charged Cherkashin. "You sign off on the memos then leave the unpleasant work to everyone else."

"What's got your balls in a trap, Comrade?" retorted Beria.

Abramov's desk phone jangled. The conversation was short, and as he hung up he rose, tightening his pistol belt, the Makarov 9 mm snug against his waist. "The Americans are starting to move, now it's stopped snowing. So I suggest, Comrades, that you save all your piss and vinegar for them. Remember what Rommel used to say: 'If you feel irritable, kill something.'"

"Huh," griped Beria. "I don't need to be out of sorts to kill Americans, but I don't like being accused of laziness. My battalion has always been ready to—"

"Sergei isn't accusing you of anything," said Abramov. "He's upset about El-Hage bringing the boy with him.

Sergei's a prude—either that or some Arab tried to fuck him when he was a boy. Eh, Sergei, is that it?"

"If an Arab had tried to mess with me," said Sergei, "I'd have strangled the bastard."

Quite suddenly, Abramov abandoned all levity and punched the air force general affectionately on the shoulder. "So would I, Sergei. I would do the same thing. But business is business, Comrade. Those MANPADs for El-Hage'll bring five million. Tax free."

Cherkashin, somewhat mollified by the promise of five million U.S. dollars, nodded in agreement. "The thing is," responded Cherkashin, "we don't need a suicide bomber now that we have Freeman in a trap."

"Added insurance," said Abramov.

"Are they still at the farmhouse?" asked Cherkashin.

"Yes," confirmed Abramov, "outside Kamen Rybolov."

"That's on the lake," cut in Beria. "Isn't that a bit close?"

"*K chertovoy materi!*—Dammit—Viktor!" said Cherkashin. "Didn't you read *any* of the memos I sent you? Yes, it's a farmhouse, but it's six miles from the tunnels here. The idea was to have one of the farm vehicles, a trailor rig with a white flag, approaching the American line for help. Americans are suckers for that kind of stuff."

"Americans suck," said Abramov, and they all laughed at the memory of Ramon's scroll.

"Well," began Beria, but couldn't continue until he coughed out the smoke from Abramov's Havana. "Freeman won't suck in the morning. He'll be dead!"

Abramov's tobacco-stained lower teeth were visible as his jaws closed hard on the cigar. "Dead?" he joked. "In that heat, Viktor, the bastard'll evaporate!" With this, Abramov picked up the phone again and rang the entrance DO. "You all set with the RDX?"

"All set, sir."

"Good."

"Ah, General Abramov?"

"Yes?"

"Sir, shouldn't we leave right now?" asked the duty officer. "I mean, the guard party as well as production line staff?"

Abramov was again dusting ash off his uniform. "You have the remote?"

"Yes, sir," the DO answered.

"Well, then, bring it to me. Right now. Tell the guard detail you'll be back in a half hour, unless you want to stay with them."

"You've notified the production line, General?"

"I've got your bonus. If you obey orders, you can forget about your fine. And I'll triple your bonus. If you don't, you'll get nothing."

"I'm on my way, General."

"Excellent."

Money could do anything.

"So," said Beria, who frequently annoyed Abramov and Cherkashin with just this expression.

"So *what*?" asked Abramov, getting up and grabbing his cap from the stand, hearing the rain pelting down.

"So this is it. The Americans are on the move."

"Yes, we know that, Viktor."

CHAPTER EIGHTEEN

INDEED THE AMERICANS were moving, and quickly, Freeman telling his fire team of Aussie, Choir, Sal, Lee, and Gomez, the TOW Hummer's three-man crew, and twelve other marines, including Melissa Thomas, that now speed was everything. Speed with *"l'audace, l'audace, toujours l'audace!"* The Hummer was to be their mobile missile platform. The twelve marines would form a crescent around the exit, and Freeman's team would hit the exit itself.

"Do we know approximately where it is, General?" Aussie had asked on their departure from the wood.

"Approximately," answered the general. His force was moving west southwest from the wood toward the midsection of the twelve-mile north-south rail line, between the town of Kamen Rybolov and the hamlet of Ilinka, leaving a new fire team from the advancing second wave to occupy the wood and so protect the hide of Chipper Armstrong's Joint Strike Fighter in a natural revetment amongst fir and deadwood debris at the northwest sector of the wood. For despite the all-weather capability of the JSF, the weather would have to improve further before either Freeman or Tibbet would unleash it for close air support. Freeman intended to get so close to the enemy that even with the JSF's state-of-the-art avionics and friend-or-foe detector, the danger of blue on blue was too acute to risk it.

In the air beyond the wood, errant ABC artillery was coming down in unprecedented lines of fire, a nightmare of work for ABC's gunners who, located between the H-block and the minefield, had to continually change not only the elevation but also the azimuth settings of their guns. It meant added anxiety for Freeman's force, for, unlike a creeping barrage or a fire-for-effect barrage, there was no discernible pattern that it could plan to avoid. And out here, trudging through the marsh, where snow would soon turn to a muddy slush, the high whistle of enemy artillery rounds, whether coughed out from the T-90s' main guns or by the big, brutish TOS, seemed much louder in the absence of the noise-dampening wood now a hundred yards behind them. Gomez, out on Freeman's left, saw a flash, dived, but never reached the white, soggy earth before the air-delivered incendiary bomb exploded in an intense aerosol. The blast lifted him up like a rag doll before dropping him to the earth.

"Corpsman!" bellowed Freeman, and within twenty seconds the marine medic ran fifty meters from the wood through rain and snow, Aussie Lewis using his hands to pack Gomez in snow, snuffing out the multiple globs of fire all over Gomez's body.

Three minutes later, Aussie rejoined Freeman's group of nineteen—now four in his team, the Hummer's three, and the twelve marines.

"How's Gomez?" Freeman asked Aussie.

"Third-degree burns. Those fucking TOSs, fucking flamethrower bombs. Outlawed by the Geneva Convention. Fucking Russians used them against the Chechens."

"That was against civilians," Freeman said. "Not combatants."

"Geneva Convention banned them against combatants, too," Aussie corrected him.

"Keep your voice down," Freeman told him.

"Incoming!"

They all dropped to the snow as a full salvo, thirty of the TOS rounds, screamed upon launch, a long "shoosh" overhead, and crashed into the wood. Ironically, Gomez, helped by a medic and another marine who'd come out from the wood to meet them, was momentarily safer in the open while parts of the wood were burning.

"I suppose," Freeman challenged Aussie as they got to their feet and the general spat out a gob of dirty snow, "that you don't think I should have shot those two Russians back there?"

Aussie shrugged. For him to criticize the general would have been what his mother used to call a case of the pot calling the kettle black. The war on terror was exactly that, a war, not a here-and-there situation where you had time for a seminar on human rights. It was an ongoing every night, every day thing for these and other soldiers fighting terror around the globe.

They walked on in the pouring rain for another fifteen minutes, each man lost in his own thoughts, until they paused before what Freeman believed, from the dead Korean's map, would be another fifteen-minute walk to the exit which should be recognizable by a cluster of hot air vents. "It's hard, sometimes," the general told Aussie, "when you're hunting evil not to become evil yourself. Stress. We'll all have to answer to God for that."

Aussie, his eyes temporarily focusing on the curtain of rain, wasn't surprised either by the answer or by the fact that the general hadn't sidestepped or dismissed it. It was the kind of dilemma that the general had trained all his men to examine. Here, in this cold, damp clime, Aussie recalled the hot, dry day years before in Iraq where *he* had been prepared on a mere hunch to take out a civilian who was running toward him, pleading, with a baby.

Freeman and his group continued to spearhead the

Hummer by fifty yards, the general preferring to place himself and the others in the snow- and now rain-veiled reeds ahead of the sound of the Hummer. The downpour was a subdued roar as it pelted down on the ant and termite mounds in the reeds and, along with the partially melting sheets of ice, flooded the indigent flora. Unless they kept moving fast, the ice would start crunching underfoot, giving their position away, despite what was now the shoulder-high cover of sodden reeds.

Freeman, moving and thinking fast on point, realized the Russians had been particularly clever, arranging for the incoming fresh air and outgoing bad air vents to be hidden in the tall reeds of the lake and marshlands. These were the last places anyone would suspect of having three tunnels beneath them; tunnels that, from the dead Korean engineer's info, ran for about three hundred feet back from here near the edge of the lake's southwestern marsh to directly below ABC's H-block. It meant that the land mines, like the one that had fatally wounded Eddie Mervyn, must have been sown from where Eddie had fallen all the way back to the H-block.

But there were certain things that the map, the scale of which was approximate, hadn't shown, and Freeman wondered whether or not there was any kind of security apron of mines immediately beyond the exit.

They were now approaching the area where Eddie had tripped the mine. The general's senses were in sync. Excited by the sounds of renewed battle all around him, he was absorbing and processing every sight, sound, and memory he could possibly monitor under the pressure of the looming deadline. Freeman's experience and his encyclopedic knowledge of military tactics had taught him how Russians, unlike their American counterparts, were not known for building in redundancy. In the U.S. Cheyenne Mountain tunnel complex, the rock-covered redoubt of

NORAD control, there was always more than one of anything in case something broke down. The Russian ruble's collapse, after the end of the Cold War, and the frantic drive amongst Russian entrepreneurs to catch up, to make a quick buck, had, as far as Freeman saw, done nothing to reduce the no-redundancy problem. His guess therefore was that there was probably only one exit. The scale of the map that Melissa Thomas had retrieved from the Korean engineer placed the exit in an area of about a square mile, but in the hurry he and the rest of the group were in, there wouldn't be much, if any, time to do an in-depth search, and—

"I see it!" announced Aussie. "Vapor. Eleven o'clock, a hundred yards."

Freeman saw something buck violently in the tall, rain-curtained rocks beyond the two- to three-foot rise he'd felt earlier in the day before Eddie had fallen. The heat and scream of the TOS's rounds rushed over them, exploding in the wood of Mongolian oak at the height of a man. Splintered oak, clods of sand, reeds, frozen earth, and vegetation cascaded around them, frozen lumps of ice-veined marsh mud striking Aussie's and Melissa Thomas's helmets.

The big forty-two-ton TOS-1 bucked again, the Hummer's tires churning up reeds, ice, and sand as it veered wildly left and right to avoid being hit. A TOS round— they were usually fired at distances of under four hundred yards—missed the Hummer again, this time ripping open a nearby colony of man-sized ant nests with such force that the concussion swept into the group with the strength of a kick in the back. The shock had put young Melissa Thomas into a dangerous comatose condition that, without immediate access to state-of-the-art MASH equipment, could result in her slipping into deep coma.

"Mark that vent!" Freeman shouted, but most couldn't see it. Freeman pointed immediately right and ducked. "Down!"

The Hummer's TOW missile, its control vanes and wires silver streaks through the rain, had hit the TOS, causing it to buck again. But this time it wasn't moving from the recoil of firing another 222 mm thermobaric warhead but flying apart, its metal fragments bansheeing through the rain-slashed air, the marine fire team and the remainder of the group scrambling for protection behind anthill, tree stump, anything nearby. The fragments from the TOS rained down over the minefield, setting off a score of anti-personnel mines to the right, where Freeman had been pointing when the Hummer's corporal had gotten the big, lumbering TOS in his sights.

As the shower of debris diminished, Freeman again shouted, "Find that vent. Move!" While his men spread out, Freeman called out to Aussie, "Give me a hand here." The general was kneeling by the unconscious Thomas; she had no pulse. "Help me drag her to that ant pile." Aussie did as he was told, but wondered why bother wasting time trying to get the young marine to the shelter of a damned ant heap.

"Found it!" It was young Kegg. He meant the outlet vents, not the exit itself. "They're using tree stumps to house the air vents. Looks like three, no, *four* of 'em. They're all grated and elbowed like a sink to stop leaves and crap falling in."

Freeman called out to Sal. "You, Johnny, and Choir see if you can find the exit opening in this snow. It'll probably be flush to the earth, maybe a trapdoor in that high hump. I don't think it'll be mined, but watch your step."

"Yes, sir," said Sal, shooting a quick glance at Aussie and at the prostrate marine. "Think she'll be okay?"

"We'll see," said Freeman, quickly tearing off her flak

jacket and ripping open her khaki shirt. "Bandage her eyes quickly!" he told Aussie, as Sal ran off, Kegg and the fire team forming a defense perimeter after tagging the four tree stumps that contained the tin housings that were shaped like the number 7. Two were intakes, two outlets, the shoulder-high reeds hiding them, but condensation was clearly visible where the warmer vented air met the icy Arctic air.

"Hurry up, Aussie!"

"What I don't understand," said Aussie, quickly using his own field bandage to blindfold the comatose Thomas, "is that the rumor in the group is that you told Colonel Tibbet in your message to him that we're going to attack the *entrance* to the tunnels, not the exit?"

"I know," said the general, and nothing more.

The moment Aussie had finished blindfolding Melissa, Freeman grabbed the marine's ankles and dragged her onto the ant heap. The insects immediately swarmed over the invader's chest, face, and body.

"What in hell—" began Aussie, but before he could get out the next word, Thomas's body was in spasm, her heart given the jolt it needed—not an invasive jolt of electricity but a collective jolt of poison from the hundreds of ant bites, shocking her heart back into action via her body's adrenaline response.

"Shit!" said Aussie, seeing her twitching, coming back to life. "You're a fucking genius, General."

"I'd argue if I could, Aussie," said Freeman, dragging Melissa, who was now screaming with pain, away from the insects. "Quiet!" he told her as she struggled to stand up, fell back, then succeeded with his help. "We're taking off the blindfold, Melissa. Didn't want those ants to get at your eyes."

"Ants—what—I—"

"Be quiet," Freeman told her sternly as she collapsed

again. "You'll wake up the neighborhood," a comment that added to Aussie Lewis's awe at what he'd just seen on this battlefield. If I survive, he promised himself, I'll never forget this, ever.

Freeman jabbed her with a one-time morphine syringe, and pushed out a small oval pink pill from his first-aid blister pack. "Benadryl. This'll help. Make you a bit dozy, but not too much."

Again, Melissa was trying, very unsteadily, to get on her feet, but the effect of the TOS round's concussion was still evident in her wobbly walk as Aussie, hustling as much as he dared, led her over to the high brush- and reed-covered ground where wisps of vapor could be seen bleeding from the marsh and which Kegg and another in his fire team suspected of housing the exit door.

On closer examination, Kegg saw there were other large, circular bumps of snow, rocks sticking through, the lake now turning a chafflike brown color, the glistening ice tent that had formerly sheathed them now melting in the downpour that was sending the ants into a further frenzy as they sought to repair the earthquake that had assaulted them in the blast from the explosion of the 222 mm missile and Thomas's sudden appearance in their midst.

"We'll have you medevaced ASAP," Freeman assured Melissa. "Soon as we get this tunnel business wrapped up."

Aussie handed Thomas her M40A1 rifle. "Can you still use this?" He had to repeat it in the din.

"You kidding?" said Melissa, mistaking genuine concern as criticism of the only female marine combatant in *Yorktown*'s Marine Expeditionary Unit.

Beneath the superbly camouflaged net roof of ABC's tank park near the H-block, General Abramov, with Cherkashin nearby, was issuing last-minute instructions to his Siberian Sixth's second in command, Colonel Nureyev, a short, tough, thickset man whom his tank crews called "The Dancer," in deliberate contrast to the great, nimble-footed Nureyev of ballet fame, and stressing to *all* his Siberian Sixth tank captains that, except for a few main battle tanks that had been given weapons-free status and sent out to harass the American flanks, most of the T-90s must be held back. These would be ready to surge around and into the main American force that Abramov was certain would soon launch an attack against the H-block. But no sooner had he explained the situation to the Siberian Sixth, than Abramov saw at least two platoons of Beria's Naval Infantry company moving through the safe channels in the minefield before turning south toward the exit area about a mile from Freeman's force.

"What's the point?" Abramov thundered at Beria, who was standing in his infantry command car. Abramov was incredulous. "You should have kept your men back here, Beria. Didn't you read the intercept between Freeman and Tibbet that I decoded? Why are you committing your best infantry over there on the lake side near the exit? Dammit, didn't you read the message? Freeman is only using the attack on the exit as a diversionary tactic, when all the time he and Tibbet plan to hit us here at the H-block, the entrance to the tunnels. So, I'm asking you, Viktor, why are you bothering to commit your crack naval infantry to the damned exit?"

"Because I *have* read your decode. What's more, I've re-read and re-read it and now I think that maybe Freeman is trying to pull a fast one. I think he intends to make the main attack through the exit."

"How do you *possibly* come to that conclusion? You think I'm an idiot? You think I've decoded the message incorrectly?"

"No," answered Beria. "I don't think there's anything

wrong with your decoding, but that you haven't understood what Freeman means."

"*I*'ve misunderstood, you say? What it tells me, Viktor—and, I might add, what it tells Cherkashin—is that we need everybody *here,* particularly crack troops like yours, to guard headquarters and the computer. The whole thrust of Freeman's message—if you'd read it *carefully*—is that he intends to attack the *entrance.* Freeman knows, and he's right, that if he destroys us and the computer here at headquarters, the Americans have won. Lathes—all the engineering stuff in the tunnels—can be replaced, but if the DARPA ALPHA information, is destroyed, then we're finished. *My propali!* Kaput! Didn't you read the decode, or what?"

Beria was stunned. What the hell was Abramov ranting about, asking him ad nauseam whether he understood the intercepted message between Freeman and Tibbet?

"*Da,*" Beria said, employing the sullen tone of a disrespectful peasant, staring angrily at Abramov and his big-prick cigar. "Yes, Comrade General, I saw your fucking decode, but you're so cocksure of yourself, Mikhail, you're not seeing what the hell is happening, are you?" Beria paused, using his revolver hand to angrily wave away the thick, bluish gray smoke, the Havana's stink mixing with the choking fumes of Abramov's twenty massed main battle tanks. "Aren't you watching Freeman's troops over there through your binoculars? If you ask me, they're more than a diversionary force. They're marines from the *American fleet.* They're tough bastards."

"Huh," said Abramov dismissively. "You're seeing what you want to believe."

Beria looked hard at Abramov. With the sounds of battle growing closer, he reached inside his battle tunic, pulled out his copy of Abramov's decoded intercept, and quickly read it aloud, then asked Abramov, "The reference to this Peter Rose?"

"Yes, I saw it," said Abramov. "It's probably a good-luck phrase the Americans use in the same way that we—"

"Do you know who Pete Rose is?" Beria pressed, breaking open his pistol. It was always the last check he made before going into action, like rubbing a rabbit's foot for good luck.

"No," Abramov answered testily, "I don't know who he is and, as I said, it doesn't matter. A go-code or an operational name can be anything. Operation 'Bird Rescue,' for example."

Beria, seeing that each chamber was loaded, snapped the revolver shut. "You see no other significance in the name?"

"No."

Beria, slipping the revolver into his holster, asked Cherkashin the same question.

"No," answered Cherkashin, who, up to this point, had been ignoring the argument, poring instead over his pilot's tactical charts and the meteorological reports, which called for more heavy rain.

"Rose," said Beria, "was an American baseball player. Famous."

Neither the air force general nor Abramov showed much interest.

"I don't follow sports," said Abramov, with an air of condescension, as a wine snob might address a beer drinker, after which he took obvious satisfaction, as commander of the Sixth Siberian Armored as well as overall garrison commander, in ordering that the bulk of ABC's forces, at least three-quarters of all personnel, were to secure H-block. His tanks would form a ring of steel around it so that the assault force, which the American was no doubt assembling with a fresh infusion of marines from the second wave, would not be met by a skeleton ABC force as Freeman would no doubt have it, but instead would be annihilated. And if the guards in the tunnels could not hold, the duty officer need only press a button and the RDX would vaporize the enemy in the tunnels— as well as many of ABC's soldiers. But Abramov knew that such "collateral damage" could always be replaced by ABC's danger bonuses. Russia was full of desperate men without work, soldiers without work.

"Pete Rose," Beria continued, "was disgraced and never made baseball's Hall of Fame at Cooperstown because he had been caught betting on baseball games. I think mention of him by Freeman is to tell Tibbet that everything in the message is exactly the opposite of what Freeman intends to do."

"You're crazy," said Abramov. "You've been reading too much American press. It's full of lies."

Beria ignored the remark and continued calmly, "During World War II, when English-speaking Japanese pilots tried to pass themselves off on radio as Americans, the American pilots, if suspicious, used to ask questions, the answers to which were common knowledge to born-and-bred Americans. If the American pilots didn't get the right responses, they knew there was a spy amongst them. And if you've bothered to read Freeman's file—indeed, if you know anything about Freeman—you'll know he has an encyclopedic mind about things military, and it's exactly the kind of trickery and wartime practice that he'd know about."

Abramov opened his hands, like a holy man, in the universal gesture of conciliation. "I tell you, Viktor, this Pete Rose thing is nothing. The phrase is probably merely a decryption identification key for their intercomputer traffic. You're being paranoid, Viktor. Now recall your infantry."

Before Beria could respond, Cherkashin added, "Mikhail's right, Viktor. You're making too much of this. We're all on edge. But you have to recall your naval platoons because we'll need them here. We'll finish the Americans off together, eh?"

It was two against one, so Beria compromised. He recalled two of the four platoons—eighty of the best, and now most highly paid, terrorist infantry in the world.

"Good decision, Viktor," said Abramov. "Now I should tell you both that I've ordered several company HQs to assign video technicians along the two-mile front. That means, Comrades, the pictures of the Americans being decimated as they attack us will be on CNN and Al Jazeera this evening, tomorrow morning's newscasts at the latest."

Cherkashin was a tad uncomfortable with Abramov's use of the word "decimated." The tank general was using it, Cherkashin knew, as most people did, to mean a casualty rate of nine out of ten, when in fact it had originally meant one casualty in ten. Still, this was a high rate for American commanders. Abramov's TV idea was a good one, because the American public always started to panic as soon as they saw a single body bag coming off an aircraft on CNN. And when the CNN woman with the big chest, Marte Price, started yakking about more American casualties, the Americans would start going weak at the knees. She and other American media announcers were considered by ABC's clientele such as El-Hage, Hamas, and Hezbollah as valuable, albeit unwitting, propagandists for the terrorist cause.

One of a pair of Hummers flown in less than ten minutes before from the second wave and ordered by Tibbet to assist Freeman in his attack through the tunnels' exit, skidded to a stop as its gunner saw tanks moving and snaking quickly through the minefield's safe road. The four tanks' commanders were doing an Israeli, standing up, cupolas open to see better in the pouring rain, despite the T-90s' infrared recon and laser-targeting system. The commanders, four of Abramov's best from the Siberian Sixth, were cursing the snaking course of the road, meant to keep the tanks off a straight line to prevent any anti-armor units having time to "frame" them for successful missile attack. But now that the American line was reported as being still five hundred yards southeast of the square mile of mines, it was unlikely any of them would see any more Russian armor in the heavy rain.

Radio silence between the four T-90s was maintained. Instead, the tanks' COs were communicating by the tried-and-true Russian method of using rapid yet distinct flag signals, such as those still used by such elite forces as the British Royal Navy when a ship was requested to go SID—Signals Dead—for reasons of launching a surprise attack against the enemy. Colonel Nureyev, Abramov's second in command and tactical leader of the T-90 force, took the small but distinct yellow flag he used on such occasions and held it out snappily to his left. Soon they would be out of the minefield, the crackle and spit of small-arms fire so loud now that he could see the flashes of the soon-to-be outnumbered and outmechanized American force in this area.

Because of the midair collision of the Cobras during the first wave, many marines, because their transport helos had had to take sharp evasive action, ended up being too far north of the minefield and too close to the lake. Fighting their way westward from the lake, then south, they were exhausted and desperately short of ammunition and food. Worst of all, they were now too far away to lend support to Freeman's team.

The three-man fire team of Kegg and the two other

marines, one of them with the SAW machine gun, formed a C-shaped defensive arc facing *away* from the general area indicated on the Korean's map as the exit zone. It was the C-arc's job to protect the backs of Freeman, Aussie, Sal, Choir, and Johnny Lee as Choir used his small metallic "finger" to search for mines. As he moved the two-and-a-half-inch-long battery-powered sonar-activated probe, which extended like a bayonet from the end of his M-16, he listened attentively for the probe's low-pitched return "warning," the outgoing pitch so high that it was detectable by only a few individuals whose hearing was well above the 2,000-hertz level. The instrument was so expensive that only one had been issued per four-man fire team. It might have saved Eddie Mervyn from his horrific wound, but in the pressure of battle, not knowing how far away the Russians were, there had been no time to use it.

But now that Tibbet's second wave was arriving, bolstering the first, Freeman seized the window of opportunity to press forward with the search for the exit hatch.

"No mines here, sir," said Choir, planting one of his green safety flags and sweeping the finger from one side of the suspected exit zone to the other without getting a mine "tone" over his Walkman-type earphones. Preoccupied as he was with his task, indeed precisely because he was so preoccupied searching for mines, Choir thought of Prince and felt heartsick.

Two minutes later, one of the three marines manning the protective C-arc spotted a T-90's aerial whipping back and forth and moving his way above head-high reeds two hundred yards away, its diesel engine a subdued but angry growl in the sodden vegetation. Then it disappeared.

"Shit!" said the marine. "Where'd he go?" He radioed back to the Hummer. "You see that tank?" he asked the corporal.

"Affirmative," came the answer. "Got the fucker on thermal. There are three more a ways back, coming from the direction of the minefield."

"Tone!" shouted Choir. "Ten o'clock." He moved farther left. "Tone! They've mined this side of the snow hump right up to those four tree trunks that they're using to hide the air shafts. But they've left clear ground on the other side, so that's obviously where anyone coming out of the tunnels is going to head, if this *is* an exit."

"Well," Freeman ordered, "if we find an opening anywhere in this goddamn hump, make sure we flag it correctly." He didn't want to see another Eddie Mervyn incident.

"Let's probe the snow mound on the mine-free side," said Choir. "Quickly. Use your bayonets. If that map's right, we should find a door or something."

Freeman could hear more armor approaching in the distance. The tanks were moving more slowly than the first T-90 that the Hummer's corporal had fixed in his thermal sight, but the general could see they were gaining ground nonetheless, and so he told the men to stop digging, ordering everyone back. He would use the Hummer to do the digging. "Corporal!" he radioed the Hummer. "Back up out of these reeds. Get two hundred yards from here. If we lose the radio, I'll use visuals. One wave with my helmet, hit the mound with a TOW. Second Fritz, use another one. Got it?"

"Two hundred yards, one TOW on your wave, another on each subsequent wave. Got it, sir."

With that, the Hummer made a tight U-turn, the still partially frozen reeds crunching underneath like cereal, a rush of the vehicle's bluish exhaust rising, dissipating, and wafting over the C-arc marines and into the reeds around the tree trunks now twenty feet away from Freeman.

"Let's all get back behind the Hummer!" shouted Freeman. "Soon as the second TOW hits it, we go in, no matter what. Got it?"

"Yes, sir," Freeman's marines said in unison, determination in their eyes.

Then everything went wrong.

Running back, Freeman saw the Hummer buck, glimpsed one of its TOW's contrails, then heard the distinctive boom of a T-90's main gun firing. The Hummer somersaulted, then disintegrated into gobs of fire; simultaneously a head-punching "whoomp!" told Freeman the T-90 had exploded, and he could see it belching flame and vomiting crimson fire into the dark green reeds.

He didn't pause. "Everyone back to the mound and we'll dig out that snow. *Now!* Aussie, go check the Hummer." Aussie did, by which time the general, Choir, Sal, and Johnny Lee were using their trench tools to dig, scrape, and chuck away the snow. Sweating like gandy dancers on a railroad in high summer, perspiration running down each man's face, they dug like men possessed.

Aussie came running back from the Hummer. "All dead!" he reported tersely. "Nothing usable." He began digging. They all heard the ring of metal against an entrenching tool and fell to the ground, except Choir.

"Not a mine!" he assured them. "Just metal on metal." It was a door handle; another handle became visible a second later.

"No shovels," Freeman ordered. "Hands only." He had no idea how close the exit was to the tunnels, only that the map had shown a narrow tubular exit burrowed out of the rock approximately four feet wide and less than a hundred feet long on a thirty-degree gradient which, as he noted to Aussie, was an extraordinarily sharp incline. If they were approaching the tunnel entrance, Freeman didn't want to give his team's presence away by making any unnecessary noise. Drawing on all his expertise in things military *and* nonmilitary, Freeman devised a war plan on the spot. "Aussie, Sal, Johnny, come with me. Choir, I want you to handle the grenades."

"Right," responded Choir, already donning his IR goggles and gas mask, his tone confident. After years of working as part of Freeman's team, and of always thinking one step ahead, he was ready for action.

"Good," said Freeman who, with Aussie, Sal, and Johnny Lee, began donning his IR goggles and gas mask.

"Choir," Freeman instructed, "start the proceedings!"

CHAPTER NINETEEN

NINETY FEET BELOW in a guard station at the foot of the long exit stairway, a guard unit of seven men and three women responsible for the security of the exit end of ABC's tunnel complex were bored silly. Completely cut off from the action above them and long used to the numbing sameness of production line noises in the three tunnels, there was nothing new to do or discuss, other than the American attack, about which they had been given no news whatsoever. The only thing that mitigated the sheer bone-crushing monotony of guard duty in the three connected tunnels was the substantial *tunnelnaya premiya*—tunnel bonus. But even the bonus could not keep the guard detail on their feet during the eight-hour shift. And, despite the strict rules against it, a game of Texas Hold 'Em Poker would usually be in progress, as it was now, with the latest production line inspector wandering over now and then between checking the counterfeit American, Korean, and Chinese manufacturers' serial numbers on the completed Igla and Vanguard MANPADs and the new hypersonic weapons and ammunition being made as a result of ABC's victory at DARPA ALPHA.

"Did you hear that scraping noise?" one of the card-playing four asked.

"Don't worry, Andreyovich," said the number checker, Vladimir. "The exit door must be under a ton of snow. If it is anything, it's probably one of those stupid deer rooting around for grass. Anyway, in this weather all kinds of crap's blowing around the lake and the marshes. Plus, last reports from H-block say we can just keep working, no problem. The Americans are getting the shit kicked out of them."

Andreyovich nodded. "Maybe, but someone had better check. Let's not risk the bonus. Vladimir, you come up with me." Andreyovich looked at his cards, the worst hand he'd had in months. "I'm out," he said, grabbing his AK-47. "Need to stretch my legs anyway."

"Good man!" said the numbers inspector, a big, bald, jovial man from one of the hamlets near the railhead that were now all but ghost towns, ABC having combed them for maintenance support workers.

Both guards heard several hollow-sounding bumps as Choir tossed two tear gas canisters and yellow SOS smoke grenades onto the grates of the two air-intake shafts. The yellow smoke laced with tear gas descended quickly, spreading throughout the three parallel tunnels, their connecting passages, and the entrance and exit vestibules at either end of the tunnels. The moment the terrorist guards and weapons assemblers at the exit end of the three tunnels saw the thickening malevolent-looking yellow gas pouring down the ninety-foot-long, cement-lined exit shaft, the alarm horn sounded, its deep, strangled "Arggh! Arggh!" drowning out the usual cacophony of the assembly line. The horn's unrelenting blasts, accompanied by the scream of *"Gaz!"* filling the subterranean world, turned panic to frenzy, sending the disorganized horde of three hundred terrorist workers rushing away from the exit toward the massive security doors at the tunnels' entrance, roars of rage erupting from the frantic mob when they found the inner security door locked. The terror of 243 men and 57 women clamoring, screaming for the door to be opened, fed on itself. The duty officer, who only hours before had thought himself incapable of pushing the button that would explode the RDX unless he was blackmailed, now discovered that his fear of the mob made it easier to contemplate putting his fellow terrorists out of their misery.

Up on the surface, the moment the general, Aussie, Sal, Lee, and Choir saw the yellowish green smoke rising up from the out vents, Freeman and his team ran down the stairs of the long, narrow exit tunnel, then split up at the bottom, Freeman taking the first tunnel, Aussie and Sal the second, Johnny Lee and Choir the third, running along a grated metal floor. They could hear the nightmarish cries coming from the mob of trapped terrorists beyond, hammering and yelling hysterically for the entrance doors to be opened, no doubt terrified the tunnel complex was being attacked with chlorine gas or, as their great-great-grandfathers had called it, mustard gas, which the Americans, like the Russians, still had in ample supply. Further exciting the terrorists' fear was their conviction, shared by the duty officer, who, sitting safely two floors up in one of the H-block's administrative offices, had caught a glimpse of the intruders, that the tunnel complex would soon be swarming with Americans. And when the duty officer heard Abramov's insistence that the RDX be blown, any hesitation that he might have had disappeared in the belief that he would be acting humanely, putting such tortured souls out of their misery. After all, as Abramov sharply instructed him, "You wouldn't treat an animal like that."

The duty officer pressed the button. The resulting subterranean roar reverberated through the tunnels, the concussion wave almost knocking Freeman's team off their feet, and, in the middle tunnel, forcing Aussie and Sal to grab one of the MANPAD lathes to steady themselves.

*   *   *

It was testimony to Abramov's expertise that he had calculated the amount of RDX so precisely that while the two halves of the massive door were bent and rendered useless by the blast, the door had not collapsed, acting, as Abramov had wanted it to, as a barrier between him and the enemy.

Safe above in the H-block, Abramov, Beria, and Cherkashin were cold as steel. They had no intention of waiting for what was being reported by the entrance guard detail as poison gas to leak up into the H-block. Thoroughly professional now, with no time to spare in a blame game—at least not yet—about the colossal error Abramov had made, enabling *Dedushka*—Grandpa— Freeman to heap humiliation upon them via the Pete Rose feint, Abramov declared, "Dead men can't make sales," adding, "Poison gas won't hurt the production line. We can always get more men. I suggest, gentlemen, we take our bonuses and vacate."

Without waiting for the other two's acquiescence, Abramov quickly took his cell phone out of its holster and punched in three digits, briskly instructing his quartermaster, "Transport helo for three, plus luggage. Fully armed Sharks to escort us—and yourself—on the pad behind ABC. Fuel for Vladivostok. *Now!*"

"Yes, General. We'll be there in ten minutes."

"Five!" Abramov shouted into the phone. "Five and you get double your bonus. In *gold*!"

"Yes, General."

Beria and Cherkashin now moved quickly to the safe and withdrew their keys to their respective gold bullion boxes and attaché cases, as well as the access codes to their Swiss bank accounts.

"Got your keys?" Beria asked Abramov.

Abramov, checking the slide on his Makarov 9 mm

pistol, retorted, "Are you serious? We'll be back in production next week. C'mon, let's get to the pad." They could already hear the heavily armed Black Shark escort helos hovering overhead and the rotors of a big, bug-eyed Hind transport chopper descending to the H-block's emergency pad, located only yards from the edge of the enormous T-90 camouflage net.

Beyond the mass of red-hot twisted and steaming metal that had been the inner door between the entrance vestibule and the tunnels, there was a phalanx of upraised Russian hands dimly visible in the emergency lanterns' light; were they surrendering? Many of the terrorists were crumpling to the floor in the eerie yellow-green fog, the choking impact of the tear gas in the confined space taking a rapid toll, Chester's marines above keeping up a steady rain of tear gas canisters and smoke grenades. From inside their gas masks, Freeman, Aussie, Sal, Choir, and Johnny Lee found that despite the state-of-the-art charcoal- and chemical-pad filters, the air was becoming throat-raspingly hot and thin. None of Freeman's team saw the flash but all heard the bursts of AK-47 fire. In the choking gas, the shooters' aim was way off, but they could have hit any one of the team.

"Fire!" yelled Freeman, and the team opened up, taking what shelter they could behind the assembly line machinery nearest them. In addition to firing their weapons, Freeman's team tossed twelve HE and eight flash-bang grenades, the wild terrorist AK-47 fire, presumably coming from the guard detail, absorbed by the boxes of guidance vanes for Igla and Vanguard MANPADs that lined the walls of the tunnels, the flash-bangs taking out most of the remaining emergency lanterns, what little light remained casting huge, macabre shadows on the tunnel walls. Amid the acrid-smelling smoke and tear gas, some of the terrorists managed to stand, screaming for mercy. Freeman's stentorian nasal voice boomed through his mask: "The *Cole,* the World Trade Towers, the Pentagon, Flight 93!" his AK-74 chopping them down, the barrel of his Kalashnikov so hot he wondered whether it would tolerate another mag just yet. Giving it time to cool, he whipped out his H & K sidearm and, with Aussie, Sal, Lee, and Choir doing likewise, continued putting the wounded out of their misery.

Aussie, his hand wet with flesh and bone, continued his gruesome, but as he saw it, necessary task if America and her allies were to be safer from these heartless murderers who sold their wares to the likes of Hamas and Hezbollah. He could make out a clutch of swarthy Middle Eastern faces screaming at him, not begging for mercy but hurling their hatred at him, the Arab face nearest him so contorted for a moment he looked as frightening as Aussie must in his gas mask, Aussie yelling at him, "You look like one of those bastards in Bali!" as the next burst punched the Arab back, his body crumpling beneath the waning light, Aussie seeing the name "RAMON" stenciled on the man's blood-soaked battle tunic. Immediately Aussie remembered the attack on DARPA ALPHA, one of the victims having written "RAM" and "SCARUND" on a piece of paper before he died. Now, looking down at the dead terrorist, he saw the raised, angry red scar under the man's chin.

"All right," Freeman yelled out, his voice muffled by the gas mask's filters but sounding just as resolute as it had at the beginning of the subterranean raid. "Hurry up with the C-4, guys, and let's get back topside!"

The five men, the general in the first tunnel, Aussie and Sal in the second, and Johnny and Choir in the third quickly placed the fist-sized lumps of C-4, connecting them with det cord, at strategic points along the production line of each tunnel. The det cords from the three tunnels were wrapped into one, then run topside by the team and connected to the remote initiator that, once the team was safe topside, would be activated, beginning the firing sequence that would move through the det cord to the globs of C-4, the cord's explosive detonation wave traveling at more than seven thousand yards a second, thus in effect exploding all the globs of C-4 simultaneously.

Freeman told each of the other four men to take a MANPAD and portable power pack with him from the assembly line. There was a chance, he knew, that if the weather cleared, the Russians might just risk some of their hitherto revetment-hidden attack helos to harass the marines' evacuation, if for no other reason than sheer spite. Against this, however, there was the equally good chance that without "product" to sell after the tunnels blew up, what pilot would bother to risk his life for revenge *sans* bonus?

"Son of a bitch!" said young Kegg, as Freeman and the other four gas-masked MANPAD-carrying warriors emerged from the exit. "What the fuck went on down there? Sounded like a—a war!"

"It was," said Aussie. "For the fucking terrorists." He whipped off his gas mask with his left hand and took in a deep draft of cold, rainy air. "Those pricks won't be making any more of these." He raised the Igla with his right hand. "These five are the only ones left."

"You know how to fire one, Aussie?" joshed Kegg.

"Surely you jest, boy." Aussie lifted the forty-pound missile in its launcher-sheath to his right shoulder, the rocket's aerodynamic spike in front of the heat-seeking infrared and its flare decoy analyzer piercing the air. Aussie looked about. "Where'd the opposition go?"

"The navy infantry," replied a sodden but smiling Lieutenant Chester. "Soon as the word got out that the tunnels were under attack, that Freeman suckered Abramov, I guess they thought, 'What's the point?' Anyway, they've pulled back for now."

"You ready with that remote, Choir?" called out Freeman.

"Ready, sir."

"Good." The general told Kegg and the marine's two fire team buddies to go back with Melissa Thomas. "These vents are going to start really smoking in the blink of an eye. C'mon, people, move!"

They moved, and waited for Choir to activate the initiator. The det cord—in effect a long, explosive-filled flexi-tube from a spool—had a burn rate so fast that once the initiator kicked off the firing sequence, the major explosions of the C-4 would occur in a fraction of a second.

But they didn't.

"Aw—" came Aussie's bitter disappointment. "Fuck a duck!"

It seemed interminable. Then they heard, saw, high up through the rain, five helos—a big transporter and four Black Shark gunships rising and turning above the minefield.

"Take those bastards out!" yelled Freeman. "I'll take the big guy in the middle. Let's see how they like their own medicine." Freeman hadn't even had time to take his gas mask off. The Igla on his shoulder, he placed his left foot forward, the ground power supply kit giving full surge power to the missile in four seconds. Gripping the launcher by its flanged neck, he gained visual contact, squeezed the trigger, and heard the gentle whirring of the missile's automatic target lock and launch circuits, the primary booster igniting the missile, passing through the tube, disabling the first safety twenty feet from the general, the sustainer motor firing, blowing hot air and reed debris into his gas mask, the missile now streaking at over a thousand miles per hour in the two seconds since leaving the tube. Second safety was now gone and, unless the missile's twenty-five-pound blast and fragmentation warhead hit something within fifteen seconds, it would self-destruct.

The subsequent "whooshing" sounds were the other four fire-and-forget Iglas taking off from the shoulder launchers on Aussie, Sal, Choir, and Johnny Lee. Johnny slipped on a patch of mud as he fired, the Igla going near vertical.

No one said anything, watching the five missiles, fierce orange streaks with the bluish sulfur exhausts visible.

"Terrorists are popping flares!" called Sal.

"Look at 'em panic!" said Aussie, watching the helos jinking hard left, right, right—trying to outmaneuver the closing Iglas, flares popping everywhere like hundreds of little meteorites burning up in the gray, rainy sky, but the Igla-E2, devoid of a friend-or-foe tone because terrorists didn't need any such discriminating equipment, proved a formidable weapon. With infrared decoy override, the E2 ignored the tortuous, frantic maneuvers of the helos two miles up. There were one, two, three, then a fourth explosion as the "traveling fuel tanks," as Aussie called the Russian choppers, blew up, sending down heavy golden showers of burning debris that, upon impact, detonated dozens of small anti-personnel and big anti-tank mines, cratering the snow- and rain-covered ground.

A lone Shark helo, the only survivor of the four attack choppers, obviously deciding not to risk any more MAN-PAD attacks, turned west, climbed higher and fled into the mountain fastness of China across the border. Freeman and Salvini thought they saw a chute blossom, but in the rain it was difficult to be sure whether it was that or a piece of fabric from the transporter caught in the air currents as the fuselage plunged earthward.

There was something wrong, however, as Freeman, taking off his gas mask, realized that there should have been explosions not above him but ninety feet below in the tunnels.

"Did you press that remote?" the general asked Choir.

"Yes, sir. I've checked the box and it's middle tunnel's det cord that's screwing things up. There must be a break. Nothing's wrong up at this end. Something must have fallen on it."

"Or cut through it!" said Aussie. "One of those bastards—" His voice was suddenly drowned out by the combined roar of a Super Stallion and a Cobra gunship riding shotgun, both helos dropping decoy flares. Despite the noise, the booming voice of the Stallion's crew chief managed to cut through it and the fury of the rotor wash. "Evac immediately. Mission is over."

Every one of Freeman's team and the marines around him wanted to leave, but no one thought that they should. They'd cleaned out the rats in the nest below, but not the nest, as Freeman told the Stallion's crew chief through cupped hands that reeked of cordite and tear gas from the tunnels.

"Doesn't matter," the crew chief hollered back. "We got orders from *Yorktown*. C'mon, General, I haven't got all fucking day." The Cobra gunship was rising and falling in the side draft of the Stallion's enormous rotors. "C'mon, mission's over. That's an order from Colonel Tibbet. You've run out of time."

The general was cupping his right ear. "Can't hear you."

"General!" the crew chief bellowed again. "We have to get you guys out of here *now*. Colonel Tibbet's order!"

"I outrank him," said Freeman, "but, dammit, all right," he continued, and ordered everyone aboard. "Go! Go!"

No matter what their personal feelings, they were

professional soldiers, Freeman's team and the marines, and knew orders were orders.

As the crew chief helped lift Gomez to put him in a litter, the others scrambled aboard the overcrowded helo through a jumble of other bodies and weapons. The Stallion's anxious copilot glanced back, saw no one on the ground, but spotted an armored vehicle spitting fire and bristling with MANPADs racing toward them from about a mile away on the edge of the frozen marshland that ran back to the lake. Because he too was looking in the distance at the armored vehicle even as he kept hauling the others into the helo, the crew chief noticed something in the rain-washed landscape previously hidden by the snow: a vast carpet of dead birds—thousands of them.

It wasn't until six minutes after they'd scrambled aboard the already dangerously overloaded helo, which, like all the other Stallions, was trying to get as many of their fellow Americans out before the twenty-four-hour deadline, that someone noticed that neither Freeman nor the marine, Melissa Thomas, was aboard the Stallion. But the pilot and the copilot had their orders. On the other hand, marines didn't leave their dead, wounded, or living behind.

"Those cocksuckers!" Kegg shouted. "Get a load of this shit!" He was watching the crew chief's TV feed on the twelve-inch bulkhead inset screen. CNN was running an Al Jazeera tape, which the Arab station said had just been taken in overflight by a lone Shark helo and which showed patches of yellowish smoke rising in Lake Khanka near Siberia. Al Jazeera claimed the smoke was poison gas used by Americans against a defenseless refugee camp. Then there was a CNN clip, Marte Price thrusting

her mike into the face of a nearly hysterical coed. "I—I—
never thought I'd live to see the day *my* country would
use such a—such a horrible, awful thing. It's, like, you
know, totally irresponsible."

"Oh," mimicked a marine who was also watching the
feed. "Like you're totally insane, you silly bitch. We colored the friggin' tear gas with a yellow smoke grenade,
you stupid whore. That's all we did."

"Yeah," put in Kegg. "But it sure frightened the shit out
of 'em." His laugh was contagious, the marines' pent-up
emotions suddenly finding a release. But Aussie, Choir,
Sal, and Johnny Lee weren't laughing. They were peti-
tioning the pilot to go back and pick up Melissa Thomas
and Freeman.

"Can't do it," said the pilot, quite properly. To go back
with a MANPAD vehicle on the loose and risk losing
every man he'd picked up would have been the height of
irresponsibility.

"Where the fuck did he go?" Aussie asked Sal angrily.

"And the woman," said Choir. "It was so disorderly.
We should've—"

"Never mind what we should have done," cut in Aussie.
What are we gonna do now?"

"Tell *Yorktown*," put in the crew chief, "to get a STAR
bird over here fast."

"It'd be their only chance," agreed Choir. "By the time
they drop them a kit we can have a Herk on its way out of
Japan and here in—" Choir did the math in his head.
"—four hundred and fifty miles—two hours, tops."

"Two *hours*," said Aussie.

"I know," said Choir, "but it's a STAR or nothing. We
can say the Herk's coming in to pick up our wounded.
Tibbet's boys say we're missing a few."

"We'll go plain language, if you like," said the pilot.
"Tell everyone to head for the lake."

"Bit bloody vague," snorted Aussie. "Lake's four thousand square miles. Bigger 'n Rhode Island."

"We've got a couple of dusters, Hueys," the pilot told him. "They're packed under nets near the ice as backup evac for any lost marines."

"Then shit," said Aussie, "send one of the Hueys in to pick up the general and Thomas."

"Negative," said the pilot. "A lot of guys have been given the location of those two Hueys, but those birds come out exposing themselves looking for our general and his girlfriend—"

"Hey!" Aussie was on the stairs up to the cockpit, but Sal, Choir, and Johnny Lee managed to save the pilot from Aussie snapping his neck.

"Fer cryin' out loud, Aussie!" Salvini shouted above the deafening rotor slap and engines.

"He's right, Aussie!" shouted Choir. "Calm down, boyo. Those Hueys can't risk having any MANPADs fired at them or risk anything else those terrorist pricks have left. If the general and Thomas stay where they are, they've got a chance with a STAR."

Aussie, cooler now, shook off Sal's restraining arm. "Have you ever done it?"

"A STAR? No. But—" Sal tried a smile. "—it's in the manual." He then resorted to a favorite line of Freeman's lighter moments, taken from one of his favorite movies, *Those Magnificent Men in Their Flying Machines.*

"Ja," repeated Sal, "it's in zee manual. A German officer can do anything from zee manual."

"Seriously, though, Aussie," put in Choir. "They drop instructions with it?"

"I fuckin' hope so! The marines only use volunteer crew."

"You think he went back?" said Johnny Lee.

"Of course he went back, Johnny," said Aussie. "Fucking det cord fucked up so the old man's gone back down the

hole. Alone. Stupid bastard." It was a term of affection.
"Think Thomas is helping him?"

"I dunno," said Sal. "She could've collapsed under the
belly of the Stallion. It was a hell of a rush before we left.
Not even the Cobra would have seen her."

Sal was only half right. Melissa Thomas hadn't collapsed in the evac rush. And the Cobra hadn't seen her,
nor had Freeman. In the maelstrom of swirling reeds
and muddy snow that was aerosoled by the downward
blast of the Stallion's rotors, the general, quickly pulling
on his gas mask, had slipped back into the tall reeds to retrieve his pack. Melissa Thomas, seeing him, intuitively
sensed he wasn't going to evac, that he was going back
down to rectify the broken det cord or remove whatever
had either fallen on it or been put there by a terrorist in a
last-ditch effort to stop the detonation of the C-4 laid by
the team. She owed him her life. From the moment he
had astonished his men, dragging her blindfolded onto
the ant heap, the adrenaline rush triggered by her body's
reaction to the ant bites' poison bringing her back to life,
she had incurred a debt that any human being would understand. Was she overconfident, she wondered, putting
a neophyte's faith in the corps, in the article of faith that
the marines, as always, would be back to get as many
people out as possible? Or, given the naked fact that the
deadline had now passed, would she merely be listed as
MIA, the best she could hope for to be honored in ab-
sentia?

What Marine Thomas didn't know was that what Freeman and his team member Sal had surmised might be a
chute was indeed a parachute, Abramov landing sodden
and bruised but otherwise unhurt in the reed-dense minefield. Abramov made no attempt to chase his chute or rein

it in. Instead, he stood precisely where he had landed, knowing he was in the minefield, and, though his legs were trembling with the effort of sustaining the weight of the bundles of U.S. thousand-dollar bills beneath his tank commander's uniform and the sheer weight of the twenty small gold bullion bars he wore in a belt, he remained on spot, making one call on his cell to his tank commander, Colonel Nureyev.

"Dancer. Release El-Hage and friend. And tell your men there's bullion for Freeman's head."

"Done, General," said Colonel Nureyev, who then called whatever ABC staff were still on duty. Most had fled, but a radio operator still on duty had apprised Nureyev of the intercepts that had been made of the American aircraft communication and that Abramov, Beria, and Cherkashin had left together in the transports, with Abramov, as overall commander, having taken the vital DARPA ALPHA computer disk with him. Having now spoken with Abramov, Nureyev concluded that, of the three, Abramov was the sole survivor of the Igla MANPAD attack. Nureyev then called his own private troop of four T-90s. "I know," he told them, "that the Americans are pulling out, but this Freeman bastard is still around. American channels were randomly monitored by our scanners during their first wave evac. One intercept was specifically asking, 'Where's Freeman?' So he's still out there. Strictly speaking, we're on a cease-fire order, some girlfriend deal between our two so-called presidents, following the deadline. But out here, we rule, and there's bullion on his head. Who wants in?"

One of the four tank teams opted out—they'd seen enough destruction, five T-90s taken out by marine anti-tank missiles and Hummer-fired TOWs. But the three remaining tank crews opted for the chance of bullion.

"Let's hope, Captain," Nureyev told his 2IC, "that El-Hage doesn't get Freeman before we do."

"Right," said the captain. "Do we have a GPS on Freeman?"

"No, but the Iglas that brought down Abramov could have only come from the tunnels, and they haven't been blown. I don't think that American shithead has come all this way to kill us only to leave our factory intact. Those SpecOp teams carry around plastique like you and I carry keys. They always have it. I'll bet ten to one, Captain, that the bastard is still sniffing around the tunnels with his boys."

"Very well then," said the captain. "I know where I'll take my tank."

"Meanwhile," said Nureyev, "I'll take my tanks out to the minefield road and run over some Bettys to get Abramov out. The sight of all that lovely currency going sky-high and getting burned up is enough to make you ill."

"Yes, so be careful in that minefield," said the captain.

"Ah," said Nureyev dismissively, "I can run over those Betty anti-personnel jobs no problem. They won't even rattle my beast's treads."

"Yes," the Russian tank captain agreed, "but don't get too close. You don't want shrapnel from a bouncing Betty to burn those dollar bills."

"You think I'm stupid?" countered Nureyev. "I'll get just close enough to extend the main gun to him. He grabs it and I'll swing the gun around behind us."

"But—" began the captain, until he sensed the Dancer's wide grin and understood: A tank with its gun pointing to the rear was giving the sign of surrender. "So you see," said Nureyev, "any asshole American with an anti-tank weapon won't fire at me."

"Be careful the general doesn't lose his grip on the gun's barrel."

"Would you, until you were out of the minefield?"

"No, Comrade," replied the captain. "I'd hang on like grim death."

"So would I," agreed Nureyev with a smile, his mood clearly elevated by the promise of the largest bonus ever paid by ABC—now A.

"All right, let's go," ordered Nureyev. "You get to that exit and put a few rounds down that shaft." The captain paused, and Nureyev could hear him pulling down his ribbed leather helmet. "One thing I don't get, Comrade. I thought this Freeman and his team were supposed to attack the entrance, not the exit?"

"That's what we thought, but from what the boys who are still in H-block tell me, Freeman sent a bogus message to an American colonel. Rumor is that there was a signal within the signal that deliberately misled Abramov— something about a baseball player in America who claimed he had never wagered and was thrown out when it was found he lied. So when this Freeman said he was going to attack the H-block and the tunnels' joint entrance below, our decoders, or Abramov himself, didn't recognize this thing about the baseball player. It was like a verbal wink, you see, like saying, 'I'm saying this but I'm going to do the opposite.'"

"Cunning shit," said the captain. "I'll take great delight in personally running over him."

"Watch him. He may still have an Igla."

The captain buttoned up his tunic and tapped on his throat mike. "Ivan, let's roll. We have Yankees to kill." The captain wasn't worried about Iglas. They would bring down aircraft, no problem, but he'd seen them fired against a T-90's glacis plate and its top—where armor was thinnest—and the HE charge just hit the tank and made a hell of a bang but no penetration whatsoever. "Ivan?" he asked his driver. "You watch all that TV shit.

What's that English phrase those Yankee game show hosts use?"

Ivan was thinking. " 'Come on down.' "

"Nyet," said that captain. "That's not it. You know— the one Bush Junior used against his enemies in his election campaign."

Ivan didn't know.

"Ah, I have it," the captain declared jubilantly. "Bring it on!"

"Don't freak!" Melissa Thomas told herself. "Don't freak out." It was difficult not to when she saw the huge black blob moving through the high reeds, especially when she realized it was a Russian state-of-the-art, infrared-laser-targeting-equipped main battle tank and when she didn't know whether General Freeman would emerge from the pitch-black square that had been the exit door which she had seen him enter shortly after the last evac chopper had left. Down there now the general would have only his infrared-keyed night vision goggles by which to see, all the lighting, from the snippets she'd heard as the team had come up from the tunnel, taken out in the firefight.

"General," she said on open channel, "a T-90's coming out of the minefield." If he heard her, maybe that would bring him up. "I say again, a T-90 is coming out of the minefield, heading our way."

Freeman froze in shock. By now he'd descended the ninety-foot-long stairway into the bowels of the tunnel complex. Melissa—where the hell was she? And more to the point, why hadn't she evaced? He didn't dare answer immediately. Someone near or amongst the dead bodies of the terrorists must have somehow severed the det cord and might hear him reply. His right hand grasping his

9 mm H & K handgun, he was on his knees, using his left hand to feel along the cord of the middle tunnel for a break.

"General! Are you reading me?"

Again he said nothing, and squelched the volume button. Ahead of him, through the infrared lenses, he was concentrating on the long assembly line of the middle tunnel. But it was slow, meticulous work, for no matter that Freeman had his night vision goggles functioning, the line of bodies he saw ahead was still a threat. During the firefight, a terrorist could have faked it, hiding in some nook or antechamber in one of the three tunnels which the team felt confident had been swept clean of the violently coughing terrorists who were trying to flee what they had thought was poison gas. No one else had come out of the exit since the team had gone in to "take out the garbage," as Aussie had put it. And the explosion-buckled entrance doors at the far end of the tunnel were impassable.

Maybe, Freeman told himself, no one had severed the det cord. Perhaps it could have been cut by something heavy, such as a box of MANPADs falling from one of the stacks along the tunnel walls.

In the dank darkness all about him, fetid with the stench of human waste, he could hear a faint dripping. Then he saw darts of white light crossing his NVGs' field of vision. Rats. Intuitively he wanted to hurry up, go topside, and try to position himself well enough so that he could trigger his identification friend or foe beacon, realizing there might still be a risk of rogue terrorist elements still prowling around after the marines' first evac wave. And the general prayed that Melissa Thomas would be all right until the second evac wave. Freeman had been touched that she'd stayed behind, offering him backup. But on an op like this, searching for just one det cord break, one soldier was enough. Besides, though she'd come out of her semicomatose state, she had the awful pain of a broken rib, and he was unsure how steady she was on her feet. The tunnels weren't the place to find out.

Silently he asked God to protect the young woman who had stayed behind. He had prayed a lot over the past twenty-four hours—never more for absolution as they'd gunned down the terrorists after only one, at the most, three, had fired at the team—and wildly at that.

Suddenly a body moved, then another. Freeman swung his sidearm in their direction and stayed his trigger finger. It had been rigor mortis setting in, an arm jerk of one of the dead terrorists enough to produce movement but no threat. Lord, he was tired. Now he could hear moaning, but was sure, from his long experience of combat, that it was no more than the sounds of bowel, stomach, and throats changing volume after death, bad air expelled. *Get a grip on yourself*, he silently ordered himself. *General Freeman! You're tired. Keep alert but don't overreact.*

He moved forward again slowly, his left hand cautiously sliding along the det cord.

When Melissa Thomas saw the T-90 slowing about five hundred yards beyond the perimeter of the minefield, she had hoped it would stop coming eastward, and turn about westward, and go away. The rain was still heavy and she knew that, despite her thermal clothing, she'd soon be in the early stages of hypothermia unless she started to move. Her body, despite one morphine jab, was throbbing with the sharp, needle-stabbing pain of hundreds of ant bites and her broken rib. She saw the tank's cupola open, sighting it through her M40A1's scope, resting the rifle on the gnarled tree branch at the edge of a clump of reed grass just beyond the wood. She could see a man's head or, more accurately, a man's bearded face, enclosed in the peculiarly antiquated thick, ribbed-leather helmet favored by both modern Russian and old Soviet bloc tank commanders and crews. The bearded face looked about quickly then disappeared. Now Marine Thomas was cursing herself in terms that would have shocked a longshoreman. Why hadn't she got away a quick "slap" shot? Because, she told herself, truthfully, you weren't ready, you silly bitch. You were so full of "poor me" and your ant-bitten, cold ass that you weren't on the ball. But at least the tank was now moving southward, reminding her, in the neurotic manner of its sudden and abrupt change of course, of some mad bird dog, fast right, then left, fast right again, as it passed through the shoulder-high reeds, at times only its turret visible.

In the central tunnel, still moving slowly, one of a soldier's most difficult disciplines, feeling his way along the det cord to find the break, the general's breathing echoed inside his gas mask, and he could detect faint whiffs of tear gas. Probably the filter needed to be changed or, more likely, his head strap had slipped, his neck aching from the unusual strain of having to simultaneously stay alert for danger in the tunnel and outside. If the fingers of his hand missed even one millimeter-wide break he would have to repeat the whole process. Unable to contain the itch in his throat from the whiff of tear gas, he coughed.

"You okay, General?"

Melissa's voice so startled him he lost his place on the det cord, quickly raising his handgun for a double-handed shot before he realized it was Thomas's voice in his earpiece.

"Yes," he said. "Having a great time!" It was the most sarcastic voice she'd heard since her DI's, immediately followed by a more compassionate question from him, "How you doing?"

"I'm holding," she said. "Tank's sniffing around. Think it's looking for us."

By "us," she meant not only her and the general but those other marines still dug in throughout the area of reeds and swamp-bordered woods, but "us" gave Freeman the impression that the tank was specifically looking for him and Thomas. A main battle tank with a 125 mm main gun and machine guns tended to make things very personal.

Freeman's left hand resumed its feel of the detonation cord. Suddenly his NVG's view was of a white jumble of bodies that looked like a long pile of clothes waiting to be ironed, the heat given off by the bodies sufficiently warm to register as "thermals" on his NVGs.

General Abramov reached up like a man doing his morning calisthenics and took a firm hold, wrapping both arms around the muzzle of Nureyev's T-90's main gun. Once before, Abramov had told Nureyev, this shit Freeman had caused trouble as leader of the U.S.-led "peace intervention" in Sirbir. Well, now he was going to pay for it. All legends die, whether those who embrace the legend wish to concede the point or not. After having carefully followed the GPS route and running over five antipersonnel mines so they could get safely to him, the tank now backed out of the minefield, Nureyev having reversed the gun.

When Marine Thomas saw this second tank, with Abramov hanging from its main gun, moving slowly away east of the mad bird dog tank that was busily sniffing in the reeds beyond the minefield, she estimated the distance between it and her to be about a mile, though in the downpour that obscured lenses and made a constant hiss in the reeds it was difficult to gauge, even using the scope's range finder. But she knew she *had* to move, the cold in her bones now making her feel, she imagined, like her great-grandfather who suffered 24/7 from the curse of fibromyalgia, from the despair of which nothing short of narcotic painkillers and the Good Book could help him. Every bone in her body was heavy with the ague, every muscle taut with strain, only one more disposable "jab" of morphine left. She forced herself to think of the second evac wave, which would surely be back within the hour. *Please, God.*

As dusk settled on this strangely beautiful but, for Melissa, godforsaken, reed-world west of the huge lake, she remembered the SpecWar guy Aussie Lewis telling her it was nearly four times bigger than Oahu, and she remembered stepping off the plane there and how warm it was, before the marines began their long haul to Japan. She was starting to drift; for a blessed moment her pain-racked brain was able to conjure up the fragrant kiss of the trade winds, the sound of crashing, lacy surf, and the sun of those blessed, healing isles.

Her brief reverie was broken by the bass bellow of the first T-90 bursting out of the reeds no less than a quarter of a mile away, heading straight for her or, she guessed, the tunnel exit, and now she understood why the mad bird dog tank wasn't so mad and indecisive as it had seemed While the other T-90 Melissa had seen had stopped in the minefield, only its cupola visible, its more agile comrade had no doubt been sent to scour east and west of the minefield exit to make sure there were no more tank-destroying Predator, Javelin, or TOW units whose marines might be tempted to fire, and to hell with the presidents' timeline for evac that had passed already. No doubt about it now. This mad bird dog tank was racing, doing at least forty miles per hour, running parallel to the minefield, charging through the reeds like a bull elephant in a surge of uncontrollable sexual "must," leaving a thick shower of tangled vegetation, reeds, birds' nests, dead birds, Euriale leaves, and splintered ice in its wake, simultaneously firing its

coaxial and 7.62 mm machine guns like some thundering
giant savagely obliterating any impediments before it, its
exhaust pipes all the while vomiting filthy brown clouds
over the hitherto pristine, clean greens of reeds and lotus.

When this monster came to a halt, it did so so abruptly
that a wave of broken ice, reeds, and feathers surged forward from its wake along the midline of the tank just as
the turret slewed to bring the main gun in line with the
tunnel's exit which, for Melissa, was two hundred yards
away at two o'clock but only fifty yards dead ahead for
the tank.

Melissa heard the telltale rotor slap of Cobra gunships.
Then, a few seconds later, the much bigger air-pummeling
noise of Super Stallions and other helos she couldn't
identify. Her heart pounding, she was elated, confused.
Yorktown's angels couldn't possibly have returned so
soon. Or could they? It must, she reasoned, be the pain of
the multiple insect bites that was momentarily stupefying
her brain until, her mind in excited overdrive, she realized
the obvious truth, that *Yorktown* had managed to scramble
an ad hoc second wave of helos from all around the fleet.
Any helo that could carry drop tanks of extra fuel to
cover the distance to Lake Khanka had no doubt been
pressed into service, once SATPIX or HUMINT indicated to *McCain*'s Blue Tile boys that there was still terrorist tank movement after the cease-fire deadline, and
such terrorist movement posed an undeniably clear and
present danger to whatever elements of *Yorktown*'s MEU
remained to be evacuated.

Melissa saw the T-90 belch recoil like a drunken
garbage truck, the boom of its big 125 mm gun frightening her more than anything since the "water facility" at
Parris Island. The crash of the high explosive round echo-
ing back from the base of the exit stairway ninety feet

below the surface was gut-punching and deafening. The blast wave hurled cement forward into the tunnels as well as spewing dirty clouds up the exit, hitting the T-90, the din momentarily drowning what had been the soft drumming of the rain.

While Melissa Thomas had started with fright, Freeman was knocked flat, as if some huge, invisible fist had slammed him down, winding him so severely that in order to breathe he rolled onto his back, tore off his gas mask, and gulped for air in the dust-thick darkness, his right— pistol— hand flung out in a desperate effort to take in as much air as possible. As well as much-needed oxygen, he also inhaled more residual tear gas. Still on his back, he put the mask back on and saw a white rain coming down onto his NVGs, sodden peat as well as red-hot pieces of floor grating falling indiscriminately about him, a brick striking his helmet, another hitting the chest area of his Kevlar vest, and yet another fragment striking his face, or rather the eyepiece of his gas mask, with such force that it spiderwebbed the hardened glass of the right lens, ramming the whole mask so hard against his face that the general felt as if he'd been in a barroom brawl. He could taste blood, and it was a moment or two before he recovered his senses, realizing that what had saved him from a worse fate was that as he'd rolled over the det cord, most of his head had been covered, not only by the gas mask and helmet but by the overhang afforded by the edge of the long, metallic MANPAD assembly table.

Now he could smell smoke.

Ninety feet above what had been the tunnels' guard antechamber at the base of the exit steps, the cupola of the T-90 opened, terrifyingly close to Melissa who, no more than thirty feet away, was hunkered down near the fallen twisted branch and sea of reeds and realized that what she was looking at was not a regular T-90 but an upgraded version, reminiscent of the brilliant Israeli Merkava main battle tank with its troop squad section added to the rear of the tank that contained a commander, gunner, loader, and driver. She saw the tank commander appear, babbling excitedly, his torso above the cupola, and she could hear raucous laughter from the tank crew. Before she realized it, her weapon stock was hard into her shoulder, her left eye closed, the right cupped by the M40A1's scope, only part of the commander's head filling her water-streaked telescopic sight. She held a half breath to steady—and didn't fire. The commander was getting out of the tank, followed by another crew member, then another, which told her that something must be wrong with the automatic loader. It was being replaced by a third crew member. But why were the terrorists exiting the tank?

The cupola banged shut, the tank buttoned up. The commander huddled momentarily in the downpour then drew his pistol, turning to one of the other two terrorists, one of whom handed him a flashlight.

Why on earth, wondered Melissa, would they bother venturing down the tunnel after the one HE round? Did they know Freeman was down there? *Oh, shit!* She'd been talking to him on their throat-mike radios. A scanner could have located them pretty accurately, if not with pinpoint precision. Now she could hear louder, distant sounds of Cobras and other helos of the second evac wave. Even given the normal confusion that characterizes the most elementary ship-shore-ship exercise, surely someone must remember to revisit the exit area? On the other hand, it was quite possible that as yet no one of authority in the fleet had heard about Freeman's absence, but they knew that there were dozens of marines still spread throughout the marshes, waiting.

And did the terrorists want to kill Freeman so badly that

they'd violate the twenty-four-hour deadline? She immediately berated herself for such an asinine question, excusing it as the product of her exhaustion. Here was a man, already a legend amongst men at arms, who had humiliated his opposition from one side of the globe to the other. Even his critics had conceded that he had been the soldier who, more than any other, had faced down the homegrown terrorist camps of white supremacists riding what he referred to, and was nearly fired for saying it, as "the understandable anti-immigrant mood" of the U.S. southwestern border states.

Melissa, fighting the cold in her sodden uniform, began shivering violently, her body assaulted by paroxysms of uncontrollable muscle spasms. All she had to cling to was the image of her DI at the water facility, his peaked hat, trouser crease sharp as a knife, arms akimbo, standing like the one and only God, declaring simply, but with the steel voice of utter conviction, "Cadet Thomas, you *will* prevail. Water is your friend, not your enemy. The chemical soup of your mother's womb was the same as the sea. You are in your element, marine. Swim. Swim. Swim for the corps."

She'd hated him for it, the badgering, but now it was his image, his immaculate sense of order and calm in the face and fear of chaos, that made her fight.

The three Russians walked toward the exit then hesitated, dust and debris still issuing forth too thick to breathe through. The commander returned to the tank, banged on the cupola, and shouted. The cupola opened and a crewman in a leather-ribbed helmet emerged and began passing down three biochem masks. Melissa took a half breath and squeezed the trigger. There was a bullwhiplike crack and the crewman's head jerked sideways, his body slumping, half in and half out of the cupola. Thomas worked the bolt action on her sniper rifle—up-back-forward-down—so fast she had the tank commander in sight before he could step back off the tank's front glacis plate, his hands dropping two of the biochem masks as he hit the ground where he died instantly from Melissa's chest shot. Unable to get back into the tank because of the terrorist slumped in the cupola, the other two men started to run for the tunnel exit. She felled one of them, the other running blindly into the exit's thick haze. She ignored him, her open sight back on the cupola. Her brain simply bullied her pain and cold aside, adrenaline alone stoking her determination as she smartly assessed the situation. The tank wouldn't move yet. An open cupola with Cobra gunships around was guaranteed death. All she needed was a hand in her scope. A second would be plenty. Someone was going to have to pull or push the dead man out of the cupola so they could close the thing before a grenade came their way. They had no idea whether Melissa's fire had come from one marine or more. She could hear panic in the tank, then the turret suddenly slewed, the 7.62 coaxial machine gun opening up, the turret moving through 180 degrees, but Marine Thomas kept her cool. It was something the Marine Corps held in contempt: wild, unfocused fire. At Parris they called it "Hollywood fire"—wasting ammunition. A marine's shot, on the other hand, was always aimed to kill. The fire from the 7.62 was too high—the bullets zipped overhead. She saw the man's body that was slumped half in, half out of the cupola suddenly, noisily, fall down back into the tank, then a hand shot up to grab hold of the cupola lid's inside hand grip and she fired, heard a scream, and fell to the ground as the 7.62 mm rounds began chopping into the wood close right and—damn, she hadn't warned Freeman. She flicked on her mike. "General, it's Marine Thomas. There's a terrorist in the tunnel and—"

"There *was*," came the general's nasal reply. She heard the general laugh. "Damned fool switched on a flashlight. Those stupid leather helmets they wear. ID'd him straight-away."

Freeman couldn't hear any more machine gun fire in the background; the only sound now was the muffled rotor slap of the helos' second-wave evacuation. It was the sound of promise, of getting out, of freedom in its most literal, easy-to-understand manifestation, the freedom of a human being able to go from one place to another at will, not subject to some order from a totalitarian regime where terrorists such as the Taliban ruled.

Forcing himself back to the task at hand, the general felt for the det cord again, resumed his crawl, and, after a few more yards, realized why half of what had earlier been a more or less continuous line of terrorist bodies was now partially obscured: A crate of heavy MANPAD parts had fallen in the melée from the top of a stack of crates that had been piled high in the middle tunnel, the impact of the crate's sharp edge against the metal grid severing the det cord. He pushed the box of MANPAD parts off the det cord, then, using his knife, he quickly cut the cord and overlapped the two ends by about a foot and attached det cord clips. He then took out his time-delay pencil initiator and crushed the vial, releasing the acid that in five minutes would eat away a thin restraining wire that would in turn release the spring-held firing pin, the pin then striking a percussion cap which would initiate the final sequence in the explosive train.

The general now quickly moved back toward the exit. His NVGs picked up a speckled bloom of light, caused by still-falling dust particles whose radiant heat from the tank round was still enough to faintly illuminate the exit stairs. Suddenly he felt, then heard, the earth trembling above him. It was the forty-seven-ton T-90, crewless except for the driver who was screaming in agony from a bullet-smashed right hand.

With three minutes to go in the tunnel, Freeman easily cleared the body of a terrorist whose flashlight was still on, the general then crashing into a folding card table that against all odds was still standing, albeit with one severed leg. But the general was up and running, with two minutes to go. As he reached the last five stairs to the top of the exit he was aware of a flash of light "blooming out" his NVGs with overload. Though virtually blind for the next few seconds, he felt the wet draft of air on his hands and on the skin between his battle jacket and the bottom of the gas mask. He remembered to turn hard left away from the mined area, running into an uneven patch of tank-mashed reeds, falling, getting up, his feet unable to gain purchase, the ground shifting, then he heard the "whoomp," the roiling of the explosion knocking him off his feet. As if a ballistic missile had been launched from its silo, a huge V of dirt and debris shot out and up from the exit toward the higher ground, falling near the edge of the wood where he'd last seen Melissa Thomas. But now all was a cloud of dark gray dust over sodden earth, the clouds of burned chemicals and noxious fumes from the incinerated terrorists' dungeon now spreading out.

Unable to see more than a foot in front of him, all Douglas Freeman could identify with certainty was the eardunning sound of the Cobra gunships' chain guns, the Cobras' tracers, if his sense of direction was intact, streaming toward the H-block. It was a maelstrom of fire, being delivered as punishment for the terrorists having violated the twenty-four-hour agreement, a venting of the Americans' outrage against what the gunships' pilots had clearly seen themselves and heard from rescued marine stragglers who had alerted the marine forces to the presence and activity of the T-90 tanks.

Freeman flicked on his mike to contact the pilots, but he could tell immediately that that bastard Murphy had struck again. All he could hear was static. And he was worried about Melissa Thomas.

At least the rain was easing, and a fragrant wind was rushing in from the Wanda Shan to replace the harsh, hot air of the detonation, an explosion which Freeman knew had completely destroyed the three tunnels, assembly lines, and the terrorists' entire stock of shoulder-fired MANPADs, hypersonic small rounds, and torpedo prototypes. Boosting the general's weary, yet decidedly effusive, mood, was the rapid withdrawal of the T-90 that had fired point-blank into the exit and was now paying for it by being attacked by the Cobras, who had initially come into Khanka as nothing more than escorts for the evac Stallions. The general's celebratory high was quickly punctured, however, by his growing concern for Melissa Thomas. With the radio out, no flare gun, and the air around him thick with debris, how could he communicate his and her situation to the mission's air arm? "Wait a minute," he scolded himself. "Run, you bastard, run out of this crap cloud. No one can see you here. Run!" And he did, until he saw the two dead tank crewmen, whom he immediately checked for flares. Nothing. He ran on until his knees seemed to be on fire and he burst out into relatively clear air and the reeds. The choppers were gone, their gas tanks' loiter times exhausted.

The general morphed into an angry savage, cursing with such force and volume that he dared any damned Russian terrorists who hadn't had enough to show themselves and he'd personally shoot them. And when he ran out of ammunition he'd go strangle the bastards with his bare hands.

Battle fatigue, he told himself. He saw a white blur coming at him and fired two quick shots. It was a small, man-sized parachute, one of half a dozen dropped either by either the unseen Cobra gunships or the Super Stallions.

"They're message chutes. I've opened one." He swung around, startled by her voice. Relieved, fatigued, and enormously embarrassed for having been caught firing at a parachute, and a small one at that, Freeman hurried over to the voice and found Melissa Thomas shivering violently, whereas he was perspiring profusely underneath the layers of Kevlar and battle tunic, with heat to spare. He embraced her in a bear hug.

The message in the milk-pail-sized canister attached to the chute was

ENCLOSED INFRARED X FOR SATELLITE OVERFLIGHT STOP
MOTHER WILL THEN EXECUTE STAR STOP GOOD LUCK

"I've—" She was shivering so badly she could hardly speak. "—spread—the X over there." Her hand shaking, Melissa was pointing to a flattened area of reeds. Freeman could see her face was tinged with the telltale bluish hue of impending hypothermia.

She pointed to the word STAR. "I—haven't—a clue what—"

"Don't talk. You'll waste energy," he advised her, while simultaneously trying not to show his alarm at the gross violation of operational procedure exhibited by whomever it was who had sent a *message*, especially one with such specific instructions. What if the enemy had picked it up? The fact that HQ had taken such a risk, however, told Freeman just how desperate operational HQ must be, the message, indeed the drop itself, stark evidence that time was quickly running out for him and Melissa Thomas.

"We've got to get you warm," he told her. "Don't worry about STAR. It's an acronym for a recovery system. I'll tell you more about it if and when they see that X. They may wait till dark in case any of these terrorist bastards are wandering around—" He paused for breath. "—though I expect by now they know their money machine's kaput, so what's the point?" He looked around at the wood and marsh. Everything was soaking wet. "We've got to get you under cover. We'll go into the tunnel exit. We can get dry clothes down there. Wrap ourselves in those and snuggle, if you've no objection. Warm you up. We'll hear Mother when she comes." He meant *"if "* a rescue plane comes, but Thomas didn't need discouragement on top of her plummeting body temperature.

Once in the driest, least bloodstained clothes he could bring her, dressing himself only after he'd helped her, they set up an improvised machine gun nest just in from the tunnel's exit, he dragging in the dead T-90 captain and crewman to use as an ad hoc barricade on which to rest his AK-74 and her sniper rifle, he down to his last clip of thirty rounds. He embraced her with his left arm, leaving his right holding the Kalashnikov, ready to fire. "No time to be shy, Marine," he told her. "I'm old enough to be your grandfather!" he joked. "Come in close. I've got enough hot air to thaw a frozen turkey." She tried to smile, but her mouth wouldn't respond, her teeth literally chattering, but she did feel a suggestion of warmth.

As Freeman held the young woman, like other soldiers who had saved their comrades in the same manner from perishing of cold, he became aware of a smell other than their body odor and the reek of charred equipment and burnt flesh in the tunnels. It was the faint but very definite smell of a woman, and he thought of his first wife,

Catherine, and Margaret. It was so distant, as if their love-making had been a dream long ago.

"Don't you ever tell anyone," he told Melissa, "that I shot at a damned parachute." She said nothing, barely hearing him over the soft moan of the China wind whistling about the tunnel exit, the warmth of his closeness seeping into her. No one at Parris would believe it, and she sure as hell wasn't going to tell anyone for the sake of both their reputations. She felt the general start. Something had spooked him.

"What is it?" she whispered.

"A vehicle," he answered. "Maybe a truck."

"Not the plane?"

"No. If—*when*—that comes, we'll know it. They'll use a four-engined Herk for our pickup."

Although warming, Melissa still felt desperately cold. It was as if the cogs in a wheel in her brain had slowed with the precipitous drop in her temperature. For a moment she was confused by him mentioning "our pickup." She thought he'd mentioned a plane, not a pickup truck.

It *was* a pickup truck the general had heard, and it was being driven by a sallow-skinned man in the navy blue padded uniform of Chinese and Russian workers and peasants along the border between the two countries, the map line separating the two running across the top quarter of the lake, about forty miles north of the tunnel exit.

Next to the man in the small Jinlin pickup, whose motor sounded like nothing much more than a two-stroke lawn mower, sat a blue-eyed boy of about twelve, his skin so fair that he was often thought by the others in Wadi El-Hage's cell to be a European. On missions, he and El-Hage never spoke Arabic, only English, the world's language of business, El-Hage pronouncing it in a halting, schoolboylike fashion, the blue-eyed boy with the fluency and colloquialisms of an educated American schoolboy, a youngster who, at Hamas's expense, had spent five of his years in a tightly controlled madrassa in the U.S. There the boy had grown up in a North American cultural sea, his task, as he was reminded daily, to immerse himself, to learn as much as he could about the infidel nation.

"You must be happy," said El-Hage, "to be so soon in Paradise."

"Yes," said the boy. "I am ready."

"Think of Azzah," El-Hage told him, recalling the woman he'd used to help indoctrinate the blue-eyed boy. "She taught you the pleasure a woman can give a young man. In Paradise there will be seventy-two virgins like her, yes, all waiting to pleasure you. Most men much older than to you—"

"Older *than* you," said the boy dispassionately. "Not older *to* you." El-Hage always made such elementary grammatical mistakes.

"What? Oh yes. I am sorry, Jamal. Older *than* you. Well, you see, not even those older than you obtain such pleasuring." El-Hage saw yet another parachute canister, this one poking out from a clump of bushes that were barely visible amid the encroaching reeds. He and the boy had seen several of the milk-pail-sized canisters which, attached to small parachutes, had floated down from the infidels' giant helicopters before they all left, the pilots and crew unable to see any more survivors in the thick smoke that had spewed out from the tunnel explosion and soon filled the evening sky. El-Hage had already stopped several times on the narrow, raised roadway through the low-lying marshes, and had waded in knee-high water to retrieve one of the canisters and thrown it into the back of the Jinlin, though even the boy could not tell El-Hage what to make of "STAR" in the canister's written directions.

But whatever it was, the phrase "pickup," he told El-Hage, meant just that, and indicated that this infidel general and some soldier called Thomas were still missing. If they saw an infidel cross spread out, no doubt a signal for the infidel's rescue, it would also locate Freeman for El-Hage and the boy.

"There it is!" said the boy, sitting abruptly forward, pointing to a spot almost a quarter of a mile to his left. The light was fading, and while neither he nor El-Hage could see a parachute, the white cross could be seen atop a reed island.

"Yes, yes, now remember—" El-Hage, though he had switched to English, was speaking more quickly than he normally did when giving his Hamas cell its instructions. "—you are looking for help for your poor father, a pond fisherman who is ill, and—"

"I know," said the boy sharply, also in English. "I know. Our engine has broken down. Could he please help us?"

"Yes, and I will stand by the engine's hood and look into the engine and I will appear—" El-Hage now allowed himself a small laugh. "I will—I will appear *how*? The word you taught me."

"Mystified," the boy told him.

"Yes, very mystified."

The boy laughed, and El-Hage saw the imperturbable courage, the cool determination in the boy's eyes. This time the boy, unlike other martyrs of Islam, would not be wearing a bomb belt. The Americans, the British, and other degenerates had grown wise to the dynamite-belted bombers since the infidels' occupation of Iraq. "Do not speak English *very* well," advised El-Hage for the umpteenth time. "Otherwise they will—"

"*Too* well," the boy corrected him. "I know, I must sound like a peasant. I am begging the American for help." He adopted a forlorn look, his pleading, snuffling manner in keeping with the rumpled Russian garb, selected and dirtied for the mission by El-Hage himself. " 'Please, you help my father. His car. No go. It no good. You help, please.' "

"Good," said El-Hage. "But remember, if they ask how it is you know a little English?"

"At school. Yes," said the boy in the exasperated tone of a much older, more mature boy who had learned not only of the pleasures of the beautiful Azzah, but English as well.

"Who's that?" Melissa asked Freeman. The voice coming down the exit shaft from above was that of a child. It wasn't loud, but its "Hello!" was persistent, and Melissa whispered to the general that it sounded as if whoever it was must be very near the spot where they put the cross. Melissa felt resentful, then ashamed. The marine in her wanted to help anyone in trouble, especially a child, but the woman in her wanted more warmth and the safe, protected feeling she had while being held by the general, telling her she was alive, coming back from the brink of hypothermia to the present, the insect bites that had saved her now starting to itch so badly that all she wanted to do was rip off the clothes and scratch till there was no tomorrow.

"Quiet, dammit!" said Freeman, his ill temper surprising him almost as much as it did Melissa, but he had a soldier's sixth sense of danger. For an instant much of his earlier life, the times of maximum danger, flashed through his mind with a vividness he'd not experienced before but which other soldiers had spoken to him about moments before their death. For all his self-confidence, Douglas Freeman was not a man who had lived with the belief that things always work out for the best. For him, that was demonstrably false in the utterance of one word: Holocaust. And he knew someday would be his day to die. The best anyone could do was try to avoid it, but if you couldn't, then for him there was only one way to deal with it: bravely.

Extracting himself from the layers of now-warm clothing, and picking up his weapon, trigger finger on the guard, he walked up through the malodorous tunnel, up into the pale square of evening. He heard two things: A boy's voice calling, "Help, please?" and Melissa Thomas coming out behind him.

When Freeman saw the Jinlin with its hood up, apparently conked out, about a hundred yards away, he was surprised to see a peasant in the ubiquitous quilted blue jacket, pants, and thick fur cap—either Chinese or Russian, it was difficult to tell—staring into the motor as if he didn't know what to make of it all. Only now did Freeman notice the boy, probably Russian, Freeman thought, off to his left. The boy, who must have walked around the large, marshy depression nearby, was now waving at the general and asking, "Please, you help my father. He sick and truck no go. It no good. You help, please. My English not good but you, you understand?"

"I understand," said Freeman, trying to quickly assay the situation. "But you just stay where you are for a jiff."

"Jiff?" asked the blue-eyed boy. "What does this 'jiff' mean?"

"It means stay still."

From almost a mile away Abramov was watching, his nerves rattled by his near-death experiences in the shot-up transport helo and the minefield. He could barely move, so tightly stuffed was his battle uniform and backpack with three different currencies and a back brace belt he'd personally ordered to be altered so that it would carry a bag of ten big-candy-bar-sized ingots of gold.

"A walking bank," the crew of Nureyev's tank had called him as they'd fished him out of the minefield.

"What's the American doing?" Abramov demanded angrily, standing atop the tank next to its cupola with two other bonus-hungry terrorists. Abramov was using the cupola to brace himself, his legs and arms still spasming in reaction to his having had to stand perfectly still and then bear his own weight and that of the gold while dangling from the huge 125 mm gun.

"General Abramov!" called out the tank's radio operator. "Our crew in Tank 1 has been badly mauled. Only one survivor. He's withdrawing to H-block."

"What for?" Abramov snarled. "There's nothing left for him there. Doesn't he know what the Cobras did? They've destroyed H-block; it's burning. Computers and everything. Gone!"

"Sir," Nureyev cut in, "the American must be telling the boy to take off his jacket. Why is he making the boy—"

"Shut up!" ordered Abramov, the weight of his binoculars straining his wrists. "The boy's in my employ. His guardian's a big customer of ours—paid half your wages. This Freeman bastard must be suspicious."

"Looks like he is telling the kid to turn around," said Nureyev.

Despite his nervous state, or perhaps because of it, Abramov gave a short, guttural laugh. "He suspects the blue-eyed boy. Thinks he might be wired with explosives."

"Is he?" Nureyev dared to ask. He, as well as his crew, were exhausted by the ever-present threat of being taken out like the others at the beginning of the U.S. raid. "He hasn't got a bomb belt on," said Nureyev, watching through his binoculars and still waiting for Abramov's confirmation of whether or not the boy was wired. "Maybe a grenade?" proffered Nureyev.

"No," Abramov said, having to lower his binoculars, hands atremble. "But he's Freeman's death warrant."

*   *   *

Freeman glimpsed movement, side right. It was Melissa Thomas coming closer, still in Russian garb, but wearing her American helmet. Hunched over from the weight of the clothing, she looked like a crone. The boy started with fright when he saw her, the suddenness of her appearance rather than her Russian uniform and American helmet surprising him.

"Now take off your pants," Freeman told the boy slowly.

"But mister, I wish to tell I am *not* Russian soldier. I am no soldier. I am only twelve years—"

"Be quiet!" snapped Freeman. "Take them off!"

The boy first took off his boots, then the trousers, revealing khaki cotton long johns.

"I am cold," he complained.

"So am I," the legendary general told him. "Everybody's cold. Now take off your long johns."

"General!" said Thomas. "I hear aircraft—"

She was right. There were three of them. Two were less loud than the other, which seemed slower and was out of sight above the gray three-thousand-foot-high stratus. Night was almost upon them, and the man, Melissa saw, purportedly this boy's father, was still visible by the Jinlin but becoming more difficult to see in the fast-descending dusk.

"Joint Strike Fighters," Freeman answered, without turning toward her, watching the boy taking off his underwear and shivering. Melissa didn't avert her eyes. She'd been trained not to, not after the number of marines lost in Iraq to innocent-looking children who had wandered up to U.S. soldiers with a smile and a "Hi, Mac!" then blown themselves and the marines to pieces.

The blue-eyed boy had no grenades tucked into the crotch of his long johns. He was shivering violently. The rule was not to let them speak, to "chat you up," as the Brits called it, chat you up all friendly and innocent and then the grenade.

"All right," Freeman said. "Put your long johns on and pull your jacket and trousers inside out. Pockets as well. And pat them down so I can see."

To help the boy understand, Freeman, still holding his AK-74 in his right hand, patted his left leg with his left hand, miming what he wanted the boy to do. The kid seemed smart enough, older than his young, blue-eyed innocence would suggest.

Melissa Thomas saw the first two planes, black specks beneath the gray stratus, the thunder and speed of their passing so fast she had only a few seconds to see they were in fact two American Joint Strike Fighters; the third plane, the one the JSFs were obviously protecting, sounded higher and was still hidden by the clouds of stratus, its drone much heavier and slower than the low-level scream of the two JSFs.

Freeman hadn't seen the planes, "total focus," as he used to tell Aussie and Co., being the necessity of the moment. Freeman still felt there was something weird. Yes, they'd seen the road track when they landed, and he himself had told the MEU force on *Yorktown* they might see the occasional rice farmer who spent the winters huddled in the hamlets around the lake, using bundled dried reeds collected during the summer for fuel, but he was cautious nevertheless.

"All right," said Freeman, pointing down at the boy's pile of inside-out clothes. "Put your hands up, like this— spread fingers—and walk back from the clothes."

"Sir," said Melissa Thomas, "he's going to die of chill."

"He'll die of dynamite if he's got a stick or two sown into that quilting," though the general could see that none of the quilted segments was big enough to conceal a stick of dynamite. But you could kill a man with much less. Melissa Thomas had heard just how meticulous the elite forces, such as the SAS, SEALs, Spetsnaz, and Freeman's SpecFor were. And she'd heard the story about Aussie and the "woman" with the baby. Freeman was quickly but gingerly feeling the quilted clothing, fur cap, and then the boy's boots, upending and smacking them. Det cord could by itself cripple and maim.

"Sir," said Thomas. "There's a container coming down."

It wasn't one of the small ones holding white infrared X cloths but was much larger, about twice the size of a forty-five-gallon drum, under a full-size chute. Freeman figured, correctly, that this was all being coordinated by *McCain*'s Signals Exploitation Space via satellite. They'd homed in on the points of the X that Melissa Thomas had spread out, and had now given the big plane, which sounded like a Herk, the X's exact GPS address.

Freeman's concentration on the boy and the indistinct man down by the Jinlin truck didn't falter for a second. The general didn't even look in the direction of the descending chute. But as he began patting down the boy's quilted trousers he could see the peasant by the truck was standing motionless. Why wouldn't the father be over here by now to see what's going on? the general asked himself. His son had been made to strip and still he hadn't moved? But the general could not feel any explosive or triggering device or any unusual heaviness as he lifted the jacket and pants up to gauge their weight. They felt just about right.

"Okay," he told the boy, pointing down at the clothes. "Put those back on."

"Okay?" said the boy.

"Yes, it's okay."

"You help my father now?"

"Yes." Freeman turned to Melissa Thomas, who was watching the big canister float down, keeping the scope eye of her M40A1 on Abramov's unmoving tank. The tank's crew was no doubt wondering what to do now that there were two state-of-the-art MANPAD-invulnerable Joint Strike Fighters in the area, with tank-busting rockets and cannon.

"Let's go help your dad," said Freeman. "Marine Thomas?"

"Sir?"

"Inside the canister you'll find two dry, insulated boilersuits, a five-hundred-foot cord of reinforced nylex rope, and a seaman's kit bag—it's the rolled-up balloon-dirigible bladder—and a tank of helium with an easy-to-release—"

Suddenly his voice was lost in a thunderous roar as the two JSFs screamed out of the stratus in a tight turn and swept over them, rocking wings to say "hello," and assuring them that if yonder T-90 tank was to cause any trouble, there would be no more T-90.

The boy was zipping up his jacket as Freeman continued. "There'll be two body harnesses. Put one on."

"Should I start filling the balloon?"

"Just enough to get it off the ground," said Freeman. "No more till I get back. Fully inflated, the dirigible's like a house-sized Goodyear blimp." He smiled. "But no gondola." He turned to the boy. "Okay, Let's go help your father."

"Thank you."

"I'm sorry about making you cold," Freeman apologized. "You understand? Sometimes bad people use children. Do you understand me?"

"Oh yes," said the blue-eyed boy. "That's why I want to tell you that this man we're walking toward is the regional Hamas leader Wadi El-Hage and they told me all this bullshit about how Americans were evil and sent me to school over there to learn English." He paused. "And where I found that American kids were great."

Freeman was stunned by the boy's mature self-confidence and sudden switch from the halting vocabulary one would expect of a peasant to the kind of A-plus high school student he himself had been. The general almost stopped walking, he was so surprised, but the boy continued walking and talking. "But these Hamas assholes have kept me like a prisoner and told me that if I ever left them, they'd hunt me down and kill me, no matter where I went. My pants and jacket are padded with explosive—with what Hamas call spun Semtex. You know what that is?"

"Semtex, yes, but not spun."

"The detonator is a fine wire and a tiny watch battery in the jacket in a seam tucked into the collar label. The theory is that I tear it and you and I go to Paradise. I don't believe any of it." The boy paused now and looked knowingly at Freeman. "In the Middle East, girls can marry at twelve. I know about women. There's Paradise here if you're alive. Hamas is nuts. If I went with you, General, they'd chase me down, *but* if you take El-Hage and me prisoner, people'll think we're both locked up. You can take me back to America where I'll be safe. I'm young, and you have the world's best plastic surgeons in your witness protection programs."

. The boy's unemotional, businesslike tone was alarming, chilling. The child had a cold, calculating heart beyond his years, the inheritance of the terrorist heartlessness.

"Is he armed?" Freeman asked, ready to bring up his AK-47 from its casual barrel-down position by his right side.

"A pistol in his waistband," the boy told him. "He's left-handed."

El-Hage was still standing by the truck, as if frozen in time. Wait a minute, thought Freeman, slowing. What if the kid was lying—a sucker ploy to get him away from the sniper, Thomas, her shooter's eye resting in the scope's reticule. A no-miss shot, with El-Hage in her scope.

El-Hage suddenly ran to the other side of the truck and snatched up an AK-47. Freeman immediately dropped to the ground, firing as he did so underneath the Jinlin. He heard a cry of pain, the Arab's legs out from under him, and the man fell, his AK-47 clattering on the Jinlin-flattened reeds. The general unleashed another long burst, and the Hamas leader was grossly spastic in his death throes. He tried to say something to the boy, but only bright arterial blood issued from his mouth, and he was dead.

Freeman heard the rifle's crack, and wheeled. Thomas, still too weak to shout loudly, had fired a warning shot into the air from her sniper rifle, and was now pointing at the T-90 a half a mile away in the minefield, its gun lowering to slightly below the azimuth, which meant it was about to engage a short-range target. "Run!" Freeman told the boy, who needed no encouragement, having sized up the situation as quickly as the general. They heard the boom of the 125 mm cannon and felt a great rush of air.

"Down!" Freeman yelled as the Jinlin somersaulted ten feet into the air and became a ball of tangled metal and flame crashing to the ground.

Melissa now had the scope on Abramov, his head and that of the other two crewmen by the cupola in her crosshairs. The tank was coming straight for her. Below the Russians were winks of orange light, the T-90's machine guns sweeping the rain-drenched reeds that Freeman and the boy were racing for.

So enraged was Abramov, kneeling on the tank with one hand on the cupola, that, despite the T-90's superb suspension, his head kept bobbing around in Melissa's IR scope. The furious terrorist's instructions to his driver didn't allow for any zigzag pattern during the T-90's charge. He wanted to run Freeman down.

Melissa lowered the M40A1 for a seventy-yard chest shot, and fired. Abramov flew off the tank into its wake, the impact of Thomas's sniper round against Abramov's Kevlar vest such that while it didn't penetrate all the way through, it knocked him ass-over-tit, *verkh dnom*, as the Russians say, his money-filled backpack leaking a trail of assorted currencies as his body, wrapped in gold, rolled in the tank's wake.

Though badly wounded and bleeding, Abramov rose in feral rage, screaming at the now-stopped tank, from which Nureyev, his driver, and two other terrorists escaped, risking all to get his money for themselves. The general was waving his 9 mm Makarov menacingly at them as Freeman, emerging from the reeds, fired a long burst. Abramov's body was sent reeling back, his face a bloody pulp.

The four terrorists, would-be millionaires, held up their hands. One, with a green signal flag, frantically called, "Don't shoot. No shooting!"

"You'll take the money and leave?" shouted Freeman, his AK-74 aimed at the four Russians.

"Sure," said one of them. "No problem."

Without taking his eyes off the four Russian terrorists, Freeman told the boy to climb quickly up on the T-90 and drop his jacket in, the Russians mesmerized by the brightly colored Euros and thousand-dollar U.S. bills still falling out of Abramov's torn knapsack and being sucked away by the faint but frigid breeze.

"We get the money now?" asked the man who had been waving the maneuver flag.

"Sure," said Freeman. "It's yours."

The boy had taken off his jacket and, without a glance at Freeman, tore the collar label, dropped the jacket into the hole with his right hand, and slammed the cupola lid down with his left.

There was a noticeably soft "whoomp" in the tank as the boy jumped off, slipped on the wet reeds, and banged his head hard against the tank's track. The Russian terrorists turned as one, and Freeman cut them down with one long burst, his AK-74's barrel steaming in the cold. "Grab that backpack," he told the boy, pointing to Abramov. The boy obeyed quickly, picking up the belt of gold bullion as well. "Here," said Freeman, stuffing the backpack and gold into a plastic garbage bag he'd taken from his DARPA "goodies" waist pouch. "We've got to get a move on. Got a plane to catch." They were running toward the X. "You okay, son?" Freeman saw fresh blood in the boy's hair.

The boy didn't answer, but kept running with Freeman and never looked back at the burning tank and river of spilled fuel that by now was incinerating the dead radio operator who'd remained inside. "Boy" seemed to Freeman a misnomer for someone so mature. But then Hamas had had him. They were a tough outfit, and Douglas Freeman knew it would take some deprogramming at home, a place which at the moment Freeman knew in his gut they had only a fifty-fifty chance of reaching, to straighten the kid out.

The STAR, or Surface-to-Air Recovery technique, was known throughout Special Forces and Special Ops command as a last resort. Indeed, it was the riskiest extraction method ever devised by man.

"You afraid of heights?" Freeman asked the boy as they sprinted to where Marine Thomas, now barely visible in the dusk, had begun preparations as per the instructions in the container as the Herk and its two Joint Strike Fighters loitered overhead.

"Fill it!" Freeman shouted at her. "Time to go. Give the valve its head."

What a moment before had been the size of a giant

jellyfish now quickly expanded into a car-sized and then a small but definite Goodyear blimp-shaped dirigible as the helium silently inflated it, and it rose high into the icy air, unraveling the first one hundred feet of the five-hundred-foot-long specially treated nylon rope that lay coiled at Freeman's and Melissa Thomas's feet as they hurriedly donned the multilayered thermal boilersuits complete with hoods, skydiver helmets, and rescue harnesses for each of them.

"You're going to have to hold on to me tightly, son," said Freeman. "What's your name, Blue Eyes?"

"Jamal."

"All right, Jamal, now the big Hercules—that plane up there—is going to come down pretty low to get us three out of here. First we'll go up like a—"

"*General!*" Marine Thomas interjected. "The dirigible's at full height. We're the only ones holding it down. The Herk'll pick it up or—" She had no time to finish; the Hercules, its four turboprop engines roaring, was coming at them at about five hundred feet, a big, metal, horizontal V sticking out from the nose like a forked tongue which, in theory, should snag the nylon rope suspended from above by the blimp. If the V snagged the rope, an automatic clamp would lock the base of the V's jaw onto the line, the dirigible, still attached to the flex rope, now high above the plane and trailing well behind it. The strain would soon be taken up by the rope, if it worked.

"Ever been on a swing, Jamal?" Freeman shouted against the roar of the Herk as he and Melissa Thomas strapped their harnesses together.

"Yes, I've been on lots of swings."

Freeman took the boy in a bear hug. "Not like this one, kid. You hang on to me no matter what, okay?"

"O—" And they were off, the plane's V-shaped proboscis having snagged the line, whisking them straight up for 120 feet before the big pendulum swing began, their initial acceleration from the sitting position to more than a hundred feet surprisingly smooth, if very fast, like being whipped up through the air at the end of a five-hundred-foot-long elastic band. The sensation of speed was so frightening and exhilarating that Freeman felt it in his loins as the three of them, in an experience for which not even Top Gun graduates volunteered, went hurtling through frigid air, the lake already far below and behind them, a silver sheen in the moonlight slipping away westward, the black Herk entering cloud. The easy part was over.

Above the Herk, now traveling at 144 miles per hour, the dirigible's breakaway cords snapped from the sheer stress of the air buffeting its huge volume. Inside the plane, at the Herk's rear ramp door, one of two volunteer crewmen set about lowering a hook line to catch the lift line, which now arced back from the nose of the Herk, now traveling at 136 miles per hour. Meantime, a second volunteer crewman began working the telescopic arm which would, it was hoped, reach out and grab the lift line so it could be brought closer to the underside of the plane, and Freeman, Jamal, and Melissa winched safely into the plane's belly.

The boom's hook missed on the first pass, but snagged the line on the backswing. The winch began its high whine, then suddenly Freeman, Jamal, and Melissa Thomas felt an arm-ripping jolt so severe that Melissa thought their harnesses had split apart, her shout of alarm ripped away by the Hercules's roaring slipstream. While the jolt, which Freeman thought he'd readied for, failed to loosen his grip on the boy, the general heard something snap, probably, he thought, one of the many wire cables that ran through the aircraft, looming two hundred feet above them, the noise of its big engines reverberating in every bone.

Three minutes and fifty seconds after the enormous jolt, they were being winched into the plane, the night ahead filled with stars. The plane, having climbed and increased speed to 315 miles per hour, was now an hour and half out of Sapporo, Japan. Chipper Armstrong and Rhino Manowski put their escorting Joint Strike Fighters through a synchronized barrel roll for victory as they crossed over Cape Titova and to the southeast saw the metallic glints in the moonlight that were the ships of *McCain*'s battle group, another two JSFs already aloft to take over escort duty for the Herk. But, apart from the JSF's barrel rolls, no signal came up to greet the Herk or its passengers who, like those in the carrier battle group, were on strict radio silence, with no running lights showing. The United States was still in a state of war against terror.

One of the two volunteer marine crewmen, coiling the lift rope, greeted the general with a hearty, "Welcome aboard, General!" It was a few seconds before a grateful and exhausted Freeman recognized Peter Norton, his courage reincarnated, his newfound self-respect purchased during the final hours of the evac when he'd repeatedly risked his own life, under fire, to help injured marines aboard.

"Is . . ." began Melissa, then stopped. "I can't remember his name." The noise in the cavernous Herk was giving her a severe headache, and in her utter exhaustion she told the general what marines told one another on a long, fatigue-plagued mission: "I'm dumbed out. Can hardly remember my name."

Freeman wasn't listening. He was bending low over Jamal. He was unable to hear the boy's breathing, which the general knew shouldn't be surprising given the thundering noise of the big transport. He stared hard at Jamal to see whether his chest was moving, but it was difficult to tell sometimes, particularly with children.

"Jamal?" said Freeman. There was no response. "Jamal?" he said louder, giving the boy a shake.

Nothing.

CHAPTER TWENTY

IN SAPPORO, THE media frenzy engulfed Freeman and Marine Thomas, reporters clamoring to be heard now that Washington, D.C., had declared Lake Khanka's ABC terrorist munitions factory destroyed after reports from the Marine Corps' Colonel Jack Tibbet and from satellite reconnaissance, which had picked up the dense "pollution debris" over Siberia's southeastern Primorski region.

"General, General Freeman!" came the shouts from the frenetic horde as flashes of varying intensity went off all around like so many flares and tracer coming at him. Adding to the charged atmosphere was the increasing cacophony of yelled questions, lens shutters clicking, clacking, and whirring, all pressing in like some unstoppable ambush. Every major newspaper, TV, and radio conglomerate on the globe was seeking the "money shot" and the Patton-like quote from the legendary general who had led the American task force into what one BBC correspondent accurately called "the world's most dangerous terrorist enclave outside of Iran." It was all too unnerving for Marine Melissa Thomas who, on Freeman's request, was whisked away by a Marine Corps chaplain and airport security guard to the U.S. Consulate's police-ringed limousine.

Freeman, a man not known for any unwillingness to help the media celebrate his true grit and daring, was, however, unduly subdued, as had been Melissa Thomas, her mood exacerbated by the bruises, scratches, and insect bites that covered her face and hands, injuries which she had no inclination to either explain or complain about.

The general, though smartly turned out in a fresh uniform that had been rushed to Sapporo, looked tired and drawn taking questions on the dais, especially so to Marte Price who, having had to elbow and fight her way through the Japanese press scrum, was close enough to see the creases of worry lines on Freeman's face. Finally he held up his hands to quell the din of the media frenzy, and when several Taiwanese reporters ignored his request, he refused point-blank to begin speaking until the room fell silent, though shutters continued to click and whirr, and the bright TV lights remained, forcing him to blink more than was either normal or comfortable.

"Ladies and gentlemen. I'll be brief. Colonel Tibbet and his marines have done an outstanding job of ridding the world of the terrorist filth who make weapons for other terrorist filth. To paraphrase a man who fought Nazi filth, 'This is not the end, but it is the beginning of the end' for terrorists all over the world, as we and our allies keep fighting, no matter how long and hard the road may be, until every stain of such scum as Hamas and company is expunged from the earth." He paused as one of the two U.S. Consulate officials behind him leaned forward, whispering advice: "Easy on the 'scum' and Hamas. Don't want to offend the Muslims."

Freeman nodded politely. "It's been suggested to me that I might be offending our Muslim brothers and sisters. Nothing could be further from my mind or from American policy. Our war isn't against Muslims. Our war is against scum like Hamas who use whatever organization they can to spread hatred of the West in general and of America in particular." Freeman now looked grim. "Today a young boy, a young Muslim boy, his name was Jamal, died en route to Sapporo from a mishap which, I must admit, I thought was relatively minor when we left Lake Khanka but a mishap that due to the stress experienced in our hasty but necessary evacuation, quickly proved fatal. That boy, a young boy, a young *Muslim* boy, was lost to us because of some scumbag in Hamas who managed to steal this boy's young life and turn him into a potential weapon."

The general stopped speaking momentarily, taking in a deep breath, his unsmiling expression now one of strong resolve. "I dedicate the memory of this mission, and all who made the ultimate sacrifice, to *all* those young people of whatever race or belief who have been killed, used, consumed by the blind hatred of Hamas and other scumbag fundamentalists. That is all."

A barrage of questions went unanswered as General Douglas Freeman strode off the dais and out into the waiting consulate limousine, around which immaculately turned-out Japanese motorcycle police and plainclothes security personnel had formed a cordon sanitaire. But the cigarette smoke was anything but sanitary, and he was coughing before he entered the limo.

Melissa Thomas, also in a fresh uniform, was sitting on the jump seat. The general indicated that the consular official take the jump seat and Melissa Thomas sit by him. "You drink, Marine?" he asked her.

"Not much. Besides, I'm on duty, sir."

"So am I," said the general, who now turned to the consular official as the limousine eased away from yet another frenzy of camera flashes to the accompaniment of the police motorcycle sirens. "You have a Coke in there, son?" he asked, tapping his combat boot against the polished cocktail-bar cupboard.

"Coke? Ah, I don't think so, General. That's a multi-channel TV."

The general frowned at the official. "You people better get on the ball."

"Yes, General," said the consular official apologetically, failing to see the smirk on the marine's face.

"Well," the general asked Melissa, "were you watching the TV?"

"Yes, sir."

"You think they bought it?"

"I don't understand Japanese, General," said Marine Thomas, "but I heard some of what you said beneath the voice-over. *I* believed you and I saw him thirty minutes ago. He was sucking on that milk shake you ordered like it was his last meal."

"It will be—" began the general. "Get them to turn off those damned sirens," he told the consular official. "We're not going to a fire."

"Yes, sir."

In the relative quiet of the limousine, Freeman continued, "It *will* be his last meal if those Hamas bastards get a whiff of the fact that he helped us." He turned to the official again. "I want everything I'm going to be debriefed on sent in code. Eyes Only, by diplomatic pouch. The only other people than us to know he's alive will be the witness protection folk who'll have to give him the usual—new name, new identity—otherwise those scumbags'll hunt him. If they—"

"He'll be all right," interjected Melissa, the consular official surprised at the ease with which this marine private was addressing the famous general.

Freeman, though still concerned, sank back in the plush leather seat. "You think so?"

"General," she said. "May I speak freely?"

"Of course."

"None of this," she told the official, "leaves this car. Okay?"

"Fine."

"Well," she began, somewhat uneasily, "that—" Suddenly she grabbed the hold strap, her legs stiffening for impact. Both the general and consular official were on the edge of their seats, looking for the unseen danger. As quickly as it had begun, it was over, Melissa Thomas burying her head in her hands in acute embarrassment. "Oh—I—I'm sorry. I thought we'd crossed over to the wrong side of the road. I forgot they drove on the *left* side over here." It gave the three of them a much-needed laugh, and it made it easier for Melissa to reassure Freeman about Jamal.

"General, that boy," she said, "he asked me if I'd—you know."

"You're kidding me!" Freeman said.

"No way, sir. No, I'm not kidding. He said things—not dirty stuff but things only a—I think that only a full-grown man should know about."

Freeman thought about it for a second. "So we should tell him he can't do that in America. Not yet—I mean, when he gets—well—I—" Melissa Thomas saw that the legend was embarrassed. Freeman could only imagine what Catherine or Margaret would have said.

"Well, I guess we'll have to reeducate him. It's one thing for damned terrorists and oil sheiks to have twelve-year-old brides, but he can't—" The general made a vague gesture which Marine Thomas took to be a stand-in for the phrase "sexual relations." "He just can't, that's all."

"He needs," Melissa suggested, "a strong male figure to look up to, someone who'll tell him what's what and not take any cra—nonsense. Who can get his respect, someone like that guy on your team. Lewis, isn't that his name?"

"Aussie?" said the general, nodding. "Yes, maybe he

could keep a sort of uncle's eye on him during the relocation program. And perhaps Jamal may be able to modify some of Aussie's antipodean phrases."

"He's a polite boy," continued Melissa. "I didn't mean to suggest he's—well, you know—vulgar. He just knows too much, if you know what I mean, General, for his age."

"I understand. I'll speak to Aussie when the team regroups. Aussie's wife is a refugee from the JAR—Jewish Autonomous Region—in the old Soviet Union. And she and Aussie don't have kids. She might help." The more Freeman thought about Thomas's suggestion, the better he liked it. "Good idea, Marine. Don't worry; we'll straighten him out." The general smiled. "Already got him started on the milk shakes."

"Oh, he knew about those," she said, smiling back.

There was a tap on the partition. The consular official pressed a button, the glass sliding down to reveal the other consular official who'd been on the dais. He'd been working his laptop and micro printer and now passed back a sheaf of two-by-four-inch pieces of paper. "Messages for you, General. I've prioritized them for you."

The general leaned forward as he reached for them. If there was one New Age expression he disliked more than the grammatically ugly "you did good" instead of "you did well," it was "prioritize." It reeked of "suit psychobabble." "Thank you," he said, and sat back.

The first message was from the president, a quotation from the inimitable Winston Churchill, ending with "well done." Freeman smiled at the vicissitudes of life: After Priest Lake he was a "bum"; now he was a "hero." Good.

The second message was from the State Department, furious that he'd linked the term "Hamas" with "scumbags." Hamas, Foggy Bottom reminded him, also served as a "charitable arm" to the Palestinians, and the general's use of scumbag in connection with it was "unnecessarily inflammatory and an affront to all Muslims."

Freeman screwed the message into a tiny ball, handing it to the consular official. "Round file this, will you?"

The consular official informed him that scores of congratulations were pouring in but that there was one message from home he might like to see immediately. The consular official was right. It was from Margaret:

Cannot work new DVD player. Will you help?
                                    A damsel in distress.